CW01202285

THE WIDENING GYRE

TRANSITS OF POWER

BENJAMIN X. WRETLIND

The Widening Gyre: Transits of Power

Copyright © 2024
by Benjamin X. Wretlind

Cover image by iobard via Shutterstock

Printed in the United States of America

This is a work of fiction. All the characters, locations and events portrayed in this novel are either fictitious or are used fictitiously.

No part of this book may be reproduced or transmitted in any form or by any means, electronic or mechanical, including photocopying, recording or by any information storage and retrieval system without permission in writing from the author.

ISBN: 978-1088263969

Library of Congress Control Number: 2023915245

www.bxwretlind.com

THE WIDENING GYRE: TRANSITS OF POWER

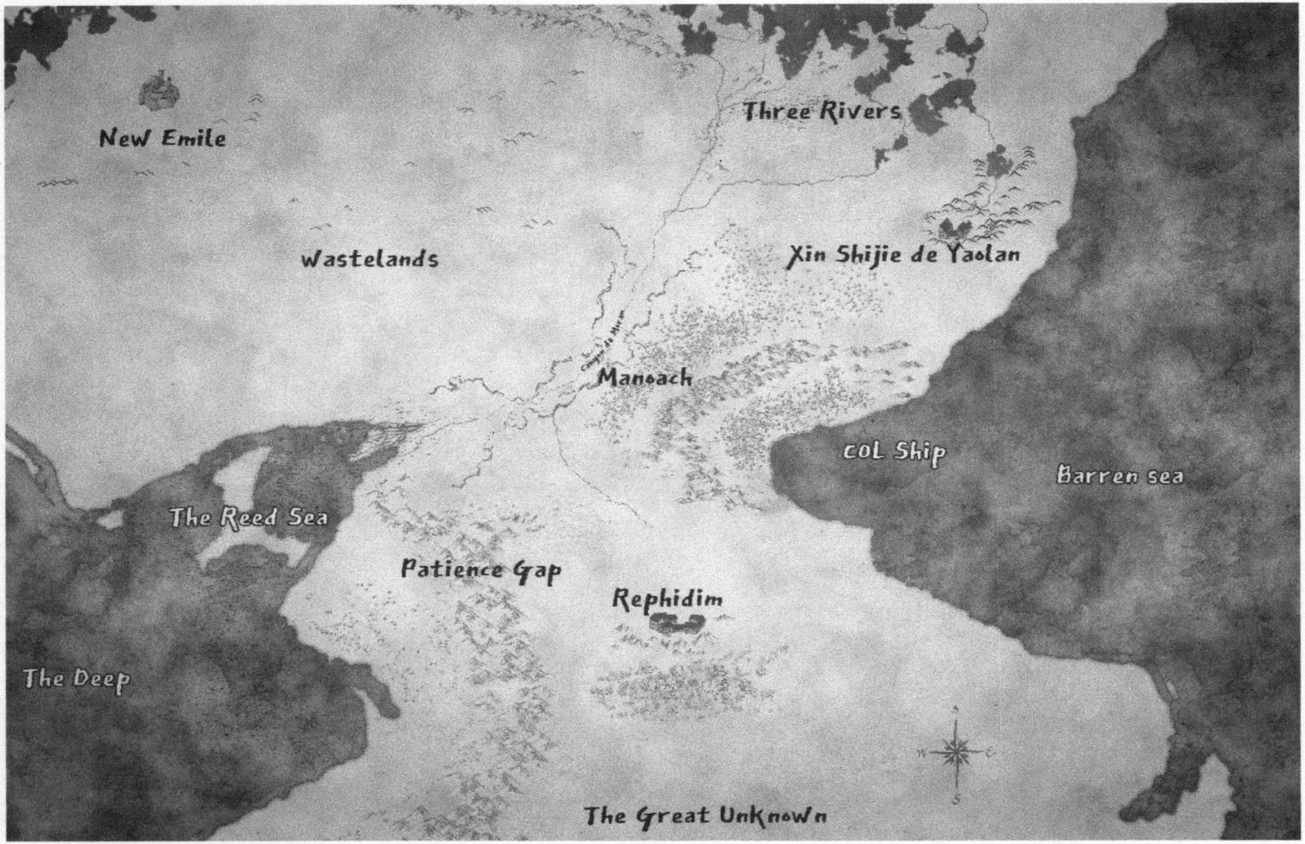
New Emile
Three Rivers
Wastelands
Xin Shijie de Yaolan
Manoach
COL Ship
Barren sea
The Reed Sea
Patience Gap
Rephidim
The Deep
The Great Unknown

For those caught in the gyre...

An Excerpt from the Book of the Col'kasid

Author Unknown, believed to have been written sometime around Year 200 AT

And lo, it came to pass in the shadowed wilderness that the caravan of the Great Mother didst venture, beset by the rychat, foul creatures of wickedness, ere two days since their departure from Manoach, that city of the damned. Encompassed, the gallant companions didst resist the onslaught, until a behemoth of the forest intervened, and verily the tide was stayed to their favor.

In the land of Manoach, a grievous pestilence did sweep through, and the rychat, crafty in their machinations, didst breach the barrier. In those days and times, the man of machines, skilled in craft, and Sojen Keeper of the Text, learned in wisdom, did labor with fervor to unravel the arcane texts of the Ancients. The Rebellious One, heedless and wanton, took up the mantle of defense for Manoach. Sojen Keeper of the Text, although filled with a righteous wrath, sought refuge in the temple, pondering his lonesome burden.

A terror took hold of the Great Mother's caravan, yet through faith unwavering, they found a hidden passage. The man of machines set forth upon a path perilous, his followers tried by maladies and avalanches. The hand of destiny did lead Sojen Keeper of the Text and his companions to traverse lands fraught with danger, where they did uncover wisdom ancient and profound. In bondage, the man of machines suffered grievously, and the Rebellious One was left to grapple with the fruit of his actions.

Thus in patterns of three, new societies were born upon the WORLD. In years hence through many tribulations, their very souls were put to the test, knit together by a common will to persevere. Shaped by resilience, their faith became a lamp unto their feet. Thus did they journey onward, their hope a shining beacon in a world fraught with uncertainty.

And it came to pass under the gaze of the first Long Moon, that two strangers arose, enigmatic and forlorn, bearing witness to all these things. And the people cried "O! Strangers! Whither the Great Return?"

And behold, the strangers, enshrouded in mystery, didst speak unto the gathered throng, their voices like the rustling of ancient leaves. "Come and see," they cried out. "Prepare the way, for the time draweth nigh. But beware the dragon which lies in wait to the North."

And the people were both amazed and afraid.

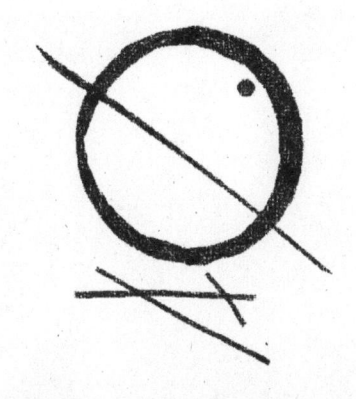

PART I: THE EXILES

Cycle 10, Day 7, Year 96

Turning and turning in the widening gyre
The falcon cannot hear the falconer;
Things fall apart; the centre cannot hold;
Mere anarchy is loosed upon the world,
The blood-dimmed tide is loosed, and everywhere
The ceremony of innocence is drowned;
The best lack all conviction, while the worst
Are full of passionate intensity.

—William Butler Yeats, "The Second Coming" 1919

CHAPTER ONE

ABEL FELT A SHARP RUSH OF ADRENALINE AS THE XIALITI attacked. The sunlight created a dazzling display of light as it bounced off the animal's scales in the early morning. For the seventeen-year-old boy, exiled from Rephidim, survival was all that mattered.

The beast had already taken the life of his mount, the quvianaq he'd been granted to keep. Now that trusty animal lay gutted, wedged between two massive rocks.

The xialiti spat, its venom missing Abel by a hair's breadth as he dove to the side. As he stood up, an acrid taste of dust on his tongue mixed with the sharp, metallic scent of beast and blood. It was a scent he dreaded. A monstrosity, the xialiti thrived among the rocky crags and crevices in the mountains west of Rephidim. Its segmented body coiled, poised for a second attack.

Despite the beast's bulk, the xialiti was deceptively agile, its short legs built for leaping onto unsuspecting prey such as khopa who foolishly poked their heads out of their burrows. Today, however, Abel was that prey. The morning sun rose higher and cast long, surreal shadows that played tricks on his eyes.

Barefoot and weaponless, Abel assessed the terrain, seeking any advantage he could find. The rocks were sharp and uneven but familiar. He had been exiled here for his heretical actions, shunned to the unforgiving wilderness surrounding Rephidim. But the mountains had become his home, and he would defend it. It was all he had.

The xialiti uncoiled and launched itself toward him. Abel side-stepped, narrowly avoiding the deadly leap. The creature crashed into the rocky terrain where Abel stood seconds ago, and the echo of the animal's frustrated roar reverberated through the mountains.

Abel's heart raced as he ran, favoring his left side. The initial confrontation had left a scrape along his thigh, a searing pain that he pushed to the back of his mind. He scanned his surroundings, spotting a narrow crevice nearby. If he could lead the xialiti there, he might trap it or at the very least, hinder its movements. It was a desperate plan, but he had no other option.

Abel ran for the crevice as the xialiti twisted and turned to prepare for another attack. His weaponless state had left him at a distinct disadvantage. The rocky terrain was uneven under his bare feet, and his exile-worn clothes were barely protection against the chill of the early morning air, much less against a xialiti's venomous spit.

He edged slowly to his left, maintaining eye contact with the beast. Its yellow eyes tracked his movement with cold, predatory precision. They were intelligent, these creatures, solitary hunters capable of waiting hours, even days, for the opportune moment to strike.

A sudden lurch of movement was all the warning Abel got. With a thunderous roar, the xialiti launched itself once again. Loose pebbles skittered away under the force of the animal's leap. The beast was a blur of color and muscle.

Dodging was not an option, not with the rocky outcrop at his back. As the xialiti closed the distance, Abel threw himself to the side, but he was not quick enough. A sharp pain lanced through his leg as the xialiti's tail caught him mid-motion, sending him sprawling to the rocky terrain.

Abel grunted. His leg throbbed with a white-hot intensity that made his head spin. He felt the warm trickle of blood staining his tattered clothes, but he pushed the pain aside. He had to get up. He had to fight.

Pushing against the rocks with his palms, he forced himself upright. His vision blurred as his body screamed in protest, but he gritted his teeth and fought against the encroaching darkness. He would not pass into shadow today. Not like this. This was not his road to Eldorado.

The xialiti coiled again to prepare for another attack. Its slitted eyes focused on him, the morning light illuminating the streaks of venom dripping from its mouth.

Abel couldn't outrun it, couldn't overpower it, but maybe...just maybe...he could outsmart it.

The sun finally crested the mountaintop and bathed the landscape in brilliant gold. The xialiti recoiled, momentarily blinded by the sudden influx of light. Abel seized his chance. He lunged towards the beast, aiming for the only weak spot he knew — its eyes.

His fingers scraped the edge of the creature's scales, but the beast was too quick. It spat, venom flying, narrowly missing Abel. However, it raked a clawed limb across the boy's side. Another searing pain erupted across Abel's flank, blinding him momentarily. He collapsed, gasping for breath, clutching at his side as warm blood seeped between his fingers. Any more of this, and he was done for.

The xialiti loomed above him and uncoiled, ready to deliver the final blow.

Abel refused to give up. He summoned his will, pushed against the ground, and attempted to get back onto his feet.

A low growl escaped the xialiti's throat, a cruel amusement in its eyes as it watched him struggle.

Abel's mind whirled, searching for anything in his environment he could use against the beast. His eyes fell on a jagged rock within his reach. It was far from a weapon, but it was all he had. A spark of hope ignited within him as he stretched his arm, fingers closing around the cold, hard stone.

The xialiti moved, slithering closer. Abel held his breath, waiting for the right moment. The beast towered over him, its body blocking the sun and casting a cold shadow. It opened its mouth, revealing rows of sharp teeth glistening with venom.

As the xialiti lunged forward, Abel acted. With a primal yell, he thrust the rock upward, aiming for the beast's underbelly. The creature's roar of surprise echoed off the mountains as the rock penetrated its thick skin, a second weakness which surprised Abel.

Pain exploded across Abel's shoulder as the xialiti's claws raked one last time across him. It fell to the side with a hiss of frustration that reverberated in the thin mountain air. The xialiti writhed, the rock embedded in its scales. It was injured, but far from defeated.

Gasping for breath, Abel scrambled backward, putting distance between himself and the beast. He could hardly stand, his body wracked with pain from multiple injuries. His vision was speckled with spots, and he was barely holding onto consciousness. But he'd landed a hit, and he'd hurt the creature. He wasn't prey.

Looking back at the beast, he saw it slither away into a nearby crevice, leaving a trail of blood behind. The animal would remember Abel, and next time, it would be more careful.

So would he.

Abel collapsed onto his back. The cold hard rocks beneath him provided a cruel comfort. The adrenaline ebbed away, leaving behind nothing but searing pain. Breath came in short, ragged gasps as he stared up at the clear morning sky.

Today, he had fought a xialiti and lived. Tomorrow, who knew what other trials awaited? But one thing was for certain—he would face them head-on, just like he did today.

Maybe.

The mountains echoed with the faint call of distant birds as the sun heated the cold ground. Amid the rocks and crags, a young man lay injured but alive, his spirit broken.

He was Abel, the exile, the abomination...

...and this was his punishment.

IT WAS as good a place to die as any other. Maybe it was better. Abel figured his body would wash away or at least feed the various critters that he'd encountered during his exile. Perhaps the xialiti could find him once again and finish him.

In the distance, a half Short Moon dipped further toward the horizon, descending into the Reed Sea. Its light drew a glittering path across the water, illuminating what might very well be a path to Eldorado. That assumed Abel believed there was something after this, a heaven, a better life than one of servitude to a beleaguered settlement that wanted nothing to do with him. He was weak from the wounds sustained in the fight against the xialiti. Headaches and muscle cramps were routine.

He looked back in the dim light of the nearly full Long Moon high overhead, following his footprints through the sand, past a myriad of maroshet, past boulders dislodged from the cliff face he'd recently left. In a crevice not a mile from where he stood, the only thing the Assembly allowed him to leave with—his quvianaq—lay rotting. Those elders of the colony had once called the animal a strider, a loyal mount creature with six arms that stood tall on two powerful hind legs who enabled transport. It had vastly improved their lives in the burgeoning days of Rephidim. Now they called it something different, a word given to them by two strangers who had visited long before Abel had been born into sunshine. Those strangers came with other words, other names they could give the various plants and animals that called the planet home.

Names. That was what the strangers brought with them. Not help, not news, not safety. Just names. And even though Abel had not yet been born when they visited, he once harbored dreams of meeting them and asking questions. As a religious tribe who looked to the sky for signs, the Col'kasid revered the strangers. That they had come from the mountains was no less miraculous to anyone who had witnessed it.

Abel turned away. How was he expected to live without the support of a community? It was apparent the Assembly didn't care. He had been exiled from home, now just a place which conjured images of hate for the person he was, sour memories of a society that worshiped a god he had never seen and followed rules from a book he was not allowed to read despite his position as a scribe.

One creature the strangers had named sat on the ground about ten feet away. The maroshet, a word that meant something like "bitter sand," was one of those animals you would not suspect had it not moved or chittered. It was black, about three feet wide, and looked more or less like a circular rock. Its hard shell apparently protected it from the elements and predators while tendrils underneath dug into the sand for nutrients. When the maroshet had its fill, it would drop the tendrils and move a few feet this way or that. More tendrils would grow and dig and feast. The cycle would continue for its entire life.

What a way to live.

There were at least ten maroshet that Abel saw. He could use a rock and crack one of them open to get at the meat inside, but that's where the word "bitter" came from. They were not the most palatable, and no amount of herbs or spices could nullify the acrid meat. Thus the maroshet were safe from Col'kasid hunters and gathers. They were safe from Abel.

Abel stumbled past the maroshet toward the edge of the Reed Sea. In the light of the Long Moon, it felt as if this was the edge of the world. Here, among the reeds that waved gently in a quiet breeze, Abel could lie down and pass into shadow. Here, with tiny waves lapping at his body, he could give himself to nature. Perhaps his rotting corpse might feed a family of maroshet for a few weeks, maybe even for a full cycle of the Short Moon.

At least then his life would have meaning.

Far to his right, the corpse of a large creature lay lifeless in the sand. It was about seven feet long. A branchlike appendage, a full three feet longer than its body, stretched out toward the cliffs. Abel knew this creature from stories the elders told of a beast that had risen from the Barren Sea and forced them all to flee. The animal could be food, but Abel knew also that there was a price for eating the raw meat of a Barren Sea shrimp. His cousin, a hunter, had tried once and was paralyzed for days.

No, this was no godsend, no manna from heaven. For Abel, there was no food here. He had not eaten in three days, and the only water he'd found had been stagnant. Since then, he'd felt dehydrated with a sickening burn in his stomach. He was failing fast, and it wouldn't be long until the Col'kasid punishment was complete.

What had he done? Nothing that anyone in love wouldn't have. That they caught him was the true sin. His kind did not belong in a society determined to grow, to abide by rules, to always prepare for the Great Return. His kind was an anomaly, a birth defect, an abomination. So the Assembly had said on the day they opened the gate and kicked him out with only a satchel of food that was now long gone and a quvianaq who was long lost.

What would the strangers have named his kind?

How long had he been in exile?

Abel felt his eyes grow heavy. He couldn't think straight. It wouldn't be long before he lost his mind and hallucinated. Perhaps he would see his quvianaq again, carrying his lover Asher aloft to him. That would be a pleasant image to have right before his world turned black as the shadows took him away.

"You should have listened." A woman's voice. His mother. She stood among the reeds, her hands stretched out to graze the tops. She looked no different from the day of punishment when she cried at the gate, her brown woven rags just as dirty as ever. She had been a lot like him—brown hair, brown eyes, brown skin. She had also been the only person to really understand.

"They're a hateful people," Abel whispered, his throat raspy. He knew this was a hallucination, or perhaps a vision come to take him home to Eldorado. For a moment, though, it was nice to not feel so alone. "They follow rules no one has seen."

"They mean well."

"They have no heart."

"They are preparing."

"For what?" Abel tried to chuckle, to show his derision to this phantom in front of him. Instead, he coughed. "The Great Return? That's a myth used to keep everyone in line."

His mother's lips turned down in a worried frown. "Did you ever believe?"

Abel did not answer. Yes, he believed once, but it didn't matter any longer. He would not be a witness to the Great Return. The gods would not descend from the sky in his lifetime. He would never know the truth. His life—all seventeen years of it—was over.

He collapsed to his knees. The muck and wet sand at the edge of the Reed Sea gave slightly to his weight. In front of Abel, his mother's image wavered in and out, flickering into and out of view before disappearing all together and leaving him once more alone.

Abel looked up at the night sky. A million stars glittered brightly, with a swath of white crossing from horizon to horizon. One of the prelates on the Assembly had called that the Milky Way, something he had heard from one of his elders who had, in turn, heard it from one of the original members of the real Circle of Light who came to this world to make it their new home.

He didn't know what a Milky Way was, but it was a beautiful last sight to see before the end.

CHAPTER TWO

KAIUS SURVEYED THE WORLD IN FRONT OF HIM. EVER SINCE he'd been tasked with Discovery—a fancy word for "get out of my city"—he'd found a lot of nothing. He was to take four scouts and head southwest toward...whatever was out there. Liorah the One Voice was ambiguous with her orders.

Standing on the top of yet another rise, he couldn't see much of anything. According to legend, the original settlers of this world had brought along something called "binoculars" which would magnify anything in the distance. Even if he had those, however, he suspected they would only magnify emptiness. A bigger nothing is still nothing.

"You see anything, sir?" Luca, a younger scout who had been eager to join this Discovery mission, climbed the last few feet to the top and stood next to Kaius. The leader regarded the boy with some disdain—he was tall, skinny, pale, and could probably slip down any one of the thousands of animal holes they'd encountered during this trip. To top it off, his recently shaved head had nicks on it. The boy needed to sharpen his blade. You'd think after twenty-one years since being born into sunshine, there were some things a person could master.

"Same." Kaius figured he didn't need to explain much more than that. They had been traveling for one and a half cycles of the Short Moon, a good thirty-seven days—perhaps not always in a straight line, but in a more general direction, a vague "that way." The hope was that there might be something of use that could be reported back to the city of New Emile—new resources, a robust food source, an ancient alien temple filled with magical things that would make everyone's life that much better. Liorah was not clear about the latter. While Kaius was aware of the history of the founding of New Emile—from the journey his ancestors had taken from a flooded Barren Sea into the Barrier Mountains and eventually to an abandoned temple called Manoach before the Great Mother Miriam led her people home—he was not sure what had been meant by "magical things."

Yet more ambiguity from the New Emilian leader.

"We should rest." Kaius turned from his view of nothing and headed back down the hill toward his three other scouts, Raphael, Nico, and Ivan. He didn't know how they ended up on his scout team, but there they were, a ragged bunch of misfits, all with their heads shaved poorly, as if they too had forgotten how to sharpen a blade.

The scouts had been busy skinning three Tishbian moles for dinner under a nearly full Long Moon which hung in the sky. If they could find enough spices, the meat might be palatable. The fat creatures with their tiny legs and needle-like noses had been the only consistent source of food for the last few weeks. It was getting on everyone's nerves, and there were only so many ways you could cook the same thing.

The temperature had dropped rapidly after the sun set. A gentle breeze in the valley between two hills was just enough to require extra clothes. Snow was for another season, and yet it was still chilly. Clouds which had gathered in the distance to the west showed a promise of unwelcome weather. More damn rain.

"Hey!" Luca, still on the hill, waved his arm. "I think I see something."

Kaius turned around. "More of nothing?"

"No, a glimmer."

Raphael chuckled. "Kid sees a few stars."

Kaius did not want to walk back up the hill. "What's it look like?" He was tired, and if he had to admit, grumpy.

"A...a shimmer of something, like when it rains around New Emile."

"What? When the moors fill?"

"Yeah. Something like that. Come see."

With a groan, Kaius returned to the top of the hill. Luca pointed toward the distance where a half Short Moon was setting. "See? There. It looks like water."

Kaius squinted. He had to admit that after forty-nine years of life, his eyes no longer worked the way they had when he was younger. Things far away seemed fuzzy unless he forced his eyes to focus.

"Huh."

"You see it?" Luca sounded like a child. "You see the water?"

"I'm not sure what I see."

"Do you think it's the Barren Sea? What we learned about in school?"

Kaius shook his head. "The Barren Sea is to the east, past a canyon and beyond a range of mountains. This...this is something else."

He couldn't be sure, but the size of the glimmer indicated something large. He looked to the right and left, but hills blocked his view of the horizon.

Ivan appeared to the left of Kaius. He stared for a moment and squinted. That irritated Kaius a little. Ivan was only in his twenties, just like the others. They should have better eyesight.

"What do you make of it?" Kaius asked.

"Looks...um...kind of like a lake." Ivan shrugged. "Maybe. Discovery means we're supposed to find things, right? Looks like we might have finally done just that."

"Hmm." Kaius squinted again. The Short Moon was now touching the horizon, casting a fainter glimmer on the water or whatever it was out there. "Guess we have a destination for tomorrow."

"Think it's within a day?" Raphael asked. He had appeared to the right of Luca without alerting Kaius.

Great, now my ears are going out, thought Kaius.

"We won't know until tomorrow." Kaius shrugged and turned away. "And I'm hungry."

They ate their meal of bitter meat around a small fire. After a few songs sung by Luca and a made-up story by Raphael about the time he bested a ku'vatar while patrolling the outside walls of New Emile, the day's travels caught up to them and they slept. Rather, everyone slept but Kaius. After an hour of tossing around, he returned to the top of the hill and looked out into the darkness. The Short Moon was long gone, but in his mind he could paint images of whatever was out there. Perhaps it was just a lake, but something in his gut told him differently.

He trusted his gut. It had served him well over the years.

THE NEXT day, after a long hike over several more hills, each smaller and smaller, they came to the edge of what could only be called a sea of reeds. It stretched out in front of them seemingly forever, as if they had reached the end of the world. The water was not deep, but the ground was nothing if not mud. Thick ooze clung to their boots, trying to suck them down into the reeds. In that way, it was a little like the moor upon which New Emile had been built. But unlike that moor, there was a smell that could only be called rancid. It grew worse as they trudged through the muck along the edge of the reeds toward the south. At nightfall, they were forced to head inland for a mile to find ground hard enough to pitch their tents and make a fire.

The following morning, Kaius led his four scouts further south along the edge of what they were now calling the Stinky Sea. The name fit. A sea breeze during the day did nothing to keep the smell away. If anything, it grew worse, like the bodies of a million rotting animals floating in the water.

By the end of the second day, there didn't seem to be anything different, save the gentle rise of a cliff to the east. At first it was maybe twenty feet high, but had grown to several hundred. It blocked out the sun after a while and left them in cool shadows. Boulders and other rocks which appeared to have fallen from the cliff face littered the ground. Between them, other odd rocks spotted the wet sand nearer to the edge of the water. They were black, some two or three feet long, and nearly circular. When a curious Luca attempted to pick one up, it chittered.

"What in the Mother's name is that?" He dropped the rock and stepped back. "It's...it's alive."

Raphael chuckled at his fellow scout's jumpiness. He stood near a second rock and tried to pry it up with a walking stick. Underneath, roots or maybe tendrils wiggled.

His rock chittered, too.

Raphael dropped the stick. "What is that thing?"

"Serves you right for laughing at me."

Kaius knelt by the rock nearest Luca. "I think it's an animal of some sort. Doesn't look to be dangerous."

"It talks."

"You talk, and you're definitely not dangerous." Kaius

stood and stretched. He looked toward the south and then out over the water. "We'll rest here for the night. Away from these things, though."

By the time night fell, they had their tents set up and a fire going. Raphael had attempted to break open one of the chittering rocks with the butt of his lance, but didn't have any luck. They were stuck with their remaining stash of Tishbian mole.

It tasted as horrible as always, and sleep was uneasy.

The scouts broke camp at sunrise without saying much. They had been each other's company for two cycles of the Short Moon, and no one had much left to say to one another. It wasn't as if they had ever been friends, just scouts who worked together and had little in common.

"You think there's anything to report?" Raphael asked as they continued their trek south, breaking a long silence. "Seems like this goes on forever."

"Discovery requires patience," Ivan said. "At least, that's what I was told."

"You told you that? We could have returned weeks ago and reported exactly the same thing we're going to report now. There's nothing out here except a big body of water."

"Well, there are those rock things that move. I think that's something."

"Another animal we can't eat. Probably tastes like this place smells."

Kaius, in the lead, halted. He held up his hand, his eyes locked on something in the distance. "There's something up there."

A few hundred feet away, a shape, maybe five feet long, appeared stuck in the mud at the edge of the reeds.

Luca stepped forward. "It doesn't look like one of those rocks with roots."

Ivan joined in. "No. If anything, it...looks...looks like..."

"Like a man?" Nico, who rarely said anything, climbed up on a boulder nearby. He shielded his eyes from the glare of the sun off the water.

Kaius swung his crossbow around, quickly loaded a bolt out of caution, and ran toward the shape. Of all the things to find on Discovery, this was a first.

ABEL OPENED his eyes, expecting to see angels on a cloud or even a lake of burning fire. Either was possible, according to the Assembly. What he did not expect to see was a man with a shaved head slightly older than himself urinating on a maroshet. The man was half dressed in what appeared to be linen, completely unlike the threads he wore. The scent of urine invaded Abel's nostrils as the man, tall and thin, held his head back and expelled a large breath.

"Piss on that one over there," the man said. As he did so, he pointed to some place Abel could not see. "I think it's pretty close to softening up."

"Not much piss in me," a voice said. "Maybe we can turn the thing over and dig out its guts."

"You don't want to do that. Did you see what happened to Nico? Damn thing wrapped its tentacles or whatever those things are around his arm and wouldn't let go."

"Nico's not the brightest."

Abel lifted his head up slightly. There were actually three men, two with their pants around their ankles and one standing off to the side, picking at something on the ground.

"Hey," a voice behind Abel called out. It was rougher and sounded much older. "Think he's awake."

The three other men turned. A slight smile crept across the closest man's face. "Lucky you," he said. "You were going to be a dinner if you didn't make it."

"Don't scare the kid," the older voice said. Abel tried to see the other man, but his head wouldn't move much in any direction. He was sore all over, but expected to feel much more pain than he did.

"Who—?" It was hard to speak.

"Relax," the gruff man said. He appeared in front of Abel and knelt down. "You're safe. I put some haelen in you, so you should be fine in a few hours. Miracle stuff, that is."

"Hae— What's haelen?"

"Water." The man held up a small vial. "Cures just about everything, from broken bones to cuts to sex diseases. You count yourself lucky we had some on us. Not much of the stuff left. Had to use some to stop Nico's bleeding."

"Water...of Life?"

The man blinked. He didn't respond right away, but cocked his head to the right.

"What's he saying?" one of the other men asked. Abel noticed for the first time that they all weirdly had their heads shaved. "Is he crazy talking?"

The older man shook his head. "No, Luca. Water of Life. I haven't heard it called that since I was a little boy running around New Emile naked."

Luca looked confused. "Is that what haelen is? The Water of Life? Never heard of it."

"You wouldn't have. Mother Miriam changed the name long before you came into sunshine. It's what it was called before New Emile was founded."

"Learn something new every day."

"You still got a lot more to learn," one of the other men said. He stepped closer as he tied a rope around his pants. Unlike Luca, this man was much larger, with sharply defined muscles. "What's your name, kid?" the man asked.

"Abel."

"Well, Abel." He spat on the ground. "They call me Raphael and that one is Luca."

Abel wanted sit up, but his body refused to move. How long had he been out at the edge of the Reed Sea?

The older man put a large hand on Abel's shoulder. "I'm Kaius. In case you're wondering, we found you in the mud a ways back. Were you with anyone else?"

Abel shook his head and suddenly felt dizzy.

"How did you get out here? Where is your home?"

It was a question Abel did not want to answer. He could have said he was exiled, but then these men might ask him why. Without knowing who they were—or where they came from—it was best not to say anything. What if they were the people he had been warned about, the people the strangers said were coming? Instead, he looked away. In all honesty, he couldn't answer the question; he no longer had a home.

Perched on a rock, catering to a wounded arm, was a fifth person. He, too, had his head shaved. Judging by the red striped wounds on his skin, Abel figured that man to be Nico. *No, you don't get near a maroshet's tentacles. How could they not have known that?*

"Need something...to eat." Abel swallowed. His throat hurt, and there was a distinct metallic taste in his mouth.

"We have little," Kaius said, "but you're welcome."

AS THE sun dipped below the horizon, Abel's body finally cooperated. He had devoured enough food to feel some of his strength return. The conversation with his new companions had been confusing. Kaius, the gruff leader of the group, had been leading them on a mission they called Discovery for almost two cycles of the Short Moon. They claimed to hail from a city named New Emile, nestled in the middle of a moor far to the northwest. And the Water of Life Kaius had given him, haelen, was no ordinary liquid. It was the stuff of legend, able to cure all illnesses and extend life beyond measure.

According to the Assembly at Rephidim, the Water of Life had come from a pool inside a temple in a rainforest guarded by unspeakable terrors. But as Abel had listened to the stories of these travelers and their wild fantasies, he couldn't help but wonder if the old folks had lost their minds. Their stories had begun to sound like the fevered dreams of the senile. And yet the magical water was real? That made him wonder if the ship that had brought people from a far-off world was real as well.

After being prodded with questions he couldn't—or wouldn't—answer, Abel eventually collapsed onto the ground, exhausted. They had set up camp near a towering cliff face, far to the northwest of where he'd almost met his end. As the stars twinkled above, Luca handed him a warm blanket, and Abel fell asleep under the watchful eye of the Long Moon. That night, he dreamed of Asher once again, his body rotting under a full sun.

"I'M TELLING you," Abel said, "you don't want to eat that."

Raphael had finally weakened the shell of a maroshet and cracked it open with the butt of a lance. The white meat inside looked tasty, but Abel knew the truth.

"We've tried cooking it twice, boiling it, covering it in herbs, making jerky out of it, and even eating it raw. It's horrible, and your stomach will rebel."

"There isn't much else out here," Kaius said. "You have any other ideas about food?"

Abel looked around. They had been making their way along the cliff face toward the northwest. It was clear that they were going to allow Abel to stay with them, and hopefully the people of this new city would welcome him with open arms. Much better than being kicked out and left to pass into shadow. He wondered if he would have to shave his head.

"There are a few roots on top," Abel said, vaguely pointing to a crevice in the cliff face. "You'll need to climb."

Luca looked up and shielded his eyes from the glare of the sun. "What kind of roots?"

"Baca. It has a green spike on the top filled with water, but under the ground there's a purple bulb. It grows near the Reed Sea but only on elevated surfaces. There's a sweetness to it once it's roasted."

"My stomach is rumbling just thinking about it." Luca set his lance on the ground and moved toward the crevice. "Who's going with me? Nico?"

Nico held up his arms, still striped red from his battle with the maroshet. "Not a chance."

"Ivan?"

Ivan shrugged and followed Luca to the cliff face. It wasn't a tall climb, maybe a hundred feet, but it was steep enough for Kaius to warn them. "Fall, and you're on your own," he said.

Kaius turned to Abel as Luca and Ivan started their climb. "Help me understand. You were out here at the edge of—" He waved his arms toward the sea.

"The Reed Sea."

"Right. The Reed Sea. No food, no water, nothing on you but an empty satchel. You're not exactly the warrior type, no offense meant. How did you get out here?"

There would be a time to explain further, but this was not it. "I got lost," Abel lied. "I was trying to find my way around the cliffs when my quvianaq took a fall. He broke his legs and passed into shadow in a crevice. I didn't have anywhere else to go but down."

"What's a qua—quvi—"

"Quvianaq. I've been told they were originally called striders. It's an animal that stands on two legs, but you can ride. My people have been using them to get around, chase down herds of Tishbe bison, and keep predators away."

"An animal you can...ride?" Raphael had been listening in on the conversation. His eyes were wide with wonder. "What a miracle would that be? Hell, I'd love to get me one of those. We'd be back in New Emile in no time."

"They aren't found out here by the Reed Sea," Abel said. "Only along the edges of the desert near my..."

Kaius waited a moment for Abel to finish. "Near your what?"

"Where I came from. Rephidim."

"Rephidim? That's the name of your city?"

Abel nodded. "I'm... I'm not welcome there."

"Why not?" Raphael asked. "You're not some sort of killer, are you? A criminal?"

Again, it was a question Abel was not ready to answer. "No, not a criminal." He quickly asked a question of his own. "Where did you come from? There were two strangers who came to visit us long before I was born into sunshine. They said that everyone at the temple in the rainforest had been murdered and we were it. Is that not true?" He decided at that moment to leave out the warnings. If the group of men he was with *were* from across the Barren Sea, Abel was in trouble. Then again, he would probably already be dead.

"You're not making any sense," Raphael said. "The only humans on this planet are at New Emile. Everyone sent out on Discovery in the last fifty years has proved that."

Kaius looked at Raphael, then held his hand up. "Obviously not true. I think our guest here is proof enough of that."

Raphael scrunched his face. "So...Liorah. She lied?"

"Let me answer this," Kaius said. "This is before your time."

A tumble of rocks alerted them to where Luca and Ivan were climbing. "Hey!" Luca shouted, his voice distant but loud. "You almost hit me with that damned rock. Watch where you're going!"

Ivan called down. "If you were any bit of a man, you'd be up top by now."

Kaius turned back to Abel, shaking his head briefly. He looked at Abel and waited a moment before continuing. "What did your elders, the Assembly you speak of, tell you?"

"Just that they left a temple in a rainforest. I can't remember the name. The way they tell the story, though, seems all made up."

"How so?"

Abel shrugged. "Well, for one, they kept telling us that their elders—their ancestors—came from a planet called Earth on a ship that's now under water in the Barren Sea. They said they had once lived in a city on the edge of that sea and had to flee when the waters rose. After a long journey to find shelter, they ended up in a rainforest surrounded by animals that didn't want them there." Abel paused. "What I never understood was why they said they had to leave to find a new home."

Kaius nodded his head. "Our Great Mother Miriam, who passed into shadow years ago, led our people across a canyon to an abandoned city she found and called New Emile. Most of what you just said is what I learned growing up."

"You did?" Raphael had a look on his face that said all of this sounded made up. "We learned nothing like that."

"Long story about why," Kaius said. "Anyway, the temple your elders mentioned was called Manoach, if I remember right."

They were silent, the only sound the distant lapping of waves against reeds and the occasional pebble dislodged from the crevice where Luca and Ivan were still climbing. Abel felt more confused than ever. He had always believed the Assembly had crafted stories to tell their children, stories to keep the Col'kasid in line. He never really trusted any of what they had said, and he had been in training to be a scribe. It was one of his duties to listen and record all of these tales. But honestly, even the legends of the two strangers, who it was said confirmed the Assembly's accounts, were hard to believe.

"How far away is this...Rephidim?" Kaius asked at long last.

Abel swallowed. He knew what would happen if he went back. "I...I don't know. I walked for weeks. Your New Emile might be closer."

THEY ATE baca, the purple root roasted according to instructions given by Abel. By the time night fell, they were satisfied and ready to sleep. In the morning, Kaius would lead them back to New Emile.

He didn't want to. He wanted to find this Rephidim and learn more about whoever was out there, whoever apparently exiled this strange kid—although that was a word Abel would never use. It was still obvious. Kaius had seen it before, many times—the look of those unlucky to have been born after the population lottery was put into place, the look of the dissidents and those who had been exiled from New Emile for having conflicting beliefs. They were outcasts, the Marokai, and they longed for a home they would never have.

Kaius had been lucky in that regard. Born into sunshine just ten years after the founding of New Emile, he and the others of his generation had been spared the results of the population lottery instituted by Master Eilian, Miriam's son. A booming population in the first forty years had caused a need to construct more and more buildings, but supplies were limited and construction was difficult. It was too hard to build outside the wall on the moor itself. As a result, it became obvious to many that the colony would run out of room quickly, and drastic measures needed to be enacted. Shortly after the passing of Mother Miriam and Eilian's ascension to power, he decreed that anyone born in the third and fourth generation should be enrolled in a lottery. Those selected in the lottery were given the mark of the Marokai and escorted out of the city. Age didn't matter. Once a person became eligible for labor at sixteen, their name was placed into the lottery. While a claim was made that it was the only fair way to deal with the population boom, it was not a popular law despite everyone's agreement that something needed to be done. And in order to carry it out—to mark the Marokai and escort them out of the city—the sentinels were called in to enforce it.

It was one of the first jobs Kaius hated. While he didn't mind escorting the dissidents or the religious nuts out, it felt morally repugnant to take a sixteen-year-old child who had not yet learned a skill and move them to the Hollows where they may or may not be welcomed. That, and burning a mark into the forehead was worse than gutting an animal with bare hands. Despite the use of haelen to heal a person quickly, marking was something he hoped to never have to experience.

Like most rules, however, the lottery didn't apply to those in power. Eilian's child Philip was exempt, as were those born of the Elite—the advisors on the council. Eilian's concubine later gave birth to a second child, Liorah. For reasons still unknown, Philip passed into shadow when he was just thirty-eight—long before he was to take over the duties of the most powerful person in New Emile. That left the heir to Liorah, who was just eighteen. Two years later, Eilian passed into shadow of the same disease that had taken Philip, and Liorah assumed power—the reincarnation of the Great Mother Miriam herself. New Emilians were confident she would reverse the lottery. She was a woman, after all. Surely she could better empathize with all the mothers among the population who had been forced to watch their children leave.

Liorah did not change the law. The Marokai were not welcome in New Emile and dissent was not to be tolerated. Community opinion did not matter when it came to Liorah's council. Truth be told, Kaius never believed her council had any say at all, and all power rested with one. Liorah, the One Voice, was not to be disobeyed.

While the others slept, Kaius kept watch perched on a boulder overlooking the Reed Sea. The Long Moon was lower in the sky and stars speckled the night. They still had muck to trudge through before climbing hills into the Wastelands between the Reed Sea and New Emile. Kaius was sure their journey would be shorter given that they had a destination in mind and were no longer wandering around on Discovery. He estimated they might make it back in one cycle of the Short Moon, maybe a few days longer—provided the weather remained decent and storms were few.

There were some oddities about recent discoveries on this trip that he couldn't place his finger on. First, the boy— younger than any of his own scouts—did not look strong enough to have made the journey he claimed. He was emaciated, and no amount of haelen was going to fix that. Abel claimed to have come from a place called Rephidim, but its very existence bothered Kaius. When he learned about the history of the humans on the planet from schools set up by Mother Miriam, the teachers made much ado about the fact that those living in New Emile were it. How the Great Mother knew that, Kaius never questioned and the teachers never explained. There was no need. If the founder of New Emile said that the world only extended to the edge of the moors, the people would believe it. They had to.

So if this Rephidim existed and the people there had descended from those who were once at Manoach—a point in common with New Emile—were they related? And what else had Mother Miriam been wrong about?

Abel stirred a little and sat up straight. He wrapped a blanket around himself and shifted closer to the still glowing embers of the fire they had made that night. Kaius regarded the boy for a moment before finally letting loose a quick whistle to get his attention. Slowly, the boy stood and joined Kaius on the boulder overlooking the Reed Sea.

"Can't sleep?" Abel asked.

"I don't get much of that." Kaius did not look at the boy, but he had to admit he was pleased to have the company. "I normally stay up and watch for threats while the others sleep. Before sunrise, one of them—usually Raphael—will take over for me and I can get an hour or two in."

"I haven't slept much, either." Abel pulled the blanket tightly around him. "Keep thinking there's a something in the rocks, but I know that can't be."

"Why is that? Other than that rock that stung Nico and the carcass of a shrimp, we have encountered little in the way of wildlife."

"There isn't much out here near the Reed Sea. Something about the smell keeps the animals away."

"I don't blame them." Kaius made a face. "Smells like rotting flesh and vomit."

"You get used to it."

They listened to the gentle swell of waves passing through the reeds. As they sat, Kaius reflected on this boy, this stranger from a strange land. He had never had a child—sentinels were forbidden—but he often wondered what it would be like. Luca had been as close to a son as he could have had, but it was difficult to talk to him, as if they shared nothing in common. Talking to Abel seemed easier. Natural, even.

"Is Rephidim the only colony you know of?" Kaius asked.

Abel took a moment too long to respond. "Before I was born into sunshine," he finally said, "there were two strangers who came down from the mountains. The Prelatic Assembly tells stories of what they told us, and no one ever questioned them."

"Prelatic?"

"There are five people who make decisions in Rephidim. The man in charge, Elder Levi, is the Keeper of the Text. The others—Mateo, Malachi, James, and Levi's son Gideon—are all prelates."

"Sounds complicated."

"Not really. But what they say is the law."

"Who were the strangers?"

Abel shrugged. "I don't know. Some say that Sojen Micah, the leader of the Col'kasid for the first twenty years and the first Keeper of the Text, knew them both. They were brother and sister, lost souls from that temple in a rainforest."

"Manoach?"

"Right. That's it. But legends change the more they're told around campfires, and by the time I first heard it, the strangers had become more like prophets than humans."

"Prophets?"

Abel picked up a small twig near the boulder they were perched on and drew in the sand at their feet. At first, Kaius thought the drawing might be related to these strangers, but after a while it looked no different than a few squiggles with no meaning.

"There is another tribe far to the north," Abel said. "According to the strangers, they live across the Barren Sea. They are more advanced with things like electric power, transports that move on their own, and many weapons."

Kaius perked up at the mention of these things. When he was younger, he had heard Mother Miriam tell stories about what she had learned from her grandfather—stories of the electric power that existed on Earth and how things called auto—autocars?—moved people around with no need for animals to pull them. That was on Earth, though. This was Tishbe, and as far as Kaius knew, no advancements like that had ever been made in New Emile...or anywhere else, for that matter.

"Did the strangers have a name for this tribe?" Kaius asked.

"Oh, they had names for everything." Abel chuckled and pointed at two rocks about fifty feet away. "The maroshet. The xialiti. The quvianaq. It's really all they really gave us. That, and a story about what they apparently witnessed at the temple."

"What about it? Our Great Mother Miriam told us tales, too. I never knew what to believe, since I knew she never returned across the canyon. It would be interesting if their stories matched, however."

"I don't know." Abel returned to his drawing. "Everything the Assembly said the strangers told us changed each time. Who knows? They left quickly and never returned. According to legend, they disappeared looking for more people. I assume they never made it to New Emile."

The maroshet nearest to them chittered. Kaius watched as the animal crept an inch, perhaps in search of more food. It was at once both fascinating and disturbing to watch.

"Who is the tribe to the north?" he asked after a moment.

"Um..." Abel stopped moving his stick around in the sand. "The Zhanshi, I think. According to the Assembly, we should always be prepared to fight if they ever showed up. That was the real message the strangers gave the Col'kasid. What happened at Manoach might also happen at Rephidim."

"What is that supposed to mean? What happened?"

Abel stuck the stick in the sand and sat back on the boulder. "Genocide."

CHAPTER THREE

CHEN TSENG SURVEYED THE INSIDE OF THE DERELICT SHIP. There were signs of water damage, but not as much as he had expected. For nearly fifty years, the ship had rested on the bottom of the Barren Sea. Now, inexplicably, the vehicle that supposedly transported his ancestor Mathias the First — the founder of their great city — from Earth to Huolong Yaosai was on dry land.

The water had receded quickly. It hadn't been a completely dry few years, but there had certainly been a shift in the weather patterns. Rain, which normally kept the rivers and reservoirs near their home valley filled, had been coming less frequently. He wasn't currently worried about what that would do to the hydroelectric power stations erected fifty-six years ago, but he had to admit it made him nervous. The village of Xin Shijie de Yaolan, the cradle of the new world, did not get a lot of power from the stations — enough for a modicum of lights and to power a few small machines — but it would be a loss, nonetheless.

According to the oral histories of Yaolan, his ancestor Mathias Tseng had been forced to flee this very ship the day it arrived. The others had discriminated against him because of the color of his skin, the way he looked, and how he held honor above all else. The many times Mathias had attempted to contact the colonists to seek help or offer his intelligence, they had rebuked him. It was a story told many times, and a reminder that the other humans on the planet—the *gulao*, wherever they were—were ruthless killers who must be dealt with. The Circle of Light, as they called themselves in the beginning, was a dangerous cult of fanatics worshiping a god whom they'd called Elijah. They were cruel. At least, that's what the histories said. Chen didn't know if any of it was true, as this ship was the very first sign of any proof of that history. For all he knew, stories could have changed as they were passed down from generation to generation. The lack of reliable evidence often shrouds the truth of legends.

Now he was in the ship's belly, wondering what other proof he could find.

The inside was weird. Not only was the ceiling low— Chen had to duck most of the time—the walls appeared to be made of an organic material, certainly not metal. They were dark, gray green in most places. Contorted shapes with knobs and recesses with no apparent purpose were dotted about. It was unlike anything Chen had ever seen, but reminded him a little of the caves to the north of Yaolan.

As he meandered through what might have been the main corridor, he tried to picture humans living within the ship. According to those same oral traditions about Mathias the First, there were other stories brought from those who had lived with him in the earliest days. They told of approximately three hundred people living and working inside the ship, each with their own purpose. There were agriculturists, chemists, biologists, janitors, cooks, and even some security personnel. It was a vibrant community for nearly three years, growing even until the time came for the event called Transit which had brought the settlers to the new world.

Chen believed less in those stories than he did about Mathias. Why would so many people choose to live in isolation and follow a leader like their Elijah?

In a room to the left, there was what appeared to be a bed frame with a dresser. It was severely water-damaged, but beside the dresser there was a metal trunk with a lock. A seal of some sort wrapped around the bulk of it, as if it had been designed to withstand submersion. Rather than attempt to open it, however, he simply regarded its size—maybe three feet by two feet and one foot thick—and tried to read what had been stenciled on the surface.

A.L. HELLE - 187 - 061475 - PER. AFF.

Chen assumed the A.L. Helle was a name, but he had no guesses as to the rest. Whatever it was, it apparently mattered a great deal to this person. He picked it up, noticed its weight, and placed it outside the room in the corridor for later retrieval.

The other three men he had been with on this journey to the ruins had been placing items outside rooms as well. Most of them were trunks like A.L. Helle's, but there were a few other interesting items—something that resembled a bone with bristles on the end, a figurine of an animal, probably from Earth, and a flat rectangular object which surrounded what appeared to be a faded picture. He'd seen pictures before—Mathias the First had carried one himself and never let it out of his sight when he was alive. Following his death, that picture became part of a shrine set up to honor the man's legacy. All Zhuren—leaders of his tribe, the Zhanshi—were expected to maintain the shrine and add one or two items from each of the leaders over time. There was a crossbow, a broken bolt made of metal with a black tip, a piece of rock that had a silvery appearance, and a carved figurine of a rychat—a beast known to frequent the rainforest far to the southwest past the mountains which loomed over the derelict ship. Each of these items held a personal meaning to the Zhuren who owned them. Chen often wondered what he would leave behind when it was his turn to die.

"Empty-handed I entered the world, barefoot I leave it," he said to himself. It was a mantra, one of many handed down to Zhuren over the years.

"Zhuren Chen." Lucien, one of Chen's advisors, moved around the trunks placed in the hall. He approached with his shaved head low, not necessarily to avoid hitting the ceiling but more out of respect for Chen.

"What is it?"

Lucien kept his head bowed. "There is another room down a floor. It is like the caves at Yaolan."

Chen's eyebrows rose. "The caves?"

"Yes, Zhuren. A deep well."

"Show me."

Chen followed Lucien down the corridor and to the left, where a room led to a set of stairs. Approximately twenty feet down the steps to the right of the cluttered hallway, there was a substantially larger room. He tried to map out where he might be relative to the size of the ship as viewed from the outside. Near the middle, maybe? Underground?

They were in a room with rusted metal panels and buttons and switches, which sat below an enormous transparent wall. On the other side of that wall was indeed a cavern, much like the one discovered in a cave north of Yaolan. From deep inside, a green glow emanated, while around and through it all, a few broken wires hung along metal boards large enough to walk on.

Below those wires there was...nothing. It wasn't exactly nothing and Chen knew it, but it certainly felt that way. Looking down into the vast expanse below was like trying to see out the back of his head. It hurt. It wasn't a blackness so much as an image of nothing, a void that played with the brain in bad ways.

"It is like the legends say," Lucien said, leaning over one panel to get a better view. "The Well of the ancestors."

Chen could not disagree. It was like the legends, but again, those were oral stories passed down for decades. Things could have changed.

"Did the ancestors not say there was a machine in their ship, Zhuren?"

Chen nodded. "They did. It is said the recusant Zachary had been there, deep in the Well with others. They had traveled to another planet and hoped to return one day."

Lucien spit, as was customary when mentioning anyone who was not a blood descendant of the Zhanshi. "The recusant spoke truth, but are we to climb down to find this new world?"

"No." Chen leaned over himself. "The Well needs repair, and no one who understood how to fix it is still alive. It was said there is a mineral in the mountains which must be mined first."

"Like the silvery walls of the caves near Yaolan?"

Chen shrugged. "Perhaps. But for now, there is nothing we can use from this hole." He turned to go. "We take what we can carry and we will figure out the rest at another time."

"Yes, Zhuren." Lucien nodded and quickly left the room.

When they returned to the main corridor, the men he had been with had already gathered together a few of the trunks and other items and placed them near the entrance — more a hole torn in the ship's side than an actual door.

"Load these," Chen said, "and then we will visit the city of the damned. Perhaps there is more we can learn of these barbarians in the ruins of what they left behind."

THEY LOADED what they could carry onto a cart powered by a small battery. The battery would not last long with the additional weight, but at least they would get much closer to Xin Shijie de Yaolan before it ran out. He had men to pull it the rest of the way.

He was proud of his men, just as he was proud of all the Zhanshi. They were, themselves, a proud people—all four hundred thirty-nine of them. They worked hard, loved deeply, and were prepared to defend the village should anyone come to visit. Chen had a feeling it would be soon. He had read it in the shift of the weather, felt it in the chill at night, and found signs in the stars above. Those who had punished Mathias the First so heartlessly would come to Yaolan soon enough.

Animals who have tasted blood once always return for more.

The Zhanshi had to keep preparing.

Rather than move the cart to the ruins of the City of Nod—a stupid name, if ever there was one—they opted to leave it next to the derelict ship and return once they had scavenged what they could carry. There would be time to return should they need to retrieve more than they could haul on their backs. Chen honestly did not believe there would be much left. When the waters had risen—an event which happened during his grandfather's time—it fully submerged the buildings and farms, laying waste to everything the Circle of Light had built in the forty-one years they had staked a claim on the edge of the dry lakebed. They could not have known the waters would rise from the ground, or perhaps their hubris blurred their own suspicions. Whatever the case, the city was in ruins.

Chen and Lucien hiked toward the shore of the lakebed

together, while his two other men, Martin and Tye, walked farther ahead. There were holes peppered all around, some large, some small. In them lay massive creatures, likely hibernating until the waters rose again. One of those creatures lay dead on the ground to their left—a reddish beast with a body about six or seven feet long, and two tentacles which withered in the sun. There was a smell in the air, something like death and rotten food mixed together.

"What is that thing, Zhuren?" Lucien asked as they passed the carcass.

"Barren Sea shrimp, or so my grandfather called them. He told me a story of how these animals lived in the holes and came out to punish the others when the waters rose. Mathias the Third was a wise man, who remained above the flood waters and out of sight as the people of this city fled in fear of the unknown."

Lucien looked at the shrimp, then around at several of the holes. "They live under our feet, Zhuren?"

Chen nodded, a sly smile on his face. "Do not let the ground crumble."

Lucien looked down, careful where he stepped. The ground felt hard to Chen, but looks could be deceiving. Only when they reached the edge of the lakebed did Lucien finally appear to relax.

Martin stood with Tye, their crossbows slung around their shoulders. The sun was relentlessly hot, and had already burned their shaved heads. Chen had been smart enough to wear a cover.

"Zhuren, what do we look at first?" Martin asked.

"Whatever you can find." Chen regarded the ruins. It was clear there once was a vibrant city—with over eight hundred people, according to his grandfather. But now there was little save for rotted wood and debris. Some of the wood had kept its shape, likely the Tishbian Oak that grew in the forests on the other side of the city. It was an incredibly sturdy wood, hard to cut and shape. There were few trees like that in the valleys around Yaolan. Only softer woods grew there. On the one hand, construction was easier with those trees, but on the other, the buildings were not as sturdy when the rains fell.

As they hiked through the debris, they each found at least something to remark upon. Tye found a muddy skull, while Lucien and Martin both uncovered broken plates and other dishes. There were a few leather belts, degraded and rotted beyond use. Some bricks of an unknown material were present near what might have been building foundations, but even those were worn down after so much time underwater. A sizable piece of metal, with signs of rust and pitting, was positioned up against the remains of a building. It was possible that it could have been part of a roof, but this was simply speculation. Chen did not know. He poked around with a stick, but nothing really seemed to grab his interest save a metal smelting pot. It was too heavy to carry back, however.

In the end, the hope that they could find something to salvage from the City of Nod faded even as the sun sank lower in the sky. It would be nightfall soon, and Chen already had a plan to set up a camp near the powered cart for the night. They could use some of the wood to build a fire. It would take three days to return to Yaolan, and they would need to rest first.

Tye volunteered to go with Lucien to find an animal to eat for the night, and in the morning, they would start the journey home with whatever spoils were in those trunks. Chen hoped this trip would be worth it in the end, but he did harbor doubts.

He would not tell his men that, though.

—

THEY TRIED to open the first of the trunks after eating a meal consisting of huan and some herbs. Despite the huan's nasty disposition, its succulent meat made for a delectable meal when cooked over an open fire. Provided the eyes were tossed into the fire, the rest of the animal was edible. Lucien had lost the tip of a finger when he checked to see if his bolt had killed it. For all the pain it caused him, he was happy to gut the beast when it was still squirming. It was hideous—four eyes, two each on the side of a pink nose and two near tiny ears. The thing needed to die.

"Why do you think they left these trunks behind, Zhuren?" Martin examined the box in front of him, unable to get it open. "They stripped out most everything in there, including bedding and wires. Surely they must have taken it all."

"It is most likely that the people who brought these trunks with them from Earth did not live long." Chen looked at the trunk in his lap. "Like this A. L. Helle. If he or she did not survive, then perhaps their quarters were kept as a shrine."

"Like the Zhuren Shrine in Yaolan?"

"No, not at all like that. We honor our leaders by remembering them. The colonists who withheld help from Mathias the First had no honor. I am sure there were no pilgrimages to pay their respects to their fallen companions."

"How are we supposed to open them?" Tye picked up a rock next to his feet and banged against a latch once. Nothing happened.

"Persistence pays," Chen said. He demonstrated by using a rock of his own, coupled with a small metal rod he had picked up from the ruins of the City of Nod. He repeatedly banged the rod with the rock until the metal holding the box together snapped. The other three followed, and soon all four trunks were open. Chen watched as they rummaged through their finds, an excited smile on his face.

In the trunk in front of Martin, there was nothing but frames with pictures, a piece of paper with a crudely drawn scene of what could have been a house and a stick figure family, and a few books. The seal had protected them from the water, but their utility was unclear. Why would you save worthless items such as these? He held up one book and read the title. "Harry Potter and the Sorcerer's Stone." Martin's face scrunched up as he flipped through the pages. "What is this?"

"Probably a book of fiction," Chen said. "Something that is not real. It would be good kindling for the fire, though."

Tye had no better luck—a few items of clothing, a stuffed animal that appeared nearly new, and a white ball about the size of his fist. It looked to be stitched together with red thread, a name written on the side. He opted to keep the ball and stuffed animal, and threw the rest of the contents to the side.

Chen regarded the contents of his trunk. There were three books and a stack of papers. He had learned to read as a child from his grandfather, who had learned from the earlier settlers of Xin Shijie de Yaolan. But not all words were known to him. Some of them still had to be sounded out slowly. "An... Anar... Anarchist's Cookbook." He flipped it open to a page near the back where there were crudely drawn diagrams of what looked like weapons. "It is no cookbook I am familiar with," he said, more to himself. "I do not know the word Anarchist, but I do know some of these things."

"What is it, Zhuren?" Tye asked as he stroked the fur on the stuffed animal.

"I... I am not sure, but if what I read is correct, there are ways to make explosives and other weapons in here, as well as ways to grow something called marihuana."

"Marihuana?"

"An herb, it looks like. Must grow on Earth as I have not seen a plant like this here."

Chen flipped through a few more pages. There were drawings of weapons that had handles on them, instructions for making "psychedelics," and ways to build a bomb. So many of the words were hard to understand, but he knew a few people in Yaolan who read better. This might actually prove to be very useful, indeed.

This he would keep.

The second book he pulled out of the truck had a useful title—*A Guide to Canning, Freezing, Curing and Smoking Meat, Fish and Game*. The animals mentioned in the book were unfamiliar—what was Canadian bacon or a chicken?—but the ideas seemed to make sense. This A. L. Helle appeared to have been a very smart man or woman. There was no doubt in Chen's mind that this was a valuable find.

"Any luck, Lucien?" Chen asked, setting the book back in the trunk while picking up the third.

Lucien held up a colorful book and turned it to the side. A page fell forward, opening the book more. A large comic grin crossed the man's face. After a moment, he turned it around for all to see in the fire's light. On the page was a naked woman with red hair kneeling on a bed.

"Yes, Zhuren," Lucien said. "I think I have found true treasure."

DURING THE return trip to Xin Shijie de Yaolan, Chen absorbed himself in the two books he'd found the most useful. He couldn't believe the amount of information found inside its pages. Not only did they explain how to cook and preserve certain foods—something his village needed right now—they also discussed how to develop weapons for both defense and offense. There were very few threats in the valley other than animals, but always in the back of his mind, he was reminded of his grandfather's words: "Seek them out first. Vengeance is the fruit of preparation and desire. You must feed the dragon for it to survive."

As expected, the cart ran out of battery power before leaving the dry lakebed on the second day of their journey to their home in the north. Martin and Tye were forced to attach ropes and pull the cart themselves. The batteries they had been using were an intriguing discovery from the past that had been refined over time, but their limitations were becoming more apparent. A small enclosure contained a blue-green material extracted from the caves around Yaolan, lanluzite. When it was exposed to sunlight, it glowed and produced a small electrical current. Provided the battery received light for a few hours three or four times a week, the current could last up to half a year. Only when it was used to power small machines did the usefulness wane. For a light that was only a few hours a day, the battery might last two cycles of the Short Moon. When it was coupled with other batteries of the same type and placed in a cart, the user had about two weeks of power. If the cart was overworked—for example, by hauling salvaged items from the Circle of Light ship up a slight incline—those same batteries would last only a few days. They could be recharged, but that would mean getting more lanluzite from the caves, something that would have to wait.

The Zhanshi had been working on a way to use the power generated by the hydroelectric stations built along the rivers north of Yaolan to augment the lanluzite batteries. Progress had been made, but there was still work to do. Chen believed that once his people learned how to keep a charge active in a larger battery, they could do great things. Perhaps they could develop carts that would last for weeks and haul more than supplies or make machines that would aid in the agricultural fields and orchards surrounding the village.

"What have you found, Zhuren?" Lucien asked. He and Chen had been walking behind the cart, absorbed in their reading. Lucien had finally put away his book of naked women and now seemed to take an interest in something more useful.

"I believe we may have a way to bolster our defenses if we are ever attacked."

"We are but one small village in a valley protected on all sides. Who would attack us?"

Chen shook his head. "We are not protected enough. When my grandfather was alive, he told of a group of refugees from that same ship who promised to continue their attack on our people. They were animals, seeking first to destroy. My grandfather was able to eliminate one threat, but he soon learned that there were many more who would wish us harm. Like cowards, these animals fled."

"Where? We have seen no signs of others except the ruins back there."

Chen looked toward the west and the mountains in the distance. "Over those mountains, there is a rainforest and beyond that, a canyon. Exploration has shown us that there may be a way around it if we go farther north before moving west. Out there, somewhere, are the descendants of those who caused our ancestors pain."

"If so, Zhuren, they are far away." Lucien spit on the ground. "Why not let them be if they cannot threaten us?"

Chen stopped walking. He measured his words well, considering how best to explain to this man what vengeance meant. "Lucien, when the huan bit you, did you not get angry?"

Lucien looked down at his injured hand. He had wrapped a piece of cloth around a finger. The cloth, now soaked with blood, needed to be replaced. "The animal did not deserve mercy," he said with a snarl.

"No, it did not. And if that animal had fled, perhaps as a coward might, would you pursue it?"

"I would not have rested until I cut off its head."

Chen nodded. "And if you did not?"

Lucien did not answer right away. No doubt in Chen's mind, the man was trying to figure out how to equate the huan with their enemies. "I would expect the huan to have come back again," he said finally. "An animal like that does not stay away for long once it has tasted the flesh of another."

"And that is the same with those who came to our planet, to Huolong Yaosai, with Mathias the First. The gulao are animals, and while they fled in fear from what they did not understand, they still had a taste of flesh. They struck out at our people first. Unless we eliminate them, they will lick their wounds and prepare to attack again. No doubt, that is what has been happening now for years beyond that canyon."

Lucien looked toward the west. "So we must always be ready, Zhuren."

"Yes." Chen put his hand on Martin's shoulder. "Yes, we must always be ready. And if the time comes when we learn where these animals have fled, we must be prepared to take the fight to them. For our children and our children's children."

"And you believe you have found a way in that book of A. L. Helle?"

Chen nodded. "More than just a way, Lucien. This book may be what finally feeds the dragon the vengeance it needs."

CHAPTER FOUR

NEARLY A WEEK LATER, ABEL AND HIS NEW COMPANIONS had crossed the muck of the Reed Sea delta and entered what Luca called the Wastelands. And what a waste it was. There were few plants that reached higher than their ankles, and the grass—jivara, as the New Emilians knew it—grew in dense yellow and red clumps.

Before his exile, Abel had never left the land surrounding Rephidim. There was no need. The buttes upon which Rephidim was constructed were all that Abel knew. He was too young to have joined the scouting parties which had found places such as the Reed Sea and explored the mountains to the west of Rephidim. It shocked him the day he first laid eyes on the ocean, however. How the Col'kasid hunters who had ventured so far described it was nothing like reality. Even as a scribe, he had trouble putting it into words.

Now Abel was in territory that was strikingly different from anything even those scouts had known. As far as the Col'kasid were concerned, there was nothing beyond the river that fed the Reed Sea, or at least nothing that interested the Assembly. As a result, they had directed most exploration south of Rephidim into forests of massively large trees that could provide enough building material to expand as the Col'kasid grew, and to the west where herds of Tishbe bison roamed. Beyond the southern forests was the unknown, and it was forbidden for anyone to travel north. Those lands were sacred to the Col'kasid by decree of the leader emeritus, Sojen Micah.

What wonders they would never see if they kept to their rituals.

"What do you think?" Luca asked Abel as they crested a small rise and faced more of the same. They both stopped and stared while the other four in their party continued on. "Wastelands, eh?"

Abel let his eyes wander across the landscape from left to right as far as he could see. "It's, um, different." The wind had picked up over the last two days and the air had a scent to it, like wet soil.

Luca smirked. "That's a word for it — different. It's like this all the way to New Emile. A lot of nothing punctuated every once in a while with more nothing in shades of gray. If you see a stick or find a bush, grab what you can."

"For?"

"Fire. It won't be easy to find fuel as we go, so collect early."

Abel looked down at his feet and saw a small stick, maybe a foot long. "I don't get it," he said as he picked up the stick. "Why do you stay in such a dismal place?"

"Where are we supposed to go? That's the purpose of Discovery, I suppose. We've found building supplies far off to the north, but it's colder there. Not exactly the best place to move."

Abel had learned a little about New Emile in the past week since being rescued, from its strange customs to its basic government structure. He knew that their leader, Liorah, had the only say in matters but that she occasionally listened to advisors, if only to have someone to blame should her decisions turn out bad. That there was another settlement of humans at all was miraculous, but even more so was the size of the population—five times more people than lived at Rephidim. And that was just inside the walls.

"You say there are too many people to fit inside the city?" Abel asked.

"Right." Luca's smirk disappeared.

"Where do they live? These others. You say you call them the Marokai?"

"Those who disagree with Liorah, people charged with a crime, and some people who just don't want to live in the city—they live outside the walls on the edge of the moor."

"That doesn't seem like there would be that many people. Are there other reasons why people live outside the walls?"

Luca's face darkened. "New Emile has a population lottery." He paused for a moment as if gathering his thoughts. "When a person reaches the age of sixteen, they're put into a lottery. You either win a labor and get to stay inside the walls or you're asked to leave. It has something to do with resources. Too many people in one place would put a strain on our food supply and shelter from the storms we get. At least, that's what Liorah tells us."

"Sounds awful."

Luca did not respond.

After a moment of silence, Abel asked a different question. "Do you have a brother or sister?"

"I do. Both, twins. Elena and Diego. Younger." He looked down and away. "They are Marokai."

Abel opened his eyes wide. "You mean they *both* lost the lottery?"

"Twins are treated as one." Luca turned to face Abel. "Look, there are laws for a reason. I'm sure the Col'kasid have laws you don't agree with, customs that you'd like to see end. It's not like my brother and sister were put to death."

Abel could not dispute that. Rather than say anything else, Luca motioned for Abel to continue down the side of the hill. The others were ahead by about three hundred feet, making their way toward another small climb.

"What is that place called?" Abel asked.

"Place?"

"Where the Marokai go?"

"It has no official name. We call it the Hollows just because it's easier to say than 'that place outside the walls where the Marokai live.'"

"Seems like a horrible thing to break apart families like that," Abel said quietly after a while. "Doesn't your Liorah see that?"

Luca shrugged. "It's not so bad if it's all you know. It's not like the Hollows is filled with children. Everyone knows what the rules are. If you don't want to break up a family, don't have children."

"The name Marokai. Where did it come from? It sounds like maroshet, the animals on the beach by the Reed Sea."

"It does, doesn't it?" Luca kicked a rock. "I think it was Master Eilian who came up with the name. There's a stupid legend that he gathered all his advisors in a room for two days straight to debate what to call the people living outside the walls. Eventually he just got angry and made up a nonsense word. Ironic that it sounds so similar to those things on the sand."

Before Abel could say anything else, Luca continued. "You ask a lot of questions. And here I am thinking you might tell me a little more about where you're from. Reph— Rephi—"

"Rephidim."

"Right. Rephidim. What's it like there?"

Abel considered how best to answer. He wanted to tell Luca all about life with the Col'kasid—from its rituals to the dictates of the Prelatic Assembly—but at the same time he didn't want to think about it. He was at once relieved to be away from them and heartbroken to be an exile. Thinking about Luca's brother and sister, he suddenly missed his own family and realized just how similar he was to the Marokai—unwelcome.

Before Abel could answer, a flurry of motion and a shout came from up ahead. "Ready bows!" Kaius called out.

Luca was quick. He immediately swung his crossbow around and pulled a bolt from a quiver. Before Abel could blink, his new traveling companion rushed forward to join the others.

Abel could not run as fast as Luca. By the time he reached them, all had their crossbows drawn. They were at the top of another rise, and there in front of them, four animals each about four to five feet long blocked the path, their bodies crouched down in what looked like a position ready to pounce.

Abel regarded them. He had never seen such creatures, which was not surprising given how much of the world he had not been exposed to. The animals all had limbs that looked muscular, with red and yellow spotted fur. They could no doubt run fast and change direction quickly. Across their muscular necks were stripes which spiraled down onto their spines. It was perhaps the slenderness of the body that was the most disconcerting, however, like they would know how to slither into tight spaces. They didn't make much of a target when facing you.

"Ku'vatar," Raphael said, probably in response to the scrunched up confused face Abel wore. "It's a predator that normally eats moles."

"Where did you come up with that name?"

One animal was slightly ahead of the other three, sharp teeth shockingly clear as it snarled. Rather menacingly, it cooed.

"Oh. I get it." Abel felt his heart beat faster in his chest, memories of fighting with the xialiti fresh in his mind. "Why aren't you shooting at it?" How he had wished he'd had a weapon on him then. He tried to keep his voice low and even.

"They don't normally hunt like this," Kaius said. His crossbow was aimed at the one ahead of the others. "They're solitary animals, adapted to hunting large areas for food. And they don't take kindly to our little bolts."

"You mean you can't kill them?"

"One, maybe. Two, if we're lucky. But unless we split them apart, one of us is going to be in trouble the minute we unload."

"Why are they together?" Nico asked in a whisper. He stood to the right of Kaius, looking down the sight of his bow. "I thought they didn't share."

"Your guess is as good as mine." Kaius took a small step backward, something Abel did not expect. "We might have stumbled across a den."

"A den?" Abel asked as he stepped back himself.

"Adults live and hunt alone, but they're brought up in packs."

"So this is a pissed off mother."

"And father," Ivan added.

As if knowing it had been identified, the ku'vatar to the right stepped forward. It was larger than the others, maybe four or five feet long. Abel guessed the thing probably weighed a good sixty-five to seventy pounds.

"Move to the right," Kaius said softly. "One step at a time, and keep your eyes open."

Nico did as instructed. He sidestepped slowly, all the while keeping his bow up. Abel felt better behind Kaius and tried his best to remain there. No need to make himself an easy target with no weapon.

The animals watched the humans as they all shifted slightly away, eyes locked on potential threats. It wasn't until Abel put his foot into a burrow and slipped that things went from bad to worse.

The largest animal leaped at Luca, who had reached down to help Abel up. Immediately, Kaius let loose a bolt which struck the ku'vatar in the neck while it was still in midair. With a screech, the animal's momentum carried it forward until slammed into Luca. Animal and man tumbled down the side of the hill just as Abel righted himself. The other three creatures were already in motion.

Abel panicked. He'd never been in a situation like this before. His instinct was to run, but he knew he had to help Luca. While Nico and Raphael launched their bolts and Kaius attempted to reload his crossbow, Abel tumbled down the hill after Luca and the larger ku'vatar.

They were about fifty feet away, and the animal was not dead. If anything, it looked angrier. Luca had pulled himself out from under the beast, but blood soaking his tunic told Abel what he needed to know—the ku'vatar would easily overpower his new friend with one more attack.

About twenty feet from where Luca and the animal faced each other, Abel spotted a dropped crossbow. There was no bolt, but it was cocked. As Abel reached for it, Luca glanced up. "Shoot the damn thing."

"There's no bolt!"

Luca reached behind him and withdrew a bolt from a quiver. Without looking, he threw it back up the hill.

"Load it!" Luca called out. He crouched and steadied

himself. The ku'vatar shook its head, the bolt that Kaius had launched into it still sticking from its neck. "Aim for the chest."

Abel had never been good with a bow, and he had never wielded a lance. He had been a nervous child, preferring to gather herbs and fruits with his mother rather than ride quvianaq on hunts for Tishbe bison like so many other men his age. They had mocked him, of course. That was the way of the Col'kasid — differences are not tolerated.

He picked up the crossbow and scrambled toward where the bolt had landed. Another strange high-pitched coo erupted from the ku'vatar, and behind him, up the hill, he heard the all too gruesome sounds of a different battle taking place between his new companions and the other three animals.

"Hurry," Luca said. He didn't shout, just growled the words between his teeth. "The chest. Before it moves again."

Abel slid the bolt into the groove, hoping it was in the right place. With a shaking hand, he held the weapon up just as he took a position next to Luca.

"The chest," Luca pleaded once again.

The ku'vatar stopped shaking its head and assumed that same pouncing pose as it had before. With the body low to the ground and the neck of the animal jutting out, Abel had no way to see his target. He looked down the path of the bolt as he had seen others do in the past. With a deep breath in and then out, he pulled the trigger.

The bolt sailed harmlessly past the animal and embedded itself in the ground far behind it.

Rather than immediately pounce, however, the ku'vatar leaned forward. It took a single step and shuddered. With another coo, this time much fainter, it fell over on its side, finally succumbing to Kaius' bolt. Air escaped from its chest one last time.

Abel shook. In his moment to be the hero, at exactly the precise time that someone needed him, he had failed. The bow in his hand fell to the ground. Quickly, Luca picked it up and Abel felt a hand on his shoulder.

"You did good," Luca said softly.

"I...missed."

"Did you?"

Abel tore his eyes away from the dead animal in front of them. He looked at Luca through watery eyes. "The bolt. It—"

"It's okay." Luca cracked a small smile. "I won't tell the others."

WHILE ABEL and Luca were uninjured in their battle with the ku'vatar, the others had not fared as well. When they reached the top of the rise prepared to help—Luca with his crossbow once again and Abel with just adrenaline—they saw the three other animals dead. All of them had bolts sticking out of their chests and neck and one had been impaled on a lance. Blood pooled around each animal, but rather than revel in their victory, Kaius, Raphael, and Nico were huddled around Ivan.

Ivan had a gash in his leg. From the amount of flesh missing, Abel figured he would either lose his leg or pass into shadow right there.

"Get the haelen," Kaius said to Luca as they approached. "In my satchel."

While Luca left, Abel knelt beside a shivering Ivan. The wind had picked up and a very real threat of a storm was on the horizon. Raphael pulled a strip of cloth from a blanket and wadded it up. When he pressed it into the wound, Ivan screamed.

"Hold him still," Raphael said. "I need to get this bleeding under control."

Both Kaius and Nico held Ivan down the best they could. Raphael nodded at Abel. "Put your hand on this and push down as hard as you can. Keep the blood from pouring out."

Abel did as instructed, despite repelling at the sight. The blood had already soaked the cloth and felt warm on his hands. Raphael reached into a satchel and pulled out a small rope. He threaded it under Ivan's thigh, then pulled it tight.

"What's that for?" Abel asked.

"Tourniquet. Hopefully, he'll bleed less and we can get him some of the haelen."

"Is that really going to help?"

Raphael glanced up at Kaius. His expression told Abel all he needed to know. The tourniquet, the rag, and even the haelen would not do a thing for Ivan. The man was sure to pass into shadow soon.

The scene briefly reminded Abel of how his uncle looked on the day he'd passed into shadow and gone to Eldorado nearly a year ago. He'd been one of the few people to accept Abel and even talked him through some of the more difficult times. There, in his bed in the middle of the night, his uncle had shivered as well, a gash from a xialiti refusing to close. No doubt if Ivan's eyes were open, Abel would have seen that same realization in them.

Ivan screamed again as Raphael pulled the tourniquet tighter. "Sorry, Ivan."

Luca returned with a leather bladder and what they had left of the haelen. Abel didn't know how much of it had been used on him when he was recovering next to the Reed Sea, but he recalled Kaius mentioning that he hoped they'd have enough for the trip back to New Emile.

Ivan was not long for this world. Was it wise to use any of the precious miracle water on him?

With another shuddering scream, Ivan arched his back

and kicked. The sudden motion knocked Abel backward. He righted himself then reached for the rag once again, but Nico had quickly taken over. As Abel stood, he realized there was nothing he could do to help. He would only be in the way.

While four people huddled around Ivan trying their best to save the man, Abel took a step back. Out of the corner of his eye, he saw a wall of dark clouds. The wind picked up with more ferocity and there was a notable drop in the temperature. In no time, torrential rain would be upon them. There was no way they were going to get themselves to shelter.

"Rain's coming," Abel said, not expecting anyone to respond.

Instead, Kaius stood. He wiped blood onto his shirt and turned to look toward the northwest. "Not just rain. Hail. We need to find shelter."

"Shelter?" Abel was confused. There was no shelter in the Wastelands that he could picture in his mind. They were on a rise on a plain that was spotted with nothing but jivara as far as he could see.

"I don't understand," Abel said, feeling stupid.

Kaius ran toward his satchel where he'd kept the haelen. Ivan was no longer screaming, but his chest rose and fell with great effort. In seconds, Kaius returned with a long piece of metal topped by what looked like a foot-long piece of wood. "Go down there," he said, pointing toward where the ku'vatar that had attacked Luca lay dead. "Find a hole about a foot wide on this side of the hill. It's where the moles live."

"You want me to...dig it out?"

"Not all of it. Just enough to fit a body, maybe two feet deep. When you're done, find another hole and do the same. We need six." Kaius glanced at the storm. "Hurry. We have about an hour before that storm gets here."

Abel looked at the piece of metal in his hand and then where the ku'vatar lay. It was an impossible task.

Within a few minutes of starting to dig into the first hole, however, Luca and Nico appeared, each with their own pieces of metal. Abel did not stop, but he had to know what had become of Ivan.

"He's on his way to Eldorado," Nico said, his voice breaking. "We'll think about that later."

Kaius and Raphael joined soon after, and between the five of them, they were able to dig out five separate holes, each about three feet deep and seven or eight feet wide. It was easy to dig around where the Tishbian moles had dug into the ground, and Abel had to admit it surprised him at how deep their nests went. That they never showed their faces was not as surprising, however. He would have hidden, too. Breaking up the ground with the metal was easy, and it made sense to dig out the holes on what would be the leeward side of the hill when the storm hit.

After the five holes were dug, Kaius dug one more for their supplies while Abel followed the lead of the others and crawled inside. Abel was directed to put a blanket over his head, curl himself up into as tight a ball as he could, and find some solace in calling out to his god. Soon, darkness enveloped the hole as the hail—clattering and pounding on the blanket—grew deeper. Thankfully, it hadn't been too large.

Despite his anger at the Col'kasid for exiling him and his ravenous distaste for all they held sacred, Abel prayed.

AFTER A long night trying to keep as out of the elements as he could, Abel heard the call of Kaius.

"Safe!"

Abel pushed the blanket off him. There was about two

inches of hail on the ground around his hole, looking more like snow than anything else. Much of it had washed into the valley between two hills, piling up in mounds about a foot high. The rise had protected them a little, and despite an incredible chill in the air following the storm, Abel felt warm inside. His fingers, however, were numb.

The barren Wastelands had transformed from yellow and red jivara to a world filled with stones made of ice, each one between an inch and two inches in size. It was something Abel had never seen before. Hail was as rare as snow around Rephidim. He pulled a blanket around his body, covering his head and face as much as he could. Puffs of air condensed in front of him with every breath he took. How could it get so cold so fast? He glanced over at Luca, who was busy retrieving his supplies. Raphael and Nico headed up the hill once more, following Kaius.

At the top of the rise, a lump of ice showed where Ivan's body lay. Under three other lumps lay the ku'vatar, once a family learning to hunt together, now nothing but flesh soon to decay.

"Clear here," Kaius said. "Set up a fire with whatever you picked up." He looked out toward the northwest from where the storm had come. Blue green skies greeted them as the sun rose higher. "This ice will melt soon."

"What do we do with Ivan?" Abel asked. He had no intention of brushing the hail off their fallen companion's body, but he certainly wouldn't be left there. Would he?

Luca answered. "We leave the flesh for the animals. New Emilians bury nothing."

"So...you just leave him here...to rot?"

Kaius turned. "Not to rot. To fulfill one more purpose. To give back to nature what nature gave to us."

"It's just... Well, in Rephidim, we have a ceremony with

a fire. I thought you might do something similar."

Now it was Luca's turn to look confused. "A fire? Don't tell me you burn the bodies that pass?"

Abel nodded. He'd been a part of so many funerals in his seventeen years of life. There seemed at least one per Short Moon, and over the past few years, more than that as diseases or famine struck the Col'kasid. "'All the valiant men arose, and went all night, and took the bodies and burnt them. And they took their bones and buried them under a tree and fasted seven days.'"

"What is that?" Raphael asked. "Some sort of speech you give those who passed into shadow."

"A part of it. I've heard it so much, it's easy to recite."

"So..." Luca looked at the mound of hail under which lay Ivan's body. "You burn your bodies and don't eat for seven days?"

"Oh, we eat. That part is always ignored."

"Good thing," Raphael said, punctuated by a whistle. "Because I'm starving and those three ku'vatar will cook up nicely."

CHAPTER FIVE

GIDEON, SON OF ELDER LEVI AND FUTURE KEEPER OF THE Text, stood at the bottom of the butte and looked out past the brush and rocks and emptiness that was the land between Rephidim and Patience Gap. He knew Abel was not there, but he had been coming out here for days just to be sure. No, his friend was gone. The boy he'd played with as a child, the boy he'd been tutored by, the boy who had become a man and then found love was not equal in the minds of the Col'kasid.

It sickened Gideon. He hated the rules, hated the dictates of the Prelatic Assembly, hated the way his father made a mockery of what was in Father Elijah's Bible.

As the sun rose higher into the sky and the temperature increased, a tiny gust of wind tousled his hair. Who could he talk to who wouldn't reprimand him for thinking that the Assembly's decision was wrong? Worse than the exile, both Abel and his lover Asher had been sent in different directions, never to be seen together again. He had a feeling that Asher, another good friend, had already passed into shadow. Had Abel found his way to Eldorado as well?

Gideon turned toward the west. Beyond the mountains in the distance, over what was called Patience Gap, there lay the Reed Sea. Gideon had never been there, but he'd heard stories from those who had explored the land around Rephidim in the early years of the colony. It called to him, yet a walk of two days was not possible. He would need to return to the Assembly soon, to perform his duty as one of the five prelates. It didn't matter to them that he needed time to mourn. He had a job to do.

What was that old saying his father, Elder Levi, often preached? For everything there is a season, a time to do things. That included a time to mourn, although the responsibilities of the Assembly were often too great to allow for such frivolities.

With his mind wrapped in the loss of his friends, Gideon wandered a good distance from the butte. Here the land was flatter, spotted with tiny bushes and a few clumps of grass called koralitha, used in many ceremonies. The midday sun was unkind, downright hot, as if the world were out of balance.

He could have taken a quvianaq, that loyal mount animal. Mournful journeys, however, should be made on foot and barefoot. Gideon was not about to unstrap his sandals, though, as the desert would certainly tear up his soft flesh. Then again, that was the point — to suffer.

Gideon stopped and looked up. Ahead of him, in front of the foothills of the far mountains, there appeared a small cloud of dust, most likely an approaching traveler. The hunters, his last remaining friends Isaiah and Jacob included, had been preparing for a long hunt, but the dust clouds they would have created would have been much larger. No, a single person and most likely someone on foot was creating this cloud.

Who would be out here alone if not to mourn? *Abel? No, it couldn't be.*

Of all the places to be bothered. Gideon believed that if

he walked far enough, he would be left alone with his tears. There were only so many people in the colony and all of them had things to do, from gathering crops, to collecting water, building shelter, and cooking food.

As the figure approached, it took on a more defined shape. There was a distinct limp, too, and without a doubt Gideon soon knew who it was. Sojen Micah had returned from his own mournful walk. The original founder of Rephidim—a legend with stories to tell of massive animals, escapes from floods, and horrific sights to see in a faraway rainforest—slowly made his way toward Gideon with the aid of his walking stick. That stick, Gideon knew, was nothing like the one his father had. It had been said that Micah carved the earliest histories of his life on the stick, starting when he was younger than Gideon was now. How long ago had that been? Fifty-five years? Micah was over seventy now.

Micah's wife, Patience, had passed into shadow a few years ago, the first casualty of a disease that had ripped the Col'kasid apart. After, the man had slipped deeper into his cave, where he and his wife had lived together for over five decades. Gideon had heard occasional noises as Micah dug his love's grave and eventually laid the woman to rest in a ceremony attended only by himself. To have that much love for each other was inspiring, and all the Col'kasid mourned with Micah.

As the Sojen approach, Gideon dipped his head in reverence. Micah slowed even more and eventually came to a stop just before the boy. The old man looked Gideon up and down before finally speaking.

"Perhaps you feel sandals are appropriate for a mournful journey."

Gideon blinked but kept his head down. "How did you know I was on a mournful journey, Sojen?"

"Have you ever seen someone come out to the desert without food or water and not on the back of a quvianaq who was not?"

"No, Sojen. I have not." Gideon regarded Micah's feet. Rocks and brush and a week or more in the desert had left them bruised and caked with dried blood and dirt.

"Tell me, son. What has happened in my absence? Has your father made a new rule that I should know? Do have to wash my ass before sitting down now?"

Gideon smirked. Old men could have a sense of humor. "None that I know. Nothing much has changed since...since, well, the exile." The smirk was quickly replaced with a frown.

"Hmm." Micah leaned forward on his walking stick. "I am sorry for your loss."

"All we do is for the glory of God."

"Hmm. Do you believe that crap?"

Gideon looked up, shocked. "Crap, Sojen?"

"Crap." Micah tapped his walking stick on the ground and twisted it a few times. "I'm sorry I didn't intercede the way I should have, but the truth is your father has his own beliefs. Once he casts his stone, his mind is made up."

"It's not right."

"Who said it was?"

"My father. The other prelates."

"No. Your father, sure, but there was only one prelate who cast his stone toward exile. The other two wanted to let Abel and Asher off with nothing more than a warning to change their ways."

"Who? And why should they have to change their ways?" Gideon felt his face flush with anger. "There was nothing wrong with what they did."

"It doesn't matter who. Once you were banned from casting your stone, the decision was ultimately in the hands of your father. I'm just sorry I didn't intervene."

"None of this is your fault." Gideon took a deep breath and looked out toward Patience Gap, the last place he figured Abel would have been. "It is what it is."

For a moment, the only sound was the rustle of brush as a gentle breeze blew by.

"Shall we return?" Micah nodded toward the butte where Rephidim lay secured several hundred feet up the side. "The evening will come eventually, and I don't want to be out here in the night again."

Gideon said nothing but agreed with a nod. He turned around and walked slightly behind Micah to the left, where custom dictated he be. Only Patience had been allowed to walk to Micah's right.

After a while, where the only noise was the tick-tick of Micah's walking stick on the ground, Gideon felt comfortable enough to ask a question he'd been dying to know.

"Sojen. How did you and Eldress Patience get together?"

"Hmm." Micah didn't answer right away, and for a moment Gideon feared he had crossed a line. The tick-tick continued, but seemed to be a little louder.

"Patience was not in my sights when I was younger," Micah said finally. "I was caught up yearning for another woman, Christina."

"What happened?"

There was an extended pause before he answered. "She passed into shadow while we were at Manoach. A creature of sorts from under the pool where the Water of Life was kept reached up and grabbed her. That event is how I ended up with a limp."

"What kind of creature? A xialiti? Or one of those Barren Sea shrimp I've heard tales of?"

"Neither. We never saw the animal again, but I suspect it

still lives there, in the pool. Call it one of many reasons we should never return to that temple. That, and the damned rychat in the trees."

"So if you had been so focused on Christina, how did Patience come into your life?"

Micah smiled slightly. "After Christina passed, I fell into a deep depression. Patience talked me off the ledge many times, and for that I could never repay her." He stopped walking and turned to face Gideon, his eyes narrowed. "Why are you asking this?"

Gideon's cheeks grew warm from embarrassment. "Just curious."

"That's not true, and you know it." Micah tilted his head slightly then smirked. "You're thinking about a wife, aren't you? You come out here on a mournful journey and your mind goes to women."

"I'm too young for that."

Micah shook his head then poked Gideon in the chest. "You're no older than I was when I married. You're sixteen. Did you know that on Earth you would be around nineteen? At that age, you could vote in elections, be shipped off to war, or get married. It makes sense to me that you'd feel this way now."

Again, Gideon felt his cheeks blush. He'd never shared his thoughts with anyone before, except Abel.

"Who are you thinking about?" Micah asked.

Gideon looked up at Rephidim built into the butte high above and still a distance away. He saw small dots, people who were milling about, some in the garden over the waterfall, some moving from place to place with purpose. It was a vibrant community, but it was also small.

Very small.

"No one, actually," he said finally. "That's the problem.

A man cannot be whole without a wife, as my father has repeatedly said." He shook his head. "Because of that, I can never be Keeper of the Text, and to tell you the truth, I don't even know if that's what I want."

"Do you believe everything that man tells you?"

"He's my father. How can I turn a deaf ear?"

"Look, Levi may be my grandson, and I love him, but that doesn't mean I have to agree with everything he says. It doesn't even mean that I have to like him. The man can come up with some ridiculous rules."

Gideon furrowed his brow. *Why allow it, then?* he thought.

As if reading his mind, Micah shrugged. "Why do I allow it? I'm not the leader any more than you are. We have an Assembly for a reason, and at the head of that is your father. If he makes mistakes, then so be it. People will learn. If I were to intercede every time the man opened his mouth, I would never get a moment of rest."

"So you don't think a man has to be married to be whole?"

"Look at me." Micah held his arms out wide. "Am I no longer whole because Patience has gone to Eldorado? Am I no longer a man? Could I not lead?"

"Of course not, Sojen. I just mean—"

"You take care of you." Micah put his arms down and resumed walking toward Rephidim. "When the time comes, you'll meet someone. You may not even realize what's happening. Love doesn't come in with a roar, but silent like a thief, there to steal your heart."

—

MICAH SETTLED down in what had been his home for fifty-five years, a cave really, naturally formed and nestled behind the room where the Prelatic Assembly met. A torch flickered near the entrance. His feet were sore from the mournful walk, but his spirit felt renewed. Patience had passed into shadow exactly five years ago, and he had honored her memory with a walk each year. Sometimes he'd be out for weeks, sometimes only a few days. This time, he left the day Abel had been exiled and followed the boy at a distance until it seemed he was safe.

He prayed nightly for a miracle.

Abel's exile weighed heavy on him. In a way, Micah understood what it felt like to be an outcast, though not for the reasons that set Abel apart from the other men. Rather, Micah had always felt...different. He had been a boy stuck in his own mind, unable to let others in. Friends were few, and it wasn't until Patience started hanging around him that he finally felt like he belonged somewhere. Perhaps Abel could find that, wherever he was.

But would he? As far as Micah knew, there was no one else on this damned planet. Whatever happened to his cousin Miriam was still a mystery, one even a visit from the strangers couldn't solve. How would a boy, trained as a scribe, survive in the harsh wilderness?

Not for the first time, Micah chastised himself. He should have intervened. It was unfair to allow his grandson Levi to make such a decision without a true quorum. There was an odd number of people on the Assembly for a reason, but when Levi decided Gideon should be banned from the decision because of his friendship with Abel, that left an opening. If just one person sided with Levi, he would win the debate.

Micah rubbed a rock placed over the grave of Patience. It was smooth from years of his gentle touch, like a kiss he could give his love before saying goodnight. Bodies in Rephidim were burned, but he would not allow that to happen to his wife. He had promised to stay with her until he passed into shadow himself, and that was taking a little too long.

Next to the grave lay an ancient text, one gifted to him by the two strangers who visited Rephidim years ago. It was well worn, and, like every other ancient text Micah had ever laid eyes on, untranslated.

He had tried. For years, he and Patience poured over the strange logograms and symbols of this alien race to figure out their meaning. Progress was painful, and while the notes left in Father Elijah's Bible had helped some, they were not enough.

Something about a seed.

Something about a third race apart from the sa'ja'veil and sa'ja'peet.

Something about a Well.

It was frustrating. Micah pushed the text to the side and rolled out his blanket. He grabbed a pillow Patience had made for him and lay down, staring up at the smooth ceiling of the cave. A tiny tendril of something white winked at him, one of the many bugs that dug their way in and out of the homes of Rephidim. They were small, maybe the size of a man's thumb, and they were lonely. Rarely would a person find more than one, and if there was another nearby, they seemed to repel each other.

He felt that—alone, repelled.

Ever since Patience had passed into shadow, Micah's mind had been filled with doubt. Doubt in his ability to lead, doubt in his worth as a man, and worse of all, doubt in his knowledge. She had been a rock, keeping him forever steady, on the right path, and mentally sound. Now she was gone.

Like Christina.

Like his sister Candice.

His parents.

His cousins.

His son.

Rephidim was full of strangers. He should have been proud to have founded the colony, to see the Col'kasid grow and flourish. He should have been elated at each birth, rejoiced with each marriage, and cried at each passing. Instead, none of it mattered.

He thought of a koralitha seed, protected by a hard, spiky shell, nestled in the dark soil. This seed contained the essence of life, waiting patiently to emerge.

As the seasons changed, the seed absorbed droplets of water. Tiny fractures appeared in the shell, allowing the first tender roots to push through. The seedling strained upwards, driving its stem through the soil and shell fragments. It burst forth into sunlight, spreading its embryonic leaves open wide.

The koralitha plant grew tall and strong. It unfurled tall leaves, grasses, to soak in the sun's energy. Roots expanded deep and wide to drink in moisture and nutrients. As seasons turned again, flower buds formed, opening into radiant blooms. These buds yielded ripe koralitha seeds, which spiraled down to start the cycle anew. On and on, the koralitha spread its grasses, each season bearing more abundant seeds protected in their spiky shells. Generation after generation, the plants traced their lineage back to that first seed that shed its shell and embraced the light.

Yet what happens to the shell? It is still there, decaying beneath its creation until it is no more.

Micah was that shell, and Rephidim no longer needed him.

A single tear fell from his right eye. Quickly he wiped it away and turned over on his side to face his wife's grave.

"It's taking too long, my love," he whispered before closing his eyes and falling asleep.

CHAPTER SIX

IT TOOK ANOTHER THREE WEEKS TO REACH THE OUTSKIRTS OF the moor where New Emile stood. Trees had appeared here and there, but none of them were very tall. At the most, they reached up waist high. The weather had turned from windy with occasional showers of rain, to just windy and somewhat muggy. At least there had been no more storms laden with hail. Luca had said the Wastelands were behind them, but Abel wasn't so sure about that. Compared to the land around Rephidim, this was just as empty.

From the top of a rise, the ground sloped away into what looked like a lightly flooded plain of interconnecting streams and tiny ponds. For at least a mile, there were no trees and only a few spots of jivara, the grass that so dominated the world behind them. If it weren't for the buildings in the middle of it all surrounded by a large stone wall and a large grouping of poorly built shelters far in the distance—which Abel assumed to be the Hollows—he would have thought this was just more of the Wastelands.

Why would anyone choose to stay in all this gloom?

There, in the middle of that bleakness, was New Emile. A stand of buildings, some large, some small, which stood like blocks sticking out of the mud. Abel was struck by how many there were—a hundred, maybe more. He imagined that a thousand people could easily live within the walls, but according the Luca, that wasn't the case. There were maybe seven or eight hundred, with the rest—the Marokai— relegated to shacks that offered little protection from the wind or other elements.

Abel noticed, too, that each building within the wall appeared to be made of stone. On that point, he had to break the silence.

"Where did all those stones come from?" he asked.

Kaius stood near, his lance in hand like a walking stick. The man had been like a father to Abel throughout this trip, telling him about life in New Emile. They had compared stories they'd both been told about the original settlers of Tishbe and the lives lost at Manoach. As part of the schooling Abel had received to become a scribe, he had been given genealogies to memorize. Kaius, too, seemed to have the same education, and Abel had to wonder why the man had become a sentinel. Did he have a choice?

"Do you see that hole down to the right of the wall?" Kaius pointed with his lance.

At the edge of the stone wall around New Emile there was indeed a hole, maybe fifty or sixty feet wide. Abel couldn't see inside, but there appeared to be a structure built over it, like logs held together with rope. In the middle of that structure there was some sort of box.

"What is that?"

"That's the quarry. In the first years after Mother Miriam established the city, she learned how the original builders brought stones up from the ground. Tiny patterns are carved into the surface of rocks far below the city. We can then lift—"

A loud screech interrupted Kaius. It was at once high pitched and jarring to the teeth. Abel instinctively put his hands over his ears. In seconds, the pitch changed in tone, dropping much lower. Suddenly Abel felt his stomach vibrate.

"What—"

"Sound!" Kaius yelled over the noise. "An acoustical force is exerted on an object from below and above." He raised his voice as the higher pitch took over again. "The high pitch pulls while the low pitch pushes."

"Pushes what?" Abel did not like the noise, nor that he had to scream to be heard.

From inside the hole, a block appeared. It was small from this distance, and if Abel had to guess, he would have said it was two or three feet wide. It looked wet, like a rock he might have pulled out of a stream back at home. A flurry of men and women surrounded the hole on one side. With long poles, they pushed at the stone until it was over the edge.

With a crash, the stone fell to the ground, and the noise cut off.

Abel heard a ringing in his ears. He blinked a few times and opened and closed his mouth. It felt like those times he'd closed his mouth and nose and tried to pop his ears as a child. His stomach felt queasy.

"There's a huge deposit of stone below," Kaius said, his voice muffled by the ringing. "Workers go down, carve out a rock, etch in the correct patterns, and then position it for the sound engineers." Kaius smiled. "It's really an amazing thing and the only reason we're able to keep building shelters in New Emile."

Abel tried to blink and yawn away the stuffiness in his head. He regarded the stone, now positioned on top of two logs and being hefted by four people.

"What makes the sound?"

"Uh...I'm not completely sure. We call it a harmonic transducer, but I have no idea what that really means. It's something that was found in New Emile during the early years. Something left behind."

"Left behind? By who?"

Kaius shrugged. When Abel was in school to be a scribe, he had had heard stories of another race on the planet who had written books left in the temple at Manoach. He never believed them. It seemed to be yet one more fantasy dreamed up by the Prelatic Assembly to control the beliefs of the Col'kasid, and even though most of the stories came from Sojen Micah and his wife Patience before she passed into shadow, it all seemed too fantastical.

Yet if there had been another race, could they have been the ones who left this sound device, this harmonic machine? And how was it powered? The strangers had said nothing about this.

Abel continued to stare in amazement at the quarry, giving his ears time to recover. His eyes wandered to the left of New Emile, beyond the wall and slightly up a hill on the other side. The Hollows, with their buildings made of sticks and covered with grass, looked exceedingly fragile.

"What about the Hollows?" Abel asked as he pointed to the distance. "You don't use stone to make those buildings?"

Kaius dropped his smile. It looked as if he wanted to say something more, but just shook his head. Rather than pursue a line of questioning that would get him nowhere, Abel looked back toward the quarry.

"How many stones are brought up a day?" he asked.

"Only a few. You're lucky to have been here to see that. Down below, the walls dampen the sound a bit. The transducer is directional, so being in front of it is ill advised. If you're behind it, you only hear a fraction of the noise."

Again, Abel flicked his eyes toward the Hollows. How did they deal with the sound when it was directed at them?

"Who are the workers?"

"Come," Kaius said, ignoring the question. "We should get you into the city. Liorah awaits."

As Abel followed Kaius and the others down a path into the moor, he noted that the ground was solid but lined with smaller stones. Away from the path, the ground became muddier. As they continued toward the city, mud turned into puddles which turned into small ponds in places. The smell was...dirty.

He looked closer at the workers around the quarry. Most were dressed in rags. Another man, who wore what looked like leather over a brown tunic, stood to the side. As the stone which had been brought up from the ground was moved, one worker lost their grip on the log. With an audible thump, the stone fell over.

The man in the leather yelled and immediately held up what might have been a long stick. Abel stared in disbelief as the man swiftly brought the stick down on the worker's back. A scream filled the air, ear-piercing despite the distance. It was a woman.

"What just happened?" Abel asked. He stopped walking and stood on the path while Kaius, Raphael, and Nico continued walking as if nothing had happened. Luca remained with Abel.

The woman quickly righted herself and scrambled to help the other three place the stone back on the logs. The man said something to her, although the words were unintelligible. She seemed to cower before resuming her place and holding up one end of a log.

"Marokai," Luca said, his voice tinged with something Abel had trouble placing. Remorse, maybe? Was he checking to see if it was his sister, Elena?

"They're the workers? The Marokai?"

"They get half a ration of grain if they help bring stones

into the city."

"I thought they weren't allowed to live inside the walls?"

"They aren't allowed to live inside, but some of them still come in and out."

"Some of them?"

Luca pointed to his forehead. "The mark on the forehead is like a pass."

"What do you mean? What mark?"

"The Marokai are marked with a line after the lottery. Some of them are given labors that will bring them back into the city. Like the quarry workers you see."

"I'm sorry. You're telling me that not only are people pulled from their homes and sent to live outside the walls, they're...branded?"

Luca nodded once. "Those who have caused or will cause trouble are given a different mark — a triangle over the line. They are not allowed anywhere near the city."

"What, like criminals?"

"Criminals and people Liorah doesn't like." Luca smiled slightly. "So much to show you, Abel. I sometimes forget all of this is new to you."

"Very."

After taking a few more steps, Luca turned to look in the direction from which they'd traveled. "It's hard to imagine that there's a colony of people living out there."

Abel had to correct him. "Two other colonies, actually."

Luca shook his head and whistled. "An entire world we haven't seen. Well, maybe you can tell me about your home soon. I'd like to know more about it."

Abel smiled.

"Come," Luca said as he nudged Abel down the path once more. "Let me show you some wonders. Oh, and we'll have to shave the hair off your body."

CHAPTER SEVEN

ELENA COULDN'T WAIT FOR THE DAY TO END. SHE'D HAD enough of the quarry, enough of the dirty water, enough of the attitude of the sentinels standing watch. They could go to Hell for all she cared. The only thing saving her from sending any of them there herself was a desire to eat and the need to protect her brother, Diego. And that the latest watchman wasn't too hard on the eyes.

She glanced over at Diego, his wan, shirtless body covered in grime and sweat as he hammered away at a chisel embedded in the rock. They had been carving out a three-foot by three-foot block of stone, which would eventually be lifted and used as a foundation for a new dwelling within the city walls. It was astonishing that all this effort had to be given for buildings she could never call home. No, her home was a rickety mess of sticks and adobe that had to be patched every time a wind storm came to visit. And that was all too often. The thatched roof of jivara was bound to cave in soon.

While it was permissible for families to visit the Marokai—but not the other way around—no amount of pleading could convince that witch Liorah to let them inside unless escorted. They were filth, and filth were not welcome on the streets of New Emile. After a while, living in the Hollows was just like living on another world. Families rarely had the time or the energy to visit, and eventually people just forgot who you were. At least their older brother Luca visited occasionally, but he had not been around for a full cycle of the Long Moon—a quarter of the year. Elena often wondered if something had happened to him. He was a scout, the only respectable position a sentinel could hold in her opinion, and had one of the most dangerous of labors.

Elena felt that familiar pang of guilt. It was her name that had been selected in the lottery, and Diego, just a few minutes younger than her, paid the price. They were both given the mark of the Marokai, with the only hope of redemption being the possibility that either of them could be given a position of servitude within the New Emile Chambers. That didn't happen, and within a day, Elena and Diego found themselves living with a blended family of six in the Hollows.

At sixteen years old, it was expected that a person could do just about anything. That's about when labor in the quarry had begun. Now at eighteen, Elena and Diego had worked themselves up from the less glamorous tasks of sweeping up chipped rock and carrying it out, to cutting a form so the extraction crew could insert their acidic lines to slice through the stone. They only had to cut a foot deep, a task that took three or four days when two people were assigned.

"How far have you gotten?" Elena asked Diego. She returned her attention to the rock in front of her.

"About—" Diego grunted, then brought his hammer down against the metal chisel. The clang of metal against metal echoed in the enclosed space. "About nine inches. I think we can start on the top and bottom by tomorrow. You?"

"Ten inches." Elena winked. "You're always a bit behind."

"One of these days I'll beat you at a line."

"We'll be old and gray by then."

"Quiet!" The attractive sentinel watchman left his post and stood to the side of the two. They were deep into the quarry, about three hundred feet from the entrance and maybe forty feet down. The light from outside through the extraction hole barely reached this depth and torches had been placed into the walls at various points. The flames kept the temperature much higher.

Elena shot a look at the watchman. Bradley was his name, if she remembered right. He was nearly twenty and mostly muscle, a fact that did not escape her wandering eyes. Under his shaved brows were deep brown eyes. Although Liorah, the One Voice, had strictly forbidden sentinels from forming any relationships, a woman could dream. Not that it would matter. No unmarked New Emilian would give a second look to someone with a brand across their forehead. The Marokai were filth, but at least their marks did not have a triangle like the others.

Elena wiped sweat off her shaved head and tried to add a twinkle to her blue eyes. Maybe Bradley would see it and take it a little easier on them for the rest of the day. In response, the corners of the watchman's mouth turned up slightly. She had him.

Diego yelled as his hammer hit his hand. He dropped the chisel and cradled his arm.

"Did you break it?" Elena asked as she pulled away from her fantasy and stepped over to look.

"Back to work." Bradley approached and pushed Elena away. So he was an attractive asshole. Her dreams of wooing this one faded fast.

"I think..." Diego looked at his hand. "I think I broke a finger."

"It's your left hand." Bradley pointed at the wall. "You hold the chisel with that one and hammer with your right.

What's the problem?"

"Have you ever tried to hold a chisel with a broken hand?" Elena asked. She slammed her hammer against her chisel for emphasis.

"I've never stooped so low." Bradley smirked.

Elena looked toward the extraction hole. The light was fading, and the sun would set soon. They would finally get a break. It couldn't come soon enough. The day had been unusually warm and muggy, such a difference from earlier in the year when it had been nothing but cold and wet.

Diego attempted to hold the chisel with his injured hand and brought the hammer down again. Not as hard, but it was enough to make him scream. He dropped the chisel once more and tried to shake off the pain.

"For all the Mother's sake," Bradley said. "You're a whiny one, aren't you?"

"It hurts."

"It'll heal." Bradley looked around and grabbed a broom. "Here. Sweep up after your sister. The shift is almost over, anyway."

Diego gingerly grabbed the broom with his left hand and nodded.

"Don't say I'm not kind to Marokai." Bradley returned to his watchman's post. "Sun's almost down. You can heal your hand up and start over in the morning."

"You're so generous," Diego said under his breath, wincing as he did so. He glanced up at Elena. "Can I have another tomorrow?"

"Have another what?" Bradley barked.

"Broken finger."

The watchman pursed his lips. "Sweep."

Diego did as instructed, but slowly. He moved around Elena to an area the torchlight barely reached. Elena no longer felt the need to speed up her work. The lines would eventually be cut, the stone eventually freed and moved into position so the acoustic engineers could set up their harmonic transducer—a thing no one really understood. At least then they would have a break. It took a good half a day to prepare the stone for extraction, time Elena could use to get on the good side of Bradley. She didn't care that he had sworn an oath to remain unattached through life. It seemed more like a suggestion than a rule, anyway. Having a sentinel on her side meant more breaks and the possibility of a few additional rations.

When the light dimmed enough that it was hard to see the chisel against the rock, the quarry supervisor called down from the extraction hole. There were sixteen Marokai in the quarry, paired off and working on different sized stones. They formed a line to exit up a ladder—something Diego would probably have trouble with—and would then wait for their daily rations. Today it was an ounce of grain each, enough for a few meals of mush or to be saved to cook into bread. Elena's stomach turned at the thought.

"Wait," Bradley said to Elena as she put her tools away and walked with Diego toward the exit. He put a hand on her shoulder. "Take this." In Bradley's hand was a small vial containing only half a swallow of haelen—his emergency supply.

"You don't need this?" Elena felt the watchman slip the vial into a pocket in her pants.

"Your brother needs it." Bradley leaned forward and lowered his voice. "And if you get caught, I'll deny everything and say you must have stolen it."

Elena nodded, appreciative of the gift. He didn't have to do this. Haelen was a highly guarded elixir and only sentinels and the Elite—those "graced" by Liorah—were allowed to use it. There had even been rumors that Liorah intended to withhold it from the medical doctors, suggesting they should only use it in the most dire of emergencies. The fear wasn't that there wouldn't be enough for the sick. No, the real fear was that there wouldn't be enough for the Elite, for her. Restricting its use and guarding it as the most valuable asset in New Emile didn't stop people from attempting to get their hands on the stuff, though. Rather, it made it that much more appealing.

"You'll repay the favor someday," Bradley said with a wink, then turned away.

Elena had no doubt that was true.

ELENA HAD wrapped up Diego's finger with a stick to keep it immobile, even though he didn't need it. The "broken finger" had been a ruse.

"There's a crack back there," Diego said. "I'm not sure how far it goes, but we need to check it out."

"You think it might lead into the city?" Elena still had the vial of haelen in her pocket. That was another part of the ruse. The more haelen they could get, the better off life might be for the people who really needed it.

Diego shrugged and looked at his wrapped-up finger. He'd need to wear the fake bandage for the next few days. "I think the sentinels are getting wise to the other ways in. It might come in handy if they close off the passage on the north side."

They both sat around a nightly fire just outside their home, or what was left of it. The thatched roof had indeed slid off the supports and part of it was lying in a pile on the dirt ground below. At least the walls were still standing. A bowl of wet grain sat between them, barely enough for both. They each took turns bringing the sticky, sweet, and bitterly cold mush to their mouths with spoons carved out of sticks.

With the sun down, the Hollows was a busy place. The Marokai who had labors in the quarry, the farms, or running supplies to and from the gates of New Emile had all returned. People were busy going about their lives, cooking grain, resting, chatting. It was a simple life of people who were unwelcome anywhere else. Half of them, mostly older, had branded triangles on their foreheads given to them by Liorah for crimes against the Elite. All the others with their single mark were mostly between the ages of sixteen and twenty-four. There were a few younger children, babies and toddlers who had been born of the union between outcasts. They had not been branded yet, but that would come.

Elena watched as a child of maybe three ran between homes naked, his butt covered with mud. Since the snows of winter had given way to rains and the temperature during the day had been higher, the children were often naked. It probably irritated their parents to no end to be cleaning the dirt off them constantly.

"What do you call a Marokai child?" she asked Diego.

"What?"

"A child, you know, made from two Marokai who got together."

Diego shoveled another spoonful of mush into his mouth but didn't answer.

"They don't have the mark." Elena continued to watch the naked child bounce up and down in front of his mother.

The child sat on the ground suddenly and slammed his fists into the mud. He titled his head back and cried. Apparently, the child wasn't happy about something. As Elena watched, though, a thought of being that age crept into her mind. Long before the lottery, she likely threw the same fits in front of her mother. Luca would have probably stood by and laughed, or maybe he would have caused the turmoil. Sibling rivalry, or something similar.

Elena sighed. "Luca should have been back by now." She turned away from the crying child and scooped up some mush from the bowl.

"He'll return."

Elena chewed quickly and swallowed. The grain concoction wasn't the best tasting, but if you forced it down, you'd get full enough. "I thought I saw a Discovery crew come back a while ago, but I didn't see Luca."

"Doesn't mean he wasn't there. It's pretty far from the road to the quarry. Can't see everything."

"Why wouldn't he have stopped by, at least? He used to never go more than a cycle without bringing us something."

Again Diego shrugged. "Maybe he's been promoted, given a squad to supervise or something."

Elena laughed. "Luca?"

They ate in silence for a few minutes, each taking turns until there was little left. Elena considered the possibility that Luca had been hurt or worse, passed into shadow. It wasn't unheard of. Discovery was a dangerous job, always facing the unknown to bring news back to Liorah, the One Voice. What she did with the knowledge gained from risking the lives of others, Elena could only guess. Probably nothing.

Discovery had let to some finds, however, things that had not only helped New Emile and those living within the walls but also the Marokai. A forest had been found northwest of the moor, about five weeks away and across a string of lakes and ponds. It was damn cold and the animals there were vicious, not caring at all for the encroachment of humans. It took a large group of armed people to surround a cutting crew to fell trees and drag them back, but once that wood was available for construction, it made the work in the quarry less intense. New Emile wouldn't need as many stones to build new structures if there was wood to make frames. They certainly had enough mud and muck to create an adobe that could then be used for walls.

That Discovery led to the formation of a Marokai construction labor, something that Elena had hoped to be on. It would be nice to work outside of the quarry and in the sun for the day. They sent the wood scraps to be disposed of, which meant there was new material for homes in the Hollows. Having a roof that wasn't made of jivara would be ideal.

Discovery had also found seeds that could be cultivated into vegetables and roots that had necessitated a farm. Built far from the Hollows on the other side of New Emile—about a day's walk away where the soil was somewhat fertile—the farm produced enough food to keep the Elite well fed. The leafy parts of the vegetables were cut off and placed into a bin, then carried back to the Hollows where they could be used to add a little flavor to the daily mush.

Noise from the right drew Elena from her wayward thoughts. A woman approached from a nearby home with something wrapped up in a blanket. Her face was drawn and her steps were slow. Elena knew her name—Ruth—but little else. She had the mark on her forehead of someone who had been exiled by Liorah to the Hollows. Elena had seen her a few times, but Ruth was rarely friendly. She kept to herself mostly and never had Elena seen Ruth with a man. In fact, she hadn't seen Ruth for several weeks.

As she got closer, it was obvious Ruth had been crying. Her cheeks were red, matching the redness in her eyes and the triangle-shaped red scar of her exile.

"Ruth," Elena said. She stood, wiped her hands on her pants, and walked over. "Are you okay?"

Ruth looked at Elena, her eyes unblinking. She appeared to be in shock, and the bundle in her arms looked heavy.

"Do you need some help?" Elena moved to take the bundle from Ruth, but the woman pulled back. She shook her head vigorously but said nothing.

"What is it, Ruth?"

The woman pulled the bundle in tighter to her thin body. In that moment, Elena's eyes went to Ruth's midsection, where a large stain of blood was apparent, running down her dress. Her shins, visible below the hem, were bloody as well. She shook lightly.

Ruth had just given birth.

"Is that..." Elena pointed at the bundle and swallowed. "Is that your child?"

Ruth still said nothing. She backed up a few steps, then looked down. With a shaking hand, she pulled the blanket back from a child's face, a child who had clearly passed into shadow already or was quickly on its way.

"Oh." Elena's heart sank. Stillborn children or children who lived only a few hours were not uncommon in the Hollows, but that didn't make it any less painful. She wanted to reach out and wrap her arms around Ruth, but she also knew this was a highly personal trauma.

The baby in Ruth's arms stirred and coughed. Elena took a tentative step forward to see better. Perhaps accented by the nightly campfires, the baby's face looked yellow, its lips blue, its eyelids swollen. A tiny coo emanated before Ruth pulled the blanket back over her child's face.

"Do..." Ruth started to say something then choked up. Tears fell from her eyes. "Do you have...a shovel?"

Elena's heart sank in her chest. She had one, but there was no way she was going to allow this child to go into the ground. Not yet. "What's her name?" she asked.

Ruth shook her head. It was customary to withhold naming a child until a week had passed. Apparently, that made it easier to put a lifeless body into the ground, but Elena had her doubts. If you carry something for so long, you must feel a connection as a mother that wouldn't matter. It was a New Emilian custom, not one meant for the Hollows. No, they had to be more moral than that. That was one reason the Marokai buried their fallen rather than take the bodies out to the Wastelands for the animals.

Elena wanted to take the child from Ruth, but knew it wasn't possible. She put her hands in her pockets as she felt an upwelling of emotion that threatened to drown her in tears.

The fingers of her left hand brushed against the vial.

Haelen could cure just about anything, and it took very little. Would the tiny amount Bradley had given her help this child?

Slowly, Elena withdrew the vial. She looked at it—a tiny metal cannister that was no bigger than her thumb—and then held it out. "Here," she said.

Ruth looked at the vial, her red eyes widening slowly. "Is that...?"

Elena nodded. "But first, tell me her name."

The woman looked at the vial, then pulled the blanket back from her child's face again. A tiny hand rose, bloodied and bruised.

"Lika," Ruth whispered as her body shook. "Her name will be Lika."

CHAPTER EIGHT

JOSIAH, THE SENTINEL COMMANDER AND SWORN PROTECTOR of Liorah, watched as she seethed. Liorah, the most high, the One Voice, holder of the vials of haelen, and granddaughter of the Great Mother Miriam, was furious. She sat with her council around a table set up in the one room Josiah knew she hated the most—the inner chamber. From the lone window, Josiah saw the Tree that Owned Itself, the symbol of New Emile's growth, with its wilted leaves growing out of the haelen pond.

Wilted leaves. How fitting.

The pending shortage of grain, reported by Marius Holmes, the Provisioner, had caused a deadlock among the council members. Liorah looked at everyone, willing solutions from an inept group of advisors. Josiah couldn't help but feel frustrated with his comrades' lack of creativity. Russant Baldwin, the Chief Constructionist, had no suggestions, and even seemed indifferent to the situation. Food was not his concern. Josiah looked over at Roland Blackwood, Liorah's Kept, who lounged beside her at the table. That idiot couldn't come up with a suggestion if Liorah had whipped him with a chain. Then again, Roland had no other purpose than to be a plaything for Liorah. It was rumored that he couldn't father children, which made him all the more useful. The One Voice was far too young to have children, and who would raise them anyway? Certainly not her.

Piper Lucientes, the Keeper of the Law and man responsible for enforcing Liorah's edicts, stared into space. The man was creepy. He picked at his fingernails and put whatever he found into his mouth. He could certainly offer no suggestions, only repeat anything Liorah said. Why he ever came to these meetings was beyond Josiah.

Among the council, only Alistair Thorne, the oldest member and the one responsible for special projects and health matters, had anything to offer. It wasn't a solution, of course, just another problem to throw on top of a mountain of problems. He cleared his throat, capturing everyone's attention. "The Marokai need something, Liorah. To deny them any more grain would be inhumane. They're already passing into shadow in increasing numbers because of malnutrition and disease. The Hollows is becoming a grave. But since it's apparent we need to ration, we can do so equally."

"Fifteen barrels will not last us through another winter even if we cut the rations to the Marokai entirely and our own in half," Marius argued. "Our growth is unsustainable."

"The Marokai are not permitted any more than a half a ration of grain." Piper yawned. "Liorah's word is not to be questioned. It is well known they have built farms to the south and west of the Hollows. If they're so ingenious, let them grow their own food."

"Farms?" Alistair looked disgusted. "Nothing much grows outside the moor, and those farms yield a pittance."

"And yet they have farms." Piper licked something off his fingers and flashed a creepy smile.

"You bring me no realistic options?" Liorah sneered. She glanced at Roland, who was just as busy as Piper at picking something out of his fingernails. She rubbed her hand across the dark skin on her shaved head, her brown eyes glinting with anger. "The Marokai are free to find their own food. Our only focus should be on those within the walls. We cannot distribute what we have to everyone equally."

Alistair glanced down. "With all due respect, Liorah, the farms are a waste of their time. Where else would they look for food?"

"Do I care? Let them migrate. Their little settlement is an eyesore as it is."

"But they have provided muscle for the quarries. They are Russant's laborers. What would you have us do if they were to rebel?"

"Rebel?" Liorah's brow rose. "I give them life. If you recall, Eilian's suggestion was to send them away into the Wastelands. It was only through my mercy pleading with my father that they were allowed to remain on the outskirts of the moor, to build new homes. They will not rebel."

"They will," Josiah said. He looked up, but not at Liorah. His eyes wandered toward Roland and rested there for a moment. The moron was a distraction in so many ways. "There has already been reported dissent in the quarry and incursions into homes within the walls. Theft of property is on the rise. It's only a matter of time before they organize, if they haven't already."

"It's your job to make sure that doesn't happen."

"The sentinels are small in number." Josiah held his hands out, and let slip a smirk which he quickly wiped away with a gloved hand. "We cannot be everywhere at once."

Liorah fumed. She was too young to be a leader, too young to take on the role of the One Voice. If it hadn't been for the untimely—and still mysterious—passing of Master Eilian, her father, then decisions would have already been made. Even Philip, Liorah's half-brother, would have been a better leader. Unfortunately, he also passed. That left Liorah to captain a series of meetings with nothing but bad news.

Roland the Kept winked at Liorah. If only Josiah was allowed to carry a knife into these meetings.

"Cut the rations for the Marokai by half," Liorah said finally. "If they rebel, find out who's in charge and throw them in the hold. Make an example, if you must. You can string one or two of them from the southwestern gate, if it makes you feel better. The marked can watch their supposed leaders rot in the sun."

"They will get in," Josiah said.

"What do you mean?"

"The tunnels, Liorah. We've been through this, and last time I believe Russant was supposed to find a way to close them all off."

Russant shifted in his seat. "We're working on it." He did not look up.

Liorah shook her head. "Surely, you have enough sentinels to post both at the gate and where you know of tunnel incursions."

Josiah shrugged. It was the best he could offer. "You sent a lot of my men away on Discovery."

"They will return soon enough. In the meantime," Liorah turned to Russant, "close off any breach you find in the walls and figure out how to keep expansion going with no Marokai laborers. Build up, if you must. If we can get the materials out of the quarry and into the city with fewer laborers, do we really need the Marokai?"

"Not if you don't mind delays." Russant shifted again. "There is lumber and jivara in the north, but the weather is horrendous. We might be able to bring some of that in with another expedition, especially if we enlist more of the

Marokai to harvest and haul the material." He looked down at the table. "It could help the marked build better homes in the Hollows, too."

Liorah slammed her fist on the table and stood. "Not at the expense of our needs here! The only thing that matters is what goes on within these walls. We did not ask for this. The lottery is fair, and the rest of the Marokai are nothing more than criminals who deserve no mercy. Our resources are limited in the moor. There is only so much available, as you all well know. To divvy up what we need to those who can fend for themselves is unthinkable."

"What if Discovery shows us another way?" Alistair asked. "Would you end the lottery?"

"What's the point?" Piper interjected. "The marked are no safer within the walls than they are in their little huts and hovels outside."

Liorah narrowed her eyes. "If you care so much about the Marokai, Alistair, you are more than welcome to take your healing whiles and your damn texts with you."

Alistair opened his mouth to say something, but Liorah cut him off. "But not the haelen. That stays here, no matter what."

"I would never suggest such a thing." Alistair crossed his arms and sat back in his chair. "I don't think even the haelen would heal some of the diseases which are running rampant through the Hollows."

Liorah tightened her eyes further into slits, irritated that much more. "That is yet one more rationale for us to not allow them to live within our city walls. It's bad enough we let the filth near the gate."

"Only to trade for goods," Alistair countered.

"Trade what? Beads and baubles? Trinkets and tassels? I would rather there be meat and muscle."

A knock on the door turned Liorah's focus away from the table. "What?" She spun around and waited for a page to open it.

Kaius stood at the threshold, unable to cross into the sacrosanct chamber. Just a few years younger than Josiah, Kaius was the one sentinel he wished would never be sent out on Discovery. If Josiah were asked if he ever had a friend, Kaius would be the only one he could point out.

"News from Discovery, Liorah," Kaius said.

Liorah relaxed slightly. "What news?"

"We have a visitor," Kaius said.

UPON HEARING that there was a visitor to New Emile—someone not from the Hollows—the room erupted into a flurry of questions. Abel waited outside behind Kaius. He'd been told to remain back by a few feet in case Liorah had no intention of seeing him. Neither Luca, Raphael, or Nico had been allowed to get this far. Already, Abel felt as if he would never see them again. Sweat beaded on his forehead.

His walk through the gate and into New Emile and then through the streets had been nothing short of amazing. For all his life, he had known only Rephidim, with its dirt walls, dirt floors, and dirt streets. It was so different here, so unlike anything that he'd imagined. There was still dirt here, but it was more yellow and somewhat muted by the amount of stone. The wall itself was a marvel to see, perhaps twenty or twenty-five feet tall, constructed of massive stones stacked on top of each other and held together with what Luca had called cement. A platform on top, five feet wide, allowed scouts an unobstructed view of the world around them. Abel had wondered what they might be looking for, but no one with him would answer. Maybe they didn't know, either.

Once inside the walls, the muddy ground of the moor

disappeared, replaced by streets of worn stone, all irregular round shapes joined with mud. Buildings, also made of stone, lined either side, most about twenty feet long and fifteen feet high, some taller. Some leaned slightly, as if the ground underneath was incapable of supporting their weight. The walls were spotless and nowhere did Abel see signs of the jivara grass sticking up out of cracks. A few of the buildings had windows about six feet off the ground where faces and shaved heads curiously peered out. Other buildings, however, had nothing but doors, mostly open, with yet more curious onlookers.

When they reached what Abel assumed to be the middle of the city, they came upon a pool of glistening silvery water about twenty feet wide. Growing out of it was a tree that had to be just as tall with a flared base, white bark and yellow leaves. Despite overcast skies, the whole tree seemed to glow.

"The Tree that Owns Itself," Luca said pointing. "The source of haelen."

"This...this is the Water of Life?"

"The same," Kaius added. "Just like the legends you heard of the water at Manoach."

Kaius pointed toward a building off to the side. It was more ornate than the others and rose about forty feet into the air. There was one large window set high overlooking the pond and the tree. "In there," Kaius said.

"What is it?"

"The New Emile Chambers, the heart of the city, where Liorah awaits."

Abel felt nervous as Luca, Raphael, and Nico turned away. "Where are you going?" Abel asked Luca.

"We're done here." He nodded toward the Chambers but kept his eyes low. "This is as far as we go. I'll see you when you come out." Luca looked up at Abel and winked.

Now Abel stood behind Kaius at the threshold of the room where he heard a woman's voice talking to Kaius.

"What do you mean, a visitor, Kaius?" Her voice sounded younger than Abel expected.

"A boy from lands far to the south."

"A boy?"

Kaius stepped slightly to the side, exposing Abel to those in the room who looked out. There were six men sitting at a table while a woman — Liorah, he assumed — stood. She was young, maybe only a few years older than Abel. Like everyone else, her head was shaved, but a white rope was tied just above her ears. It matched the color of the cloak which draped loosely over her slight frame. Abel could not help but feel suddenly captivated by her looks, from her light brown skin, deep brown eyes, and just the slightest hint of a smile from thin lips.

"Send him in," Liorah said. She stepped around the table and approached Abel. She walked with grace, like the prelates in the Assembly back at Rephidim. But unlike those prelates, she seemed to glow with a cleanliness Abel didn't think was possible.

Kaius stepped back and motioned for Abel to enter while he remained outside the room. Was he really going to meet this leader alone?

"You may go, Kaius." Liorah did not take her eyes off Abel. "Return to your station and I will send for you when we have finished here."

Abel swallowed.

"Let me have the room," she said. Immediately, five of the six men seated at the table rose. As they passed Abel, he noted in each of them a certain deference to Liorah as they kept their eyes low. Only one remained, a man no older than Abel. He had fairer skin than anyone Abel had ever met back in Rephidim. He was, in a word, exotic despite the lack of hair on his body. He also looked a lot more relaxed than the other men had been. In a way, Abel thought he looked bored.

"Please sit." Liorah returned to the table and waited for Abel to find a chair. He wasn't sure if he should sit at the opposite end or closer. Meanwhile, the young man yawned.

"What is your name?" Liorah asked as Abel finally sat in the one chair that wasn't too far away or too close.

"Abel, ma'am."

Liorah smiled. "No one calls me that. Liorah is fine, unless, of course, you're in trouble. You're not in trouble."

How is one supposed to respond to that? Abel thought.

"Where are you from? Kaius said you were found south of New Emile? About how far out would you say?"

"We walked for a full Short Moon." Abel shifted a little, unable to relax. His eyes flicked toward the man. "My home is called Rephidim, across from the Western Mountains near to the Reed Sea."

"The Reed Sea? I have not heard of this place."

"It's, um, a big ocean. Mostly weeds and other grasses grow for about a mile out before the depth drops. The mountains which border the sea are not horribly tall, but they provide some protection from storms which come in from over the water."

Liorah continued to smile, and Abel was further transfixed. Ever since Kaius and his team had rescued him from certain death, he'd imagined her as a formidable woman, someone you didn't mess with. They feared her.

Why?

"Is this your first time out of... What did you call it?"

"Rephidim. And yes, ma'am— I mean Liorah. This is the first time I've been away from home."

Liorah clasped her hands in front of her. "What about

your family? The people in this town? Do you think they miss you?"

"No." Abel realized that he may have responded to that question too fast. "I mean, I don't know." Did he tell her he was exiled, or would that equate him to the Marokai? "I got lost, and Kaius and the others found me."

"By the Reed Sea?"

Abel nodded. "It was probably faster to go with them here than it would have been to return to Rephidim."

Again, Liorah nodded, her smile refusing to drop at all. The line of questioning was relatively simple. Abel felt his body relax a little as he found comfort in the presence of this woman. Who the other man was—and why he'd been allowed to stay—left a slight knot in his stomach.

"How many people would you say live in this Rephidim?"

"About two hundred, maybe a little more. We're not a large colony, and there have been times over the past few decades when things were rough. A lot of people passed into shadow then."

Liorah did not ask another question right away. Instead, she stared at Abel with that same smile, those same deep eyes. It became more uncomfortable the longer it lasted. Perhaps he should break the silence.

"Can I ask a question, Liorah?" Abel shifted again in his seat.

"Absolutely. And I may answer."

"What... Who are the people in the town I saw coming in?" He was suddenly aware this was a question that would make him sound foolish, but he was already committed to asking it. "One of the men I was with, Luca, called it the Hollows. Are they the Marokai?"

For the first time since walking into the room, Liorah's

smile faltered. It was quick—a tiny down turn of a lip—but it was enough for Abel to catch. Her eyes darted toward the young man and then quickly returned. Liorah took a breath. "They are the Marokai, yes," she said. Her full smile now seemed more forced than before. "They help New Emile in many ways. Are you hungry?"

A change of subject. "Yes, Liorah. We ate some jerked meat early this morning, but I have had nothing since."

"Then you shall be fed." Liorah clapped her hands loudly once. From a door on the opposite side of where he had entered, two young women appeared, heads shaved. They were dressed more like Abel in brown tunics and pants held up by a rope. One woman, maybe sixteen, carried a bowl of something that looked like fruit. She carefully placed it on the table as the other woman filled up two clay cups with water and gently positioned them in the center of the table. Neither of them made eye contact with Abel or Liorah, and it was not unnoticeable that they did not provide the young man with water. Both of them had a single lined burned into their foreheads. Marokai.

"Vermillion aichmiri." Liorah motioned to the bowl. "A delicacy here, but found in abundance where my grandmother came from."

"Your grandmother?" Abel did not reach for fruit right away. It looked good, and he could not deny his desire for food in his stomach, but something felt wrong about it.

"Miriam Michaels, the woman who founded New Emile. Our Great Mother led the only remaining colonists from the temple at Manoach, across a deep canyon, through many perils and across the Wastelands to come here. She is our savior, and we owe her a great debt for our existence and prosperity."

Those last two sentences sounded rehearsed, like the sermons given by the Assembly at Rephidim. "There were other colonists," Abel said. He still wouldn't reach for the fruit.

Liorah's smile dropped perceptibly this time, and it did not return.

"You speak as if you know something I do not."

"You mentioned Manoach. The prelates of the Assembly at Rephidim speak of that temple as well, a place of sorrow built in the forbidden rainforests to the north."

"And what do your prelates say about it?" Liorah spat out the word "prelates" as if it had given her an unpleasant taste in her mouth.

Abel realized it was his turn to recite history. "Our histories say that twenty-six people, led by Sojen Micah and his wife Patience, traveled a great distance from the temple at Manoach to the safety of Rephidim. It was there that they established a new tribe called the Col'kasid."

"Col'kasid? What is that supposed to mean?"

"The Col is in reference to the great Circle of Light ship which brought our ancestors to this planet. As it has been passed down from generation to generation, 'kasid' is a word given to us by Father Elijah in the ancient texts. It means follower."

A brief chuckle escaped Liorah. She sat up straighter and reached across the table to pick a fruit from the bowl. She rolled the spiky food around between her hand and the table several times until the skin cracked. While the man next to her watched with what looked like hungry eyes, Liorah peeled the fruit and took a bite. "The Circle of Light is a myth. We, too, have heard that tale, but it is one worth forgetting. All of life began with the Great Mother, as it was she who brought New Emile into sunshine."

"What of my people, then?" Abel asked. He watched Liorah chew. "Are they not from Manoach?"

"I don't see how. When Mother Miriam sent scouts back to the temple, they found nothing save hundreds of bodies who had been torn apart by the beasts of the trees, the rychat. There was nothing left. Perhaps your elders told you stories to cover up the fact that they had descended from those who abandoned the Great Mother on the quest across the Wastelands."

"I... I would not know the truth, only the legends I have been told. As a scribe for my people, it was my labor to record the words of the prelates."

Liorah nodded and chewed some more. When she was done, she wiped her hands on her cloak, then folded them in front of her. "Tell me, Abel. What other legends have you been told?"

Abel had been told many things in his seventeen years, many stories recited around fires by the Assembly. Some felt made up, while others were just believable enough to have been true. He weighed his words so as not to further upset Liorah. He missed her smile already.

"There is another tribe," Abel said finally, "across the Barren Sea. They are more advanced, and we were told to always to be on the watch for them."

Liorah's eyes opened wide. If she'd had eyebrows, it would have been more obvious. For the first time, the young man next to her appeared to listen. "What tribe?" she asked.

"They are called the Zhanshi. They are responsible for what happened at Manoach."

"Animals were responsible for what happened. Rychat."

"No, Liorah. It was murder."

At that, Liorah scowled. She obviously didn't like to be countered. The man next to her shifted uncomfortably in his seat. "Tell me, Abel," she said slowly. "You said you are a scribe. What have you written about this...this history?"

Now it was Abel's turn to shift uncomfortably. "I have

only been a scribe for a year, Liorah. The stories I have written have all been told to me by the prelates, the four members of our Assembly led by the Keeper of the Text, Elder Levi. They all speak of two strangers who came to Rephidim long before I was born into sunshine."

"Two strangers? Did they not have names?"

"If they did, only Sojen Micah knew them."

"What did these strangers tell you...or tell your Assembly?"

"Many things. They gave us names for animals, told us how to find resources we desperately needed. But their main message was about another tribe, the Zhanshi who had murdered everyone left at Manoach."

"What did they say?"

"Other than tell us the story, they said we should always be aware of the dragon which lies in wait to the North."

The chamber fell silent. Liorah tilted her head just slightly, while outside the noise of a city full of life filtered in through the open window. It was uncomfortable, a moment that seemed to stretch on as if Liorah expected Abel to say something else. What could he say? That was the message the strangers gave, and now, sitting in this chamber in front of this woman far from what used to be his home, Abel had to wonder if "the dragon" was here.

Without another word, Liorah stood. Her mood had changed from the moment he'd been brought in. Even the air in the room felt different to him. Unsure of what to do, Abel quickly followed.

"You are welcome here." Liorah directed Abel to the door with her hand on his back. "Kaius can show you around, or you may find company with someone closer to your age. If I have more questions, I will call for you."

Just as Liorah reached for the door handle, she paused.

"I advise you to keep your legends to yourself. And Abel..." She paused and ran her fingers through Abel's hair. "It's important that you shave. The bugs here can be...nasty."

When Abel was beyond the threshold, the door closed behind him with a loud click.

What did I say?

KAIUS STOOD in the corner of the room, unwelcome at the table. It was not his place, but he had been called in to this meeting, nevertheless. Roland the Kept was at the table, though, and that irritated Kaius to no end. At least Liorah's famous anger had not been on full display. Kaius never liked that about her.

He watched as Liorah leaned across the table and pointed at Russant. "What do you know about this third tribe? You sent people to the east in the direction of the Barren Sea. From what I recall, they were gone for nearly a full cycle of the Long Moon. Were they playing or did they find anything?"

Russant shrugged. He dabbed at a long scar running across his right cheek. "As I reported, lumber. There is a range of low mountains to the northeast, a few weeks away. One scout took a detour and found an animal path that wound through the valleys and came out on a plain filled with lakes and rivers."

"And beyond that?"

"The scout returned before he ventured farther."

"No other signs of life? No hints of this third tribe?"

"No, Liorah. Nothing like what our visitor describes."

Liorah twisted her lips in thought. "Why didn't the scouts go beyond the mountains?"

"It was not their directive."

"And you trust the reports? They would not have kept any secrets from you?"

"I don't see why they would. We trained them like any other scouts, those sent on Discovery in every direction. Investigate, find, report."

Liorah sat back. Kaius considered what Russant had been saying. Perhaps there was nothing to report to the east. When Mother Miriam was alive, she sent scouts in all directions looking for signs of life, other places that might be more hospitable than this moor. Of the five teams that went out, four returned, and only one of them mentioned anything of note. That was the team who had returned from Manoach.

"And this Abel says this third tribe is more advanced?" Josiah asked. "What does that mean?"

"Electric power," Kaius said.

The room erupted in a murmur of confused exclamations.

"That's impossible." Alistair scoffed and shook his head. "Electric power is a myth of old Earth. There has never been a hint of anything like that since humans arrived here. The only thing that has power is the harmonic transducer, and that's certainly not something we can tap into."

Of all the people in the room, only Alistair, Kaius, and Josiah were old enough to have heard the stories told by those who arrived with Mother Miriam. Schools had been set up to teach the children about their history, stretching back to the days when the settlers first arrived on the edge of the Barren Sea and established the City of Nod. But that history had changed when people questioned Miriam's decisions. Within twenty years of their arrival at New Emile, it was decreed that schools would no longer teach about this period of time or even of the exodus. What did it matter? History began at Manoach and the only focus should be on the future.

Kaius remembered that shift well. Everyone else at the table—from Russant to Marius to Piper and especially

Liorah—was clueless. History before Manoach was a blur to almost everyone, even the One Voice, the ruler of New Emile. Both Russant and Piper had been toddlers when the schools eliminated history...or at least rewrote it. Marius and Liorah had yet to be born into sunshine.

"What were you told in school?" Liorah asked Alistair. She then turned to look at Kaius. "You, too. What did you hear growing up?"

"A good many things," Alistair said. "Can you be more specific?"

"What happened before Manoach? You are most familiar with the written texts of the scribes of the Great Mother. What did they say?"

Alistair glanced at Kaius before answering. "Before Manoach, there was a city on the edge of the Barren Sea. A flood forced the settlers there to flee into the Barrier Mountains, and Mother Miriam led a group out of those mountains into the rainforest, where they found shelter at Manoach. From there, by decree, history begins."

"Before that, I mean." Liorah waved her hand impatiently. "Before the flood."

Russant and Piper leaned forward, and Kaius could tell they were as interested in hearing this as Liorah was.

Alistair did not answer right away. Instead, Kaius answered in his place. "Pain."

Everyone in the room turned to look at Kaius. The attention did not bother him.

"Explain yourself," Liorah said.

"When I found Abel, he told me a story about where his ancestors came from. I did not discount it because it matches up with what our early schools had told us. That made me think that perhaps the other stories I had heard growing up were also true, or at least part of them."

"What stories are these?"

"When the Circle of Light ship—"

"That's a myth," Russant interrupted. "One told by parents as a bedtime story."

Liorah held her hand up. "Continue."

Kaius took a deep breath. He really wanted to punch Russant, but in this venue, it would not be appropriate. "As I was saying, when the ship arrived on Tishbe, there was a stowaway, a man named Mathias. From Mathias descended a new tribe of people who lived to the north of the Barren Sea. When Abel called what happened at Manoach a genocide, that story made more sense."

"It was rychat who killed those remaining at Manoach." Liorah's face revealed a sort of betrayal, as if all she'd been told had been a lie. "Animals and nothing more."

"Not according to the reports out of Rephidim, where Abel is from. If it was genocide, I believe it was perpetrated by this third tribe."

"What makes you think that?" Josiah asked. "Hundreds of people cut down by a small tribe of outcasts?"

"It's the only thing that links our histories together. If we trace all our lives backward, we come to one event. The arrival. Transit."

"Do not use that word." Liorah clenched her fists.

"My apologies, Liorah."

"So what of this Col'kasid?" Alistair asked. He stroked his wrinkled face. "Is what this Abel says true? There were survivors from the temple?"

"I'm not so sure I believe that," Liorah interjected. "During Mother Miriam's quest, a group of about fifty people were said to have broken off to return to Manoach. But the canyon was probably too difficult to cross. It's more likely that this Abel descends from that group, not from anyone still left at the temple. It was clear whatever happened in the rainforest left no one alive."

"But it is also clear there are more people out there," Josiah said, "regardless of where they came from. And if that splinter group broke apart, are there more than three tribes?"

"Master Eilian told us there were no other humans left on Tishbe." Russant leaned forward onto his elbows and clasped his hands together. "Was that a lie?"

"The written texts of the scribes of the Great Mother's day are clear," Alistair said. "The people escaped the horrors of the forest and found a new home on the moor. Their promise to return to the temple to bring the others along was impossible to keep when scouts found no one left alive."

"How many people were there?" Josiah was not about to let this go.

"About two hundred."

"Did they count the bodies?"

"That's enough," Liorah said. "The written texts of our Great Mother's scribes were dictated by Miriam herself and have been proven to be infallible. We do not dispute the words of our Great Mother."

"I'm just saying." Russant spread his hands out. "Master Eilian had to have been wrong. If what this Abel is saying is true, and what Kaius here confirms, it may be possible some people left the temple before they died out, before this supposed slaughter—by man or beast. Maybe the Col'kasid descends from an offshoot that Mother Miriam would not have known about."

Josiah nodded. "It's what I would have done—left of my accord. If the conditions there were so bad, I don't see why people didn't leave and find new homes, go on Discovery themselves."

"Perhaps those schools should not have been

redirected," Alistair said, his voice lower than before. "There is a lot to learn from history."

"What my grandmother decreed is not to be disputed, either." Liorah's anger was back. "And certainly not any decree I make. Is that clear?"

"Yes, Liorah." Alistair lowered his eyes. "History begins at Manoach."

Liorah looked around the room, but it seemed no one wanted to argue any further about what had happened when. Only Roland the Kept was animated as he stretched and yawned.

"Kaius," Liorah said, turning. "Have Abel return you to this Rephidim. I want to know all there is to know about this tribe, the Col'kasid. Where they came from, who their ancestors are, and what skills they have that we might use."

"Abel will not return, Liorah."

"Why is that?"

"He would not say, but I suspect it was because he was exiled."

"Exiled?" Liorah knitted her hairless brow. "The boy doesn't look like a criminal or a threat to anyone. Why would he have been exiled?"

"I do not believe he looks at women the same way he looks at men."

Roland's eyes flickered up at Kaius, then back down.

"And? This is a problem?" Liorah asked.

"It may be to the Col'kasid. They are a religious tribe with certain customs. As we were all warned, religions are not to be trifled with."

There was something in Liorah's expression that Kaius couldn't pinpoint, but he had seen it before, long ago. It was the same look Mother Miriam had whenever religion was brought up in her presence. "Invite a few of them here," she said finally. "We should talk. Perhaps there is something we can trade—grain for our people in exchange for maybe clearing the Hollows of the filth."

Kaius nodded.

"And Russant." Liorah leaned across the table. "Take a group of scouts and head back east. I want to know what's past those lakes and rivers. Is there another tribe, and if so, what do they offer? If they have electric power, I want to know how it was done, and if they have anything else we can use, seize it."

"Seize it?" Russant looked troubled. "I'm a constructionist, not a sentinel."

"If you can swing a hammer, you can swing an axe. Don't argue. Just go."

Russant nodded and pushed himself back from the table. Before he stood, Liorah spoke once more. "Alistair. Read through all the written texts again and tell me something I don't know. Where did these tribes really come from and why are they not with us here? The answers are probably in those ancient texts you've been sitting on."

"Those texts are unreadable, Liorah." Alistair looked annoyed. "As I've mentioned many times, we have no place to even start translating them."

"Do I look like I care? You have a job to do. Find me knowledge and share it."

"And what would you have the rest of us do?" Josiah asked.

Liorah smirked. "You can guard me with your life. It's about all you're good at." She looked at Marius and Piper. "As for you two, figure out what we can do about our grain. Can we annex the Marokai farms?"

CHAPTER NINE

ABEL STOOD WITH LUCA IN THE MIDDLE OF THE HOLLOWS. Around him, people gathered to gawk at the stranger's hair, some even daring to reach out and touch it. It was unnerving.

"They haven't seen hair this long before," Luca explained. "From early on, we're forced to shave everything off to keep the mitters away."

"Mitters?" Abel allowed a small girl with dirty clothes and an even dirtier face, to stroke the hair he'd tied up which fell to the middle of his back.

"Nasty bugs. Like I said before, you'll need to shave. It's not for looks. If you don't do it soon, you'll find out what I mean." Luca winked at Abel. "They come at night. Mostly."

Abel took in the sights of the Hollows with curiosity and sadness. The homes were basic and run down, built from mud bricks and thatched roofs made of jivara that provided little shelter from the elements. The streets were dusty dirt paths winding between the clusters of houses, muddy in spots where recent rains had pooled.

The people looked just as weary and malnourished. Their skin was sallow and stretched thin over protruding bones, while their clothes hung loose and tattered on their skinny frames. The lack of hair made them appear sickly, almost alien to Abel. He couldn't help but notice the mark of the Marokai—a line cruelly branded on the forehead. With the exception of the children, some of whom had distended bellies indicative of malnutrition, the marks were everywhere.

There was a sense of hardship and lack hanging over the place. The Marokai scraped by with what little they had, but at the same time Abel felt there was a community here in the way they gathered around this newcomer. Though Abel felt saddened, he also felt the first stirrings of admiration for these people. They were exiles, no different than him.

"We should find Elena and Diego," Luca said, gently nudging Abel forward. "I'd like you to meet my siblings. They both should be away from the quarry by now."

Near the middle of the Hollows, Luca found them, both watching a bowl of mush cooking over a small fire. It did not look appetizing despite the fact that he had not eaten in a while. Diego, Luca's brother, was the first to stand. His skin was as dark as Luca's and he was wearing a bandage over one hand. Elena stirred whatever was in the bowl, but did not look up.

"Diego, Elena," Luca said. "This is Abel, a stranger from a strange land. We found him on Discovery."

As Diego held his hand out, Elena scoffed. "You took your time coming to see us."

Luca dropped his smile. "I've been busy. I'm sorry—"

"Sorry, my ass." Elena finally stood. Without hair and no eyebrows, she looked almost exactly like her brother Diego. It would be hard to tell them apart save the more obvious differences between a man and a woman. Both of them had the mark of the Marokai across their foreheads. It looked painful. "You could have stopped by. It's been nearly a full cycle of the Long Moon."

"Kaius had—"

"Save it." Elena held her hand up. "You have an excuse for everything." She nodded toward Abel. "Who's the weirdo?"

Abel was taken aback for the first time since he'd come into the Hollows, and he felt his cheeks grow warm. "I am Abel, from Rephidim, a city—"

"Don't care. Nice to meet you." She turned to Diego. "Food's almost done."

"Elena," Luca pleaded. "Please don't do this. I've brought a guest. It's been a long journey of Discovery, and I'm sorry that I didn't stop by earlier."

Elena's shoulders slumped...a little. She straightened her back. "Welcome, Abel of Rephidim," she said holding out her hand in greeting and forcing a small smile. "Why my brother showed you the underbelly of New Emile is beyond me, but here we are."

"What's with the hair?" Diego asked. He reached out to touch it, but Elena quickly swatted it down.

"Don't touch that." She shook her head. "You don't know where he's been."

"It's so...long. You don't have mitters in your Reph...your home?"

"Rephidim," Abel said. "And no, we don't have them. Luca says I'll have to shave my hair soon or they'll get to me."

"Oh, they will," Elena said with a curt nod. "They will bite and bite until your body is filled with sores. The pain is unbelievable, like fire to your skin. You'll wish you were dead."

Luca stirred. "That is no way to talk to someone," he said. "You don't have to scare people just to make your point."

"Think of it more as a warning." Elena's lips turned up in a cruel smirk. "You'll thank me or curse me, but one way or another, you'll need to take a blade to that mane of yours."

"Thank you," Abel said. He felt suddenly uncomfortable. "In the meantime, I'm curious about you, about the Hollows. This place is fascinating."

Diego's eyes opened wide. "Fascinating? This place is a disaster, barely standing. If you want wonder, have Luca show you the New Emile Chambers. I hear the walls are lined with shiny metal."

"I've been there. I don't recall seeing the walls as anything more than stone, but the lady there was nice."

"The lady?" Elena spit on the ground. "Liorah? She's no lady. More like a witch who hoards what she can. I'm surprised she gave you the time of day. You must have something she wants."

"To be honest, it was an uncomfortable conversation."

"She was probably trying to find a reason to mark you and send you out of the city. She's not known for her kindness."

"How do you mean?"

Elena tilted her head a little and looked Abel up and down before continuing. "Come," she said finally. "Let me show you the type of woman Liorah is."

Abel looked at Luca for assurance. He merely shrugged. "My sister has never been a woman of few words."

IT WAS a small farm filled with nothing but tiny grasses. Elena had escorted Abel and Luca to the west of the Hollows, on the opposite side from New Emile and hidden from view. Diego followed, quickly downing the mush in the bowl in a few quick bites.

Abel looked over the small farm in dismay. Back in Rephidim, farms teemed with rows of lush crops, vegetables bursting with ripe fullness and grains growing tall and golden. But here, the farm was barren and sad. Instead of healthy plants, scrubby tufts of jivara were scattered thinly. They were stunted, barely ankle high, with spindly stalks and few seed heads. It was less a farm than a vacant expanse of weeds.

"This is your farm?" Abel asked in disbelief.

Elena nodded. "Not exactly overflowing, is it? The soil here is worthless. We can barely coax anything to grow."

Abel knelt and tugged halfheartedly at a clump of grass. It came out in his hand, roots dangling meagerly. Left over was a sickly-looking root plant, its leaves brown.

"The jivara takes over everything out here," Diego said. "We try to rotate plots to let the ground rest and recover, but it doesn't do any good. Our harvests grow more pitiful each year."

Abel felt dismayed looking over the struggling wisps of vegetation. His heart went out to the Marokai, trying to survive off this desolate land.

"I have a feeling," Abel said after dropping the clump of jivara and kneeling again to check the soil, "you're going to tell me there's another farm that grows plants for everyone else." He stood and wiped his hands on his shirt.

"Come," Elena said with a frown. She looked up at the sky. "We still have some time before nightfall. You'll want to keep your head down. There are sentinels everywhere."

They walked for a while, skirting the moor behind a small rise that offered some protection from those along the top of the wall who might see them. When they reached what Diego said was the northwest corner of the city, they turned slightly to the left along a path that was well trod. Rather than walk along the path, however, they kept at a low crouch on the other side of a berm, hidden from view. To their left, a small irrigation stream flowed from someplace unknown in the direction they were headed. Abel caught a few words from Marokai who walked on the other side of the berm, their conversation seemingly focused on the cruelness of some sentinel that apparently guarded them that day.

By the time they reached another berm where Elena directed them all to duck down, the sun was much lower in the sky and dusk was showing its colors of indigo, green, and orange. Far to the east, a nearly full Short Moon was rising.

Abel poked his head above the berm and looked out over rows upon rows of vegetables stretching for what seemed like a mile. Now *this* was a farm, and while the variety of plants was limited—Abel only counted two different crops—the amount was surely enough to feed a thousand people.

"This is the real farm," Elena whispered. "Patrolled day and night by the likes of my brother."

"Hey." Luca kept his voice low as well. "I'm a scout, and I've never been on watcher status."

"You will eventually."

Abel cut off the sibling argument before it could start. "I don't understand. If these plants grow here, why can't you grow the same near the Hollows?"

"Soil. Far to the north of New Emile where we are now, the ground is rich with nutrients and easy to plow. South, it's packed more densely. There are some irrigation ditches here fed from wells, but in the Hollows, the water table is lower and we don't have the tools to dig deeper."

"The soil is that different? It's not that far of a difference."

"Far enough."

Abel watched as a sentinel moved from left to right, his crossbow slung. He looked bored.

"Where are the workers?" Abel asked after the man was out of sight.

"It's late. They've all returned to the Hollows. The

Marokai who have labors in the farm grow and then harvest the vegetables and pull the greens off. The good stuff is pulled by cart to the northern gate where they're unloaded by New Emilian cooks. The greens are thrown into a compost pile on the other side of where we are now."

Abel's eyes opened wider. "Thrown away? You can't use the greens?"

"Bitter," Diego said, "but we've managed to sneak a little out when the sentinels aren't watching. I'd say it adds flavor to the grain rations we get, but that's not true. It still tastes like shit. The real prize is the seed, but every Marokai worker is searched thoroughly before returning to the Hollows."

"How—?"

Elena cut Abel off with a quick hand to his mouth. The sentinel had returned from the right, apparently alerted by a noise from their direction. Tension increased as Abel and the others slowly lowered themselves further behind the berm. Next to him, Luca scooted closer, and along with the tang of dirt, Abel caught the man's scent, sweet and alluring.

Sneaking around was not new to Abel, but it was nonetheless exciting. His memory flashed back to times when he and Asher would sneak past the gate of Rephidim and try to remain hidden from all the judgmental eyes. Even as a boy, he would sneak into the Assembly meetings just to see if he could catch any secret discussion. A sadness he hadn't felt in a long time threatened to well up.

The sentinel moved closer, boots crunching softly against the ground as he approached. Abel held his breath, willing the sentinel to move on.

Elena signaled for them to lower themselves even further behind the berm. They pressed themselves to the ground, feeling the dirt beneath their palms. After what seemed like too long, the danger passed. As the sentinel moved away, the four of them breathed a silent sigh of relief. Abel had no idea what would have happened had they been caught, be he didn't want to find out.

Once the sentinel was out of earshot, Elena cautiously raised her head. "We need to head back. Nightfall is approaching, and we don't want to be caught out here."

Abel nodded. Sneaking around was one thing, but challenging a sentinel's watchful eye in a foreign land was an entirely different level of risk. For a second, he longed for Rephidim...

...until Luca winked at him.

CHAPTER TEN

Abel did not want to return to Rephidim, and he made sure everyone he met knew it. From Kaius to Luca, he pleaded for another way, another path that would both satisfy the desires of Liorah to learn more about the Col'kasid and also keep him out of trouble. He had little doubt that if he returned, he would be strung high over the waterfall and left for the zarcoa, a nocturnal hunter with a wingspan twice its four-foot body length. His flesh would then be picked at until he passed into shadow.

He'd witnessed that before, and it made him shiver.

In the end, however, Liorah would not relent. Abel, with his newly shaved head and hair-free body, was to guide a contingent of seven New Emilians to Rephidim, led by Kaius and including Luca, Raphael, Nico and two others with whom he was unfamiliar. Their goal was to learn what they could about the ways of the Col'kasid and invite some of them back to New Emile as a gesture of goodwill. They were well armed, and assuming the weather held out, they figured they should not be delayed.

Now, near the end of the third week on a path that was becoming well-worn and easier to follow, Abel found himself at the delta that led to the Reed Sea. Kaius had sent two of his men, Eli and Paul, ahead to find the easiest way to cross, while the rest set up camp and erected a cairn to mark their path.

Abel had not wanted to be a burden to any of his new companions, and so he took on duties as they were assigned. This evening, he was to help skin the three Tishbian moles they had killed today. The moles were interesting creatures. A small, sandy-furred mammal perfectly adapted to life underground in the Wastelands , they carved extensive burrow systems with strong claws to feed on roots and invertebrates. Most striking was the strong smell as they bathed in familial urine. They would serve two of them for dinner, while the third would be jerked and preserved in case they came upon a day where no food was available. They had been doing this since they left New Emile, and now each man carried a satchel full of extra meat.

Luca joined Abel, and together they skinned the animals. The two of them had grown close over the past few cycles of the Short Moon, starting when he had been rescued from sure death on the shores of the Reed Sea. They were the same age, and Abel had taken a liking to Luca more so than as friends. He did not know if Luca felt the same, and after his previous disastrous relationship with Asher in Rephidim, he did not want to chance exposing his feelings.

"How are you doing?" Luca asked as he pulled a full hide off the animal in his hand. "We're getting close to your homeland. I imagine that has to make your heart sink."

Abel pursed his lips. "I'll feel better once we're headed back to New Emile. They won't be happy to see me come down through Patience Gap and march toward the gate."

"Patience Gap?"

"A tight squeeze. Probably the easiest way to get through the mountains from the Reed Sea. It's a windy place, but once you're through, Rephidim is just maybe a day or two away."

"What's it like? I mean, what things do you do during the day? Surely you can't pray every minute."

Abel cut the stomach of his animal open and reached in to pull on the guts. "If the Assembly had their way," he said, "that's all the Col'kasid would do—pray to Father Elijah's God that the Great Return would happen soon."

"The Great Return?"

"According to the teaching of Sojen Micah, our first leader, The Great Return was foreseen by the Prophet Jackson Liao in the first years after our arrival, after Transit." Abel pulled harder at an organ that seemed to be stuck. "I had to memorize it as a kid. 'A time may come when humans will return to Earth, to spread the great news of the paradise we have found and bring with us those who believe. This Great Return may be initiated by us or because of us, but it will happen.'"

Luca said nothing. He pushed a stick through his animal's mouth and back out the rectum. It was almost ready for the fire.

"When I got older," Abel continued, "I stopped believing that the Great Return would happen. The Col'kasid—or the Assembly, at least—was so sure that the time was near, all our lives were spent in preparation."

"Why did you stop believing?"

"Are you kidding?" Abel chuckled. "The Assembly preaches from this book, Father Elijah's Bible. They worship it and hold it in higher regard than their own family members. The problem is, very few people outside of the Prelatic Assembly have seen it, and even if it was made available, even if the scribes made copies for all, there aren't many people who can read."

"No?"

Abel shook his head, then yanked out the final bits of the

inside of his animal. It wasn't quite ready for a spit. "There are two schools—one for those who hunt and one for those who are destined to help build the colony. Only the builders are taught to read. Some of those are also taught to write, but only what the Assembly dictates."

"What school were you put into?"

"What do you think? You saw how good I was with a crossbow. I started off with the hunters when I was little, but that didn't go so well and they moved me. I became a scribe."

"You're lucky you were taught to read at all. There are schools in New Emile, but once you're chosen for the sentinels, that stops."

"Read, write, and pray. As a scribe, I had one of the few labors in Rephidim that could be a witness to the inner thoughts of the Assembly."

"That sounds neat, like being in Liorah's council while she yells at people."

"It's not what I wanted to do."

"No? What would your life have been like if you could have chosen your path?"

Abel shrugged. "I don't really know. Certainly nothing to do with the Assembly."

Luca quickly skinned and gutted the third and final mole and placed it with the other over the fire, while Abel finished up with his own animal. It would take a while for the meat to cook, and with little more to do, Abel reclined on the jivara and looked up at a moonless sky. These were rare nights, nights when both the Short Moon and the Long Moon had yet to rise. The sky exploded with stars, a million little pinpricks. Somewhere out there was Earth's sun, and around it was a planet no one on Tishbe would ever see...at least according to some of the Col'kasid. The Assembly still held out hope.

Luca lay down next to Abel and took in a deep breath,

knowing it would probably be one of the few times he would be this close. They were essentially alone while the others set up tents, bathed in a nearby stream, or rested their weary legs elsewhere. The moment reminded Abel of the last time he'd been with Asher. They had quietly left through the gate and located a peaceful spot beneath the waterfall. There, after enjoying each other's company hidden away from judgmental eyes, they fell asleep under the stars, naked, sweaty, and in each other's arms.

That was the mistake.

When the sun had risen the following day, a woman coming to fill the water troughs found the two men. There was no denying what they had been doing, and no way for either of them to escape the coming punishment. Love was to be between a man and a woman, and anything else was an abomination. Abel was well aware of what would happen to him should his tendency to love men ever be known. He had risked it all for a chance at the happiness he saw in others.

Why shouldn't he have that?

The New Emilians were different, though. They were accepting of who he was. Abel had the impression that gender was not an issue and people could love who they desired. For that very reason, Abel would have stayed in New Emile, a beggar on the streets, just to feel that acceptance. He certainly didn't want to go back to Rephidim and face his accusers once more. Living in the Hollows as one of the marked Marokai would be better.

"Don't worry," Luca said after a while of silence. "Kaius will be there to protect you."

"Protect me? What do you mean?"

Luca shifted himself to a more upright position and rested on an elbow. "I see it." He touched Abel on the nose. "Right there. That fear."

Abel attempted to conceal his thoughts with a smirk and an uneasy laugh. There was no way to hide it, though. He really was afraid, and Luca had picked up on it.

"Believe me," Luca said. "I understand. But know that not everyone in New Emile is accepting. You've been lucky so far with the people you've met. You've seen the good in people. In many others, there is only judgment, more so in the Hollows."

"You—"

Luca bent down and gave Abel a kiss on the forehead before the words were out of his mouth. In that moment, hope replaced fear.

"Like I said, Kaius will be there to protect you." Luca rose and flipped the animals over above the flames. "And so will I."

IN THE morning, they followed a path across the delta, through the mud and then along the shore where Abel had once thought he would pass into shadow. In one more day, they had reached the point at which he had to explain how to get to Patience Gap. It would be a day's hike up the side of the cliffs through a crevice where his quvianaq probably still lay rotting, and into the Gap. Once they were on the other side, they had about a two-day hike across an open plain. He no longer feared running into a xialiti, however, as they often shunned large groups of people and were not likely to come out of hiding.

Once into the Gap, the wind picked up. It was hot and moist at first, heavy with a salty scent. Soon, however, the temperature dropped, and a chill forced them all to wrap leather around their bodies. Once they were through Patience Gap and headed down the other side, the temperature would jump again, and they would sweat before reaching the plain that stretched between Rephidim and the mountains. But for now, it was cold. Luca kept Abel warm when they rested for the night. While there was certainly no privacy in their present situation, they could at least be together without repercussions or questions. No one cared.

With the sun still not up, Abel woke with a start. There was a commotion on the other side of the camp near to a sharp rise, partially illuminated by the waning embers of yesterday evening's fire. Luca was already awake and had joined two other men standing around what looked like a xialiti. It was not as large as the one that had attacked Abel, but it was no less frightening.

Without putting on another layer of clothing, Abel quickly grabbed a nearby lance and ran over to join in the fight. The animal hissed as it tried to back away into a crevice. They were good at squeezing through tight spaces and disappearing, but not backward. The animal lunged forward at one man, backed up and lunged again at another. It appeared uneasy on its short legs and fat body, the mouth open wide, baring its teeth.

"Going to make a meal of this one," Raphael said. He jabbed his lance at the xialiti. "Damn thing tried to nibble on my toes while I slept."

"Let it go," Abel said. He pointed at the crevice. "Through there. There's no point in killing it."

Raphael looked back. "Why would I let it go? We need food for the trip."

"You don't eat xialiti. You'd have to cook the meat twice to get rid of the poison in its flesh, and even then it has a nasty taste. You'll be squatting in the rocks for hours."

Raphael frowned, and the men slowly dropped their offensive stances and backed away. The xialiti hissed again, saw its moment, and turned around. Quickly, it slithered into the crevice and disappeared.

Raphael put a hand on Abel's shoulder and looked longingly at where his potential meal had been. "Any other animals we shouldn't eat?" he asked. "I'm tiring of mole."

Abel nodded toward the east. "Once we're out of the Gap, there might be some khopa. Look for the burrows. Take the baca root, cut it open, and leave it at the entrance of any hole you see. A whole family of them will come out and you can take your pick."

"They bite?"

"No."

Raphael shook his head. "Strange world you've got here."

After a meal of tough and stale jerked meat for breakfast, they were ready to head out again.

"How much farther?" Kaius asked Abel. He had pulled back from the lead just as they neared the eastern edge of the Gap.

"There's a break to the right up ahead. Once we get over that, you'll see the buttes. Rephidim won't be visible for a while, but you'll be able to see the butte it's built into. When the sun hits the waterfall at the right angle, it'll be like a beacon."

"What would you say? We have a day?"

"Probably two. I never walked the distance, only rode it on the back of a quvianaq. You could make the distance in a day on their backs if you drove without rest. So on foot, give it two. At the most, three."

Just as Abel said, a break appeared in the gap and far in the distance, flat-topped mountains rose into a blue-green sky. Dark green plants dusted the plain in front of them, but most of it was red dirt. Abel felt a tightness in his chest at seeing his home for the first time in a full cycle of the Long Moon. He did not want to be here—would have done anything to stay in New Emile—but at least he was not alone. That had to amount to something.

A cloud of dust appeared on the horizon, and Luca pointed. "What is that?"

Abel squinted in the sun's light. "Tishbian bison. They herd on the plains and enter the orchards when the sun sets. They're probably running right now because of that hunting party you see to the right."

Luca watched for a moment, transfixed. "Huh. Did you ever want to ride with them?" he asked.

Abel shook his head. "No. I'd rather do other things with my time, but Asher..." Abel trailed off without completing his thought. He hadn't mentioned Asher to Luca, and now that there appeared to be something between them, he didn't know how much he should say. There was still a pang of regret that he had lost the man he once loved, driven out to the north to pass into shadow in the forbidden dunes, while Abel was forced to go east toward the Reed Sea.

"What about Asher? You don't talk about him much."

Abel took in a deep breath and let it out slowly. "No, I don't."

They exited Patience Gap and took a winding path down toward the plain. There were multiple holes in the ground at the foot of the mountains, too small for xialiti and too large for rodents. These were khopa burrows and that meant food. Raphael found and dug out a baca root, then did as Abel had suggested. Within just a few minutes, a furry creature no bigger than a man's foot with no ears and a smashed-in face emerged from the hole. It sniffed at the cut baca root, then reached out with a claw to grab it.

A bolt from Raphael's bow skewered the animal and pinned it to the ground. It took seconds for it to stop squealing.

Raphael reached for the baca root.

"What are you doing?" Abel watched from nearby. "You can leave it right there. Another will come out and then another until you have a family. You don't need to move the baca root. These are not the smartest animals."

Raphael left the root and stepped back. In one more minute, a second khopa emerged from the burrow and sniffed around. Another bolt pinned it to the ground, as well. When Raphael had killed five of them, he whistled.

"Any more? That's like target practice."

"Families run between five and six, so you probably cleared the den." Abel helped Raphael pull the bolts from the khopa and drop them in a pile. "Let me show you something else."

Abel approached the burrow, and using the tip of his lance, poked around inside. After a moment, he pulled it back out. Stuck to the end was a brown sticky substance that reeked lightly of vomit and shit.

Raphael scrunched his nose as all of them approached warily to see what Abel had pulled out.

"It's khopa dung," Abel said, "but you can use it for medicinal purposes. Put this over a cut and a natural seal will form. After a day, your skin will have healed."

"Who decided that was a good idea?" Kaius said, studying the tip of the lance.

Abel shrugged. "Don't know, but it works. We— I mean, the Col'kasid collects the stuff and stores it in jars. We can keep it there for at least a Long Moon without it rotting. It might be good to take with you on Discovery. Along with the haelen, you'd have enough to survive most things."

Nico ran his finger along the dung and brought it to his nose to smell. "Not too bad. Might have helped Ivan back in the Wastelands."

Before anyone could respond to that, a sudden eruption

of chaos to their right shattered the moment. Abel pivoted, his eyes fixed on a billowing cloud of crimson dust that loomed ahead of them. In a heartbeat, the haze cleared, revealing five figures atop quvianaq, brandishing lances.

Immediately, Kaius and the rest of the group swung their bows around and cocked them. With bolts loaded, they were ready for a fight. The air was thick as the strangers in the distance thundered closer, their mounts tearing up the ground beneath them. Abel felt his heart pound in his chest as he braced himself for the inevitable.

"Friends of yours?" Kaius said, as he raised his crossbow.

Abel stepped back, the lance in his hand feeling worthless. "No. I have no friends."

THEY WERE surrounded quickly. One rider quickly noticed Abel and pointed a lance in his direction. "You shaved your head," he said. "You still look ugly."

Abel felt helpless, even as Kaius and Luca put themselves between him and the riders.

"We mean no ill will," Kaius said. "We come from afar bringing news from the One Voice."

The rider who had singled out Abel slowly made his way over, his quvianaq snorting. Abel couldn't help but notice that his companions, from Luca to Nico to all the others, seemed more intrigued by the strange creatures than by the danger their riders posed. He had to remind himself that they had never laid eyes on such a beast before. In New Emile, nothing even remotely similar existed. Their curiosity was weakening their defense.

"The One Voice?" the rider said. "What is that?"

"Our leader." Kaius remained motionless, the man in charge. He lowered his weapon slightly. "We only come to talk."

The rider scanned the group with a piercing gaze, seeming to size up each of them one by one. Finally, his eyes came to rest back on Abel, narrowing to slits.

"Why did you bring this one?" His voice was laced with suspicion.

Abel felt their stares. He knew each of the riders, all hunters who had bullied him in the past. The man speaking was Saadya, the Keeper's help. His long brown hair was braided in the back and wrapped up with twine. Sweat on his dark skin glinted in the afternoon sun, and across his face was the sign of the hunter—a slash burned diagonally from the left of the man's forehead to his right cheek. Muscles rippled as he adjusted himself on the back of his mount.

"He is with us," Kaius said. "He has been our guide and is under our care."

Saadya spit on the ground toward Abel. "He is the apostate, the heretic. He cannot enter the gates of Rephidim again except on punishment of death. Unless you want to die here, boy."

Luca stepped forward and stood next to Kaius, his weapon still drawn and this time aimed at Saadya's chest. "You will not leave him to pass into shadow out here. He is no longer Col'kasid. He is New Emilian and therefore no threat to you or your people."

Saadya laughed, and in unison, the other four riders laughed with him. "We will see about that," he said finally. With a snarl, he nodded toward the buttes and turned his mount. "Come."

One man picked up the dead khopa and quickly threaded a long spike with a rope through their necks. When they were all tied together, he strapped the bundle to his mount and winked at Raphael, who had watched with disappointment on his face. They then hiked toward the buttes at a pace befitting a quvianaq, not men with satchels to carry. At this rate, they would make it to the base of the buttes by nightfall. Abel would have gladly turned and run back to Patience Gap to not only escape the heat, but to get away from the punishment he was sure to face.

Although Kaius attempted to start a conversation with Saadya several times by asking a multitude of questions, the only response he ever received was a curt "That is for the Assembly to answer."

Abel tried to keep pace with the speed of the group, his legs burning with the effort. Luca walked beside and lowered his voice. "You know them?"

"I do." Abel nodded ahead. "The man in the lead is Saadya, the Keeper's help. He's the leader of the hunters. I never liked him, and it's best if you stay on his good side."

"He has one?"

"Only when he's been drinking. To the right, up ahead, is Adam. His brother, Malachi, is behind. On the left is Asher's brother, Michael."

"I suppose you knew Michael well."

Abel shook his head. "Not at all. Asher never got along with him and the two rarely spoke, except at Assembly meetings and only then to argue."

"At least he knew his brother." Luca did not elaborate, and Abel didn't press. "Who's behind us?"

Abel glanced back. "Thomasson. He cannot speak."

"Because he doesn't want to, or was he born that way?"

"It was a punishment for talking back to Saadya last year. The Assembly ordered his tongue be removed."

"Great Mother!" Luca exclaimed. "What is it with you people?"

"Not my people."

"Well, just the same. You and Asher were exiled and left

to die. That man had his tongue ripped out. And that scar on Saadya's face. Was that a punishment, too?"

"No. It was an honor."

Just as the sun dipped behind the buttes, the New Emilians and their Col'kasid escorts arrived at a road dug into the side of the mountain. Saadya stopped his quvianaq and dismounted. The other four men followed.

"We will walk from here," Saadya said to Kaius.

"What are you going to do with these...things?" Kaius pointed to the animals.

"The quvianaq will graze and not wander far. I suppose you keep your animals in a pen."

"We don't have animals like this, so no. Are you sure they won't try to escape?"

Saadya smiled, revealing two broken teeth in the front. "They are our companions. Would your friends try to escape from you?"

The trek up the narrow road to the gate of Rephidim was arduous. Abel remained behind Luca, while Nico brought up his rear. At least he felt a little protection, though his stomach churned with a sickening sense of dread. Of all the places he could imagine in his worst nightmares, this was the one that haunted him the most. The last time he had traversed this road, he had been exiled and cast into the shadows. Somewhere out there lay Asher's body, likely picked apart by animals. Perhaps he, too, had stumbled upon a group of people on Discovery, but that seemed highly unlikely. If he had been forced to go north, only danger — and the dragon — awaited him.

As they climbed, a light mist from the waterfall cascading down from the butte enveloped the men. While Abel had always been curious about the source of the water, he had no answer for Luca when asked.

"We are told it's a gift from Elijah's god," Abel said in explanation. "'Behold, I will stand before you there and you shall strike the rock, and water will come out of it, that the people may drink.'"

"More stuff you had to memorize?"

"Not exactly. It's something spoken during every meal. You'll hear it more than once, if they decide to feed you, that is. After a while, it sticks with you, no matter how ridiculous it sounds."

After a good half-hour, the road opened up wider, revealing a breathtaking view of the ground some five hundred feet below. As they approached the gate to Rephidim, Saadya turned to Abel and eyed him with disdain. "You will not enter."

Luca apparently wasn't having any of it. Leaving Abel out here was simply not an option. He stepped in between Saadya and Abel. It was a noble move, but Abel knew it was also futile. The rules of the Col'kasid were absolute, and no one dared challenge them.

"You cannot leave him out here to pass into shadow." Luca's nostrils flared in anger. "It would be inhuman."

"He's an abomination," Saadya spat. "Regardless of your feelings towards him, he cannot be allowed back into Rephidim."

"So what do you suggest he do?" Luca protested. "Wait out here by himself until we're done?"

"I do not care, nor would even one member of the Col'kasid lift a finger otherwise. Even his parents have disowned him."

That hit Abel hard. It was true, and cut deep. He couldn't shake off the feeling that this was just the beginning of his troubles. Blood would soon flow.

Before that happened, Kaius stepped forward and put a

hand on Luca's shoulder. "It's okay, Luca. You can stay out here with him."

Luca's face showed just how much he didn't agree with that idea, but he wasn't about to argue with Kaius. He kept his eyes on Saadya, his fists clenched.

"Fine," Luca finally said. He pointed to Malachi, the man who had skewered the khopa. "Leave us the meat, then."

Malachi looked at Saadya, who nodded in agreement. "One only," Saadya said. "And if you get hungry later, you know how to hunt." He smiled wickedly as he glared at Abel. "Don't you? And while you're out here, maybe you can take a bath in the water below. You stink like shit."

Saadya turned and headed for the gate. "Come," he said. "The Assembly awaits."

While Luca and Abel stood together and watched their New Emilian companions and the Col'kasid approach the gate, Abel felt a burning nervousness in his stomach. Something terrible was going to happen, and it would be his fault for bringing them all there.

CHAPTER ELEVEN

KAIUS SURVEYED THE FACES STARING BACK AT HIM. He wanted to bring Abel along, yet he already figured out that defying the customs of this enigmatic tribe would not bode well. After all, he was there as a messenger of amity, not as a bearer of hostility. It was still bewildering to him that other humans existed on this planet, even after spending so much time with Abel. And now, amidst the unknown, he felt utterly vulnerable.

Saadya guided Kaius and the small group of New Emilians—Raphael, Nico, Paul, and Eli— toward the heart of a cluster of structures nestled into the mountainside. While the edifices had wooden fronts and doors, their roofs were snugly tucked beneath a rocky outcrop. Even in the dim light of evening, Kaius had to concede that the place was a wonder, crafted with ingenuity and inspired by nature. It was a stark contrast to New Emile, where crude blocks of stone had been hauled from the quarry and stacked together, creating a jarring juxtaposition with the surrounding amorphous moor.

The streets were nothing more than packed crimson dirt, teeming with people who all wore brown tunics over brown trousers. Lengthy hair was woven into plaits regardless of gender. The sole distinction between males and females, it seemed, was the men's beards. Even the children—standing alongside what Kaius surmised were their parents or guardians—were strikingly similar in appearance. Their skin was a fusion of olive and dark tones, like himself, Saadya, and Abel. Almost everyone looked like they could use a meal or two.

Positioned near the far end of the city of Rephidim and surrounded on two sides by larger structures, the Assembly, as it was called, was an oddity in a group of oddities. The front wall was all adobe, rising to meet the outcrop some forty feet over their head. There were no windows, but five small openings near the top. Blue smoke rose out of two of those openings, met the rock above, and wafted by toward the more open evening sky. Saadya ushered them through a single door made of a reddish wood.

Inside, the space was enormous, as if the edifice was nothing more than a cover to a cave. Torches set into the walls illuminated a room that stretched beyond the reach of the lights. In the middle, five men sat around a small fire, each one dressed in a white robe. They were not old, and in fact, one of them could have been in his late teens. Despite their young age, however, all but one wore long beards, cut in the middle so that they fell to both the right and the left of the wearer. At the end of each beard was tied a small rock. The youngest only had stubble on his face.

The smell of the cave was horrendous, as if the fire had never once been put out. The walls were covered with gray, and Kaius figured by the time he left, he would need to wash his clothes in the nearest stream. How could anyone stand to be in this room for long? Were they used to the smell?

The oldest looking man stood. He was shorter than Kaius but held himself regally. His skin was brown, brown hair fell in waves behind him, and he wore a brown sash across his white robe. The man approached Kaius and looked him up and down.

"Messengers, Elder," Saadya said.

"From?"

"They claim to be from a city called New Emile."

The man in the robe and sash tilted his head to the left as if contemplating something.

Rather than wait for an introduction, Kaius spoke. "We bring a message—"

The man held up his hand, cutting Kaius off. He continued to stare, first at the clothes, then the shoes Kaius wore, and finally up at the man's shaved head.

"Where is your hair?" the man asked.

"It is shaved."

"Why?"

"We...um..." Kaius did not expect this to be the first question. "Bugs in our city. They feed on hair stopping just before getting under the skin. The best way to rid ourselves of the pestilence is to shave."

The man nodded, tilted his head to the right, then clasped his hands together in front of him. "Welcome, shaved man," he said finally. "I am Levi, Elder of the Assembly, and Keeper of the Text."

"I am Kai—" Again, Levi held his hand up. Kaius noted the man had to be in his mid-thirties, judging from the scarcity of wrinkles on his face. His hands, however, looked to be from a man in his seventies.

"I hear you have a message," Levi asked.

"Yes, well." Kaius shifted uncomfortably. If he had pictured the way this meeting would go, this was not it. "We come from New Emile, a city far to the northwest. Liorah, the One Voice and holder of the vials of haelen, bids you greetings."

Levi's eyebrows rose slowly. "The One Voice?"

"That's what she calls herself."

"Why?"

"Um...well...I'm not exactly sure." Kaius knew why, but it wasn't for this man to know. "She is our leader."

"A woman?"

"Yes."

"And what is this colony, this tribe, called?"

"It's not so much a tribe as a city. New Emile."

Levi nodded. "Not the Zhanshi?"

It was Kaius's turn to raise his eyebrows. "We had not heard that name until recently."

"So your answer is no."

"No." Kaius decided it was time to throw a little knowledge at this Elder, show him he knew some things. "Abel talked about a third tribe, people who caused a genocide at Manoach. Are the Zhanshi the people who live north of the Barren Sea?"

Levi took a step back. His eyes flickered toward Saadya, then came back to Kaius and his group of men. His expression in that moment changed from one of guarded interest to both fear and anger. Something in what Kaius had said evidently didn't sit well with him.

"Where is the apostate?" Levi spit to the left. "He is not welcome here."

"He is outside, Elder," Saadya answered. "With one more of their tribe."

"He stays out there."

"Father," the young man with the stubble rose and approached. "We do not turn anyone away."

"Not unless they turn away from us." Levi, still facing Kaius, narrowed his eyes. "You will forgive my son, Gideon. He has not yet learned the ways of respectable conversation."

Kaius nodded. "We mean no ill will in coming here."

"No?" Levi asked. "Then why are you here? It cannot be

to return the apostate to our gates and be on your way."

"No. We are here as ambassadors from New Emile. We had always been under the impression that we were the last humans left on Tishbe. Our discovery of Abel led us to another reality."

"Indeed." Levi stroked one part of his beard. "Come. Sit. We will talk while we eat."

Kaius and the others followed Levi to a table set up beyond. Past the table, the room continued in darkness. Kaius briefly wondered who—or what—lived down there. Perhaps a beast kept in captivity and fed the bodies of wayward travelers. He would need to keep his guard up.

With no instruction, three women entered through the door at the front of the room. Each of them looked emaciated, much like Abel when he'd been found on the shore of the Reed Sea. Their brown clothes hung on their frail frames loosely. The women brought with them bowls and trays filled with fruit and meat. Kaius heard his stomach growl at the sight and only then realized just how hungry he was. When the trays and bowls were placed on the table and the women left, two more equally thin women entered and filled clay cups with some sort of red liquid. It looked like juice from a berry.

"Eat. Drink." Levi waved his hand over the table. "Let no man go hungry. 'For I was hungry, and you gave me food, I was thirsty and you gave me drink, I was a stranger and you welcomed me.' The words of Jesus from the Gospel of Matthew. Are you familiar?"

Kaius looked on as his men grabbed food from the bowls and plates and began eating. He wanted to reach for the meat, but suddenly felt it would be rude. "I am not."

"These are the words passed on to us from Father Elijah. We are to honor him in all we do."

"Father Elijah? You mean Elijah Jonas, the leader of the Circle of Light cult?"

Levi's right eye twitched. "We do not refer to our ancestors as members of a cult. They were pioneers, and we will honor them as we honor our living. If you are from this tribe as you say and can trace your histories back to the temple at Manoach, you know then that we are likely related."

Kaius did not know how to respond to that. Instead, he reached for a loaf of bread and tore off a bit. As he chewed, relishing in the taste of something other than stale jerked meat, he considered a response. "It is possible," he said as he swallowed, "that our paths might lead us back to a common beginning. But I would not say we are related."

"No?" Levi tilted his head again, then laced his fingers together. "We all descend from Adam and Eve, given life by God."

Kaius did not come for a sermon. It was time to change the subject. "My name is Kaius, by the way. And these men are Raphael, Nico, Paul, and Eli."

Levi's eyebrows rose again at the mention of Eli's name. "Eli? Named after our Father?"

Eli chewed his meal and was about to respond when Kaius broke in. "Eli stands for Elias," he said quickly. "No man should be named after something he cannot live up to."

Levi chuckled and looked at his son. "Did you hear that, son? I should have named you something else instead of Gideon, the judge. You can never live up to that man."

A nervous laugh filtered through the room, starting with Gideon. Kaius was unsure how to take it. In fact, this entire meeting had been odd from the start. He filtered through Liorah's instructions and wondered if he'd satisfied enough of them that he could now take his men and go.

He had not.

"Can you tell me more?" Kaius asked after the laughter had subsided. "About your tribe, your ways. We, of course, will reciprocate. It is not often that two tribes who are not aware of each other should meet."

"You wish to know about the Col'kasid?" Levi reached for a loaf of bread himself. "I would have thought the apostate told you plenty."

"Abel only said that you live here, in Rephidim. And that we have common beginnings at Manoach. He did not give us much of a history lesson beyond that."

"Oh, our history goes much farther back than Manoach. That was but a way-stop on the journey of life."

FOR THE next few hours, while the night wore on and the fire in the Assembly continued to burn bright, Levi told the story of the Col'kasid, starting with the plans of Elijah Jonas to bring three hundred people from Earth to start a new life and correct the mistakes of the past. He told of the City of Nod, the bounties given to them by Elijah's God, of the prophets Jackson Liao, Zachary Miller, Kayla Boyer, and Tigger Jones. He also told of a man named Mathias Tseng and of his treachery, his attempts to destroy Nod and wipe out all that Elijah had built. Finally, he told of the Flood and the great Exodus to Manoach where they were given words from the ancients—texts written in a strange language.

This intrigued Kaius, but he did not interrupt.

Gideon had joined them at the table, while the other three men—other prelates, Kaius assumed—had left, climbing stairs built into a wall of the Assembly. Kaius wondered if these men lived and ate where they met to discuss matters of policy. Did they ever leave? *Great Mother, the smell.*

When the subject of leaving Manoach came up, Kaius had questions.

"When Micah and Patience arrived at Rephidim," Kaius asked, "why didn't anyone return to Manoach?"

Rather than Levi answering, a raspy voice spoke from within the darkness. "There was no need."

An older man, maybe in his seventies, stepped out of the shadows. He walked with an ornately carved stick taking slow steps, a slight limp evident. Immediately, both Levi and Gideon stood and lowered their heads.

"Sojen," Levi said. "I did not know you would be awake."

"At this age, you get up a lot to pee." The man approached the table, but did not take a seat. Kaius regarded the man's frail frame and long white hair pulled back and tied with a leather strap. Unlike the other Elders, he did not wear white. Instead, his robe was brown and stained in many places. Glancing down, Kaius also noted a lack of footwear and feet that had seen better days.

"May I present Sojen Micah, founder of Rephidim and Great Scribe of the Col'kasid."

Kaius nodded, but he did not stand. He didn't know the custom of the Col'kasid, but he did know the customs of New Emile. And there, the only person a man deferred to was Liorah. "I am Kaius of New Emile."

"So I have heard. I wondered what Miriam would have called that city on the map. Emile. That was my grandfather's middle name. Did you know that?"

"No. That is definitely news to me."

Sojen Micah shifted his eyes around the table. "My grandson leaves too much out."

Gideon moved a chair behind the old man and helped him sit. "Now, my great grandson," he said, patting the younger man on the hand, "he would tell you the truth."

"I have told many things, and none were fabrications,"

Levi said. "I have told of our shared histories."

"It is not the shared histories that these men want to know. It is the new histories, the stories of how we came to live here. I, too, am interested in knowing what became of Miriam, my cousin. For too many years, I have let my imagination fill in the gaps."

"Your cousin?" Kaius sat up straighter. "This is also news to me."

Micah nodded, then quickly wiped his nose with the back of a hand. "She was determined to find the city on the map the ancients gave us. It was buried in one of the texts in the temple. To her, the map was a sign that there was another place to settle and so she left."

"Why didn't everyone travel with her?"

"Age, disease, depression. All these and more. In the end, a third of our tribe went with her toward the great canyon west of Manoach. That is where we lost their trail." Micah adjusted himself in his seat, then leaned forward on his walking stick. His right hand rubbed one of the carvings on the top, something Kaius wished he could get a better look at. "You ask why we did not return to bring the others back, nor why we did not follow Miriam to your new city, this New Emile."

"The Great Mother sent scouts back after arriving there," Kaius said. "Their discoveries are what led us to believe that no one else had survived."

"The Great Mother?" Micah smiled slightly. "That's an honorific I would never have expected of her." He shifted again. "Anyway, there were three groups who left. Did you know that?"

"I was only aware of Miriam's journey, and now that of yours."

Micah stared ahead at the table. He did not appear to be

focused on anything in the present, but rather the past. "Joel, another cousin of mine, took a group back to the Barrier Mountains to set up a mining camp. About seventy people went with him, and none returned."

"What happened?"

"We did not know for many years. After what happened to my sister, we all agreed not to return to the north. We had a new home, food and water, and a chance to build something. Rephidim was a miracle in the desert, and you do not ignore gifts from God. Years later, two strangers appeared at the base of the mountain of Rephidim—Petra and Nemeth, the last survivors of Joel's group. It was they who told us of the genocide at Manoach and the eradication of most of those who went into the mountains, all at the hands of Mathias Tseng's grandson."

"The Zhanshi?" Kaius asked, although he knew the answer.

Micah nodded. "Petra and Nemeth warned us to always be on guard, to beware the dragon in the north. Should the Barren Sea's water recede, it was believed the Zhanshi would come looking for more survivors. They were—are, I still believe—determined to wipe out the descendants of those who slammed the gates shut on Mathias in the earliest years."

"Abel had said there were two strangers who came to visit you. These were Petra and Nemeth?"

"Strangers to just about everyone here, but not to me or my wife, Patience. They did not stay long. They said they had been searching for survivors of the temple and still had not found Miriam. It was their mission to spread the word of the Zhanshi threat."

Kaius considered all that Micah had said and compared it to what he had learned in his early years. No one else in his group—from Raphael to Nico or Paul and Eli—had ever been told the complete history of New Emile. To them, history started at Manoach. That was the way Master Eilian, Miriam's son, wanted it. It was rumored that the Great Mother had lost her mental faculties in the years after arriving at New Emile, and her paranoias informed her son's later beliefs. Eilian then passed those same beliefs on to his son, Philip, and later his daughter, Liorah. It was as if they wanted to wipe out everything that had happened before in order to focus on rebuilding the future.

The Col'kasid, on the other hand, seemed content to learn from the past. While they would not return to Manoach, they were more aware of all the dangers on Tishbe. Micah's intonation showed reverence to that past rather than ignorance of it. Kaius didn't know what was better.

"What my grandfather is saying," Levi said after a moment of silence, "is that we have had no sign of a third tribe in existence on Tishbe. No sign of you."

"That's not what I'm saying at all." Micah looked at Levi and shook his head slightly. "I've always believed that Miriam's group didn't survive, but if they did, I'm sure that she and her husband Tobias found a way. Where they would have ended up, however, was a mystery. This is all news to me, and I am grateful for these visitors who have come to us."

"My apologies, Sojen." Levi bent his head in reverence.

"But you did not come simply to tell us of your existence," Micah added. "Did you?"

"No, we did not." Kaius leaned forward. "We come to extend our hand and welcome a contingent of yours to return with us to visit New Emile. It is Liorah's desire that we see what we can offer each other in trade."

"Trade?" Levi perked up. "We have everything we need right here."

"Maybe not all, father," Gideon said, then turned to

Kaius. "You called your leader, Liorah, the One Voice and the holder of the vials of haelen. What is haelen?"

"I believe Abel called it the Water of Life."

At that, Micah suddenly sat in a more upright posture than Kaius expected. "From the temple?" he asked excitedly. "Surely Miriam could not have taken that much. I was there myself when she filled two containers, but after all this time, it must have been used up."

"There's another pool at New Emile, in the middle of the city. It contains the same healing properties."

"Another...pool?" Something flashed across Micah's face.

Fear?

"What's...in this pool?"

"A tree."

"White bark with yellow leaves?"

Kaius nodded. "You describe it well. Is that what was in the pool at Manoach?"

"That...and something else."

Again, Kaius noted Micah's expression. His hands, shaky as they were for his age, gripped his walking stick more firmly.

"If this is the Water of Life," Gideon said excitedly, "we can surely find benefit."

"You have sick?" Kaius asked.

"Many of—"

"We are fine," Levi said, interrupting Gideon. "Our Lord will provide. There is no cure that can beat prayer."

"But father." Gideon turned to Micah. "Sojen, surely you see the benefits this would have."

Micah glanced at Levi, but did not answer. Instead, he pushed himself off his chair with his walking stick and stood. "I am tired," he said.

There was no mistaking the look on the man's face just then. Kaius had seen it before, many times, over many years.

It was the look of someone who had lost a loved one.

ABEL AND Luca had found a small indentation in the rock at the bottom of the butte, away from prying eyes. A small fire near the entrance kept them warm while the temperature dropped after the sun had set. There was no way Abel was going to let his feelings for Luca get him in trouble again, however. He made that clear quickly. No matter how openly New Emilians expressed their love to one another, being caught by the Col'kasid would put them both in danger. Abel couldn't let that happen to Luca, especially after so many reminders of the pain he and Asher went through.

When the morning arrived, Luca set out to find a khopa to kill for some food. Abel remained by the fire, considering all that he had been through and what it really meant for him to be back at the gates of Rephidim. He was an exile, unwanted by his family, with a name that was unspeakable in the community. If they all left now, they could make it back to New Emile in just one cycle of the Short Moon. There, life could begin again.

Luca would be gone a while. Abel mentioned they found most of the burrows about a mile past the buttes, where the ground was softer. This close to the rocks, the only animals that might be found were xialiti—which were poisonous—and maldoric, four-winged white birds that were damnably difficult to shoot down with a crossbow and bolt. There was little threat of someone coming by on their way to the orchards or to pull water from the pool below the waterfall, but Abel was still anxious. Perhaps it was just the memory of his prior experience with being caught, tried, and sentenced that had him on edge.

The relationship Abel had with Asher was almost a lifetime ago. They had been neighbors growing up and could be found playing in the streets long after the sun had set. When both of them had been assigned to the hunter's school, Abel was thrilled. It wasn't long, however, before ineptitude with a bow and bolt put him on the path of the builder and then scribe. There he was to learn how to read and scribe any new dictates of the Prelatic Assembly. He was also taught how to read nature, from the weather to any signs in the sky that might foretell the Great Return. The time Abel had with Asher had been significantly cut short. Every opportunity they found to be together, they would enjoy to the fullest, acting foolishly and being the teenagers that everyone expected them to be.

Abel pushed embers around the fire he and Luca had set up. With the sun rising, the temperature would jump. He did not know how long it would take for Kaius and the others to complete their ambassador duties, but he hoped it would end soon.

A scuffle just past the indentation in the rock alerted Abel to the approach of another. It couldn't have been Luca so quickly. He moved as far back into the shadows as he could and hoped whoever it was would pass unaware.

"Abel?" The voice was that of Gideon, and Abel relaxed a bit. While Gideon was Levi's son and expected to become the Keeper of the Text when his father's time was up, he had always been a good friend. Gideon had not been a part of the trial, nor had he been present for the exile—the day Abel was sent out of the gate to pass into shadow on his own.

Abel stepped forward. "Gideon? In here."

Gideon appeared near the fire and looked inside the indentation. "I've been here before. This is where you used to come when your parents were mad at you."

"As good a place as any to hide out and wait."

Abel ushered Gideon inside and sat against a dirt wall. Neither of them could look at each other. Abel felt shame. What did Gideon feel?

"Your new friends are interesting," Gideon finally said. "I like the shaved head."

"It's comfortable but takes work."

"What's it like, this New Emile? I heard a little last night from Kaius, but he didn't really go into detail and my father rarely let the man get a word in."

Gideon's simple query felt...investigatory. Still, he had once been a friend.

"It's completely different from here." Abel took in a deep breath. "For one, it's built on a moor in the middle of nowhere."

"A moor? What is that?"

"It's wide open, like a marsh but with few plants. There are pools of muddy water everywhere. Imagine putting your face in dirt and taking a deep breath. That's about what it smells like."

"Doesn't sound very pleasant."

Abel shrugged. "Not the moor, but New Emile is an interesting place. They make most of the buildings out of stone that they pull out of the ground. The streets are stone as well, so that you don't get dirty walking everywhere."

"And the people?"

"Nice." Abel thought of the Hollows and the way he'd seen the Marokai treated. He did not need to go into that much detail. "I have yet to meet someone who would kick me out for being me."

Gideon must have caught the implication immediately. "I wasn't a part of that, and you know it. I am sorry about what happened to you."

"What about Asher? Whatever happened to him?"

Gideon picked up a small stick and began moving dirt around in front of him, drawing circles then scribbles with no shape. "He was forced to go north."

Abel opened his eyes wide. "Toward the dunes?"

"If he didn't make it past, then that's where I suppose he passed into shadow. There's little water there, even if you stick to the edges of the sand."

"How could they do that?" Abel felt sick to his stomach. He had a feeling Asher had passed into shadow, but to the north? There was nothing that way. "They could have sent him south or east."

"They should have sent him with you. Maybe you'd be happy then."

Abel felt a surge of emotion. Although he and Asher both knew they could never have a life together in Rephidim, that didn't mean they couldn't have had one if they had left together. It was something they had talked about many times. At one point, they had made plans to head into the forests south and build a new home there. They wouldn't have been the first.

"Why didn't you say anything?" Abel asked softly. He didn't want to cry, but he couldn't help it if his voice cracked.

"What was I to say? I won't be Keeper of the Text until my father's time is up. He is only thirty-four. His time does not end for six more years."

"But you have a seat in the Assembly. You have a voice."

"I am one voice. Between my father and Malachi, James and Mateo, I am outnumbered. Believe me, I argued, but in the end, my father wouldn't allow my vote. Why do you think I wasn't at the gate when they sent you out, or why I never took part in your trial?"

"I thought you were too ashamed of me."

"Not at all." Gideon dropped the stick and crossed his arms. "My plan has always been to reverse many of the laws Sojen Micah and Patience set down. To do that takes time, though. And it takes people like you who will join with me in protest. I don't believe this is what Father Elijah had in mind when he arrived here, and from the stories Sojen Micah tells around the fires, I don't think it was what his generation wanted, either."

"So say something now." Abel tensed the muscles in his hand. "Go up there and tell them what you think. Throw your stone. You have a voice, even if it's one of five. With enough passion, you could—"

Gideon held his hand up. "It's a nice thought, but I'm too young, and not one person respects me. I have no wife and no prospect of a family, meaning I am not whole. Until then, youth taints my voice. You know the rules."

Abel shook his head. Rules. It was a poor excuse, and Gideon knew it. That a man could not gain respect until he reached a certain age and took a wife was just as ridiculous as the idea that only the prelates should have access to Father Elijah's Bible. Knowledge should be gained and shared, not hoarded for power.

"Keep telling yourself that," Abel said. "You were always good at hiding behind the rules to keep from getting in trouble."

CHAPTER TWELVE

THE STRANGERS WERE GIVEN FOOD AND WATER AND ALLOWED to stay together in a room near the gate—except for Abel and Luca, who would remain wherever they were. Gideon had told Kaius that they would not leave until the Assembly had decided whether to send a contingent of ambassadors back to New Emile or simply give them a message for Liorah. The offer of haelen was too good, though, and surely there would be other items to trade between this New Emile and Rephidim. Perhaps together they could even stand against the Zhanshi should they ever attack.

Gideon sat with his father around the Assembly fire, an eternal flame that had not gone out since it was first lit on the day Sojen Micah and his new wife Patience arrived. The Assembly was their first home, or so the stories went. It was a deep enough cave that had housed the twenty-eight survivors from Manoach until they could build adobe and wood structures under the overhang and over the waterfall that fell from the cliff face below.

Micah was the only person remaining from that original group who still lived in the cave. The rest had made their own homes and started their own families. Micah would not leave his wife's side, however, even after she passed into shadow. The only exception to that had been his mournful journeys which he took every few cycles of the Short Moon.

Gideon looked toward the dark maw of the cave beyond the table where just last night the New Emilians and Col'kasid had their conference, the first summit of two very different tribes who had, until now, been ignorant of their existence. In that darkness, Patience Victor had been buried, a grave dug into the rock by an aging Micah. She'd had a long life—seventy-two years—but bore just one child, Gideon's grandfather. That child, Micah the Second, passed into shadow on his fortieth birthday during the Red Death, just a few days before his son, Levi, turned twenty.

On that day, Sojen Micah decreed that no Keeper of the Text should remain in power past his fortieth birthday in honor of his son's life. Instead, he must sire a replacement, and that replacement must be old enough—and be married to a woman—by the time it came for him to be handed Father Elijah's Bible.

Gideon was next in line, and he didn't want that Bible. He still had six years to go before his father's reign was over, but there was no way he was going to find a wife before then. He'd had no luck with any romantic endeavors in the past. Then again, he was only sixteen.

"What are our options?" Malachi looked at each of the men around the fire. "I say we send them back and wash our hands of the idea of any sort of trade. We know they are there, and that should be enough. If the time comes when we need something, we'll ask."

Mateo stroked the left side of his beard and stared into the flames. "But we need something now. They have the Water of Life, and what do we have? Khopa dung? That's good for scrapes and cuts, but if what the legends say is true, the Water of Life will give us a fighting chance. There have been signs of illness recently, perhaps another Red Death. I cast my stone toward a meeting."

"And what are we going to offer them? That's why I say we wash our hands of this." Malachi scoffed. "It's pointless to send representatives on a journey that will take a full cycle of the Short Moon or longer to a place we don't know is safe just to say we have nothing. Oh, but please give us your Water of Life. I'm sure this Liorah, the One Voice, will be all for that. Besides, a woman in charge? These people are animals. I do not see the point in risking any of our men's lives in this foolish endeavor. A society set up under a woman's rule cannot be anything we wish upon our children."

The men fell silent, the crackle of the fire the only sound within the Assembly. Gideon's mind wandered elsewhere, as he never really felt a part of their discussions, especially when they denigrated others. He rarely contributed to the conversations around the fire, and even though he had cast his stones for a vote, they rarely went against his father. He wouldn't dare. No, Abel was down below and needed comfort. This was a waste of time, and he itched to return to his friend.

"I for one," Levi said after a moment, "am not inclined to send anyone back. Their attitude seems a little too liberal for my tastes, and the longer they remain in Rephidim, the more they will infect the others. They have already accepted the apostate as one of their own. God knows what else they will accept." Levi looked at Gideon. "What do you say, son?"

Gideon blinked. "I...You want to know what I think?"

"Yes." Levi spread his arms out and smiled. "You're a part of the Assembly and you'll eventually take my place. This is a momentous decision, and we need the collective wisdom of all of God's men to know what to do."

"Well...I don't...I mean...I think we shouldn't sit here and pick fruit, kill bison, and have babies forever."

Levi's smile faltered. "Is that what you think we do all day?"

"I see nothing more. I see no purpose."

"What do you mean?" Malachi asked. "Our purpose is to prepare for the Great Return. There is no other responsibility so great as to grow."

"That's what I mean." Gideon shifted himself to get more comfortable. If they really wanted to know what he thought, he would share it. "We lost sixty-five people, nearly a third of our population, to the Red Death a year before I was born. The signs of that are back, as Mateo has mentioned."

"We don't know that," Malachi interrupted. "And to spread rumors this early is to invite unrest."

"I am only saying what I think."

"Let him continue," Levi said.

Gideon sat up straighter. They really should use the chairs instead of sitting on the ground. "New Emile has this haelen, the Water of Life. Do you know what that could have done for us in the past? And what of the future? The Red Death will come again—soon or years from now—and we must be prepared. If we've all fallen victim to another disease and the Great Return happens, what glory will that have shown Father Elijah's god?"

"So, you cast your stone toward trade?" Levi asked.

"No. I cast my stone toward the future of the Col'kasid." Gideon looked around at the other elders. "Mateo casts his with me. Malachi and you, Father, have cast yours toward the past."

Now Levi's smile was completely gone. Gideon had stepped over a line, and he knew it. But his father wanted to know what he thought.

Levi stared at Gideon for too long, his eyes narrowed into

slits. No one else dared say anything, lest that famous rage turn on them.

"James," Levi barked. "You have said nothing. What about it? It is two against two. Where do you cast your stone?"

James looked confused. He often disagreed with Levi, but this was no ordinary decision. Gideon had noted that he had said little during this meeting and seemed to be lost in his own thoughts. Something else had been weighing on his mind. "I need time to think. There is more to this than just black and white."

"What are you saying?" Levi asked. "It's simple. You cast your vote to send a contingent back with Kaius to New Emile, or you cast your vote to bid them well and rid ourselves of the temptations they bring."

"You're swaying the vote, Father." Gideon had witnessed this behavior many times before.

"I am doing no such thing." Levi did not look at his son. "James. Your stone?"

James took a deep breath in, then let it out slowly. "I will tell you in the morning. Perhaps a walk with God will clear my mind."

"There is no time for a walk. Decide."

"There is always time, Elder. When that day comes when we are too busy to walk with Him, we will become apostates ourselves. Grant me this, and I will return with my vote."

Levi fumed, but did not respond to the request right away. Both Malachi and Mateo looked anywhere but at their leader. Not only did Gideon not feel comfortable with the proceedings, he was even more uncomfortable when angers rose, either in his father or in someone else.

Somewhere in the cave's darkness where Sojen Micah lived, Gideon heard a noise. His great grandfather was awake, listening in on the proceedings. How would he have cast his stone?

"Fine," Levi threw his hands up in the air. "One hour. Return with your stone and no excuses. Perhaps a walk will do us all good."

GIDEON STOOD in the garden built on the edge of the butte above the waterfall. From his vantage point, he could only see where the water forcefully exited the rock and little else. However, the rush of water as it fell hundreds of feet below was a pleasant noise, one that often lulled him to sleep. Not tonight, though. A waxing Long Moon cast a dim light on the surrounding plants, while the Short Moon hung high just over the butte. The stars were spotty, some covered by clouds.

The garden was built more as a place of contemplation than as anything practical. While there were fruits, vegetables, and herbs which could be picked when ready, its purpose was to be the Col'kasid's Gethsemane, that refuge in Jerusalem where Jesus had been arrested days before his crucifixion. Gideon had to admit the stories in the Bible were hard to understand, perhaps because if they were true, they happened on a planet far away surrounding one of those stars. A planet from which his ancestors had fled. Earth sounded like a violent place, and even if humans had made thousands of years of progress between the events of the Bible and Transit, it felt as if they had never found the right course.

What was so different now?

Gideon was not alone in the garden. Every one of the five prelates of the Assembly had taken up space there to contemplate their own thoughts about what the existence of New Emile meant to their community. For years, the Col'kasid lived with the belief that they were alone on Tishbe. It wasn't until the strangers came—Petra and Nemeth—that news of another tribe was revealed. That tribe, the Zhanshi, was safely on the other side of the flooded Barren Sea. It posed no real threat.

Just last year, however, hunters returned with word that the Barren Sea's waters were receding. Only Sojen Micah understood what that meant. To everyone else, it was just another mystery of the world upon which their ancestors had settled. When the waters were gone, the Zhanshi would have easier access to Rephidim. In the meantime, the strangers said the Col'kasid should focus on growth while always keeping their eyes open.

Rather than across the Barren Sea, however, news of a new tribe came from the northwest. New Emile, a place that sounded devoid of religion, with a unique set of societal norms and mores. Gideon could see himself living there, or at least embracing some aspects of their culture. He still believed in the Great Return, but what was wrong with also believing that all of God's creatures were equal? Under Micah the Second's leadership—and with no rebuttal by Sojen Micah—the Prelatic Assembly had relegated women to child bearers, subservient to their husbands. Men were considered mature only when they had wed. Schooling was based only on expected positions within the community. And no one outside of the Assembly was permitted to look at Father Elijah's Bible.

Gideon strongly doubted those rules were what the original settlers of Tishbe had in mind when they set out to start a new colony.

Most troubling was the treatment of who they considered "deviants," those who eschewed most, if not all, aspects of the teachings of the Assembly. Gideon had taken part in many trials over the past few years—his first when he was only twelve. People who accused others of heresy or questioned the dictates of the Keeper of the Text were given stern warnings, usually in the form of a lashing. If the heresy did not stop, more drastic measures would be taken, such as that which was given Thomasson when he dared argue with Saadya. Having one's tongue removed had been the pinnacle of punishment. That is until Abel and Asher were caught together.

Until that day, the Assembly had never exiled anyone, and there had always been a chance at redemption. But for this most abominable act, exile was not enough. Both of the boys' families were forced to not only disown their children, but wipe their minds of their memories. Their names were never to be used again. It was the harshest punishment Gideon's father could come up with, apart from death. And Levi promised it would not be the last time it happened. Aberrant behavior must be stopped at the source.

Did New Emile have the same laws? Were their people as afraid of this Liorah, the One Voice, as his people were afraid of Levi?

And why had Sojen Micah never intervened?

A crunch of sandal on rock alerted Gideon to another nearby. It was followed by another crunch and then a third, the pattern of a man with both a limp and a walking stick. Gideon turned to see Micah approach slowly. Why he was coming to see him and not any of the other four prelates, he did not know.

"Sojen," Gideon said with a slight nod. The sound of the waterfall would mute whatever conversation they would have. That was good.

"I heard your arguments in there," Micah said as he stopped next to Gideon and looked out toward the north. "I don't know where James will cast his stone, but I am in agreement with you."

"Thank you, Sojen." Gideon wanted to ask a multitude of questions—like why the founder of the Col'kasid never argued with the Assembly—but it was not his place.

"I would love to go with you, you know, to New Emile."

Gideon regarded Micah. There was no way he would make the trip, even if the Assembly eventually allowed it. "I don't know if we'll get the chance. Father seems very set in his ways."

"Your father is only one man, and one man should never be the only voice. That is why we have an Assembly."

"But he usually gets his way."

"Through weakness of the others only." Micah put his hand on Gideon's back. "If more of you would stand up to him, you might get different results."

"Is that what happened with his father? Micah the Second?"

Micah did not answer that question. Instead, he kept his eyes on the distance. "You're related, you know."

"Related? Yes, he was my grandfather."

"No, boy. Related to Liorah. Miriam was my cousin. No doubt the New Emilian line of succession stays in the family, which would mean this Liorah is her grandchild, or, like you are to me, her great grandchild."

"That's a rather thin relation."

"Blood is blood. Most of the people here could probably trace their lineage back to New Emile. We all have a shared history at Manoach."

Gideon followed Micah's gaze toward the north, toward the forbidden dunes. Whatever had happened there—and it was not one of the stories told around the fires at night—had been painful to Micah. Gideon saw a glint of sadness in his eyes.

"Do you trust these visitors?" Gideon asked after a while. "I mean, Kaius and the others?"

"Have they given you a reason not to trust them?"

"Not to me, but my father seems to think differently. He called them more liberal and worried that their presence might infect the thoughts of others."

Micah chucked softly. "Your father is a fool. Don't tell him I said that, though. He has never been one for change."

"No, he hasn't. But I'm just like him, aren't I? Nothing more than a future Keeper of the Text who follows the laws set before me?"

Micah finally tore his eyes away from the dunes and turned his body toward Gideon. "What did you feel when you heard the visitors brought Abel with them?"

Gideon swallowed. He wasn't sure how to answer that question, at least in front of this man, their most respected elder. Did Sojen Micah feel the same as the Assembly? If not, he'd never argued with them about it. "The apostate should never have returned."

"You don't believe that at all. And he has a name, despite what the trials said."

Gideon lowered his head. "I...I talked to him earlier today," he whispered, hoping the noise from the waterfall would drown out his confession to Micah. "Down below."

It did not. "I know," Micah said. "And how do you feel about it?"

Gideon's shoulders slumped. "I'm...angry. Abel and Asher only wanted to be together. So what if that meant they could never father children and advance the Col'kasid? They would have gone off together and harmed no one had the Assembly voted differently."

"But you never cast your stone. It was three to one for exile, you know."

"I was forbidden. Father said I was too close to both of them for me to make a rational decision."

"What would your stone have said?"

Gideon thought about it for a moment. As a rule, the stone cast—not an actual stone, but a figurative one—could say anything. It did not have to be a simple yes or no, but could come with a completely different outcome altogether. "I would have cast my stone toward getting rid of the laws that forbid love."

Micah nodded. "Then you are nothing like your father. Take that attitude with you to New Emile. It may do you—and us—some good."

Gideon shook his head. "I don't think my father will allow that."

THE FOLLOWING morning, Kaius and his companions were invited back to the Assembly. This time, however, they were not allowed to sit at the table. They were to stand between Saadya and some other sack of muscles with an equally hideous facial scar. All five of the prelates surrounded the fire, sitting on the floor. They had reached a decision to either send someone from the Col'kasid back to New Emile or to just let them be on their way with a message that said "Thanks, but no thanks."

Kaius didn't care either way. The Col'kasid had been kind enough offering to let them stay for two nights in a dwelling with real grass-filled mattresses, and there was certainly no shortage of food. But the attitudes were something else entirely. They were...barbaric, for lack of a better term. He was ready to go, one way or another, grabbing Luca and Abel on the way. The lack of any task during the day had grated on his nerves. He was the type of person who had to be moving always, doing something.

When Raphael and Paul had offered to check on Luca and Abel yesterday, two Col'kasid hunters had followed them. They immediately shifted to pretending they were simply taking a walk and purposefully did not look for the exile and their companion. Upon return to Rephidim, no less than four people questioned where they went and what they discovered. That was only the beginning of their mysterious stay.

Women, all teens, brought the food and drink. They were thin with baggy clothes. Given their age and the fact that the New Emilians had only been with other men for a full cycle of the Short Moon, Eli had attempted to talk to one of them. She hurried away, and Kaius had to wonder if the fear in her face was less about a stranger wanting to get to know her better and more about what others might think.

The food was good—meat that was said to be from Tishbe bison, fruit from orchards growing down the mountain, and baca root—but the drink seemed to make them all sleepy. Even the water which was left for them smelled a little off, like it had been filtered through dirt and mold. In New Emile, there was a standing rule to boil all water, mostly to kill off any bacteria but also to improve the taste. The Col'kasid didn't appear to care.

During their stay, the only men who talked to them came with questions—about their weapons, what training they received, how their women were treated, and what they thought of the teachings of Father Elijah. No one seemed pleased that aside from Kaius, no New Emilian had heard of Father Elijah nor believed in anything called the Great Return. Yet they didn't offer to explain it any further.

For two days, it had felt as if they had been tested and probed, and now on the heels of this momentous meeting between two tribes of people who had previously known nothing about each other, Kaius felt slightly irritated.

Elder Levi stood, his white robe seeming to glow in the

fires of the Assembly. He approached Kaius, clasped his hands together in front of him, and cocked his head.

"We have decided," Levi said. "It is the custom of the Col'kasid to seek guidance from Father Elijah's God and to cast stones in the direction we feel we are being compelled. We have spent the night and a good part of this morning walking with God and have decided that we wish you well on your journey, but we will send no one with you. We ask that you respect the Col'kasid's desire to be left alone as we prepare for the Great Return, and that you send no more people in our direction."

Kaius shifted, uncomfortable in the presence of Levi and also itching to get his stuff and leave. He glanced at the other four prelates and noted that two of them were visibly upset at the decision. "We understand," he said finally.

"You do not." Levi took a step forward. "Regardless of the fact that we may indeed be relations, our paths have diverged at Manoach. Where one seeks to bring glory to God, the other seeks to destroy all that Father Elijah built. There is no common ground between our two tribes, and our differences will not aid in the fight against the Zhanshi should they come. We fear that you may be tempted by their claims of technological advancement and join with them. We also fear that your customs and disregard for the teachings found in Father Elijah's Bible are inconsistent with our future."

"Like I said, we understand."

"You do not. We respect your desire for trade, but the Water of Life will be an unwelcome salve for wounds we can heal through the bounties of our Lord here. While it may be easier to heal our wounded, it is through our suffering that we get closer to God. We have survived for fifty-five years under the leadership of the Keeper of Text because that leader knows the answers are not found in the ways of men but in what has already been provided."

Kaius was about to say "We understand" again since it was obvious this man wasn't getting it, but he opted to remain quiet and hope they would be released soon so they could get on the road back to New Emile. They had plenty of daylight left. If only they were given quvianaq to make the trip that much faster.

Levi stepped back and tilted his head again in the other direction. "Do you understand?"

Finally. "Yes."

"Leave the apostate at the gate."

Kaius blinked. "No. We will not do that. Abel is a New Emilian now, and we will not abandon our brothers or sisters."

Kaius noticed Raphael's feet shift to a fighting stance and his hand move closer to the knife strapped around his waist. He must have sensed something in the room.

"The apostate is not yours to save," Levi said, his voice filled with derision. "He willingly returned to Rephidim to face his true punishment. It was God who guided his decisions and showed the Assembly that our punishments were not complete. You will leave the apostate at the gate and be on your way."

"No."

Saadya stepped forward with his well-muscled companion. There was going to be a fight if something wasn't done soon.

"Father." Gideon stood quickly. "Abel has been given his punishment by decree. To add more punishment would be to go against what God has decreed through the casting of your stones."

"You are to sit, Gideon." Levi snarled. There was no love lost between these two.

"I will not." Gideon walked around his father and stood next to Kaius. "I stand with the future, as God has impelled me to cast my stone. Abel is not to be harmed any more than he already has. We stripped him of family, name, and tribe. We will not strip him of life as well. That is not for us to decide."

Now Paul and Eli had their hands on their knives, and Saadya's grip on his lance tightened.

"You will not disobey me, son," Levi said through gritted teeth. "Return to the fire."

"I will go with them to New Emile as an ambassador of good will."

Kaius glanced at the boy. He was no older than sixteen, but taking him along would not be any different from taking Abel. Perhaps this one could shoot a bow.

Levi was having none of it. "Sit, Gideon. When these men have left, we will cast our stones toward *your* fate."

"You will cast no more stones. I will not sit by while the Col'kasid suffers at the hands of future trials that will test us while we have an opportunity to bolster our defenses and our medical knowledge through the trade of information and goods. You swayed the decision of the Assembly and broke the rule of law."

Levi's voice rose. "I did no such thing. All elders cast their stone as God impelled them, according to the rule of law."

"Only after making it known how your stone would be cast and influencing their decisions." Gideon looked around at all those gathered. "I call for a quorum."

Whatever that was, Kaius could not help but notice a redness rise in Levi's face. No one in the Chambers at New Emile would dare speak to Liorah in such a way, but there seemed to be a precedent here. It was almost as if the

Col'kasid had put a check in place to limit the absolute power of the leader, something that Kaius had to admit was a good idea.

"You need a second for a quorum," Levi said. "And I should remind you that it must be done before the casting of the first stone. No man present will second your motion, even if I were to allow it."

Sojen Micah stepped from the shadows. "I second the call." He limped forward, supported by his ornately carved walking stick. "No decision like this should ever rest in the hands of a select group of people, regardless of what you think." He approached Levi and stopped in front of him. "Grandson, you try my patience."

"We all cast our stones after an appropriate debate," Levi argued. "There was never a call for a quorum during any of that. If there had been, I would be more than happy to oblige. But as it stands, no call prior to casting our stones means no right to a quorum after."

"That's a coward's rule, and you know it."

"It's a rule you put into place years ago." Levi raised his hand as if he planned on poking his grandfather in the chest, but quickly lowered it. He took a deep breath instead. "If a quorum is to be called, it must be done before we cast stones. Otherwise, it would be pointless to debate anything in this Assembly. We might as well give the vote to the community and let decisions be made by those who have no direct knowledge."

"You can give them knowledge."

"With all the respect I owe you, Sojen, it is not your decision any longer."

At that, Micah's left eye quivered. It was a rebuke of the man who had apparently led the Col'kasid to safety coupled with a rebuke by his own blood.

What was wrong with these people?

"Father," Gideon said. "What is the harm in my presence? If I am to be Keeper of the Text, should I not expand my understanding of the world more so than I have stuck here on the side of a mountain? I can bring word of our ways and what we have to trade for the knowledge that New Emile possesses. To stay here is to go against the future of the Col'kasid and spit in the face of the Great Return."

Levi tore his eyes away from Micah and looked at his son. There was no relaxing of facial muscles, no sign that Levi's stance had wavered at all. There was only a visible rage rising in the man's eyes. His hands opened and closed; all the tension of the room was now focused on this one moment.

"If you leave," he said after taking a deep breath, "you are no son of mine."

"Then I have nothing to lose."

PART II: THE LIBRARY

Cycle 13, Day 12, Year 96

Where is the Life we have lost in living?
Where is the wisdom we have lost in knowledge?
Where is the knowledge we have lost in information?

—T.S. Eliot, "The Rock" 1934

CHAPTER THIRTEEN

THE FIRST EXPLOSION KNOCKED CHEN ON HIS REAR, ELICITING a stream of expletives from the leader. The second went off prematurely and burned the arms of an armorer, rendering him too injured to do anything after. In this case the fuse was determined to be too short. With the third explosion, Chen hoped to have better luck.

It had taken weeks to decipher what was in the *Anarchist Cookbook* and even longer for his chemists to find and secure the material needed to make just a handful of bombs. The books found in the ruins of the Circle of Light ship had helped, but it was Mathias the First's insistence on retaining and passing on information about anything from Earth that was the real savior. If these bombs worked, the Zhanshi would have a weapon like no other, something never seen by anyone still living in Xin Shijie de Yaolan.

"Ready for three!" Lucien called out.

Chen joined Lucien behind a barricade in the hills far from the population. "How long is the fuse?" he asked.

"We set it to a minute, but the last one burned faster than expected. We cannot seem to get it right."

As soon as Tye lit the fuse, it rapidly burned toward the explosive charge.

"Run Tye!" Lucien called out. "Keep your head down!"

Before Tye could reach the barricade, the ground shook and a fireball larger than either of the previous two bombs bloomed in reds and yellows and oranges. It flared outward in a deadly arc at a sickeningly fast pace. Tye threw himself on the ground as a wave of fire rolled over him.

In seconds, the fireball was gone, replaced by a smoldering crater about ten feet wide. Rocks and other debris rained down from above. Tye remained on the ground, his arms over his head. A piece of his shirt had caught fire and Lucien rushed to throw dirt on it.

Chen rose from behind the barricade and looked out at the crater. They had placed the carcass of a pua'a ono next to the bomb to judge the impact. There was no sign of the floppy-eared animal, and only blackened dirt remained.

Success.

Tye let out a whoop of exhilaration as Lucien helped him to his feet. "That was great!"

Chen nodded, but did not respond. It was great—or at least it worked as expected—but the timing of the fuse was going to be a problem if they couldn't get it right.

"We have another ready, Zhuren." Lucien smiled and put his hands on his hips. "We might try the secondary fuse."

"No." Chen walked toward the crater, his eyes darting back and forth. There was so much destruction, and it would be the perfect defensive measure...if only they could figure out the right trigger. And if they could figure that out, they might be able to make it into an offensive weapon.

Lucien and Tye followed their leader, and all three of them approached the blast site.

"What are you thinking, Zhuren?" Tye asked as he brushed dirt off his clothes.

Chen still did not respond. His mind formulated what he would have said to Mathias the First or to his grandfather,

Mathias the Third. Would they have approved? Could the Zhanshi use these weapons for vengeance and fulfill the dreams of their ancestors or were they better suited to be defensive weapons should the outsiders—the *gulao*—arrive unannounced?

Yes, it was possible to be on the offense, provided his scouts could find out where the survivors from Manoach had gone. There had been no signs past the wide canyon far to the west of the temple at the edge of the rainforest. If they had crossed, their trail was gone. But Chen had a feeling there might be other refugees who had fled before his grandfather arrived. And as long as there was still one descendant left of those who unfairly punished Mathias the First, the Zhanshi would not rest.

The ground suddenly caved in under Tye's feet. He yelped as he slipped into an ever-widening hole, his arms and hands clawing at the surrounding dirt, making things worse. Lucien reached down to pull the man up, but his weight was too great.

"Need help, Zhuren!" Lucien called back as he pulled with all his might. "I think there are caves under our feet."

Chen watched, unmoving. "Let him go," Chen said after a moment.

The order must have confused Lucien. He glanced back at his leader, and in that instant, Tye's hands slipped, and he fell into the hole completely. Lucien dropped to his knees and looked over the edge.

"It is not deep," he called down. "You can climb out."

"I need a rope or something."

"Leave him," Chen said. "It is good for a man to have time to think."

Lucien backed up and stood. He would obey. He had not been a problem.

As Tye continued to call out from the hole, Chen and Lucien walked closer to the center of the crater. The ground was soft, black, and still smoking. Again, there was no sign of the pua'a ono. It had vaporized.

"Set up the fourth bomb," Chen said. "Put it on the hill over there and let's see what happens when we shoot it with our bows. Perhaps we can get lucky with a disconnected fuse."

"A lit bolt?"

Chen nodded.

Within an hour, Lucien had anchored another bomb on the side of a hill above the previous blast site. Tye had crawled out of the hole by creating a small mound of fallen dirt, fashioning some steps and using roots. Chen felt a sense of satisfaction knowing that one of his lieutenants had used his mental capabilities to resolve the issue. Men should always learn new things. Tye may not have been happy about it, but it was not Chen's place to ensure his people were happy.

With the men once more at a safe distance, Lucien handed Chen a tipped bolt. The design had been around since the days of Mathias the First, and it worked wonders. Once lit, the tip would remain that way until it impacted something else and spread out. People who had been targets would quickly be engulfed in flames, screaming as their life burned away. There hadn't been a reason to shoot people of late, though. Most of the Zhanshi followed the rules, and those who tried to alter the system without the Zhuren's permission faced exile or a quicker death by the blade.

Chen took aim with his crossbow and steadied himself. He had always been an excellent shot, ever since he was old enough to draw the string back himself. As soon as Lucien lit the tip of the bolt, Chen pulled the trigger.

With incredible speed, the bolt flew in a curved arc and hit its mark. All three men tensed up, readying for the blast, but when nothing happened, Chen's hopes faded. Flames should have ignited it upon impact, just like a fuse.

This bothered Chen to no end. He stood with the crossbow down at his side, watching the hill for anything, something to tell him the weapon was ready.

"What happened?" Tye fidgeted, appearing eager to rush toward the hill. "Did you miss?"

Chen slowly turned toward Tye.

"N-no, Zhuren," Tye stuttered. "You would never miss."

"Perhaps you should see where my bolt landed," Chen said slowly. "Go. Retrieve it and tell me if I have missed my mark."

Tye nodded quickly and ran toward the hill. Chen watched the man scamper up the side over a few larger rocks, slipping twice and then recovering. He had been loyal and ready to please, always doing his best to improve both his physical and mental state. He could be brash, but he would grow.

As Tye approached, a sudden explosion sent shockwaves through the air. The resulting fireball illuminated the hill, and Tye disappeared in a bright flash of light. The blast obliterated a significant portion of the hill, scattering debris and rubble in all directions. The ground shook and rumbled violently, causing Chen and Lucien to dive for cover behind the barricade.

The air was thick with dust and debris. Chen coughed and covered his mouth with his sleeve as he peered through the haze. It was difficult to see anything clearly, but he made out the silhouette of Lucien huddled next to him. Chunks of rock and what looked like charred flesh littered the surrounding ground. The acrid smell of smoke filled their nostrils and made it difficult to breathe. After a few moments, the haze slowly dissipated, revealing a scene of utter destruction. The ground where Tye had been standing was now a massive crater, much larger than the one left by the previous bomb. The force of the explosion had been so intense that the ground had been completely torn apart, leaving only charred and blackened soil in its wake. Nearby trees had been reduced to smoldering stumps, their leaves and branches scattered about.

The hillside was almost unrecognizable, as if a giant fist had punched a gaping hole in it. Where there had once been lush grass, there was now nothing but smoldering, ash-covered dirt. The grasses that the blast had not annihilated were still burning, and the flames licked hungrily at the remaining bits of vegetation. The crackling of the flames mixed with the sound of the still-settling debris. Chen stood in stunned silence, taking in the full extent of the devastation.

"This will work," he said at last.

Lucien coughed in the thick air. "Tye is gone."

Chen slowly nodded. "I will burn joss paper and incense for him tonight. His sacrifice will be remembered."

CHEN STOOD solemnly before the altar of past Zhuren, his hands clasped together in silent prayer. The scent of incense wafted through the room as the flickering flames of candles danced in the darkness. Before him, a small pile of joss paper was arranged neatly on a tray, ready to be burned in honor of Tye. He hated to lose any member of the Zhanshi, let alone a young man who had been eager to please.

Taking a deep breath and closing his eyes, Chen called to mind memories of Tye. After a moment, he reached for the joss paper and lit it with a match. It crackled and burst into flames, sending up a plume of smoke that filled the air.

"Rest in peace, my brother," Chen whispered, his voice

soft. "May this offering bring you comfort and guide you on your journey to the afterlife."

These were words Chen had said many times for many people. Death was a part of life for the Zhanshi and something you accepted as the yin to the yang. Just last week, he had stood in the same spot honoring a child of eight who had wandered into the den of a huan in the woods to the south of the village.

As the joss paper burned down to ashes, Chen bowed his head in a show of respect. The ritual had been performed, and Tye's spirit could now receive the offering and find solace in the afterlife.

The night air was still as he emerged from his home. The village was abuzz with life. Children played on the dirt paths in front of their parents while many others ate their daily meal. The noise was comforting to Chen, reminding him of the prosperity that they could all have. Electric lights powered by the meager bit of hydroelectric power generated by the rivers to the north illuminated the faces of the Zhanshi, his people. He was proud of them all—proud of the way they came together to work out problems, proud of the way they carried on the legacies of their ancestors through education, proud of how motivated they were to make a better life for their neighbors. Most of all, he was proud of the sacrifices they made to ensure no invaders would take away what they had.

He knew they were out there. It was just a matter of time.

"Your meal is ready, Zhuren." Chen turned to see an aide, a boy of twelve with his head shaved.

"Thank you, Tian. But I am not hungry. Tonight I will fast for our fallen."

Tian nodded once, then turned. Before he could scamper off, Chen called him back. "Spread the word that I would like a meeting with the men tonight."

IT TOOK no longer than a few minutes for all Chen's lieutenants to arrive, save one—Tye. They all had a distinct physical appearance—shaved heads and stout builds and scars obtained through years of pain and sacrifice for the glory of Xin Shijie de Yaolan.

The first to arrive was Lucien, easily recognizable by his down-turned lips, which always suggested he was unhappy about something. Martin was next, also sporting a recently shaved head and a sturdy build like the others. Lin Xi was not far behind, joining the group with his signature green eyes and muscular physique. Finally, the oldest member of Chen's circle of trust, Luke, arrived. Unlike the others, Luke had been granted permission to grow his hair once again. The white hair on his head was a mark of respect among the Zhanshi, indicating his many years of service and experience. It was a symbol of honor that commanded respect from others.

That the man was still alive was a miracle. He was eighty, the only person left who remembered Chen's grandfather and was present when the gulao were eradicated from the temple in the rain forest. It was becoming more apparent that he had little time left, yet it was that age that Chen respected the most.

Chen ushered them all inside. The men bowed their head toward the Zhuren shrine before taking a seat at a table set up nearby. The incense still lingered in the air and the lights from the candles flickered under the dull glow of the overhead electric lamp. Spread out over the table was a map of the valley in which Yaolan sat. Each building within the village was meticulously drawn and every tree and bush within the boundary was labeled. A topographic representation of the surrounding hills showed locations of all nearby caves, where deposits of the lanluzite used for the batteries had been found. Red marks or small boxes indicated dangerous areas where huan dens had been uncovered, while black marks showed deaths, each one a tiny shrine to the life that had been extinguished there. The most recent black mark was where Tye had fallen.

"We are victorious," Chen said after his circle of lieutenants had settled. "Today we mark a new beginning in protecting Yaolan."

Luke shook his head while the others remained mute, their eyes anywhere but on Chen.

"You disagree?" Chen asked.

Luke sighed. Tye had been like a grandson to him, and no doubt the man's death was a great weight to bear. "I still do not see what the need is," Luke said after a moment. "We lost a good man today, and for what? The last outsider to visit the village was the gulao, Aaron, and while his betrayal led to the deaths of many of our people, he was but small — a huan in a pit of dragons."

"Your words are true." Chen interlaced his fingers. "But we have all seen the signs in the sky and felt the change in the wind. There were survivors from Manoach, that temple of the followers of the Circle of Light. And from that great tragedy, we learned that they had crossed the canyon and made a new home. If they look to their own past and apply pressure on our community, it is not unreasonable to assume they would greedily take from us what they have not earned."

"We do not know they made a new home," said Luke. "We only assume. There have been no signs during any of our expeditions to the west or north. Even when Lucien took his men around the canyon two years past, no signs were found."

"Even without signs, they are out there. I feel it. It is not beyond reason that our next expeditionary group will find a clue to their whereabouts."

Chen did not find Luke's argumentative nature to be bothersome. In fact, he found it to be refreshing in a way. Most of the Zhanshi, excluding his lieutenants, kept their opinions to themselves, and while this helped to maintain order, sometimes the expression of alternative viewpoints was welcome. This was why Chen had advisors.

Luke looked at the map spread out before them. He pointed to a narrow gap between two sharp rises. "There is but one way into the valley of Xin Shijie de Yaolan. That way is protected already, although our guards waste away with nothing to do. Do you really believe these explosives—these bombs—will be needed?"

"If not for defense, then perhaps for offense, should the need arise."

"They are like angry dragons, dangerous, and we do not truly understand how to contain them. And if we were to use them for offense, how would you transport them? They are unstable, and as you have seen from the loss of Tye, they have minds of their own."

"You were not there," Chen said. "Inanimate weapons have no minds. They only do as men willing to wield them instruct. And we can work on the design. I will not waste the sacrifice of Tye and abandon development."

Throughout the debate, none of the other lieutenants had offered any input. They listened intently to the conversation between Chen and Luke, but no one spoke up to provide a different perspective or idea. This was highly unusual given that Chen had chosen the lieutenants for their strategic thinking and ability to contribute to the growth of the Zhanshi.

Luke dominated the conversation, and while his passion for abandoning the development of the weapons may have been sound—even if based on emotion—it would be beneficial to have another voice in the room. Chen looked at each of them. Perhaps the lack of input resulted from the recent death of their comrade. That was acceptable. It was not acceptable if their quietness was because of a lack of assurance in their own thoughts.

"Lucien," Chen said. "You have said nothing. Do you agree with your comrade that we should abandon the development of this gift we have been given?"

"You are baiting him with your opinion," Luke said quickly. "A curse can be a gift in disguise."

Chen did not respond to that. "Lucien? Martin? Lin Xi? Your thoughts."

Lucien was the only one who looked up from the map. "I do not believe Tye's death should be in vain," he said, his words measured. "Nor do I believe any threat out there would dare return from across the canyon to attack us. But if one were to come here, to approach the gates to the valley, we can maintain peace through a show of force. The protection of the Zhanshi should be our only priority. One cannot fight aggression—should it ever come to Yaolan—with pointy sticks and slung rocks. I am with you, Zhuren."

Luke raised an eyebrow at Lucien's response, clearly not expecting such a reply. Chen nodded in agreement with Lucien's assessment, but as he was about to respond, a loud rumble echoed through the valley, shaking the ground beneath them. The room filled with smoke and debris, and for a moment, no one spoke.

When the dust settled, Chen looked around the room at his lieutenants. The shock had left them speechless. The door burst open, and Tian rushed in, his eyes wide with fear.

"Zhuren!" Tian was breathless. "The hills are falling!"

Luke shouted, "And that, my dear leader, is why we should *not* tamper with things we do not understand."

CHAPTER FOURTEEN

THE ENCROACHING EVENING PAINTED THE SKY IN HUES OF fiery crimson as the sun receded, its soft glow cast upon a motley group of Marokai huddled around the warmth of a modest fire. At the head stood Elena, while Diego knelt beside a rough sketch etched into the dirt representing New Emile.

Slightly detached from the immediate glow of the fire, Angela, Jeremiah, and Cain engaged in hushed conversation. Angela and Jeremiah were both twenty, Cain, the most senior of them all at nearly fifty, had a face scarred by the events of his exile and the realities of living in the Hollows. He represented those who had been accused by the Elite of some crime—from simple robbery to, as in Cain's case, stealing haelen for his ailing wife. As with all those exiled for "treasonous acts," Cain's forehead was marked with a brand that looked as painful as it probably was—a triangle burned into the flesh over the line that marked the Marokai.

The rest of the council, half a dozen other dissenters of varying ages, alternated their attention between Elena, Diego, and the crude map strewn across the ground.

"We've trampled this ground a hundred times over," Elena said. She was annoyed. "A direct charge on the city gates is a fool's errand. The sentinels would cut us down before we'd cover half the distance to the Chambers."

Murmurs of agreement rippled through the gathered council.

"What about what we found in the quarry?" Diego suggested. "The crack. It's not much, but it's something."

"And where does this mysterious crack lead, Diego?" Angela's voice sounded tired.

Diego shrugged. "I don't know yet, Angela, but I'm intent on finding out. There are ways into the city from the north. We know where they lead, and perhaps this will be just a good."

"Your watcher will notice. You might as well turn yourself in to the sentinels and be thrown in the hold for all the good it will do us."

"It's a better idea than any of you have had. We need a plan that ensures we take control of the haelen and make it accessible to everyone, not just the privileged Elite."

There was a moment of silence as Diego turned from Angela. As his sister, Elena knew he was angered easily and just as easily gave up when pressures became too much. They were twins who shared so many traits, but had vastly distinct personalities.

"What about the Marokai who are allowed into the city?" Cain broke the silence. "The ones who barter for goods during the day or have labors within the walls?"

Elena shook her head. "At nightfall, they are required to leave. New Emile is not our home...yet. There have been many who've tried to stay the night, and each time some sentinel is there to throw them out." She pointed to her forehead where the mark was permanently etched into her skin. "We're not exactly able to blend in well."

Elena considered their ultimate goal—the overthrow of the dictatorial rule. Not that she hadn't thought about it since she was first marked. "Liorah is the problem," she said at last.

"Not so much the Elite. We need to get close to her."

"That's obvious," Jeremiah said, "but it's how we do that."

Elena thought about Bradley, her watcher during her labor in the quarry. If he could be manipulated, what about the others? "We need to consider the possibility of insider help."

Jeylin, a woman just slightly younger than Cain with a matching mark, raised a hairless eyebrow. "Are you suggesting we put our own into the witch's nest?"

Diego rubbed his chin, a small frown forming on his face. "No, she's suggesting we use someone who's already in the nest." His eyes flicked toward Elena.

"Luca? Your brother?"

"Yes, Luca," Elena confirmed, meeting each pair of eyes that looked her way. "He's away on Discovery now, but he'll be back soon. He has access, and he has the trust of the sentinels and the Elite. If anyone sympathetic to our plight can get close to Liorah, it's him."

"But can we trust him?" Jeylin asked. "He's been with them for too long. He's one of them, now."

Elena raised her voice. "Luca is our brother, our blood. He may not be marked or sleep in the Hollows, but he's no different from anyone here."

Arguments erupted around the fire, but Elena held back, listening as the council debated, knowing they were far from making any decision about how to get at Liorah. For now, this was a brainstorming session.

"There is another angle we could consider." Ruth stood at the edge of the council meeting, her newborn child Lika wrapped in a tattered blanket as she nursed the girl. All eyes turned to her and a hushed curiosity overtook the meeting. The woman rarely spoke.

"Liorah has always had her entourage of handmaidens," Ruth said haltingly. "All Marokai. They stay with her all day and night. As you know, I used to be one of them, and I can tell you all the ins and outs of Liorah's bed chamber and her routines."

"No offense, Ruth," Cain said, "but you were exiled like myself. You're marked and not even allowed near the gate."

"Not me." Ruth looked heartbroken at the comment and no doubt at the memories her exile brought up. "Others. Find the handmaiden who is most vulnerable, the child who lives with Liorah and would take our side. They are young, helpless, pliable."

"And how do we do that?" Angela questioned, crossing her arms over her chest. "You once told me that handmaidens were not allowed contact with anyone outside of the Chambers. If one of them went missing, even for a day, the sentinels would be on high alert. They would question everything when she returned."

"I'm not saying it will be easy," Ruth said as she adjusted Lika in her arms. "They bring handmaidens in at an early age, and none of them really know what it's like beyond the Chambers. I sure as hell didn't until I came here. But if you want to get close to Liorah—if you want to end this tyrannical rule—you'll need to start from within."

The silence following her proposition spoke volumes. Elena looked around the council at each of those present. Were they actually considering it?

IN THE heart of the Hollows, where a mosaic of makeshift dwellings sprawled across the edge of the moor, Elena approached Ruth and her child Lika. Their home was nothing more than a patchwork of scavenged materials, just like hers nearby.

Ruth sat on a tattered rug, mending a piece of clothing, while Lika cooed quietly on a blanket next to her. As Elena stepped in, she eyed the child. "She's growing so fast," she said with a warm smile. "What is she now? Six cycles?"

"As of today," Ruth said, "Six more than she would have had without your help." She set her work aside and made room for Elena to sit. The question, when it came, was not unexpected.

"Elena, where did you get the haelen?" Ruth asked.

Elena didn't answer. Some secrets were dangerous to share, even with those you trusted. "Sorry, but I can't tell you that. I wouldn't want to put you or Lika into a situation."

She settled herself beside Ruth and watched the growing child before them. Elena's brows furrowed in thought, her lips pursing slightly. "What was it like, Ruth?" she asked.

"What was what like? Childbirth?" Ruth winked. "You've heard the screams. I'm pretty sure you can guess."

"No, sorry. I mean in the Chambers, serving Liorah. How was it?"

Ruth's smile dropped, and she looked down. "It was...it was an honor, first," she said after a moment. "You're given a labor like everyone else, and most think it'll be in the quarry or out in the farms. To serve directly under the One Voice felt...exciting. In the beginning, anyway." She looked up. "But then you realize that the honor is a heavy shackle, more of a punishment than anything else."

Elena nodded, encouraging Ruth to continue. "Liorah...she's never content," Ruth continued, her voice dropping to a whisper. "She's always in need of something, always wanting, always demanding. It could be the middle of the night and she'd have us prepare a feast fit for the sentinels. Or she could wake up with a desire to have a dress made before sunrise. The worst... Well, the worst was cleaning up the mess she made with Roland, her Kept."

Ruth's hands tightened around the piece of cloth she had been mending. "The handmaidens...we were constantly on our feet, constantly working. There was no rest, no moment of peace. It was all about Liorah."

"And your banishment?" Elena asked softly, a delicate question she knew, but one that needed to be asked.

Ruth sighed heavily, her gaze moving to the quiet child by her feet. "I crossed her, I suppose. She never gave a reason, just ordered me out." Her voice wavered, as if the memory were fresh. She put her hand to her forehead where the mark of banishment painfully sat. "I don't know why she didn't have me killed. Maybe it's a punishment worse than passing into shadow, to be banished from the city and forced to live in the Hollows."

Ruth was leaving out the real reason for her banishment, and that had been expected.

"Why do you ask?" Ruth's eyes narrowed. "We haven't spoken much since I arrived here."

Elena wasn't sure if she should answer. Instead, she changed the subject.

"Her father?" Elena pointed to Lika. "Is he around?"

Ruth's face darkened. If asking about banishment was taboo, then this was beyond reproach. But Ruth didn't lash out. She simply looked at Lika and breathed deeply for a moment. "He found his own way to Eldorado."

Elena shivered. That phrase—found his own way— could only mean one thing. Whoever Lika's father was, he'd taken his own life. It wasn't uncommon in the face of all they had to endure. You either suffered under the conditions thrust upon you for being unlucky enough to have been picked in the lottery, or you walked out into the Wastelands, never to be heard from again.

Ruth remained silent as her eyes shifted away to a point somewhere in the distance.

ELENA LEFT Ruth's dwelling, her mind full of the shared stories of suffering and unspoken secrets. She walked down the beaten path that wound through the Hollows, past the scattered settlements. Children's laughter echoed in the distance, a reminder of the life she and Diego had growing up with Luca.

The Hollows was a cluster of makeshift homes, cobbled together from scraps and salvaged materials. Fires were lit here and there, and curling smoke rose in thin tendrils against the dim light of two half-moons. Despite the hardships, the Marokai made do. There were small, neat but pathetic-looking rows of vegetables in tiny gardens planted from seeds stolen from the farms. People shared their talents with each other—if you could cook but couldn't mend a tunic, someone else would be there to help. If you could mend but couldn't build a wall, someone else would be there, too. While they didn't trust everyone, they were forced at times to trust one another out of necessity. That's how the council worked, as tenuous as it was.

Elena didn't know what it was like to trust anyone fully.

She passed a group of men, their faces grim under the weight of their struggles, their hands hardened from toil. They were quarry workers, men she knew who worked with her cutting rocks from the ground so that true New Emilians could have sturdy homes. They silently acknowledged her with nods.

Further along, a young woman with a child strapped to her back smiled at Elena, her eyes bright with unshed tears. Elena returned the smile. These were not filth, as Liorah called them. They were people, born into sunshine with the same rights as anyone else. Yet fate had given those who lived within the walls of New Emile permission to look down on them. They were no different in appearance, save the cruel mark across their foreheads. Elena was determined to fight, not only for those around her, but for Diego and for herself.

Liorah's reign had to end.

As she reached the edge of the Hollows, she stopped, her gaze falling on the desolate Wastelands. Lika's father likely passed into shadow somewhere out there. Her thoughts turned to her brother, Luca. Would he ever return from his Discovery mission? It was strange, two missions heading in the same direction back-to-back. A shiver of worry ran through her. Luca was a seasoned member of the sentinels, but the Wastelands were unpredictable and ruthless.

She missed him, missed his friendliness and his steady presence. She couldn't help but wonder what he would think of the rebellion they were planning. Would he understand? Would he join them? Or would he remain loyal to the city, or worse, to Liorah?

She pushed the thoughts away and forced herself to focus on the present. There was a revolt to plan, a city to reclaim, and a people to save. For now, she had to lead the Marokai to reclaim basic human rights.

As she turned to leave the edge of the Hollows, the sound of hurried footsteps drew her attention. Diego ran towards her.

"Elena!" He panted, hands on his knees, as he struggled to catch his breath.

"What are you doing here, Diego? Shouldn't you be resting?"

Diego straightened up, his chest still heaving. "I went to the quarry. The watchman...he was asleep."

Elena frowned, a sudden worry settling in her stomach.

"Diego, that's dangerous, and you know better. If anyone saw you—"

"No one did," he interrupted. "But that's not important. I think...I think I know where the crack leads."

Elena's eyes widened. "Where?"

Diego glanced around, ensuring they were alone, before leaning in closer. His voice dropped to a whisper, barely audible. "The hold...inside New Emile."

Diego's words lingered in the evening air. His revelation resounded with an implication that invigorated Elena. The hold wasn't just another part of the city. Rumors told of its strategic location—a place beneath or at least very close to the Chambers.

"Under the Chambers?" Elena's voice came out softly as she stared at her brother Diego. Her mind raced with all sorts of possibilities. The Chambers, the heart of the city, Liorah's sanctuary. If this were true...

Diego nodded. "That's what the rumors say, right?"

If the hold indeed sat beneath the Chambers, it would provide them with an unparalleled advantage, a chance to infiltrate New Emile without notice. As far as they knew, there were other places to sneak in, but none so close, none so...dangerous. Yet the proximity to the heart of power in New Emile—to the problem—was not to be underestimated. And if they were close to the Chambers, they could get close to the haelen.

Elena felt the pieces of the puzzle fall into place. If they could use this crack, this secret passage to the heart of the city, they could change the course of the Marokai's future. Coupled with Ruth's knowledge of how the Chambers were laid out and Liorah's routine, they were close to action.

But at what cost?

CHAPTER FIFTEEN

They were maybe a week from New Emile, and Abel was tired of walking. Gideon had convinced his father — through Sojen Micah — to let him go as an ambassador of the Col'kasid and take two others with him, two others who were accepting of Abel. They weren't easy to find, and only one of them, Jacob, knew how to use a bow and lance.

The love lost between father and son was unmistakable, but Gideon would not disparage the Keeper of the Text throughout the journey. It was the position he respected, not the man. Jacob, Gideon's right hand, had led the way on the back of his quvianaq with the New Emilian Nico as a guide, while the third member of his entourage, Isaiah, took up the rear on his own mount. Kaius and his men, along with Abel and Luca, had remained walking in the middle.

The path they were on was more apparent than it had been the first time Abel trekked toward New Emile, and every mile or so, they quickly built a tiny mound of rocks — a cairn, according to Raphael — with a stick pointing in both the direction they intended to go and the direction from which they'd come. They were trying to build a road of sorts. Or, at the very least, a string of rock piles that connected tribes. Should trade eventually be established between the two communities, the road would fill in. Abel imagined small settlements being set up as way points between the cities, but this was far too premature. What if Liorah rejected the Col'kasid altogether?

The return trip almost didn't happen. While preparing to leave, one of the New Emilians, Eli, had approached a younger Col'kasid woman and attempted to start a conversation. The woman's father, a hunter, found out and threatened to castrate the man on the spot. Isaiah quickly escorted Eli out of Rephidim and, together with Abel and Luca, rounded up three quvianaq against the wishes of a raging Elder Levi. The animals were not the property of any one man at Rephidim, however, and so there was nothing that could be done about breaking up the herd that lived below the buttes. The animals were fine with it. Abel would have liked to round up more mounts, but three was all they were getting. They would, however—at least according to Kaius—be an outstanding display for Liorah, the One Voice, as a possible item of trade. There were no beasts of burden or animals who would accept a mount at New Emile. Most were small and served only as food or existed as pests. Some had nasty dispositions and would prefer not to be bothered by the encroaching humans. Quvianaq would be a highly valued prize, should Liorah be willing to trade.

That was the real issue. Would Liorah be willing? The Col'kasid had suffered many plagues over the past few years, ones that Abel had witnessed firsthand. Abel and Gideon had explained this to the New Emilians during one of their nightly rests.

"Why couldn't you have used khopa dung?" Kaius had asked.

"Khopa dung is good for wounds," Gideon said. "It's useless against diseases which affect the internal organs of the body."

"What happened with this Red Death?"

Abel looked at Gideon, who nodded his head. As the future Keeper of the Text, Abel still deferred to the man's position within the Col'kasid. He was the leader, and Abel didn't want to overstep his boundaries, even if he was no longer a part of the community.

"I lost both of my grandparents to the Red Death," Abel answered. "A rash develops on a person's body after they're affected. Could be a week, could be a full cycle of the Short Moon after it gets in the body. In just a few days after the rash appears though, the person passes into shadow. I hadn't yet been born into sunshine before the first wave, but my schooling taught me that Rephidim's population was about one sixty-five just before."

"How many after?" asked Kaius.

"One hundred forty-five," Gideon said. "Khopa dung does little, and no matter how many tinctures our people develop and try, nothing seems to work."

"Haelen might have saved them all." Abel looked into the fire. While no longer a part of the Col'kasid, the passing of so many people had still affected him. How could it not? "It can do so again. A few years ago, Rephidim had blossomed to over two hundred people."

"What happened?" Luca asked.

"A new Red Death came," Gideon said. "Following that wave of illness, twenty-six people passed into shadow. The worst was after. Thirty Col'kasid took off toward the south, hoping to build a new home in the forests there. It's believed that the Red Death comes from the soil around Rephidim, so moving south might have kept them out of danger."

"Where are they now?"

Gideon shrugged. "No one knows. Maybe they formed a new tribe, a new settlement. Or maybe they're just bones for the soil."

"If moving away saved them," Kaius asked, "why didn't Levi opt to move the colony?"

"No one knows if it saved them. Besides, Sojen Micah will not leave the side of Patience, and the Col'kasid will not leave the side of Sojen Micah. Rephidim was a promise kept."

Kaius knitted his brow in the fire's light. "Patience passed into shadow years ago, did she not?" He looked thoroughly confused, and Abel understood why. New Emilian customs after a person passed into shadow were different than those of the Col'kasid. No one in New Emile would "stay" with a body.

"Five years ago, yes." Gideon laced his fingers together and bowed his head. "My great grandmother was the first to die of the second wave of the Red Death. It sent Sojen Micah into a deep depression."

A coo from afar alerted the group to a ku'vatar nearby. It sounded like only one, but Abel felt his heart beat faster.

"What is that?" Isaiah asked. He darted his eyes around in the light of the two moons.

"That," Raphael said standing, "is dinner."

JUST A day from New Emile, Jacob fell off his mount and smacked the ground with a crunch. He had signaled no trouble, and no one who had been near him thought anything was wrong. Gideon dismounted his quvianaq and joined Abel by Jacob's side. The man's chest heaved with effort and his face was splotchy in spots.

Red.

"Is that what I think it is?" Abel asked. He knew the symptoms of the Red Death, but so far from Rephidim, it made little sense.

Gideon checked Jacob's heartbeat. "He must have picked it up before we left."

"Wouldn't we have known that?" Kaius asked. He pulled his satchel around and rooted for something inside.

"There is no warning before it strikes. It festers in a body until something triggers its release."

"So we could all have it? Is it contagious?"

"Only if you get infected blood on you."

Kaius pulled out a vial similar to the one that had held the haelen which saved the life of Abel so long ago. "Try this." He handed the vial to Gideon. "It's haelen. Call this a test for establishing trade."

Gideon lifted Jacob's head a little and prompted him to drink. Puffy red eyelids blocked the man's sight.

"Blindness is first," Abel said. "It's usually followed by a loss of hearing and then control of the limbs. If his throat swells up, he won't last long."

"People starve to death?" Luca asked. He'd pulled out a blanket and set it up near Jacob. They would move him once he was able. The quvianaq stood nearby, uttering soft clucks in sympathy.

Jacob swallowed what he could of the haelen. His body relaxed slightly.

Kaius stood and looked around. "We're about a day out," he said. "We should see New Emile over that far rise tomorrow."

"It's still early." Raphael looked anxious. "A few of us can go on ahead."

"No." Kaius pointed to a flat area. "Set up camp with Eli and Paul, and build a fire. Nico, go with Luca and find us some food. We'll wait it out here on the off chance this is contagious."

Raphael nodded, but he didn't look happy about it. Abel really couldn't blame him. He'd been gone from New Emile for nearly half a year, and while relationships were something sentinels could not form, that didn't mean he wouldn't miss the comforts of home. In the strangest way, Abel himself suddenly missed Rephidim.

Jacob leaned over and vomited. Undigested food lay in a pile next to his face, tinged red with blood.

"Don't touch that," Gideon said, pulling Jacob away. "There's blood in it."

Kaius backed away. "You won't get any argument from me."

JACOB'S HEALTH mended with remarkable speed. By morning, the crimson blotches that marred his face had nearly vanished. His vision remained impaired, however, a fact that vexed Gideon. Though the haelen's potency in eradicating the Red Death seemed undeniable, the illness left behind residual symptoms, including a faint quiver in Jacob's limbs. Kaius proposed a brief delay, a few hours to ensure the malady did not reemerge. Following a meager meal of dried ku'vatar, the troupe resumed their journey.

With Nico offering to carry Jacob on the back of a quvianaq, the group continued on their journey, traversing the rugged terrain. Five New Emilians, three Col'kasid, and one exiled member of their party made their way towards the moor, the promise of a partnership spurring them on.

As the evening sun cast long shadows across the landscape, they finally descended the hills and approached the moor. The quvianaq, ever cautious, were reluctant to tread upon the muddy ground, and it took some effort and cajoling to keep them on the rocky path which crossed the muck.

The city of New Emile loomed ahead, with its block buildings and massive walls built around it. Though Abel and Luca had described it to Gideon before, the reality was far more surreal than anything he could have imagined.

Having spent his entire life in humble adobe structures framed by wood on the side of a butte overlooking vast desert-like plains, Gideon was awestruck by the grandeur of this new world. The vistas he had witnessed during his travels across the Wastelands paled compared to the sheer magnitude of what he saw now. It was as if the planet itself had experienced a great tremor, expelling perfectly hewn rocks and structures in an orderly fashion, just right for a burgeoning society.

According to Kaius, that was almost true.

"Do you see that structure over there?" Kaius asked, pointing to what looked like frames of wood with dangling ropes. "That's the entrance to the quarry. Workers carve out the construction material, lift it, and bring it into New Emile."

"Are all the buildings made of stone?"

"Not the newer ones. We were lucky in finding a forest to the north where there was material to use in framing new structures. It takes a bit to get it back here, but worth it. The stone is mostly used now as a foundation, since the moor doesn't have the most stable ground."

"How do you get the rock out?" Gideon asked, his curiosity piqued.

Abel smiled knowingly. "Sound," he replied.

Gideon felt confused. "What do you mean? How does that work?"

But Abel only offered a cryptic wink in response. Suddenly, a deep, resonating hum filled the air, and an inexplicable feeling of dread sent chills down Gideon's spine.

"What—?"

The quvianaq beneath him trembled, the enormous creature's muscles locking as the hum grew louder, its resonance reaching an unnerving crescendo. The hum seemed to vibrate at a frequency that targeted the creatures specifically, as if the machine had been designed to disorient or paralyze them.

Gideon struggled to stay astride the animal, feeling his mount's muscles tense with fright. He glanced to his side, seeing Isaiah and Nico with Jacob on their own quvianaq experience the same paralyzing effect. They were just as terrified.

Without warning, the quvianaq dropped to its knees, its body trembling uncontrollably. Gideon was thrown forward but hung onto the reins, narrowly avoiding a tumble onto the rocky terrain. Jacob and Isaiah weren't as fortunate; they were thrown from their mounts, landing roughly in the mud beside the path.

The strange, paralyzing hum slowly receded, replaced with the panicked breaths of their group and the terrified whines of the quvianaq. As the sound faded, so did the paralysis gripping the beasts, though they remained on the ground, visibly shaken and reluctant to rise.

"Huh," Kaius said. "Who knew?"

"Is this going to be a problem?" Gideon asked.

"The sound is directional and never points toward the city. As long as we're inside the wall, I wouldn't worry about it."

AS THE contingent of nine, accompanied by their three strange and exotic animals who were still rattled by the attack on their senses, approached the city gate, a group of children ran at them from some dilapidated buildings built outside the city walls. It was clear that the sight of these creatures was something the people of New Emile had not encountered before. Giggling and pointing, the children, with their dirty faces, shaved heads, and ragged clothes, stared with awe at the quvianaq. Their young minds buzzed with a multitude of questions that no one from Rephidim could answer. Gideon listened as Abel tried his best to explain, but there were too many queries that went in too many directions.

Isaiah couldn't help but smile as he surveyed the scene. "Quite the welcoming committee," he remarked, glancing down at a child of only four or five years old who peered up at him with wide-eyed fascination. "They haven't seen animals like this before?"

Luca shook his head in response. "Not like this. The biggest creatures we have around here are ku'vatar, and they're only ever seen dead. To encounter a live one out on the moor would be a miracle. It would also scare just about anyone."

At the gate, they were all surrounded by what looked like guards, each with a crossbow drawn and a lance in a sheath attached to their backs. They didn't appear happy, but at the sight of Kaius, they all lowered their weapons and moved back. Two men pulling on a lever opened the gate, and the Col'kasid entered.

Gideon's eyes widened as he took in the breathtaking sight before him. New Emile stretched out in front, a marvel unlike anything he had ever encountered. Buildings, fashioned from stone and wood, were grouped together with little space between. It was a world beyond his wildest dreams, a place where the impossible seemed possible.

The ground beneath their feet was littered with gravel and rock, lending the city a rugged feel. Gideon felt a shiver of excitement run through him as the quvianaq sauntered forward, taking tentative steps on the unfamiliar terrain. As they made their way deeper into the heart of the city, people of all ages emerged from their homes to gawk at the strange creatures and their riders.

Gideon picked up bits of conversations that were not only about the animals but also about the men riding them.

He noticed that all the onlookers had shaved their heads, like Kaius and the rest of their New Emilian escorts. Amidst the spectacle of New Emile, the uniform baldness of the people had struck him as odd. Clearing his throat, he turned to Kaius. "Does everyone here have a shaved head?"

Kaius, riding next to him, glanced sideways before breaking into a brief smile. "You'll probably want to do the same. As I told your father, there are tiny insects here that seem to have a particular appetite for hair. Mitters. The best way to avoid them is to shave it off."

"Any hair?" Gideon asked, suddenly self-conscious about his own full head of brown locks.

Kaius chuckled and nodded. "If it's anywhere on your body, you might want to consider taking a blade to it."

As they journeyed deeper into the city, the sights, sounds, and smells of the place intoxicated Gideon. And yet, everything seemed...confined. It was, he knew, a place he would never forget, and one that would forever be etched in his memory.

His mind was restless, though, an uneasiness tugging at his thoughts until he could bear it no longer. He turned again to Kaius.

"The people outside," he began tentatively. "They seem different from those within these walls."

Kaius, seemingly unsurprised by Gideon's inquiry, replied with a dismissive air. "Marokai," he said simply.

But this explanation was not enough for Gideon, who probed for more. With a sigh that bordered on annoyance, Kaius relented. "Liorah, the One Voice, can enlighten you on the matter. It's a complicated history, and one I'd rather not delve into."

Though Kaius had not provided a direct answer, Gideon had heard the term during the long journey from Rephidim, and Luca had mentioned that his brother and sister were both Marokai. He slightly understood that they were a separate group, distinct from those who lived within the walls of the city. But why? It was almost as if there were two colonies coexisting in this realm—one filled with well-fed inhabitants adorned in clean garments, while grime marked the other and sustenance appeared scarce from the look of the children who had approached them on the moor.

Having lived through a famine himself, he could empathize with their plight. "They don't get enough food?" he asked Kaius.

But once again, Kaius was dismissive, offering only a single word in response. "Liorah."

As they continued on, Gideon's attention was drawn away from the people to a central location, where a pool of water glimmered like a gemstone in the fading light of day. Several men encircled it, and at the center stood a tree with white bark and golden leaves that glowed with a soft radiance.

Luca pointed to the pool. "Haelen," he said, "or the Water of Life, as you call it."

Gideon's throat tightened at the realization of what he beheld. The pool held the power to heal any ailment that nature could inflict upon the Col'kasid. From the infamous Red Death to unknown diseases and fungal infections that could ravage a body—this water held the potential to save his people from any harm. It had already saved Jacob's life.

"Come," Kaius said. "Liorah awaits."

CHAPTER SIXTEEN

GIDEON'S HARSH EXPECTATIONS OF LIORAH, THE ONE Voice, were quickly shattered as he took in her appearance. She sat at the far end of the table, her head shaved like everyone else, but adorned with vibrant jivara banded around her scalp. Her robe, a clean and crisp white, fell gently over her small frame, accentuating her rounded features. Her eyes were a deep, rich brown, and her smile was a thing of beauty, revealing perfect teeth that glistened in the soft light.

As Gideon surveyed the rest of the room, his gaze settled on a bored-looking younger man sitting next to Liorah. The man never spoke nor was he introduced during the meeting. The three other men around the table asked most of the questions. To Gideon's left sat Kaius, whose company he had kept for the better part of a cycle of the Short Moon. He had apparently been allowed to sit in by the "grace" of Liorah, something that he admitted privately to Gideon he had rarely done. Opposite him was an older man named Alistair, whose nervous fidgeting betrayed his discomfort any time Gideon spoke. The final member of the group was a stout man named Josiah, the leader of the sentinels. He wore leather armor that looked as uncomfortable as it was practical, and his bald head gleamed in the light as if it had been polished. Empty chairs indicated that there were others missing from this meeting.

Gideon answered the questions posed to him by the others, but he couldn't help feel slightly uncomfortable in Liorah's presence. He had come to this meeting as the future Keeper of the Text and ambassador of the Col'kasid, yet here he was, befuddled by the One Voice. Her calm demeanor and piercing gaze made him feel exposed, vulnerable even. But he pressed on, answering each question with care. Where Jacob and Isaiah were, he couldn't say, but he trusted their needs were being met. Especially Jacob, who still had not fully recovered from his brush with the Red Death.

"Where does your food come from?" Alistair asked. He picked at his fingernails and did not look up.

"Rephidim is built near an orchard filled with poralima and mirakulu trees," Gideon answered. "The mirakulu trees produce small red berries, which the women turn into wine. From the poralima trees comes a long fruit that, while slightly bitter and has the consistency of dirt, is filled with nutrients. We have brought some of the wine along as a gift, but the poralima fruit doesn't last long."

"What keeps your trees alive if, as you said before, there is very little rain?"

Gideon knew the answer to this question was bound to cause a stir. "When my great grandfather, Sojen Micah, arrived at Rephidim with the Col'kasid, they passed through the orchard. There were already a multitude of agricultural ditches that ran through it, filled with water. These ditches support the growth of the trees."

"Where does the water come from?"

"That's actually still a mystery. There are two principal water sources—the ditches and the waterfall. Both come from somewhere underground, and no source has yet been found."

Alistair finally looked up, and his gray eyes narrowed into slits. "You mean you don't know?"

"No, but it's suspected the ditches were dug out many years ago by the Ancients."

At the word Ancients, Alistair's eyes opened wide. "What do you mean, Ancients?"

"Sojen Micah called them the sa'ja'peet and sa'ja'veil, and the two strangers who visited us years ago called them the Orinate and Ikoli. It is unknown who they were or where they came from, only that they left written texts in the temple at Manoach, where our common history lives. Surely you have a record of that."

Alistair glanced at Liorah as she sat forward, clasping her hands together and resting on her elbows. "The sa'ja'peet," Liorah said, "are said to have written the texts, while the sa'ja'veil are mostly likely the original inhabitants of New Emile. We have some knowledge of that history."

Gideon felt speechless suddenly. The Ancients had built this city, this vibrant community of nearly a thousand people on a moor! It was something he did not expect to hear, and although Sojen Micah would tell tales of what the Ancients had built at Manoach and the clues they left behind of their lives, the stories felt like nothing more than fables told to put children to sleep. Even when the strangers came to visit long before he'd been born into sunshine, they too told stories.

Now this woman was confirming a myth.

"I..." Gideon struggled to find the right words. "I never believed the stories."

"Why not?" Liorah smiled. "You said the Ancients had built the ditches, and you appear to revere this Micah. Why would you not believe?"

Gideon shifted in his seat. "There has never been a sign outside of the straight agricultural lines in the orchard." He realized he was leaving out the fact that Sojen Micah had one of the texts in his possession, but no one here needed to know that. "My great grandfather once told us the story of his sister and the moment she passed into shadow in the deadly dunes. He'd said they had brought some of the Ancient's texts out of Manoach but that they were lost when sand creatures attacked the Col'kasid during their traverse across the dunes."

"No one went back to retrieve them?" Josiah asked. "I would think something so important would be guarded with the utmost care."

Gideon shook his head. "Everything to the north of Rephidim, past the orchards, is forbidden land. It was one of the first decrees of Sojen Micah that no man enter what he called his sister's grave. No one has ever questioned that decree."

The room was silent for a moment, and Gideon stared at a pattern on the wood table. He suddenly felt disassociated from the meeting at this news of the Ancients and the confirmation of legend. But how would the New Emilians know outside of the history of Manoach? What would have made anyone think New Emile had been built by the sa'ja'veil?

"These texts," Alistair inquired. "What were they?"

Gideon shrugged. "Words of the Ancients. Sojen Micah said they couldn't be read. Most were squiggles and archaic drawings. He had spent much of his time at Manoach in a library attempting to translate them with his cousins, one of whom was your Great Mother, Miriam." He looked up in time to see Alistair glance again at Liorah, as if they were hiding something.

"So you eat fruit and drink wine," Liorah said, changing the subject. "What about these qu... these animals you brought with you? Are they food?"

"No," Gideon said, shocked at the very idea of eating a quvianaq when they were so sociable. "The quvianaq are mount animals who follow us around. They're predators, but welcome us as one of their own. The meat that sustains the Col'kasid comes mainly from Tishbe bison, which naturally graze to the east of Rephidim, closer to the shores of the Barren Sea."

"They let you ride them?"

Gideon nodded. "You don't even have to train them much. Once the animal gets comfortable around you, you become an extension of it. It knows more about where you want to go and what you shouldn't do than you will."

Liorah's face lit up, almost like a child's. "I would love to ride one of them."

"You shall get a chance," Gideon offered. "I think any of the three we brought with us would welcome you on its back."

"So, meat from bison, fruit from orchards, water in abundant supply," Josiah recounted. "And you live in a protected village high above any natural dangers. What else would the Col'kasid ever need?"

Gideon glanced at Kaius, who had said little during this meeting, nor had asked any questions. Not that he really needed to, since the two of them had conversed so much during the journey from Rephidim.

"Haelen," Kaius said. "They have...medical problems."

Liorah's eyes widened. "Medical problems? What would so plague you that haelen would be your only recourse? Are there no healers within the Col'kasid?"

"There are," Gideon said, "but they have not been able to combat two specific diseases which have affected the population since arriving at Rephidim. The first is the Red Death, which we believe to be a fungal infection brought in from the soil during dust storms. It lingers in the body for weeks or even full cycles of the Long Moon before attacking the body."

"What makes it attack?" Josiah asked. It seemed the only time he had a question was when it was related to some sort of battle or defense.

"That isn't known. Something triggers the fungus and within a week at most, the host passes into shadow."

Josiah looked around the room at each person before continuing. "How do you know haelen will help?"

"It is the Water of Life," Gideon said. "And we have seen it cure the Red Death recently. One of our own, Jacob, was infected before leaving Rephidim. It attacked him just before we arrived here. It was only through the grace of Kaius that he was saved."

Liorah, Josiah, and Alistair all turned their attention to Kaius, who seemed, in that moment, to withdraw into his seat.

"You gave up your haelen?" Liorah asked, her voice no longer pleasant. Suddenly, it sounded...harsh.

"I..." Kaius stuttered. "The man was going to pass into shadow. I wanted to see if it would work on this Red Death. It was a sacrifice I was willing to make as we were only a few days away from New Emile."

"I don't understand," Gideon said, coming to the man's defense. "Why wouldn't you use it to heal a disease if it works?"

"The other disease?" Liorah asked, again diverting the conversation. "What is it?"

"Tishbe fever."

Liorah looked stunned. "I can tell you right now that haelen doesn't work on the fever. The Great Mother, Miriam, had it. All it ever did was arrest its spread, but it did not remove it from her mind." Her demeanor was oddly defensive.

"Nevertheless," Gideon said, unphased by the admission of haelen's limitations, "the Col'kasid could benefit from the Water of Life, and we come as ambassadors to offer trade."

THE CONVERSATION between the Col'kasid and New Emile shifted more and more during the meeting. Kaius grew tired as the night wore on, his eyes becoming heavy with sleep. He had yet to have a moment for himself to rest and recover from the journey to and from Rephidim. He felt as if he'd been walking for years, and if something exciting didn't happen soon, he feared nodding off in the presence of the One Voice, who was much less interested in what the Col'kasid offered.

Kaius had feared this, with his suspicion that this was a waste of time growing each day he had learned something new from Gideon. If anything, the meeting of the two tribes was nothing but an introduction, something that could have been accomplished with a simple message. He suspected that Elder Levi may have been right all along. Aside from the haelen, there was nothing New Emile could offer Rephidim that would improve their society. On the other hand, the quvianaq and knowledge concerning agriculture could have an immediate impact on the lives of those on the moor—particularly the Marokai. Whatever trade was eventually agreed upon, New Emile would have the upper hand.

Kaius half-listened to the conversation, or rather the answers Gideon gave to the myriad of questions which were lobbed at him from the others around the table. Roland the Kept appeared more bored than usual and never once looked comfortable. Why was he here? The man's role was to remain by Liorah's side as both someone to look at and, when it pleased her, someone to bed. He seemed to have no other purpose in life.

Where were the others? Probably sleeping. Kaius turned his attention to the matter of Luca and Abel. While they had made their relationship known during the journey, as a sentinel Luca was forbidden from forming any sort of permanent bond. Kaius had let it go while they were on Discovery, but now he would need to reign in the boy's behavior by observing Luca closer. It would hurt Abel, but he would eventually need to find a life elsewhere. As far as Kaius could tell, the Col'kasid exile had no skills which would be beneficial to New Emile. He'd certainly never make it as a scout or as a sentinel. Abel was a man of letters, though, a reader and a scribe. Maybe Alistair could find use for him in the Library.

No one had told Gideon of the Library yet, and the Col'kasid ambassador had missed his moment to ask. When Alistair had inquired about the texts of the Ancients, a part of which Sojen Micah had apparently translated, Kaius had assumed the conversation would veer in that direction. Kaius was aware that New Emile had plenty of texts under guard, none of which could be read. It was Alistair's role to oversee the Library and poke and prod a few younger New Emilians into figuring out what they said. But there was no easy way to translate something that looked—at least from what Kaius had heard—like scribbles in the sand.

Not to mention the fact that Liorah outright refused to allow anyone other than Alistair and his wards inside. He'd heard rumors that she was ready to burn the building to the ground.

Eventually, the conversation moved away from trade and landed squarely on a topic that Kaius *had* been more interested in—the whereabouts and culture of the Zhanshi. He sat up straighter and even Roland the Kept finally appeared to finally care about something.

Josiah wouldn't shut up about it.

"Where are they?" Josiah asked, his voice tinged with frustration. "You must know something."

Gideon shook his head vigorously. "I only know what the strangers passed down to us. The Zhanshi live across the Barren Sea. Where, I don't know. While we have been to the shore, we do not venture across the water, nor do we go anywhere where we know danger might be."

"Why?"

"There's no point." Gideon sounded frustrated as well.

Josiah pushed away from the table and stood. He began pacing back and forth in the room, like a hungry animal. The veins in his forehead stood out.

"You have had no signs?" The sentinel commander stopped and turned on Gideon. "No wayward scouts who have crossed your hunters' paths? No unexplained sightings?"

"No, nothing. If they are still a fully functioning tribe, they keep to themselves."

"Josiah," Alistair said. "Perhaps you could sit back down."

"All this time," Josiah said, obviously not listening, "you sit on your mountain top eating fruit, worshiping your god, and learning nothing. You never explore? You never go out and see what the world around you is like?"

"That's not it, at all. God directs our actions, and we listen to what He says. At one point, Elder Levi, my father, had suggested we send scouts to discover the Zhanshi's whereabouts, but after a contentious quorum of the community, we decided to leave well enough alone. If trouble did not find us, why should we seek it out?"

"Because trouble *will* find you." Josiah shook his head vigorously. "I don't—"

"Sit, Josiah," Liorah said, her voice more commanding than Alistair's.

Josiah let out a deep breath but did as he was told. He mumbled something under his breath that no one at the table caught.

"What did you say?" Liorah pursed her lips.

"Nothing, Liorah." Josiah said. He dropped his eyes to the table. "I cannot live with apparent laziness. That is all. It grates on my nerves, and the fact that the Col'kasid are apparently beholden to an imaginary deity makes me furious."

"We do not know if they are lazy or just overly cautious." Liorah turned to Gideon, her curiosity piqued. "Abel said these Zhanshi are more advanced with electric power," Liorah said. "What does that mean? What else do they have that you or I don't, besides the ability to light their homes?"

Gideon shrugged. Her face showed it was not the response she hoped for. Coupled with Josiah's outburst, Kaius expected the One Voice to lash out at any moment herself.

"What are you not saying?" she asked more firmly.

"There is nothing to say." Gideon did not look at Liorah, but his eyes told a different story. "The strangers who came to us warned that the Zhanshi sought vengeance for what they perceived as a slap in the face of their founder, Mathias Tseng, something that happened in the first few years after Transit. The genocide at Manoach should always serve as a reminder of what they are capable of and why we should always be on guard."

Josiah chuckled derisively. "Of why you should bury your head in the sand. You live your life by 'shoulds' instead of doing something about it."

The length of the meeting had obviously affected everyone's temper.

"These strangers seem to know more than you do," Liorah continued without acknowledging Josiah. "It is almost as if the Col'kasid—you—are not interested in learning more."

"They do know more, but their arrival was long before I was born into sunshine. They have not been seen for over forty years."

"Then the threat may not exist. Did you ever think you may have been duped into keeping to your little butte in the desert, eating your fruits and drinking your wine? All the while, advancements are made without your knowledge."

"Perhaps, but anger boils deep in the heart and grows with each day that vengeance is not sought. If they are out there still, they have grown stronger."

"What about weapons?" Josiah asked. "Did these strangers tell you anything useful? If you are to defend against this mysterious threat, how do you know what to defend with? A crossbow and lance may not be enough if this advanced tribe has developed something more."

Gideon shook his head. He really knew little, and perhaps, Kaius thought, that was because the strangers knew little themselves. "I don't know," Gideon said after a time.

"Perhaps Russant will have better luck than you." Josiah sat back in his chair and crossed his arms again.

At that, Gideon looked up. "What do you mean?"

Josiah opened his mouth, but Liorah cut him off quickly. "That is none of your concern." She took a deep breath and leaned in, her voice softening. "You must be tired. In the morning, Kaius can show you around if you'd like. And I would love to ride one of the mounts you have brought. Perhaps you can show me?" She flashed a quick smile, disconcerting given her anger seconds before.

Kaius was suddenly relieved that he could finally get

some rest in his quarters. It had been long enough.

A page burst through one of the servant doors and rushed toward Alistair. A thin boy of only ten or eleven, he leaned down to whisper something in Alistair's ear. The old man looked suddenly stricken and pushed himself back away from the table.

"What is it?" Liorah asked. She stood from the table. If she'd had a crossbow, the boy would have taken a bolt to the forehead. "You do not come into this chamber unannounced like this. Who sent you?"

The boy looked frightened. He bowed his head deeply and shuffled backward. "I...I beg your mercy, Liorah." Tears formed in his eyes. "I was t-told to in-inform Master Alistair immediately."

"Inform him of what?"

"The L-library, Liorah. There has been a breech."

CHAPTER SEVENTEEN

IN THE DIMLY LIT CHAMBER OF A BUILDING KNOWN AS THE Library, Jacob and Isaiah stood with their heads bowed, their hands bound in front of them by a coarse rope. A lone sentinel stood nearby, a loaded crossbow in his hand. Gideon swallowed as he looked in from the doorway standing next to Kaius and Liorah. Alistair was already in the room, pacing, enhancing the weight of the apparent Col'kasid transgression.

Gideon could not believe his eyes. The room in front of him—the Library—unfolded like a sacred sanctuary of forgotten wisdom and cosmic enigmas. It was a room unlike any he had ever encountered, a place where it was more apparent than not that the echoes of ancient civilizations resonated through the very air they breathed. Walls adorned with intricate carvings, symbols of a language lost to time, reached towards a low ceiling. Despite any windows that Gideon could see, everything seemed to have an ethereal glow, casting an otherworldly light upon rows of ancient alien texts.

"Those symbols..." Gideon's voice was barely more than a whisper. The words caught in his throat.

Alistair stopped his pacing and turned to face Gideon, a look of disdain wrinkling his features. "What about them?"

"They're...sa'ja'peet." Gideon's voice faltered under the enormity of the revelation.

Alistair's eyes opened wide. "Indeed. Yet do you have any notion of their meaning?"

"No." Gideon's mind whirled, pieces of a puzzle falling into place with a thunderous crash. The secret glances exchanged between Alistair and Liorah, the Great Mother's enigmatic knowledge of who built New Emile—all paths led back to this hoard of hidden texts.

"I don't understand," Gideon said softly, his eyes asking a thousand questions. "Why are my men bound?"

Liorah stepped forward. "The Great Mother had her reasons for keeping this place off limits. Only pain can come from here. Her edict was passed down to Master Eilian and from him to me."

As much as Gideon wanted to stay and explore the wonders before him, he had another problem with which to deal. Both Jacob and Isaiah were in trouble.

Before he could say anything else, Liorah slid up next to Alistair and waved him away. She turned to Jacob. "How did you get in here?" Her eyes flickered between him and Isaiah. "The door is always locked and guarded."

Jacob shrugged, but he still looked like he was about to faint. "Not when we walked by. The door was slightly ajar, and I thought I'd look around. There didn't seem to be anyone home."

Liorah shot a glance at the sentinel, who suddenly looked nervous. "There was no one at the door?" she asked, her voice raised. The implication was clear.

The sentinel lowered his head. "I— I needed to relieve myself, Liorah. Five minutes around the corner. That's all."

Liorah balled her fists. "Why was it unsecured?"

Alistair suddenly looked sheepish himself. "Forgive me, Liorah. I was recently in here and did not think to lock up."

Gideon didn't believe she would take a swing at the

sentinel or at Alistair, but that didn't mean she wouldn't find some way to punish them for this apparent breach of order.

"Kaius." Liorah spun around. "Take this sentinel out of my sight and deal with him. We can't have this lack of security, even if there's nothing of value in here."

Nothing of value?

As Kaius dutifully escorted the anxious sentinel out of the Library, Gideon, still not knowing what was going to happen to his Col'kasid companions, spoke up. "What do you intend to do with them, Liorah?"

Liorah stepped toward Gideon until she was within a few inches. The overpowering smell of her fragrance—likely from a flower which Gideon had yet to see in this dismal place—wafted through the air, setting Gideon's heart racing. She placed a hand softly on his chest before speaking. "Nothing. You may unbind them, Alistair. But I must warn you that these texts are not to be disturbed. They have caused many troubles in the past, as our Great Mother attested, and I will not allow them to be our downfall. Why I haven't burned them for warmth yet, I can't say."

Gideon nodded as Alistair unbound Jacob and Isaiah. "These texts, Liorah. May we look at a few of them? Under your generous and watchful eye, of course."

Liorah's gaze was as tantalizing as it was stern. Her hand lingered on his chest, her decision hanging in the air as if she sought to measure the weight of her words.

"No," she decided, then brushed past him and headed for the exit. As the echo of her refusal died away, Gideon was left wrestling with a whirlwind of revelation and uncertainty.

WITH JACOB and Isaiah released, Kaius returned from wherever he had taken the sentinel and escorted the Col'kasid contingent from the Library to find a place to sleep.

The early morning's damp chill sunk into their bones as they followed Kaius through narrow, winding pathways lined with small buildings. Gideon could not fathom the idea that there was not enough room to allow the Marokai to come inside. The place seemed...massive.

As they rounded a bend, they were joined by Abel. The Col'kasid quvianaq were tied to a post outside a small dwelling. It was, as Kaius said, the home of a family whose last member had passed into shadow recently. It had not yet been reassigned. Inside, the space was tight, the air still. There was a hint of something lost, like the faint smell of a loved one long gone. Thin, utilitarian blankets were haphazardly strewn across the floor, their colors muted in the low light.

Abel looked around. "If this place is empty, why not give it to one of the families outside the walls? To the Marokai?"

"That is not for me to decide," Kaius said. "For now, sleep off your trials and we'll regroup in the morning. You can find food in a container in the corner, and there is a latrine hole in the back."

Abel looked as if he wanted to protest further, but Gideon put a hand on his shoulder. "Thank you," he said and closed the door on Kaius.

After a moment, Gideon turned to Jacob and Isaiah.

"We're sorry for that," Jacob said sheepishly. "We thought the place was empty, and we were surprised by what we saw when we looked inside."

"Forget that. Tell me what you found."

"There are hundreds of texts in that place, all written in the sa'ja'peet's style," Isaiah said. "I'm sure of it. The symbols and logograms are similiar to some of those still used in our ceremonies and in that text Sojen Micah keeps with him. I think he should see this."

"I don't understand." Abel sat on a blanket with his back

against a wall. "How can there be texts here? The stories we've been told said they were lost at Manoach and in the desert where Micah's sister passed into shadow. The only reason Sojen Micah has one is because it was gifted to him by the strangers, and yet he claims he cannot read it."

"Do you think Sojen Micah can read these?" Jacob asked, ignoring Abel's query.

Gideon shrugged. "It's possible, but he's no longer the Keeper of the Text. That honor fell to my father."

"Yes, but Elder Levi has Father Elijah's Bible, and from what you've told me, it contains a dictionary of sorts."

"It does, but it's not as helpful as you think." Abel said.

"What do you mean?"

Abel took in a deep breath. "As Sojen Micah explained it, the texts are written with a keyword or phrase embedded near the beginning. Each one is different. A circle line might mean one thing in one book and something else in another. The writer uses that keyword to establish context and from there the rest flows."

Jacob scrunched his face. "I have no idea what you just said."

Gideon slowly lowered himself to the floor. The hardness of the ground was almost comforting, especially after such a long journey. With an absent hand, he swiped at his face, as if he could wipe away the gnawing sense he was missing something.

He looked around the room. The walls felt closer, and yet there was a certain comfort in the solidarity of being the only Col'kasid in a city with strange customs and an even stranger leader.

After a moment, Gideon looked up. "Jacob. If I can get us back into the Library, do you think you might borrow a text? Concealing it, of course." He paused. "This...this mystery. It's something the Assembly at Rephidim needs to see, Micah most of all. I can't understand why this Liorah character is so determined to keep these secrets locked away. They are not hers to begin with."

Jacob flashed a reassuring smile. "You know I can," he said, as his smile widened. "Just get us inside."

WHEN THE sun rose, there was a loud knock on the door. Gideon was already awake and jumped to his feet. The events of the previous night swirled in his mind, and his thoughts about what was in the Library had consumed him. He yearned for answers, and he hoped Kaius would shed some light on the matter. He really didn't trust any other New Emilian, save Luca. But it was likely he and Abel would go off on their own for the day.

As Gideon swung open the door, he found Kaius standing there, flanked by Luca and Nico.

"Morning." Kaius gave Gideon a slight nod. "The One Voice, Liorah, would like me to be a guide or something."

"I would appreciate it." Gideon adjusted his shirt and then mussed up his hair with his fingertips. It felt both invigorating and oddly embarrassing to have such a full head of hair when New Emilians shaved their heads. He did wonder why they hadn't seen any of those supposed hair bugs yet, the mitters. "We'd wander around ourselves, but that got us in trouble already."

The corners of Kaius' mouth turned down slightly, but he did not respond. Instead, he nodded toward the quvianaq still tied up outside. "When we are done, Liorah has requested you teach her to ride one of your mount animals."

"I take it then that there are some places you can't show us."

Kaius' lips turned down further. "I should have given

you some guidelines before we came into the city. There are a few places where it is forbidden for anyone outside of the Elite to go, and a few others where only Liorah may enter."

Gideon wanted to say how much of a waste it was to keep livable space away from the Marokai, but he quickly nixed that idea. It was not for him to judge, and Kaius had no power over the situation anyway.

With Jacob and Isaiah beside him, Gideon followed Kaius and Nico into the street. Luca offered to give Abel a more private tour, something Kaius did not seem pleased about, but did not argue.

The streets stretched out before them, and based on Kaius' mention of forbidden spaces, Gideon had to wonder just what else lay hidden, what other undisclosed knowledge New Emile concealed within its walls.

The expression on Kaius' face was reserved. His footsteps were slow and steady, leaving plenty of time for quiet contemplation between pointing out features such as homes, bakeries, and workshops. That was good. Gideon's inner turmoil could not be discounted, however, and with each step, more questions filled his mind. The city was both intriguing and anxiety-provoking.

As they navigated the streets, Gideon's gaze alternated between the architecture and the fleeting interactions between the inhabitants of New Emile. There were glimpses into the lives of the New Emilians, reflecting their shared values and traditions, but little else. A man piled a cart high with bags of grain, while nearby the sounds of a blacksmith pounding away at an anvil filtered through the air. There was a mix of smells—from sweat to flowers to oil to cooked meat—which did not sit well with Gideon's stomach. The city felt both alive and reserved, its residents going about their daily lives with a sense of purpose yet less community than he expected. That routine, however, paused as the Col'kasid contingent passed by.

"Tell me about the Marokai," Gideon said. "Why are they cast out of the city?"

Kaius slowed his pace even more before answering. "Don't look at them as outcasts. They are taken care of long before they are relocated to the Hollows. The lottery that places them there is fair."

"Fair? You mean everyone is perfectly happy when fate kicks them out."

"It sounds awful, I know, but the Marokai are given a home outside the walls. We lack the space here for all the growth." He took a deep breath and looked around. "Think of both New Emile and the Hollows as one city, one community. Just because we ask the Marokai to live outside does not mean they are not welcome."

"But they cannot live here."

"No. They cannot."

Gideon considered this "welcoming" of the Marokai, but he didn't know if he believed it. The more he interacted with the sentinels and the Elite of New Emile, the more he sensed there was definitely a caste system being forced upon everyone that started with an arbitrary—and honestly unfair—lottery. That was something he'd learned about as a child when his great grandfather Micah would relate stories of what life was probably like back on Earth. Even if Sojen Micah had not lived there, he was a scholar and had spent much of his early years learning what he could from the elders, from the first generation who came over on the COL ship. Caste systems were not good.

"Are the Marokai only those who lost the lottery?" Gideon asked after a while.

"They didn't lose," Nico countered. He looked defensive.

"If the lottery had not been put into place, this city would be overwhelmed and crumble. We do what we can. For the most part, the Marokai are just like us."

"You said 'for the most part.' You mean there are people who live in the Hollows who are not Marokai, who are truly different?"

"There are some people who moved out on their own, and some of them were asked to leave for various offenses. You know — criminals."

Kaius turned a corner. In front of them stood a larger building with two stories. The second story was more recent, made discernible by the rougher cut and less weathered stones than the ones that were used for the first story. A few small children played in front of the building, heads shaved.

"The Hollows is a part of our community," Kaius said. "Everyone is treated the same."

Gideon really wanted to argue that point, but he decided to keep his mouth shut. This was a diplomatic mission, after all.

Kaius stopped walking and pointed to the two-story building. "That is a school. When these children turn sixteen, their names are placed into the lottery. Some of them are sent out and some of them remain here. There is no difference in how they are raised or how they are treated."

"Until there is."

"What?"

FOR THE rest of the morning, Kaius and Nico guided the Col'kasid contingent through the streets. Never once did they go outside the walls, and Gideon was comfortable with that for the time being. He would explore more later. Now, however, it was time to return to the New Emile Chambers with a quvianaq so that Liorah could have the pleasure of a ride. Gideon felt this was the least he could do for the hospitality the New Emilians had given them already, even if two of his contingent had been bound by rope and they were forbidden from knowing what was in many of the buildings. Provided he kept the animals away from the quarry and that sound machine, he couldn't imagine anything else going wrong.

Liorah, Alistair and Josiah stood by the pool of haelen with the Tree that Owns Itself. The sun was high, making the yellow leaves glow with a brilliance unlike any plant Gideon had ever laid eyes on. Gideon arrived on the back of his quvianaq, while Jacob and Isaiah followed close behind. After the three dismounted, Liorah broke out in a wide but disconcerting smile. She stepped toward Gideon's quvianaq and reached her hand out.

"Can I touch the beast?" she asked. "It won't bite me, will it?"

"Not at all." Gideon scratched his quvianaq on its long neck. "They are more friendly toward humans than they are to some of their own kind."

Gingerly, Liorah reached out and put her hand the side of the animal's neck opposite Gideon. "What is it, exactly?" she asked as she took her first tentative strokes.

"The original members of the Col'kasid found this animal after losing their way. They had called it a strider because of how it moves, but they changed the name after the strangers I mentioned showed up."

"Do you know what it means? Quvianaq?"

Gideon shrugged. "No idea. These are the only natural predators we know of for the rychat."

At the mention of the rychat, Liorah's eyes opened wide. She stopped stroking the quvianaq and looked at Gideon. "Our Great Mother, Miriam, had plenty to say of rychat. She believed they were Tishbe's apex predator, at the top of the food chain. You're saying these animals are more dangerous?"

"To the rychat, but not humans. They actually protected our founders in the rainforest before finding Rephidim. Or so the story goes."

Liorah resumed stroking the animal and examined it. "It has six arms," she said with a giggle. "And they're so short!" For a moment, her voice was light and childlike.

"The arms are retractable," Gideon said. For a demonstration, he removed a piece of food from his satchel and placed it on the ground about eight feet in front of the quvianaq. The animal cocked its head to the right, then left. An arm shot out, and with a single motion, it plucked the morsel of food from the ground and popped it into its mouth.

Liorah stepped back, still giggling, her smile wider. She looked beautiful, and the soft glow of yellow leaves of the tree in the middle of the haelen pond made her look like a dream. If Gideon hadn't been so uncomfortable around her—and scared of her power—he might say something.

"Come, then." Liorah swung around the quvianaq and placed her hand on Gideon's chest. Every time she did that, he felt his stomach twist. "Show me how to ride!" she said with a glint in her eyes that instantly softened Gideon's spirit.

THE EVENING came with a large dinner. Within the New Emile Chambers, the help—all children, as far as Gideon could tell—had set the table up with food, to include meat, grains, and some bitter greens. It wasn't nearly as colorful as the meals at Rephidim, but it was good to eat something. Rather than a full contingent of Col'kasid, however, only Gideon had been invited. Jacob and Isaiah were likely in their temporary dwelling, and there was no saying where Abel had gone. The boy hadn't been seen since Luca took him away in the morning. As for the New Emilians, it was just Liorah, Josiah, Alistair and that strange fellow, Roland the Kept.

The chatter around the table focused mostly on Liorah's experience with the quvianaq during the day, her face still beaming with excitement. Roland looked unsure of what to make of it. His eyes darted around the table, repeatedly landing on Gideon with a jealous stare.

While Josiah probed more about what the Col'kasid had learned about the Zhanshi tribe, Alistair tried on many occasions to bring up the texts in the Library. Specifically, he wanted to know if Gideon or any of the Col'kasid knew what was in them. So far, no one in New Emile had deciphered more than one page, and even that page was questionable. There was nothing that would help them. Micah, at least, had been given a head start.

Alistair pushed his empty plate away from him and leaned in toward Gideon. "How did your Sojen...Sojen..."

"Micah," Gideon said.

"Right, Micah. How did he translate these texts, or the texts that were found in the temple at Manoach?"

"A cipher, really." Gideon was not finished with his dinner, but he pushed his plate forward out of courtesy. "Father Elijah brought with him a Bible during the First Transit. In it were many translations of both symbols and words. Micah had said that he and his cousins had used that as a starting point for each of the texts. Once they found a keyword, they could then work on what was next. The great Elder Marcus, Micah's grandfather, helped considerably."

Gideon stopped and took a drink of wine. He had been feeling the effects of the fermented beverage all night, making his head spin. "Your Great Mother, Miriam," he continued. "She was with Micah when they translated the first few texts."

"So we've been told," Liorah interjected. "But when we arrived at New Emile and it was discovered there was a Library here, the Great Mother forbid anyone from trying to translate anything."

"May I ask why?"

Liorah shrugged. "It didn't matter. Translating the texts at Manoach led to pain, and she knew the same thing would happen here. Her grandson, Philip, implored his father, Master Eilian, to grant Alistair access to the Library for a trial."

"When was that?"

"Seven or eight years ago," Alistair said. "We haven't gotten very far in all that time."

Gideon considered what he had learned about the New Emilian experience with the texts and compared it to his own knowledge of what was in Father Elijah's Bible. Either he or Abel might be able to help, and he said as much to those gathered around the table.

"No," Liorah said sternly. Her affect had changed from one of excitement to one of irritation, perhaps anger even. "As I have said before, the texts in the Library can bring nothing but trouble. No one but Alistair and his scribes are allowed inside, and even that I feel is a foolish waste of this man's time."

"Is there something we can offer you in trade, then?" Gideon asked.

"And what do you have? Fruit that won't last the journey here? Wine? Your agricultural knowledge might be useful, but New Emile is not exactly on fertile soil. Unless you can supply us with a...a flock of quvianaq, then we see little value in the Col'kasid." Liorah smirked. "Surely you wouldn't suggest trading your animals for a peek at some old dusty texts and a bottle of haelen."

Gideon sat back, dejected. No, Levi would never consider trading even one quvianaq for something that was unreadable and probably useless. Sojen Micah once joked that the ancient texts might as well have been fanciful fables written by alien children for all the knowledge they could glean from them.

Liorah was stubborn, and Gideon doubted there was any way he could convince her to change her mind. Alistair, on the other hand, seemed very interested in what the Col'kasid might be able to offer.

Perhaps it was time for a different approach.

THERE WAS to be no real trade, and there didn't seem to be a reason to stay in New Emile much longer. Liorah had been right: the Col'kasid were not the trading partners anyone thought they would be. They had nothing tantalizing enough. Gideon needed to find another way into the Library, and in the morning he intended to approach Alistair away from the Chambers and alone, assuming that was possible. He couldn't remember if he'd ever seen the man by himself.

Gideon sat against the wall in their temporary dwelling and looked around at the others gathered. Jacob and Isaiah looked bored. No one they'd interacted with in New Emile would show them exactly how they got their meat or where it came from. Abel, who was the most learned of the contingent but no longer welcome as a member of the tribe — at least as far as Levi was concerned — had returned from the Hollows that evening after having spent the day with Luca's brother and sister, Diego and Elena.

"There is definitely a split in classes," Abel said. "Despite what Kaius or anyone else may have told you, the Marokai do twice the labor and receive half the rations." He turned to Jacob. "You want to know why no one in New Emile will show you how they hunt? It's because *no one* in New Emile hunts.

"What do you mean?" Jacob asked.

"The Marokai have divisions of labor, one of which is to collect food for the city, and that food is not shared equally." Abel sighed. "It's not a pretty sight. There's more disease, too. The haelen is only for the Elite and in emergency cases, the sentinels. Have you seen the mark?"

Gideon looked up. "The mark?"

"Across their forehead." Abel drew a line above his eyebrows. "The Marokai are marked with a permanent brand here. The criminals and those who are targeted by Liorah for whatever reason are then branded with a triangle over the line. You can't miss it."

"I guess I've been protected from seeing them up close." Gideon paused for a moment. "In fact, the only Marokai I saw were children when we first entered and only one of them had something on his head. I thought it was a scar."

Isaiah threw up his hands. "What in God's name is wrong with these people?" He rubbed his own forehead. "Branded, like with a hot metal?"

Abel simply nodded.

Jacob stood and paced the small room. "This place is not what I expected. I feel very isolated, and the fact that we have hair makes us look like freaks. Not to mention I'm starting to itch. It must be those bugs. When are we leaving?"

Gideon fidgeted with his hands, interlocking his fingers in different patterns before answering. "Not until we get one of those texts."

"Which one? There has to be a hundred, if not more."

"I don't care. Whatever we—*you*—can get your hands on."

"I can't do that if you can't get me back inside. It doesn't look like anyone will let us just walk in there. You heard the angry lady."

Gideon's eyebrows shot up. "The angry lady?"

"Liorah, their One Voice." Jacob's voice was laced with scorn. "They put a woman in charge and look what happens."

"What's wrong with a woman in charge?" Gideon's face flushed. There were so many rules he disagreed with among the Col'kasid—despite being the next in line as the Keeper of the Text. Aside from how they treated Abel, the relegation of women to support roles for men was definitely another. "I think they've done pretty well here as a community with her in charge."

Now it was Jacob's turn to raise his eyebrows. "Pretty well? Are you blinded by her beauty or something? The New Emilians are split down the middle with half of them disfigured and discriminated against simply because of some stupid lottery. Everyone within the walls gets fat while the rest labor all day for a tiny portion of a meal. You heard Abel. New Emile is sitting on the one thing that could eliminate disease for an entire generation, and the Elite hoard it."

"They gave you some, if you recall."

"And didn't you say that Kaius was scolded for giving it away? Something like the haelen should be a universal right."

Gideon raised his hands. "I don't disagree with you, but this is their culture, their way of life. It does us no good to force our beliefs on to them. Besides, half of our traditions need to go away." His eyes flicked toward Abel involuntarily.

New Emile might welcome Abel, Gideon thought, *but at what cost? Would he be shunned because he was not born here and become Marokai? Would he be marked?*

Gideon paused for a moment before speaking again, his voice quiet and thoughtful. "I'll talk to Alistair in the morning. If we can bring one of the ancient texts back to Sojen

Micah, then we will come away from this trip with more than just bugs in our hair and the knowledge that someone else exists on this planet."

"He'll say no." Jacob sat down next to Isaiah and put his head against the wall. "These people will follow that angry lady anywhere, regardless of how wrong she is."

CHAPTER EIGHTEEN

WITH A SLIGHT CHILL IN THE AIR, THE SUN SAT LOW AND CAST long shadows over the vast expanse of the lake. Russant and his group of six scouts had journeyed past the body of water, a boundary previously undiscovered. They were now in a forest, a strange mix of green and yellow trees that rose higher and higher the further they went.

The soft crunch of undergrowth underfoot coupled with rustling leaves marked their passage. Russant, who had never been good at being a scout, refused to be at the forefront. He took in every detail, ever aware of the dangers that might show themselves. Why Liorah thought it was a good idea that he should be the one to locate the Zhanshi — this mysterious third tribe — was obscure. He was no emissary, no warrior. He built homes, for all the Mother's sake.

Behind and in front of him, his men trudged on, each lost in their own thoughts. Unlike him, they were nimble, aware, and capable. And unlike him, too, they were more physically fit for this journey. What had Liorah been thinking?

A menacing growl suddenly broke the silence. The scouts froze, and Russant held his breath as he scanned the trees for the source of the sound. His stomach twisted at the unknown.

From the dense underbrush between two large trees, a

creature emerged. It was large, about the size of a man, and its form was at once foreign and terrifying. It had six legs, four of which were in a position to pounce, its body low to the ground. Muscles rippled beneath thick, matted yellow fur, its eyes hungry for a kill. In many ways, it was much like the notorious rychat of the rainforest, a legend told by those who had traveled with Mother Miriam and passed down from generation to generation.

With another roar, the creature lunged. One of Russant's men, too slow to react, was taken down with a swift strike of the creature's claws. His screams echoed through the forest, cut short as the creature's jaws clamped down. Russant watched in horror, transfixed, as the animal tore away chunks of flesh. In all his thirty-six years, he had never witnessed something so disgusting, so violent, so vile. Adrenaline surged through his veins as the remaining men backed away.

With lance in hand, Russant set his feet, unable to charge and unable to flee. In a harrowing second, the beast turned its attention towards them as if sensing some challenge. It narrowed its gaze at Russant and tensed its body to prepare for another strike.

Russant took a deep breath in and stepped forward, his lance poised to strike but heavy in his hands. Time seemed to slow as the beast turned away from its kill and closed in, its maw opened wide, blood covering its jowls. A roar echoed in the forest and in Russant's ears as the world narrowed to just him and approaching death.

Chaos erupted.

With a guttural roar of his own, Russant launched himself forward and thrust his lance with all the might he could muster. The tip met resistance as it plunged into the creature's thick hide. A shocked, pained snarl echoed from the beast as it reared back from the unexpected injury. Its claws flailed in a wild, uncoordinated manner while its eyes, once filled with a predator's confidence, now held a glimmer of fear and confusion.

Russant staggered back and joined his men. Sweat trickled down his face, mixing with the dirt and grime of the day's exertion. The scouts now beside him gasped in shock and relief as they held lances of their own. Any celebration, however, was cut quickly short as the wounded creature recovered from its surprise.

With a blood-curdling roar, the beast lunged forward again, its claws reaching out towards Russant. This time, the scout leader barely had time to brace himself. The creature was too close, too fast. Massive claws swung towards Russant, fueled by both rage and pain.

As the world once more moved in slow motion, Russant felt a sense of clarity. He saw each ripple of muscle under the creature's fur, saw the lethal glint in its eyes, and more importantly, he saw his window of opportunity. At the last moment, clarity dawned and he dove aside. He thrust his lance again, aiming for the creature's exposed flank. With a harsh squelch, the weapon found its mark, evoking a chilling roar. Its legs slipped on the undergrowth as it tried to shake off the attacker.

Russant held on, his hands wrapped around the lance. In the corner of his eye, he saw his fellow scouts, plainly terrified.

Just as he was about to drive the lance deeper into the creature, he felt a sudden jolt. With one last desperate struggle, the beast twisted its body and took another swipe at Russant. His world spun as he was flung away, nearly losing the grip on his lance. He crashed into the undergrowth, his vision swimming. Roars from the beast coupled with shouts of his men sounded distorted, muted. He struggled to his feet, the world around him now a blur of green and yellow and brown.

As he regained his footing, Russant's eyes focused on the scene in front of him. The creature was on the ground, writhing, but not defeated. With a speed that belied its size and injuries, the beast launched itself towards Russant once again. Fear surged, but within all that, there was a flicker of resolve.

This would not be his end. This was not his road to Eldorado.

Summoning his strength, Russant gripped his lance tighter. His senses heightened, he saw the beast's eyes, noted its muscles, and was keenly away of the sharp, gleaming teeth aimed to tear him apart. Instinct took over and Russant pivoted, using his momentum to thrust his lance upwards. The spear's tip pierced the underbelly of the leaping beast. A surprised and pained roar echoed in the forest as the creature was impaled mid-air. The force of the attack carried it forward, and Russant fell back, the lance still gripped tightly in his hands and the beast skewered at the end. It thrashed wildly, a grotesque spectacle of death throes.

In moments, the creature's movements stilled, its life draining away until it was nothing more than a dead weight at the end of Russant's weapon. The deafening silence that followed was broken only by the heavy panting of the scouts who stood nearby.

With great effort, Russant pushed the beast off his lance and stood. He trembled with the aftereffects of adrenaline as his team stared at him wide-eyed.

It would have been nice if one of them had helped.

AS TWILIGHT gave way to darkness, the scouts gathered solemnly around a fire. The embers cast an eerie, flickering glow on their grim faces. As tradition dictated, they had left their fallen comrade on the forest floor to return to nature, while they were now left to grapple with the harsh reality of his passing.

They ate their meal in silence—the meat of the creature that had brought them their first loss. It was a quiet acknowledgment of victory, a bittersweet feast they shared under the watchful eyes of the forest. Eyes darted around constantly, ears attuned to the next threat. The sooner they were out of the forest, the better. As the fire crackled and popped, Russant silently cursed Liorah for sending them on this Discovery.

Antony, a scout who had worked with Russant for years, broke the silence. "I think we should go back," he said with a waver in his voice.

The others nodded, and in their eyes Russant saw the same fear and uncertainty he felt. As he chewed on a piece of the meat, his gaze fixated on the dancing flames. He wanted to agree, but to return now would be wrong. A man had just passed into shadow because of their quest—Liorah's quest—to find the Zhanshi.

"No," Russant said after a moment. "We have our orders. We won't return until we've fulfilled Liorah's wishes." He wanted to add how much he disagreed with her, but it wasn't his place to disparage the One Voice. Not here among these men.

"If she wants to find this mythical tribe, she can come out here herself."

"No. Not now." Russant looked up from the fire and glared at Antony. "We lost one man, Oren. If we won't do it for Liorah, then we'll do it for him. Is that understood?"

His words were met with a groan of dissent. Russant understood their fear, shared it even, but they had a duty, and he wouldn't allow them to fail no matter how ridiculous, how brash, the charge had been. So what if some hairy kid said there was another tribe out there? So what if they were more advanced? If they were a threat, they could better spend their time preparing a defense at home. His mind had already come up with a few ways to reinforce the wall around New Emile.

As the night stretched on, the scouts fell into a disturbed silence. They finished their meal of meat, but Russant felt something odd. Gradually, the world around him warped. Trees swayed without wind, and shadows danced of their own accord. Sounds became distorted, echoing unnaturally through the forest. It wasn't just him. Russant saw the expression on the scouts' faces turn from fear to confusion then to wonder as whatever they had just consumed took hold.

One by one, the men slumped onto the forest floor. Russant fought against the onslaught of strange visions, but eventually his mind spiraled into a world of surreal dreams. Reality slipped away and, like his men, he too collapsed to the ground. The world faded into a swirl of colors and sounds. As he slipped into unconsciousness, his last thought was a silent questioned aimed at the woman who sent them here on a mission that would help no one.

Why?

AFTER A disoriented awakening, the scouts, still hazy from the night's hallucinations, quickly disposed of any meat they'd cut from the animal that had attacked them the day prior. They would find other food. As they continued their journey, Russant's head pounded and his vision still swam from whatever had been in the meat, but he had a labor to perform. Unlike the days and weeks before, he decided to take the lead, bolstered by his unexpected courage the day before.

Ahead of them, the terrain thankfully shifted, giving way to a scene that would have been picturesque had their circumstances been different. Three rivers, narrow but furious, cut their paths through the wilderness. They churned and roared, their foamy, white crests standing in stark contrast to the calm, untouched nature that surrounded them.

The rivers, though separate, were close together, each one's roar adding to the cacophony of the others. In the scouts' weakened state, it seemed like an insurmountable obstacle.

Russant squinted at the rivers, strategizing. "We go one by one," he decided, his voice strained over the deafening rush of the water.

Russant went first to test the waters. He took a rope, tied securely around his waist, and plunged in, his body reacting as the cold water engulfed him. The current was relentless, tugging and pulling, but he fought against it, step by step. If he slipped or otherwise lost his grip on the riverbed, his scouts would pull him back. After what felt like an eternity, Russant emerged on the other side, drenched, cold, and gasping. But he'd made it, and he tied the rope on a nearby tree to help the others.

Emboldened, the others followed, battling the watery fury one by one. They slipped and stumbled, but each time, they caught themselves, guided by shouted instructions from the other side. By the time they had all crossed the third river, they were exhausted. Their bodies ached and their spirits dampened. At least they were alive.

DAYS OF difficult travel passed in a hazy, fatigue-ridden blur. Having navigated the treacherous rivers, Russant and his remaining men found themselves facing yet another obstacle—a vast, bug-ridden swamp that stretched as far as the eye could see. It was as if Tishbe couldn't give them a break, something easier to cross like the vast plain of nothingness that was Wastelands. But no, this part of the world was a patchwork of various hells.

The air became thick with an unhealthy humidity that clung to their skin and filled their lungs. Each breath became a struggle. Tall, decaying trees sprouted from murky water, their gnarled branches reaching out like skeletal fingers. Russant knew immediately that this had to be a breeding ground for parasites and disease, but there didn't seem to be any other option. He considered the mitters, the bugs of New Emile—the reason for shaving all hair off their bodies—and silently wondered if the same would be found here.

As they trudged through the mire, swarms of insects emerged, their buzzing a constant, maddening drone in their ears. They bit through clothing and injected a venom that sent waves of nausea and fever through the men. The farther they trudged on through the swamp, the deeper their steps sunk into the mucky landscape, the more their bodies weakened. They swatted away the relentless bugs, but it was futile. Each bite, each attack, took its toll.

A scout named Corin fell first. His usually ruddy face turned pale as his body writhed in a fever-induced agony. Despite Russant's best efforts, nothing could be done but watch as Corin succumbed to the swamp's poisonous kiss.

Now there were five.

Once more, Russant's heart ached with the heaviness of loss, the bitter pill of another life taken too soon. He looked back, a part of him longing to retrace their steps, to retreat from this alien world that seemed hell-bent on their destruction. But the fear of Liorah's wrath if they did not accomplish the mission was stronger. The things she could do to a person were unimaginable, and he'd seen firsthand how her anger had sent strong men to the Hollows, crying.

Arguments flared up again, desperate voices whispering in the darkness about the wisdom of turning back. But Russant held firm. "We're not turning back. We owe it to Corin."

"We owe it to Oren, too," Antony shot back. "If another falls, you'll owe to them. And then another. We're building a debt here you can't repay."

"Enough!" Russant slapped the man across the face with the backside of a gloved hand and the five weary travelers moved on.

As darkness took a stronger hold on the swamp, a slight rustle reverberated through the stagnant air. The sound gradually drifted towards them from the gloom. The men paused. They'd already faced a fierce beast and been tormented by poisonous insects, but this was a sound that hinted at an entirely different danger. The world was not done throwing daggers at them. Eyes, wide with apprehension, searched the murk. It took a moment before they glimpsed the horror that the swamp belched forth.

Hulking shapes the size of a small man crawled out from the rotting undergrowth, glistening with a black sheen in the dim glow of the dying day. One. Two. Five of them. Their form resembled the harmless creatures the children of New Emile played with, but any sense of familiarity ended there. Their protective outer shells were revolting, pieces of what might have been armor that gave off a ghastly reflection of the pale light. Abruptly, they tightened their bodies and morphed into compact spheres. Then, with a horrifying hiss, they propelled themselves at the men.

Russant and his scouts, surprised, barely had time to form a thought, let alone act. These Tishbian nightmares were a jumble of hard shells and rapid motion, clashing with the humans with remarkable strength, causing them to fall into the slimy ooze. Amidst the pandemonium, they transformed again. They unfurled, bodies writhing and twisting as if unhinging. Mouths split open, dividing their faces into four distinct parts with multiple razor-sharp tendrils hanging down. They opened wide to become a black abyss, waiting to shred anything.

An ominous hiss echoed through the clammy air. The sound clawed at a nearby scout's senses with terror. Without further warning, a stream of viscous fluid shot forth, slicing the space between predator and prey, a man named Fenton. It struck him with unerring accuracy.

Fenton's reaction was immediate. His body seized. His muscles locked in place as if he'd been turned to stone. His face, previously a mask of horror, became a vacant canvas, eyes glazed over in stunned surprise. Whatever the fluid contained, it was swift, and the others could only look on, helpless as their comrade was transformed into a living statue before their very eyes.

Without wasting a moment, one creature advanced with a predatory speed that was at odds with its grotesque form. It moved toward the immobilized Fenton, the gaping maw opening wider. Within seconds, the monster claimed their friend. Mercifully, Fenton's paralysis prevented cries of terror and despair. The creature swiftly enveloped the man entirely, and swallowed the last remnants of his existence whole.

"Run!" Russant's voice echoed through the swamp and cut through the chaos. He thrust a hand out, shoving Antony, the closest scout, with a force that sent the man stumbling towards the relative safety of the trees. "Get to cover! Move! Move! Move!"

The men ran, each breath a harsh gasp, the moist swamp air filling their lungs as they sprinted. Behind them, a haunting chorus of hisses and the rumbling thunder of the monstrous creatures filled the night. They zig-zagged desperately through the murky swamp terrain finally diving into the underbrush, hoping the rotting vegetation would offer some cover from the frenzied assault.

Russant was the last to seek cover, casting a final glance over his shoulder at the scene of his fallen man. Gritting his teeth, he plunged into the underbrush, joining his remaining scouts.

Four remained now, and they yet to find any sign of a third tribe.

Only death.

CHAPTER NINETEEN

THERE WAS NO KNOCK AT THE DOOR TO WAKE GIDEON. Instead, four large men, all armed with crossbows and swords in sheathes on their backs, stormed into the dwelling and grabbed Gideon from his bed. Within seconds, the future Col'kasid Keeper of the Text was bound hand to foot, a gag shoved into his mouth. With no tenderness, he was whisked away into the pre-dawn air. As Gideon was pulled through the door, he quickly glanced back. Jacob and Isaiah were not with him, and Abel was missing once more. Gideon had been abandoned in the middle of the night.

The taste of the rough-hewn cloth gag dominated Gideon's senses, its musky tang mixing with the saliva in his mouth. As his captors pulled him along through the dark streets, his disoriented mind attempted to figure out where he was. Each building looked the same, every turn more confusing.

Finally, something that looked familiar appeared in his periphery—the yellow leaves of the tree growing out of the haelen pool. He was near the Chambers, which could only mean that Liorah had learned something and was not pleased. Before entering the building, however, his captors turned right. Near the base of a wall of a nearby structure, Gideon saw a gap about three feet wide. With no mercy, they shoved him into the hole, and he fell several feet, landing on his side with a crunch. The gag in his mouth fell away and immediately he turned his face back to the hole and screamed.

"Hey! Let me out here!"

In response, there was a loud grating sound as the hole was covered, plunging the room into darkness. It would do him no good to continue yelling.

He tried to look around. A small crack above him let in the tiniest amount of light, and after a while, his eyes adjusted. From what he could tell, he was in a small room with a dirt floor, a dank, cold air filling the space. The smell of dust and something sour assaulted his senses.

Where was he, and where were the others? As if in response to his internal confusion, a dull echo of movement disrupted the silence of the room. Squinting in the low light, Gideon noticed two familiar figures huddled in the corner. Jacob and Isaiah.

Through the gloom, Gideon saw that they, too, were bound, their usually expressive eyes now clouded with fear and confusion. Unlike him, however, they appeared to have their sandals on their feet. An uncomfortable realization hit Gideon as they both shifted forward to meet their leader: they had gone back to the Library in the middle of the night.

"What happened?" Gideon asked. He was furious that they didn't wait until he'd talked to Alistair, but he couldn't fault their initiative.

Isaiah kept his voice low. "We almost had two of the ancient texts. We waited until the sentinel had to relieve himself again and then slipped in through the door."

"It wasn't secured? I thought Alistair was going to make sure that didn't happen again."

"No. We both thought that was odd, but didn't question it."

"Now that I think about it," Jacob said, "it was probably a trap."

Gideon looked away briefly. "You think?"

"We each grabbed what we thought we could put in our satchels and then made for the door." Jacob shrugged. "A minute in, a minute out. That's all we needed."

"The sentinel was back with three more men," Isaiah added. "The next thing we knew, we were shoved into this hole."

"Where are we, anyway?" Jacob asked. "I didn't see much on the way here."

"Next to the Chambers." Gideon looked back up at the crack in the low ceiling, its soft light gradually brightening as the sun rose. "I saw that tree before they shoved me in here." He looked back down. "Where's Abel?"

Jacob and Isaiah looked at each other. "He was asleep like you when we left. You think they took him, too?"

"He's not here. Maybe he went off to meet Luca." Gideon wrestled with the bounds on his hands. "Are any of your ropes loose?"

"No," Isaiah said dejectedly. "We've been trying everything to get them off."

"Sorry about this, Gideon." Jacob lowered his head. "We thought we were doing the right thing."

"Apologize later. Right now, we need to figure out how to get out of this mess and back to Rephidim. The Assembly — and Sojen Micah — needs to know what New Emile has."

"And what's that?" Isaiah grunted as he struggled again to get free. "A few of the texts of the Ancients and a power-hungry woman in charge? A miracle water they won't share?"

"We don't know what else they have. You heard about how they move the stones from the quarry."

"Something about using sound. Remember the noise we heard when we first arrived that frightened the quvianaq?"

Gideon nodded. "If they figured out how to do that, what else can they do? There may be more that they're not sharing with us."

"What do you mean?"

"I get the feeling that Liorah sends scouts on her Discovery missions to see what else she can take. She may say New Emile needs nothing from the Col'kasid, but I don't know about that."

"What else could she want? New Emile seems to have it all."

Gideon sighed. "All is never enough for some people."

AS THE cold floor seeped into their bones, hours stretched on, each one seeming longer than the last. Silence greeting their shouts for explanation or even just acknowledgment. Food, water, and information were all equally absent.

The hours trickled into a stream of relentless uncertainty, and the magnitude of their situation weighed heavily on them. Gideon couldn't help but feel responsible for their situation; his incessant need for knowledge and disregard for the New Emilian culture had resulted in their predicament. Liorah, Alistair, Josiah and even Kaius remained unseen and unheard, adding a layer of psychological torment to their physical confinement. The oppressive silence was now oppressive in its own right. With no human contact or comfort to be found, the stillness spoke volumes.

The light coming in through the crack in the ceiling faded as the day wore on. It would be nightfall soon, and still there had been no sign anyone was coming for them. Were they expected to die in this prison, starved to death with their hands and feet bound? Is this how Liorah dealt with those who disobeyed? According to Kaius, people were exiled to the Hollows. This was different. Gideon thought he should have known something was wrong when he first spotted the Hollows before ever entering the city. No one who had any inkling of mercy would allow such depravity to exist.

As Gideon's thoughts spiraled further into the dark chasm of despair, a sudden clatter outside their subterranean prison jolted him. The unmistakable sound of footsteps crunched on the dirt street outside the hole he'd been shoved through. A fleeting shadow briefly blocked the thin shaft of light.

A grinding sound resonated through the room as the stone cover of the hole was scraped away, blinding them momentarily with the stark contrast of the setting sun's light against the darkness they had grown accustomed to. It took a moment for Gideon's eyes to adjust and take in the figure looming over the hole.

There was no mistaking the silhouette that gradually took form in the fading light. Josiah peered down at them from the hole's opening. His face was a grim mask, devoid of any trace of compassion or understanding. The dread that had been an undercurrent in their hours-long wait surged like a torrent within Gideon. Fear wove its tendrils around his heart. Josiah looked them over, his eyes lingering on each captive.

"Well, well," Josiah's voice echoed, a chilled dagger in the engulfing silence. The corners of his lips curled up. "Looks like you have some questions to answer."

Saying nothing more, he pushed the stone cover back into place, snuffing out the sunlight once more and casting them back into darkness. Josiah's words hung in the air as the crunch of his footsteps faded away. However the man intended to get answers from the Col'kasid, it wouldn't be pleasant. The promise of torture now mixed with all the questions they had.

ABEL PUSHED past Diego and Elena, who had been sitting around a small fire in the Hollows. He rushed to meet Luca who ran to meet them.

"Did you hear anything?" Abel demanded. His breath came in ragged gasps. "Where are they?"

Luca paused, bending forward to rest his hands on his knees. His face was flushed, his chest rising and falling heavily as he gulped in air after his lengthy run. After a moment, he straightened, meeting Abel's gaze. "Liorah has them locked up."

The words hit Abel like a punch. "Locked up? Why?" The dread in his voice was unmistakable.

"From what I heard," Luca explained, his voice firm despite his visible fatigue, "Jacob and Isaiah attempted to steal some texts from the Library. Gideon was taken just before morning and thrown in a cell with them as a conspirator."

A wave of confusion washed over Abel. "Cell?" he echoed, perplexed. His life in Rephidim hadn't exposed him to any such form of punishment. Disobedience there was met with public humiliation or exile, as he knew all too well. The concept of a prison cell was foreign. The endless expanse of the Tishbe desert was prison enough.

"It's a room near the Chambers, dug into the ground," Luca said, his voice adopting an eerily calm tone. "It's not used often, but there's no way out except the hole that the sentinels shove prisoners through."

"They aren't prisoners." The words left a sour taste in Abel's mouth. "They're ambassadors from Rephidim and are to be treated with respect."

"Respect is earned," Luca shot back, his gaze hardening. He straightened, his entire demeanor shifting from exhaustion to irritation. "We didn't disrespect your laws when we visited Rephidim, and we would expect the same from you."

Taken aback by Luca's impassioned defense of Liorah's actions, Abel recoiled. The bitter taste of disillusionment seeped into his mouth. He couldn't afford to succumb to despair. Gideon, Jacob, and Isaiah needed his help. They were his fellow Col'kasid, and even though his own people had cast him out, he wouldn't let friends suffer. If he had any allies left in the world, these three were it. Abel would do everything in his power to help them.

Not that he had much power to begin with.

"Take me to Kaius."

"Why?" Luca held his hands out. "He can't do anything. He may have been the leader of our Discovery mission, but that was it. He has no more power with the council than I do."

Abel fidgeted. "Maybe he can get me in to see Liorah. He did it when we returned from your Discovery."

Luca snickered. "A lot of good that will do. I'm telling you right now, if you step foot in the Chambers, you'll be arrested. There's a warrant out for you."

"Me?" Abel's eyes opened wide. "What did I do?"

"You're Col'kasid, exiled or not. You have a target on your back."

Abel turned back to where Diego and Elena were looking on with both interest and fright. He sat down across from the fire and put his head in his hands. He'd spent most of his time back in New Emile with Luca's siblings, learning all he could about life in the Hollows. "What am I supposed to do, then? Leave?"

"You're safe here," Elena said. She put a hand on Abel's

shoulder. "Apart from Luca and his humanitarian visits, the sentinels rarely venture into the Hollows. They know what will happen to them."

"Why are you allowed, then?" Abel directed his question at Luca. "You're a sentinel. What makes you special?"

"The Marokai know I have family here who I haven't abandoned. These people you see—" Luca waved his arms around "—their birth families ignored them the moment they were selected for the lottery. There isn't any good will toward those within the walls."

Elena gave a weak smile. "If you ever wanted to belong to a group of misfits, welcome." She pointed to her forehead. "We can get you one of these marks, if you want."

Abel said nothing for a moment. He still had to get Gideon and the other two out. They could run back to Rephidim and warn the Col'kasid that no good could come with interacting with the New Emilians.

But how could he do it without getting caught?

As he sat by the fire, his mind raced with ideas. It was possible he could sneak into New Emile at night, but that would be too risky. Luca had said there was one way into the pit and one way out. His only other option was to reason with Liorah, but she seemed set on punishing the three ambassadors. She wouldn't have arrested them otherwise. Of the two options, though, only a meeting with Liorah seemed to have the slightest chance of working.

"I need to see Kaius," Abel said finally. "I know you think it's a bad idea, but I have no other choice."

"You could leave with us," Elena said softly.

"Leave? Leave where? Your home is here in New Emile and you'd be abandoning your brother."

"We don't plan on sticking around," Diego said. "We had thought the only thing we could do was get rid of Liorah, but that's proving harder than we thought. Trust me when I say it's time we go on a Discovery ourselves and find a new place to live. If not your home of Rephidim, we'll make our own."

Abel shook his head vigorously. "I can't leave Gideon or the others behind. I'm sorry, but I feel responsible for what's happened to them."

"Why?" Luca's face reflected confusion. "You're risking your life for people who exiled you."

"Gideon was not allowed to cast his stone toward my exile." Abel took a deep breath. "And Jacob and Isaiah are on his side of things. There may be rules within the Col'kasid, but no one said they were good rules and not everyone agrees with them."

Luca appeared to consider Abel's words. After a few moments, he sighed. "Fine. But you're not going alone. I'll get you a meeting with Kaius, but understand if the sentinels come, I won't be able to protect you."

Abel stood up, feeling hopeful for the first time since he'd heard about Gideon's capture. "Thank you, Luca. I don't know if this will work, but I have to try. There's more at stake than you realize."

AMID THE raw wilderness, away from the prying eyes of the Hollows and the ominous presence of the moor, Luca had set up a covert rendezvous with Kaius and promptly left. Underneath the orange-tinted sky of an impending twilight, they stood close. "Of all the ideas I've heard before," Kaius began, his voice stern, "this is the stupidest. I should arrest you myself."

Abel, eyes wide, tried to maintain his composure. "I've had no ideas," he quickly countered. His palms were clammy. "Can you at least ask her for an audience?" he pleaded, his words barely above a whisper. He attempted to inject a note of levity. "The only thing she can say is no, right?"

Kaius scoffed, his laughter a sharp, bitter sound that left Abel feeling cold. "You misunderstand," he corrected him gravely. "She can say more than no. She can say whatever she wants, and as the One Voice, no one will argue differently. If she wants your head on a pike, that's where it will be."

Abel swallowed uncomfortably. He remembered his past encounter with Liorah. That memory filled him with apprehension, but he couldn't deny that a sense of duty tempered it. Gideon had always stood by him, and now it was time for Abel to return the favor.

He rallied whatever courage he had left. "Just get me in there," he said, albeit with a little less confidence than he had intended.

"Why don't you go back to the Hollows?" Kaius proposed, almost casually. "I'm sure they will release Gideon and the other two soon. Maybe they'll just exile them with a mark. Then you four can pack your satchels and leave."

Abel fixed him with a steely gaze. "You're not sure, or you wouldn't be standing here talking to me."

His words must have hit their mark. Kaius grunted, a look of dread clouding his features. Abel knew he was not wrong, and he knew Kaius was acutely aware of the looming danger. If Gideon was not freed from his confinement soon, many things could go sideways. And when Elder Levi found out about his son's fate, there was no telling what would happen then. Would the Col'kasid wage war on New Emile, on the home of Luca and his new friends? Or would Levi simply turn his back on family and move on?

Abel guessed it would be war, something that had never happened before.

Reluctantly, Kaius conceded. "Give me a few hours," he

said. "If I can get you an audience — and that's a big if — you'll be on your own." The caveat was obvious.

Abel nodded. "Thank you." A small flicker of hope kindled within him.

As Kaius left, Abel turned his gaze toward the distant horizon, where a sea of fiery colors was cast by the setting sun. His mind wandered back to the tumultuous events of the past few cycles of the Short Moon, from his exile to near death, rescue, and new found love. It was a winding road that had brought him to this pivotal point.

He had no choice, really. He would face whatever came next.

He prayed Luca would stay with him through it all.

CHAPTER TWENTY

It took three days for Kaius to get Abel an audience. Three days of hell, of sleepless nights and listening in on the plans of the Marokai. Now, Liorah, the most high, the One Voice, holder of the vials of haelen, and granddaughter of the Great Mother Miriam, was, as expected, furious. She looked at Abel across the table, her eyes burning holes into the remaining Col'kasid visitor.

"As much as you'd like to believe otherwise," she said, "we don't have many laws in New Emile. The most important, however, is that what comes from the mouth of the One Voice *is* the law." She slammed her fist on the table for emphasis. "I am that One Voice, and I forbade Gideon and the others from stepping foot into the Library. Your friends have disrespected the New Emile Chambers and me."

Abel shifted uncomfortably. Josiah, commander of the sentinels, sat to his right, picking at his fingernails, while Alistair sat in a corner, his head bowed. He'd allowed the Col'kasid to enter the Library through negligence, and for that, Liorah was none too pleased. Roland the Kept was naturally by Liorah's side, befitting his name and his position. And while Kaius had miraculously secured this meeting, his presence was not welcome. No one else was, either. It was just a small weak boy against an all-powerful ruler.

"Liorah," Abel said weakly, "the texts of the Ancients have guided the Col'kasid way of life since Sojen Micah first spotted Rephidim from a distance. Please do not fault Gideon, who is the to be the future leader of the Col'kasid, for wanting nothing more than to examine what he sees as foundational to their way of life."

"To *your* way of life, you mean."

Liorah's correction did not sit well with Abel. "No. Not to mine. I am no more Col'kasid than I am New Emilian. I was exiled from that life."

"And yet here you sit, pleading mercy for the very people who wronged you. I don't understand."

Abel didn't know how best to explain this. He was uncomfortable speaking of his amorous preferences to anyone, let alone the leader of a colony so vastly different from the one he'd grown up with. "I am not...like others," Abel started. It sounded foolish, but he continued. "And for that, I was cast out of Rephidim. It was Gideon who stood up for me in the Assembly that decided my fate, and he did so against the most powerful man in Rephidim, his father. I owe him a debt I cannot repay."

"You like men," Liorah said matter-of-factly. "That's no different than many people, Roland here included. I cannot see why it would matter to the Col'kasid who you love."

"It is their way." Abel could not add much more to that statement.

"And is it also their way to disobey the laws of those appointed over them or to thumb their noses at another's culture?"

"No, Liorah. It is not, although they have never encountered another culture before."

"Then why should I show mercy to Gideon? I might as well show mercy toward anyone who breaks the law or disrespects my position." Liorah stared for a moment before continuing. "And what then? Tell me. Where would leadership be if it cannot round up the wicked?"

Abel looked down. "I do not know."

"In the pit with Gideon. That is where. A lawless society cannot stand—"

"But Liorah—"

"Do *not* interrupt me, Abel of the Col'kasid!" Liorah's nostrils flared. "You were once a guest, and now you are a threat to our existence."

"I am not Col'kasid."

"Silence! I will not have you speak out of turn. I have not asked you a question, nor have I given you permission to grovel any further. I will not release—"

"The Col'kasid will march on New Emile," Abel burst out. It was the last thing he intended to say, but what other argument could he use?

Josiah shifted in his seat, pushing his shoulders back as he stopped inspecting his nails. "What do you mean, march?" he asked. "Is that a threat?"

Silence engulfed the room, and even the normally detached Roland looked anxious. The four New Emilians glared at the exile who slowly slid back into his chair.

"No. Not a threat," Abel said, swallowing hard. "A prediction. If Gideon and the others aren't set free, Elder Levi will see it as an act of war. The Col'kasid will come for them."

"War?" Josiah scoffed. "What would your Col'kasid know about war?"

Liorah sat back in her chair, her eyes narrowing as she studied Abel. A moment of silence passed before she nodded at Josiah. "Bring him in," she ordered.

Josiah pushed his chair back and left the room. As the silence dragged on, Abel listened to his stomach groan with unease. This conversation had gone wrong, and quickly.

A few uncomfortable moments later, Josiah returned with Gideon. The future Col'kasid Keeper of the Text was a pitiful sight, the very image of torment. His clothes were ripped and dirtied, hanging off his frame like ragged curtains. His face was no better, smeared with grime, sweat, and blood, the telltale signs of struggle.

The lines of suffering etched onto Gideon's features were stark in the chamber's light. Deep, violet shadows underscored his eyes, suggesting a few sleepless nights, while a thin trail of dried blood stuck to the corner of his mouth. Yet, for all the physical damage, it was the raw, unbroken fire in Gideon's eyes that was the most disconcerting.

Abel felt a tight knot in his stomach as he took in the sight of his friend. Disbelief and horror washed over him in waves. He clenched his hands into fists, nails digging into his palm, as if trying to hold on to the pain, to anchor himself amidst the storm of guilt and regret brewing within him.

"Sit," Liorah commanded, pointing at the empty chair next to Abel. "We must...negotiate."

"I'd rather stand." Gideon spat on the floor, eliciting a gasp from Roland the Kept.

Liorah stood, knocking her chair over. "You disgust me." Her voice was measured, yet spoken through gritted teeth. "The Col'kasid disgusts me. You are animals, and far lower on the steps of life than the Marokai. To come in here, to my home and mock my rules and try to take what is rightfully mine—it astounds me that someone like you could ever be considered a leader."

"Those texts belong to everyone." Gideon's voice sounded parched, yet he still spoke with authority. "What we could learn from them is unknowable and could very well make all our lives easier. You might even discover ways to defend against the Zhanshi should the day come. You cannot hoard was is not yours."

"Everything in New Emile is mine!" Liorah took three long steps toward Gideon until she was within inches of him. She scrutinized his features before finally speaking. "And to think," she said in a lower tone, "I once thought of bedding you."

Liorah spun away from Gideon and looked at Abel. "Tell me. What is this man's life worth to you?"

Abel swallowed. *Worth?* "I— They— They do not deserve what you have done to them."

"I didn't ask you that." Liorah stepped closer to Abel. "I asked what his life is worth to you."

Thoughts of war swirled in Abel's mind. He'd never witnessed it himself—no one had—but through stories told at Assembly meetings and tales of old told by the original settlers of Rephidim, he had a good idea that it would be just as horrific as what had happened in the temple at Manoach when the Zhanshi murdered hundreds of tired and sick settlers. But how could he answer this question?

"If it means avoiding war," Abel said finally, his voice resolute despite the trembling in his hands, "then his life is worth mine."

Liorah's reaction was a sound deep in her chest, a low, rumbling chuckle that sent an unpleasant shiver down Abel's spine. Her lips curled into a malicious smile. "*Your* life? Your life is worth less than the spit on the floor over there."

She spun around abruptly. "Josiah, take both of these wastes of flesh away. Put them in the hold."

In response, Josiah clapped his hands once, a sharp, echoing sound that punctuated Liorah's command. Two men, who until now had been guarding the door to the chamber outside, entered. Their faces were stoic, uncaring as they roughly grabbed Abel. A firm grip on his arm cut his protest off. Any resistance would be futile. Simultaneously, Josiah took hold of Gideon, who despite his condition, still held an air of defiance.

As they were quickly ushered out, the chamber door closing behind them with a disheartening finality, Abel heard a scream. It was Liorah's voice, echoing with fury and frustration, punctuated by the sharp sound of something thrown against a wall.

"Get Kaius in here! Now!"

LUCA STOOD with Diego and Elena in the Hollows. It was morning again, two days after Liorah had Abel thrown in the hold with Gideon, Jacob, and Isaiah. The hold, Luca knew, was more permanent than the pit in which they were first thrown. That meant there would be no release, no chance that the Col'kasid could return to Rephidim. It was a final destination for those were unlucky enough to be exiled to the Hollows.

They were outside their sleeping hut, the adobe walls crumbling over loose sticks. Breakfast involved some grain Luca had brought with him that morning. He was supposed to be in formation in an hour, but with all that was going on with Abel—and how it had mentally affected him—he knew he wouldn't make it.

He may never be allowed to return to the sentinels again after setting up the meeting that ended with Abel in the hold. Already he felt like an outlaw on the run, and Kaius, his protector at times, was missing.

Elena took a bite of food, made a face, then swallowed before speaking again. "She put them in the hold? They'd be more secure in the pit by the Chambers."

Luca studied his sister for a moment. "What do you

mean? The hold is permanent. The sentinels have used it several times for the more violent offenders."

"Or those Liorah wants to watch die slowly," Diego added. "Don't play dumb."

"Fine. Those, too. But why do you say it's not secure?"

Diego shot a glance at his sister and gave the slightest shake of his head. Luca caught it.

"What aren't you telling me?" Luca asked. He stared at Elena before turning his attention to Diego. "Have you been in the hold? Do you even know where it is?"

Elena put her bowl of grain down and wiped her mouth. "Are you sure Liorah isn't just trying to scare the Col'kasid?"

"You're not answering me."

"She could be sending a message, you know — don't disobey me again and I'll let you leave. That sort of thing." Elena shrugged. "It's what I would do if I was the One Voice."

"Why are you avoiding my question? What aren't you telling me?"

Diego poked at his bowl of grain, then set it down. He darted his eyes around. "Not here," he said, his voice lower. "There are ears who listen for mouths to feed."

Luca understood that. The Hollows was not entirely devoid of anyone loyal to Liorah or the Elite. There were little ears that listened to everything, and because some of them had once had labors in the Chambers and could probably be turned, secrets should be protected.

The three siblings left the Hollows and walked along the perimeter of the moor. By now, his sentinel comrades were lining up for roll call. He would not be with them, and that was okay. Recent happenings had given him a bad feeling, and it was liberating to walk away from his position. Nico and Raphael would be furious, but no matter how much he tried to understand the politics and authoritarian rule of New

Emile, the farther he wanted to run. He would deal with that problem later.

And where had Kaius gone?

Diego and Elena came to a halt near the hill where the road that had led them to Rephidim reached its crest. It was as safe as any.

"Promise me you won't go back," Diego said. He poked his brother in the chest. "You belong with us."

Luca glanced over at the decrepit buildings in the distance. Before he could respond, Elena cut in.

"Brother, we know you. Your loyalty is not to Liorah, nor is it to your leader, Kaius. When our parents passed into shadow, you made sure we were fed. When Josiah came to take Diego and me to the Hollows, you broke down and cried. Even now, you look after us. You are a family man, not a warrior." She stepped a little closer and waved her arms toward the Wastelands. "Look out there. There's more than enough room for us, and more than enough places we can go—as a family—where we can't be found. You and Abel can be together."

Luca took a deep breath and closed his eyes. "What does this have to do with the hold?" he opened his eyes and looked at Diego and then Elena. "You've been too secretive about that."

"There is a way inside," Diego said after a moment. "It leads to the hold."

Luca furrowed his hairless eyebrows. "If that's true, why hasn't anyone escaped yet? The Col'kasid are not the first guests of Liorah to land in Josiah's playground."

"We only recently found it," Elena said. "A matter of luck, really, and lately we've had to divert the attention of our watcher to ensure it stays hidden. Diego has been inside once and found where it leads. It's a crack, hardly noticeable, but if we can slither our way in, it might provide an exit for Abel and the others."

Luca swallowed. Was it possible? He'd always considered the hold to be the end of a person's life, and perhaps it always had been. If there was a way to rescue the Col'kasid, to rescue Abel, however...

"Does anyone else know about this?" Luca asked. "You're not the only ones whose labor is in the quarry."

"There are few," Diego said. "Friends. People we trust. From what we've been told by one of the Marokai who used to clean up down there before he was exiled, the sentinels are aware of a crevice opening inside the hold, but they have yet to cover it up. The vibrations from moving all this rock using the harmonic transducer have been destabilizing the ground under New Emile. It may be even larger now."

"Why haven't they covered it up? If it's an escape route, I would think they'd be boarding that up immediately."

"Not if you tie people to posts on the floor," Elena explained. "The opening is too high."

Luca thought more about the possibility, but something else bothered him, too. "Who are these people you've told?"

"People who will leave with us," Elena said. There was a moment of silence, and then she glanced down. "People who will join us when we set out on our own."

"On your own?" Luca's face couldn't hide his shock. "You have a plan?"

Elena glanced at Diego, who simply nodded his head. "For a while, now. We wanted to wait until you were ready. There was a time we thought we could find a way into the Chambers to face Liorah directly, but that doesn't seem possible. She has too many people guarding her. So we've been working on a plan to leave."

"Leave? You don't have the supplies for that. You'll die within a cycle."

"We've been hoarding supplies. Things we can use. But

the tunnel inside to the north by the farm is going to be discovered soon. The time is coming, but we've been waiting. The others may not feel the same, but we don't feel right leaving without you. Not after all you've done."

"Leave where? There's nothing out there but ku'vatar and death."

Diego's eyes twinkled with a hint of mystery. "Are you sure about that?"

"What? What are you talking about, and damn it all, Elena—what does this have to do with getting Abel out of the hold?"

"If we can get the Col'kasid out of the hold, we'll have to run now. But all is not lost. There are more options out there than just this home of Abel and New Emile. There has to be. But Diego and I can't do this without your help. Someone like you is going to have to watch our backs as we get in and get out."

"Me? What am I supposed to do? I'm a scout with the sentinels, not a watcher. You'd have to find an ally among those ranks."

"The current watcher doesn't know that," Diego said. "You can tell him you're his relief, punishment for missing formation."

"And if I'm found out? What then? You'll be digging your way into a prison instead of pulling people out of it."

Elena shrugged, and Luca found that to be most annoying. "It's our only shot. We know what Abel means to you, and we couldn't live with ourselves if we didn't do something we know is possible."

"Possible, but damn stupid."

"But *possible*. Have a little faith, brother." Elena flashed a quick smile.

Elena was right: it was their only shot. Luca's mind spun

as he processed his sister's words. The Col'kasid, his new friends, and Abel—if he could somehow deliver them from the clutches of whatever hell Josiah intended to bring on them, it might change everything.

His heart pounded at the thought. Abel, the man who had become the center of his universe, whose laughter echoed in his dreams and whose absence, he'd only just realized, had left an undeniable void. Abel, who had been thrown into the hold with Gideon and the others. Yet now, before him, lay an opportunity. A sliver of a chance, highly dangerous, incredibly stupid, but tangible all the same. And wasn't love itself a daring gamble? A leap of faith into the unknown?

A part of Luca balked at the nerve of the plan. The risks were monumental. Two Marokai and a young scout would attempt to deceive a guard, pull four people from a crevice, and then lead fugitives to an uncertain freedom...and there was no way Liorah would stand for such a betrayal of trust.

Then again, what was life without a little nerve, a little adventure? Love demanded risks, and Luca knew he would take a thousand more if it meant securing Abel's freedom. The thought of holding him close once again fueled a courage Luca didn't know he possessed.

He looked up at Elena and Diego. "What are we waiting for?"

UNDER THE cover of nightfall, with the Short Moon a little too large for comfort, Luca, Diego, and Elena had brought supplies out of the Hollows and placed them on a hill far away. Without saying a word, they then slipped onto the moor and silently moved toward the quarry. There was only one watcher at the opening, which had been expected since it was the middle of the night. While Diego and Elena held back out of sight, Luca had played his part the best he could, explaining to the stout and smelly guard that he'd been sent here as a punishment for missing formation in the morning. It was a half-truth. He'd certainly missed formation, but his punishment would have been much worse. The guard bought his story.

"Better you than me," he said. "Watch out for the Marokai. You never know what those fez-faced pests will do."

For a moment, Luca considered slicing the man's throat for his attitude toward his brother and sister. With a deep breath, though, he decided against it. After the other guard left and disappeared through the gate and into New Emile, the three of them slipped down the ladder and into the quarry. They had to do so with no torch light, and Elena explained they couldn't light them until they were deep inside the labyrinth and past the massive harmonic transducer. While the guard was gone, it was possible to see light coming from the quarry from those on the wall. They held hands as Diego guided them through the maze of stones not quite freed. After about five minutes, they reached their destination.

With a torch finally lit, Luca saw what they were up against—Elena's "possible" way in to the hold. The crack in the wall was barely wide enough for Diego, who was the smallest among them. Luca had to wonder if the others could even fit through once they were pulled out of the hold. They had little time, too. Eventually, the watcher would say something, his supervisor would realize how stupid he was, and an army of sentinels would descend upon the quarry.

Underneath the blanket of darkness, they squeezed through the narrow crevice, Luca included. He couldn't just wait outside and hope the plan worked. The stone walls pressed in around them, cold and unyielding. Diego led the way, his slim figure melting into the darkness ahead. Elena came next, clutching a torch that barely cut through the oppressive blackness. Luca took up the rear, stealing a last glance at the still quiet of the quarry before he pushed himself into the crack.

The stone passage twisted and turned in a labyrinthine descent. As they journeyed deeper into the heart of Tishbe, the weight of the world above pressed down on Luca.

About halfway through their passage, he noticed a strange offshoot. A smaller crevice branched away from their path, barely noticeable in the darkness. It was below this split in the tunnel that he saw an eerie green glow emanating from an unseen source. He paused, curiosity piqued by the anomaly.

Before he could utter a word, Diego's hand shot back, finding his arm in the darkness. He felt Diego's grip tighten, a silent urging to keep moving. His brother's voice echoed softly, barely a whisper in the stone chamber. "Not now, Luca. We've got no time."

"What is that?"

"Not now."

Blinking away his curiosity, he nodded, though he knew Diego couldn't see it. He filed away the strange glow in the back of his mind and pushed forward. Finally, after what seemed like crawling through miles of cold rock, another crevice appeared in the glow of Elena's torch. Hushed whispers fluttered up to meet them. Luca pushed forward to get a better look. The torchlight flickered over huddled forms—the Col'kasid, Abel, their friends—imprisoned and bound. They were at the hold, somewhere under the heart of New Emile.

"Over here," Diego whispered, motioning towards the crevice. He pushed himself through first. Moments later, a soft thud echoed up as he landed on the other side.

Elena was next, squeezing through with a grimace, the soft rustle of her clothing against the stone the only sound in the stifling silence. The torchlight disappeared with her, leaving Luca alone in the hushed stillness. Taking a deep breath, he followed. For a moment, he felt wedged in, trapped. But with a push and a twist, he spilled out onto the hard-packed dirt floor of the hold.

The first thing he noticed was the smell. The stench of decay filled the air, a potent mix of waste and despair. As the torchlight flickered over the floor, it illuminated the detritus of survival. Scattered bones, gnawed and bleached by time, lay among mounds of feces. A grim realization hit him—many who had been trapped here had not left alive.

Elena was moving, her face pale under the torchlight, but her hands steady as she worked on the coarse ropes that bound Abel and Jacob. Diego joined her, and Luca moved to help, pushing the grim reality of their surroundings out of his mind.

As they worked, Gideon and Isaiah's shadows seemed to grow more substantial. Time was running out.

Footsteps echoed from somewhere past the lone door, growing louder with each passing moment. Josiah's deep voice cut through the soft whispers, chilling Luca to his core. Sentinels were closer than they had expected.

Jacob's ropes fell away just as the unmistakable sound of a distant bolt being drawn back reverberated through the hold. The torchlight caught the fear in Abel's eyes, but there was resolve there, too. He helped Jacob to his feet.

"Go," Gideon said, his voice steady despite the situation. He gave a quick nod to Isaiah. "We'll buy you time."

Luca protested, but Gideon cut him off. "Get to my father. Warn him."

They didn't have a choice. With one last look at Gideon

and Isaiah, Luca turned back to the crevice. Diego helped Abel and Jacob through first, then Luca, followed by Elena.

The last sounds they heard as they scrambled through the rock were Gideon's voice, holding steady as he spoke with Josiah, and the indistinct murmur of sentinels echoing ominously behind them.

THE FIVE of them stood on a hill overlooking the moor, the landscape dimly illuminated by both the Long and Short Moons. The city of New Emile was nothing more than a faint cluster of a few lit torches in the distance, a dull glow. Tension was a living thing among them, an energy that hung in the air. Luca's heart pounded, the rhythm in time with each successive thought and worry.

Next to Luca, his siblings' eyes were fixed not on New Emile, but on the Hollows, on their former home. For Diego, with his hands clenched into fists at his sides, there was a wild energy about him, a nervous anticipation that made Luca uneasy. For Elena, there was a deep sadness, a darkness that spoke volumes.

"We can't waste any more time," Diego said, his voice carrying an edge. "We need to go. The sentinels won't rest until these two are found, and I don't want to be there when it happens."

"You're right," Elena added. "If we try to go back to the Hollows to get anyone else, we'll put them in danger as well."

"It won't happen," Jacob said, the words like the barest whisper of wind through the jivara grass. "I'm never going back there."

Luca noted several burns on the man's face and neck, most likely the result of Josiah's form of questioning. At least they had not yet been marked. He feared for what would happen to Gideon and Isaiah. Thankfully, Abel was no longer in the hold. He glanced over at his friend, his love, and observed him as he gazed steadily and unblinking at the horizon. He'd also been beaten; that much was obvious with all the bruises and broken skin. Yet still the young man had a strong aura about him, a resilience that had been hardened by his recent trials—from exile to imprisonment to a fugitive's life.

Silence fell upon them as the reality of the situation sank in. They were no longer Marokai, no longer New Emilians, no longer Col'kasid. They were a small band of five upon whose lives Gideon's and Isaiah's fate depended. They were on their own now, against Liorah, against time, against all odds. Yet, they were also together, bound by shared experiences, shared struggles, and a shared purpose.

Luca felt an anxiety he hadn't felt before. Gideon and Isaiah were counting on them. The Col'kasid were counting on them. And despite the monumental challenge before them, there was a fire of resolve in his heart that refused to be extinguished.

Without a word, the five turned almost in unison and set off towards Rephidim, leaving the vast moor behind. There would be bloodshed, but Elder Levi had to know.

In the back of his mind, mixed in with all the thoughts about how much his life had changed, Luca remembered that strange green glow he saw through a crack under the city of New Emile.

What was it, and what did it mean for their future?

PART III: THE BETRAYAL

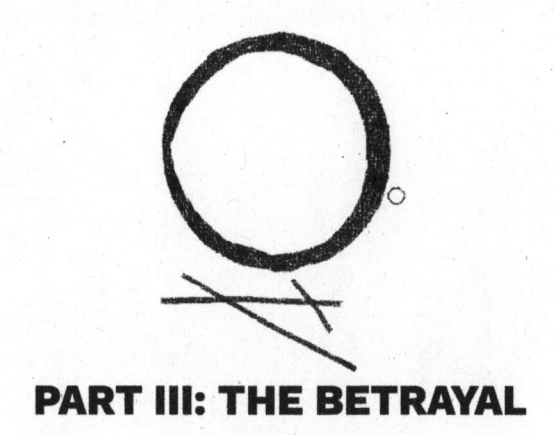

Cycle 14, Day 13, Year 96

"The murdered do haunt their murderers, I believe. I know that ghosts have wandered on earth."

—Emily Brontë, *Wuthering Heights* (1847)

CHAPTER TWENTY-ONE

IT HAD BEEN ALMOST TWO FULL CYCLES OF THE SHORT MOON since the explosion which ripped apart a side of the hills surrounding Xin Shijie de Yaolan sent a landslide into homes. Many of the northern buildings had received the worst of the damage, suffering the onslaught of boulders and debris. Twenty-three people had died, and of those, seven were children. Chen could still see their faces in his mind, hear their laughter in the wind. The collapse of the hillside had sent shockwaves through the heart of Yaolan, in more ways than one. Homes had been obliterated, the mountainside was forever scarred, and debris and detritus still littered the once tranquil valley. The physical damage had been substantial, but not unrecoverable. The emotional devastation left a more lasting impression.

Chen felt the weight of those lives lost with each breath he took, and it continually fueled his desire for vengeance against the gulao. While he would be the first to admit they were not directly responsible for this latest tragedy, the weapons the Zhanshi had been developing would not have been necessary had it not been for the threat. They could have used that energy on other things — like increasing the power output of the hydroelectric generators in the valley or advancing the technology of the algae-powered batteries powering their motorized carts.

Rebuilding the village had been as much a process of physical labor as it was a healing ritual. Each board nailed in place, each home restored, was a testament to the spirit of resilience that hummed through the veins of the Zhanshi people. Chen knew this, and he was proud. The process had been slow, marked by the sweat of the villagers and the dirge-like melody of their songs of mourning and remembrance.

In those two cycles, they had erected a barrier wall to protect them from any more landslides. The families of those lost had moved on, and none of them blamed their Zhuren, Chen, for the tragedy. No, they were in this together and would support their leader through it all. They understood what was at stake. They understood the reason for loss.

Chen's advisor Luke, however, had been more and more belligerent about his belief that the Zhanshi should abandon this "foolish" quest for vengeance. "Live in the moment," he'd said frequently. "Let the dragons rest; they will burn themselves in their sleep."

Chen did not believe that. The Zhanshi had accomplished many things in the fifty-five years since his great grandfather Mathias the First came to the planet Huolong Yaosai on the backs of the gulao (who foolishly thought it should be named Tishbe). In that time, great technological advances had been made, more the result of the elder Mathias' belief that knowledge must be constantly gained and forever passed on. It should never rest with one person. For every new member of the Zhanshi, the collective knowledge grew tenfold.

Was it unreasonable to suspect that the gulao had advanced as well? Were they not all bred from a community of scientists, engineers, and forward thinkers? Did innovation not run through their veins just as it did with the Zhanshi?

What weapons had they developed?

The victory at Manoach when his grandfather Mathias the Third eliminated a majority of the gulao was muted because some had escaped their fate. As the years progressed, how many were out there now?

Chen sat in his home at a table and tried to calculate the potential population of this colony. It had started with a seed of maybe one hundred fifty based on the testimony of some of the gulao who had been questioned and the deceit of the traitor gulao, Aaron. He didn't know what the mortality rate was, but if he calculated it based on the rate in Yaolan, he estimated that it could be well over a thousand people by now.

So many more than what they found at Manoach. And those that were there, according to the historical records left by Mathias the Third, were weak, malnourished, and near death. What his grandfather had done was nothing short of mercy.

Where were they now? He'd sent scouting parties to the west and south around the Barren Sea. None, however, had reported anything remarkable.

It was midday. The sun was high overhead and the sound of construction filtered through Chen's windows and door. He put away his calculations and stood at the Zhuren altar. He bowed slightly and lit a candle. Consumed with his thoughts of finding the other colony, he did not hear Luke knock.

"Zhuren," the old man said quietly from the doorway. "A word, please."

Chen took in a deep breath, centered himself, and let his lieutenant inside. The man shuffled toward a seat by the table and sat down with a grunt. He was getting up in age — one of the few left in Yaolan who had known Chen's grandfather.

"What is it?"

Luke wiped his face with a weathered hand. "The projectiles are ready to be tested, although I advise you again against this reckless endeavor...this pursuit of vengeance."

"I hear your advice." Chen sat in a chair opposite. He leaned back, the wood of the floor creaking under his weight. He respected Luke, but he knew they stood on opposite sides of this argument. "Have the fuses been perfected?"

"Adjustable timers, long enough to get to safety. There is a pressure trigger mounted on the leading edge which will set off the explosive once it reaches its target. Lucien has been preparing a sled for them to travel down before they launch."

"Angled?"

"With a crank for both the azimuth and angle. We can safely calculate the trajectory provided we know the speed at which the projectile will leave the sled."

While most of the Zhanshi had been rebuilding the homes lost in the landslide, Chen had ordered a small contingent led by Lucien to build a weapon capable of sending their bombs at a great distance. It was an idea he'd gleaned from one of the many books found in the old COL ship sitting derelict on the dry Barren Sea. *Jane's Defense Weekly* was an interesting read—and an even more curious addition to the things the original settlers had been allowed to bring with them. From what Mathias the First had said, the elder Elijah had forbidden such items, hoping to restart society with no need for weapons of war. A foolish utopian dream. Did Elijah really not know that humans would forever be...human?

"When is Lucien preparing for the first test?"

Luke did not answer right away. He sat forward in the chair and rested his elbows on his knees, his chin in his hands. After a moment, he straightened. "Most wise Zhuren," he began, "is this really necessary? Have you thought about the cost, the additional lives we may lose in the process?"

Chen expected this from Luke. He had been adamant about not needing to design such a powerful weapon long before Tye had died in the explosion that set the hills crumbling. It did not matter, however. Luke was but one voice among his lieutenants. Lucien, Martin, and even Lin Xi were supporters of Chen's vision. Even Tye, who'd lost his life advancing the power of the Zhanshi, would have been on board.

"There are probably one thousand gulao on the planet, if not more," Chen said. "The longer we wait, the stronger they will become, and the cost of doing nothing could be much higher. It is likely they have also perfected weapons and are right now planning to take what meager resources we have in this valley—our generators, our food, our women. That cannot happen. No matter what it takes, I will honor my great grandfather's wish."

Luke nodded slowly, but Chen knew he would never be convinced. He was too much of a peacemaker, perhaps a little like the man who would not be named, the Zhuren between Mathias the First and his grandfather. Peacemakers did not inherit worlds.

"As you wish, Zhuren. Lucien has set the projectile up at the mouth of the valley, thankfully five miles from the village. It will be ready to launch in the morning." Luke shifted uncomfortably in his chair, his old bones protesting.

"And the target?"

"A corral full of pua'a ono."

Chen's eyes twinkled with a touch of humor, attempting to lighten the mood. "Should be a splendid and celebratory feast for the village."

"Assuming anything is left."

LUCIEN MADE some final adjustments to the sled that would ensure the projectile launched in the intended direction. As Chen approached, the Zhuren noted the intensity with which his lieutenant was focused on the job. He would make a fine Zhuren in the future, and given Chen's own lack of male children, Lucien was the best pick. In another life, the man could have been his son.

It was early morning, and while his other lieutenants Martin and Lin Xi were here, Luke had respectfully asked not to be present. Chen was okay with that. The man had given many years of service to the Zhanshi and, as he had learned years ago, elders were to be respected at all costs. Tye was sorely missed, and it did not escape Chen's awareness that his lieutenants felt the same.

Lucien worked meticulously on the projectile, his attention riveted on the menacing device. Forged from Yaolan's own rugged metal ore, the weapon stretched almost six feet in length, a monolith of raw power and destructive potential. Untouched by any unnecessary embellishment, the weapon wore its raw metal complexion with stark pride. In the rising sun's light, its metallic surface shimmered subtly, the natural textures and imperfections of its craftsmanship offering an unflinching honesty to its purpose. The blacksmiths had done an outstanding job and would be rewarded.

Its ominous silhouette was broken only by the bulging section towards its tail end. This held the explosive charge—the same potent mixture of chemicals derived from the valley's abundant natural resources. They all knew it worked well. According to Yaolan's scientists, the charge had to be near the rear; if it was near the nose of the projectile, its weight would create a dangerous instability. As it was, no one knew if the thing would fly as expected.

Chen watched the scene unfold, anticipation gnawing at him. In the quiet hush of the early morning, the sense of purpose in his actions resonated with a gravity that filled the surrounding air. This was a moment of consequence. Here was a manifestation of their intent, a physical testament to their readiness to defend what was rightfully theirs—or to set themselves up to exact vengeance. It was a sobering sight, one that left a cold echo of unease threading through the crisp morning.

In the nearby background, Martin and Lin Xi observed the proceedings. Several other guards who were normally positioned at the entrance to the valley had moved away out of caution. Many people would witness the demonstration, and it made Chen proud that they had come this far.

Chen's gaze shifted to the open field that lay beyond the opening to the valley. There, in a spacious corral about half a mile away, was the target for the day's impending test—a group of about ten pua'a ono, peacefully oblivious to the spectacle about to unfold. The small group of fat animals with their floppy ears and reddish skin rooted and foraged, the morning light casting long, playful shadows that danced around the enclosure. Their grunts and squeals were soft background notes to the scene.

As Chen's attention lingered on the oblivious animals, he was acutely aware of the disconnect between the tranquility of the corral and the deadly power of the weapon poised nearby. The irony wasn't lost on him—the simple joy of life blind to the machinery of death aimed in its direction.

He imagined the pua'a ono were the gulao, and he was pleased.

"Are we ready?" Chen asked. He tried his best to mute his excitement and remain the stone-faced Zhuren they knew and respected.

"One more small bolt to tighten." Lucien moved around the sled that held the projectile and knelt down. The sled was an inventive idea, one that Lucien had come up with himself. Launching the projectile without an initial guidance could have resulted in more tragedy. The sled would help.

"Tell me again how it is supposed to work?"

Lucien tightened the bolt and stood. "While the charge in the tail of the projectile will push it down the sled, it is helped along by a catapult." He pointed to what looked like a string of metal ovals linked along a path in the middle of the sled. "We have calculated the trajectory based on the expected speed and believe it will hit the target in under thirty seconds."

"The charge in the tail is safe from the explosive charge of the bomb?"

Lucien nodded, but it wasn't the most confident nod Chen had seen. "We think so. We have a two-minute timed fuse that will allow us to get to safety." He pointed to a metal barrier about fifty yards away.

The three men were silent for a moment. The guards were away and already sheltered from anything that might happen. Other than a few birds welcoming the morning, there was little other sound.

Chen clapped his hands together. "Well, let us see what our efforts have yielded."

Lucien nodded, pulled out a flint, and stepped back toward the timed fuse. Just as he knelt, however, a sudden rustle of footfalls on loose gravel broke their attention.

Chen looked toward the sound, far to the left of the target. There, about two hundred feet away, a group of weary strangers slowly emerged into the light of the new day. There were four of them, and they were not dressed as any scouting party sent forth from Yaolan. Chen's heart quickened as he watched them slowly stumble forward. They looked malnourished, if anything, but the weapons they slung told of something else.

These men were not Zhanshi. They were not from here.

They were gulao...

...and all Chen's predictions had come true. Immediately, his hand moved toward the knife sheathed at his waist.

Dressed in tattered clothing, with shaved, scarred heads and an unkempt appearance, the strangers' haggard look suggested a journey of great length and many hardships. They paused upon seeing Chen and the weapon, their cautious eyes taking in the scene, their mouths slightly agape. Unspoken questions hung heavily in the air as the strangers faced something they probably least expected—and a formidable weapon that could destroy them in a flash.

"Stand down, Lucien," Chen commanded, breaking the silence that had descended over the scene. Lucien glanced at his Zhuren, surprised. He nodded in acquiescence.

As the weapon was held back, the group of strangers cautiously approached. Their steps were slow and measured, an apparent attempt to project peace. One of them held his hands out in a placating manner. From their midst emerged a man who, from his posture and the wary respect given to him by the others, was clearly their leader. He was tall and bore a scar across his right cheek worn like a badge of honor. He, too, held his hands out.

"Greetings," the man said, his voice harsh. He stepped toward Chen and nodded his head slightly. "My name is Russant and we come from New Emile, sent by Liorah, the most high, the One Voice, holder of the vials of haelen, and granddaughter of the Great Mother Miriam." He caught his breath after such a long-winded introduction. "We are on a quest for Discovery."

Chen bowed his head, receiving the strangers with an outward show of cordiality. In his heart, however, he wanted nothing more than to skin these men alive and send them back to where they came from—a message that the Zhanshi were coming, that their days were numbered.

If only he knew where this New Emile was or how many people really lived there. He studied the men for a moment, trying to ascertain how best to proceed.

What else did they know?

Chen tried to make his voice as welcoming as the warmth of the morning sun, masking the whirlwind of thoughts and speculations churning in his mind. "Welcome," he said with a fake smile. "I am Chen, Zhuren of my people and leader of the Zhanshi. We..." He glanced at Lucien and Lin Xi before continuing. "We welcome you to our village, as you must be tired from your travels."

That was hard to say.

The man's eyes opened wide, and he swiftly took a more defensive stance. His arms dropped to his side, and there was a hint that he might go for the crossbow slung on his shoulder. "Did you say...Zhanshi?"

Without saying another word, Chen signaled discreetly to his lieutenants with a slight twist of his right hand. Suddenly, a shrill whistle cut through the serenity of the morning air. Within seconds, the men were surrounded by others wielding weapons.

For all the questions that had been plaguing Chen for most of his life, fate had intervened at the perfect moment.

These gulao would now answer them, and the treatment of Mathias the First would finally be avenged.

CHAPTER TWENTY-TWO

THEY COULD HAVE USED THE QUVIANAQ. IT WAS A SHAME they didn't sneak into New Emile and steal them out from under Liorah's nose.

It took one and a half cycles of the Short Moon to reach Patience Gap—six weeks—following all the cairns that Abel and Luca had placed on the slightly worn path to Rephidim the last time they'd been through. That seemed so long ago, and yet it wasn't even so much as a full Long Moon—a quarter of a year. The weather had become colder in the Wastelands, with the threat of snow present nearly every day. Regardless, not once did anyone complain about the cold, the lack of food, or all the sacrifices they needed to make on the way. They were together as one, felt free for the first time, and the moments they spent on what they had jokingly dubbed the Road to Hell had bound them even more.

"Hell," Abel had said, "is where we're headed."

"Hell is where we came from," countered Elena. "The only way to Eldorado will be to get off this damn path."

Abel and Luca were in love with each other, staying together in a tent they fashioned out of some blankets and sticks. Elena had grown fond of Jacob as well during this journey, and it wasn't long before those two were together.

On a night colder than any of the previous ones, Elena

had snuck up to where Jacob was sleeping under the stars, startling the Col'kasid hunter. His breath quickened as Elena slid next to him and under his blanket.

"Relax," she whispered, placing her hand low on Jacob's stomach. "I know your laws. Besides, I'm cold."

Jacob's upbringing said everything he wanted to do with Elena right then was wrong, but he didn't think the only other Col'kasid companion with them, Abel, would mind if he sinned...just a little.

"It's not that." He swallowed a lump in his throat. "I've...I've just never been with a woman before."

Elena didn't say anything. She placed a warm kiss on Jacob's chest then settled in with her head nestled in his shoulder. For the next hour, all Jacob could do was stare up at the stars, his arms wrapped around Elena and recite Bible verses he had learned as a child. It was going to be a long journey back.

He eventually fell back asleep with a grin on his face.

That left Diego alone, but it was not something which outwardly bothered him. He seemed to be okay watching over the group.

"I'm content," he told Abel and Luca one night. "Not happy."

The road up Patience Gap and down the eastern slope of the mountains elicited varying emotional responses. Abel was once again scared, sure the Assembly would make him food for the carrion birds, for the massive zarcoa. How many times had they told him to go? The last time he had been ordered to stay outside the gate, unprotected. It was as if one punishment wasn't enough. Jacob was elated at the prospect of returning home again, even if it was bittersweet. No one could fathom what Liorah had done with Gideon or Isaiah, but they had agreed not to speculate. Liorah would probably keep them alive, if only to use them as barter for whatever it was she wanted.

And what did she want? What was her real purpose for imprisoning the Col'kasid? Was it really because they disobeyed her edict to not go into the Library, or was there something else going on under the surface? Perhaps Liorah had an ulterior motive. She had taken a liking to the quvianaq—and maybe even Gideon. Beyond animals and a rudimentary grasp of agriculture in non-fertile soil, there wasn't much the Col'kasid could offer.

Did she want something else?

At the bottom of the foothills on the opposite side of Patience Gap, the five fugitives rested. Dinner that night was a feast of khopa, courtesy of both Jacob and Abel. They were in their element now, and all Diego and Elena could do was watch as they expertly skinned and cooked the meat, topping it off with boiled baca root. Luca had seen this before, of course, but he was content staying back while the other two worked together to prepare the meal. It had been good to see Abel get along with some of his Col'kasid companions; Gideon, Isaiah, and Jacob did not care if Abel was attracted to men. But Luca knew what was to come. Would Levi or that beast of a man Saadya allow Abel through the gates this time, even with the news they brought from New Emile?

That night, they slept little. The anxiety about delivering the news of Gideon's capture weighed heavily on them all. They were bearers of bad news, and from all the lessons anyone had been taught growing up, the messenger was often vilified. It was a human trait, a need to blame someone for something.

By the time they all fell asleep, dawn was showing its face.

—

LUCA OPENED his eyes. Saadya loomed over Abel, the lance in his hand glinting menacingly. Its tip hovered at the boy's neck like a venomous animal poised to strike. A shock of adrenaline coursed through Luca, propelling him to sit upright. He longed to leap into action, to defend his friend, but the reality of Saadya's brute strength held him back. The beast was not something to be trifled with.

"Get back, boy." Saadya barked, his voice grating against the quiet morning air like stone across stone. From what Luca could tell, there were eight Col'kasid hunters on their quvianaq mounts surrounding their camp. All of them had weapons drawn.

Saadya applied a fraction more pressure to the lance, the deadly point indented into Abel's soft skin just enough to make its intent clear. "How many times do we have to exile you? And yet you keep coming back."

Luca's voice trembled with fear. "We're here with a message. An important message for Elder Levi."

"Give it to me and leave."

"No." It was Jacob who spoke this time. He stood from where he had been lying with Elena, oddly embarrassed as if he'd been caught doing something wrong. "The Assembly will have an audience with us. This is a matter of the highest concern, and only we have the details that the Keeper of the Text must hear."

Diego and Elena followed, standing strong even as the unfamiliar environment of Rephidim held its own threats for them. This place was foreign to them, but the need to protect their companions was a language they understood well.

"Sit down, fez." Saadya relaxed the lance from Abel's neck and swung it around on Jacob. "You leave with Gideon and Isaiah and return without them. It's obvious you're murders. What did you do? Run out of food and eat them on your way?"

"They're being held prisoner," Elena said, her voice more dominant than Luca ever would have expected of his sister. "And war is coming. What would your leader have to say if you denied him the information we have?"

Saadya's lips curled up in a mischievous grin. "And what would he know? We could gut you here, leave you for the zarcoa and the xialiti, and no one would be the wiser."

"Then you'll be ensuring Gideon passes into shadow."

"At your hand," Abel said weakly. He rubbed his throat. "I don't think even you're that cold."

Saadya's eyes darkened. His grip on the lance slackened just slightly, a minute shift that would have been invisible to a less keen observer. Dread filled the silent air as time stretched thin.

Without warning, a sharp, keening call echoed through the morning air. A chill ran down Luca's spine. Whatever it was, it didn't sound friendly. Within seconds, another answered the call, and then another, until the air was filled with the eerie symphony of danger.

"Zarcoa," Jacob said quietly at Luca's confusion. "Carrion birds. Scavengers."

Saadya didn't flinch at the call, but his gaze flicked momentarily towards the source of the sound. When he looked back at the group, there was a slight softening in his gaze.

"Speak," Saadya finally said, lowering his lance completely. "Speak your message and be done with it."

The words came out in a rush, the adrenaline of the moment still buzzing in Luca's veins. He rapidly told of their trip back to New Emile, of Liorah and her treatment of the Col'kasid, of Gideon and Isaiah's capture. He spoke of war on the horizon, of treachery and danger, and of the dire need for action.

"War?" Saadya's expression was unreadable. "That is a word used for humans of the past."

"Not any longer," Abel said. "We've heard tales of warfare and strife from the Assembly, but they never ruled out the possibility of it happening here. Even the strangers warned—"

"Shut it, boy!" Saadya cut him off. "You're nothing but a deviant, an abomination, and your words hold no weight with me."

Luca lunged towards Saadya, but another man quickly barred his path, the sharp tip of a lance daring him to advance further. "He's no deviant!" Luca's voice rang out. "And he's not misguided. War is on the horizon, and that's precisely the chaos Liorah seeks."

Saadya's gaze swept over the group before him, evaluating each one, pointedly excluding Abel from his scrutiny. After what seemed like an eternity, he gestured to his men. "Pack up," he ordered, his voice as gruff as before, but lacking the same malice. "Take their belongs with us."

Luca's words had hit a nerve.

Saadya turned on Abel. "You," he spat. "Stay outside the gate. This news changes nothing about your fate...or your problem."

Luca was about to protest, but Abel put a hand on his arm. He nodded slightly. "As long as Elder Levi hears what they have to say."

There was a sense of both fragile relief and anxiety. After six weeks, they were one step closer to their goal. As one, they moved forward, doing their best to keep up with the hunter's quvianaq and still wishing they had stolen Gideon's back from Liorah.

In the distance, Rephidim loomed large, as did the fear in Luca's heart about the treatment Abel was sure to receive.

ELENA STOOD outside the Assembly room...or cave...or whatever the hell the Col'kasid called it. As a woman, she was not allowed inside, and to her surprise, Jacob didn't protest. She couldn't hear what was happening behind the massive wood door that had closed in front of her. One of Saadya's men stood outside, his brown skin glistening with sweat. He refused to meet Elena's gaze, perhaps because of orders from his superiors or the fact that she was a woman, as if the women were the Marokai of the Col'kasid.

At the moment, she didn't know what to do. Perhaps visit Abel still outside the gate, be with her own kind—the exiles? What was wrong with these people?

She looked around. The women were clad in long, ragged brown dresses, and the men wore makeshift brown coverings over their legs with scraps for shirts. In contrast, Elena felt conspicuous in her gray tunic and gray pants. To make matters worse, her hair—once shorn daily—had been growing in spots, uneven. Being the same species didn't matter if you could separate the classes. As people passed, they cast fleeting glances at her, swiftly averting their eyes once Elena looked their way.

Disgusted, Elena turned. She ventured near the cliff's edge and discovered a garden filled with exotic plants that she had never encountered before. The colors amazed her the most and seemed to soothe her fury. Red and orange fruit, hanging like jewels on green and blue vines, contrasted against the tufts of yellow flowers that grew out of the red soil like a carpet of sunshine. Paths zigzagged between the plants, inviting her to walk among them. The sound of the waterfall that she had caught sight of while making the journey from the desert floor to the gate echoed in her ears. It was so much different from the Hollows, from the monochromatic life she had fled. Despite the leering looks and lack of importance, she suddenly felt at peace for the first time in years.

Had she ever felt such peace before?

A woman approached, holding a basket of what looked like herbs and grass in her left arm. Her face bore the wrinkles of age, but she appeared strong. She did not look away when Elena saw her. Instead, she smiled slightly and bowed her head.

"You must be the girl from that other place," the woman said, her voice rather meek.

"Elena. Yes. I came with Jacob and the others." She tried to return the smile, but found it difficult. She knew not to mention Abel's name given his status among the Col'kasid, but in her heart, that hurt.

"I am Ruth." The woman paused for a moment and looked around as if someone might see her talking to the outsider. Her eyes flicked up to the mark across Elena's forehead then back down and away. Finally, she stepped close enough that Elena caught a sweet fragrance on her skin. "How is Abel?" she asked, almost in a whisper.

It shocked Elena to hear anyone mention the boy's name. Throughout their journey from New Emile, both Jacob and Abel had explained just how blasphemous the Col'kasid considered Abel's actions with his boyfriend Asher. To everyone else here, Abel no longer existed, wiped off the face of the planet. This woman, however...she cared.

Elena lowered her head and her voice as well. "Are you his mother?"

Ruth looked around quickly before answering. "Is he healthy?"

"Very much so. He's much stronger now." With a

courage she didn't think she had, Elena added, "I can take you to him."

Ruth shook her head vigorously. "No, no. I cannot. They would put me out there myself, and I would not survive." She appeared to choke back tears. "I am no longer a mother."

"A mother is always a mother. No one can take that away from you."

"Oh, but they can." Ruth put a hand on Elena's arm. "They can take everything." Tears formed in her eyes, but she twisted away. Before Elena could say anything else, Ruth left.

She stood in the garden and watched Abel's mother quickly walk through the paths and toward a small dwelling built like all the others in the side of the butte. Her mind flashed back to that other Ruth, the one in the Hollows, the one whose child Lika had been saved by a small vial of haelen. She felt an overwhelming urge to cry, her throat tightening with emotion. A child given back to one Ruth. A child taken away from another.

No, the Col'kasid could not take away this woman's motherhood. That was wrong no matter how strong the cultural traditions were. This Ruth had carried Abel for ten cycles of the Short Moon. She had birthed him, raised him up, nurtured him. She had been everything to him, and Elena imagined Abel must feel the same connection. He'd rarely mentioned his parents during their journey, but that didn't mean he was emotionally disconnected. Some people just learn to tuck it all away behind a wall that no one else can penetrate. Give a person enough pain and they will turn to stone.

Ruth stepped back out of the dwelling and waved Elena over.

"Come," she said as Elena approached. An unexpected smile played across her lips. "You should see this."

ON A bed made of grass and linen, a woman's face twisted in pain, her groans echoing through the room. Breath came in short, rapid bursts. She was in agony as she tried to give birth to a new child. Elena had never witnessed a birth before, and if this was what it was like, she didn't want to experience it for herself.

She watched from the corner of the home in which Ruth had brought her. Sweat beaded on Elena's forehead as a small fire burning in the corner of the room had made the temperature uncomfortable. Another woman—perhaps a nursemaid—demanded it get even hotter.

Ruth set a bundle of grass down on the ground next to the fire, then quickly returned to where Elena stood transfixed. "Koralitha grass," she said quietly. "The heat and smell helps the birth process."

The repugnant aroma turned Elena's stomach. She had never seen such grass before and never smelled anything so sharp.

The sweat on Elena's forehead was minuscule compared to the thick layer that drenched the woman on the bed. Ruth said her name was Leah, and she couldn't have been any older than Elena. Her pale skin glistened in the flickering light while her body quivered with each moan, each scream, each sucked-in breath.

"You're almost there," the nursemaid said calmly, with no more emotion than if she had been talking about the change in seasons. "A few more pushes." She turned and placed another bundle of koralitha into the fire. "Trust in God that He will provide."

For the past few minutes, the nursemaid had been saying the same thing, over and over. Elena had learned from Jacob during the journey from New Emile that the Col'kasid colony once edged close to two hundred people about twenty years prior. Some disease called the Red Death, however, had decimated the population. Later, according to the story she'd heard, a migration of those dissatisfied with the appointment of the man named Levi as Elder of the Assembly and Keeper of the Text reduced those numbers even more. The colony eventually recovered, and nearly two decades later, this child would push the Col'kasid to over two hundred thirty people, or "souls" as the people she was now with were fond of saying.

Births here were treated differently from those in New Emile, with each one special and not just another mouth to feed, another name to add to the population lottery.

Elam, the apparent father, knelt beside Leah, gripping her hand. Sweat also drenched his face, matting his black curly hair to his head and neck. The darkness of his skin contrasted with the red-spotted pale white flesh of Leah.

A figure darkened the door, short but large, dressed in a white robe with a brown sash draped over his chest. Ruth bowed her head slightly and stepped back, pulling Elena with her.

"Elder Levi," Ruth whispered.

"Why is he here? I thought he was in the Assembly meeting with the others."

"The Keeper of the Text is to be present at all births, even if he is supposed to be in another meeting. It's been this way since the beginning, since Sojen Micah's wife Patience gave birth to the first soul born into sunshine at Rephidim."

Elena did not understand. She couldn't imagine the One Voice Liorah being present at any birth.

"For a soul to have a blessed life, the Keeper of the Text must welcome them in person."

"Why?"

Ruth smiled. "Elder Levi has a special link to God."

Elena was bothered a bit by Ruth's reverence of the man who exiled her son. Had she really forgiven him?

Levi took up a position next to Elena, gripping an ornate walking stick with a meaty hand. "How long?"

Elena didn't know if the question was directed at her or Ruth. Before she said anything, Ruth answered, her head still bowed. "A few minutes, maybe."

Leah tensed her muscles and let out a loud grunt, followed by a shrill scream through her clenched teeth. Elam leaned in and whispered something in her ear, but an angry glance quickly rebuffed it. He moved back a little and glanced over at Elder Levi.

"I see the head," the nursemaid said. "Push harder and trust in God that He will provide."

What did that really mean? Elena had heard the term God before, but there were no religions in New Emile. Those who had been the most faithful were said to have been cast out to the Wastelands during Mother Miriam's rule, and when her son Eilian became the One Voice after her passing, religion of any sort was outright banned. To confess a belief in a higher power than the One Voice was a quick road to exile or, worse, to Eldorado.

What was this God supposed to provide at this moment? If it was relief, it was nowhere to be found.

As if understanding Elena's confusion, Levi leaned in and spoke to her in a low voice. "God provides comfort to the righteous and eases the pains of birth."

Elena blinked, then pointed toward the nursemaid. The woman seemed to have no sweat on her at all. "That's easy?"

"More so than those who do not walk in the way of the Col'kasid. The texts tell us that those who do not walk with God bear only rotten fruit."

Leah let out another scream, followed by a deep gasp and a guttural groan. Ruth stepped forth and silently placed another bundle of koralitha grass on the fire for the nursemaid.

"But there is no comfort," Elena said. "The woman is obviously in pain. Why? Is it always like this?"

Levi smiled. "God said, 'I will increase your pains in childbearing; with pain you will give birth to children.' But that is more so for those who do not walk in the way of the Col'kasid, those who do not see the light. Surely you must have seen this in your New Emile."

Another scream, this time from Elam as he tried to pull his hand out of Leah's grip.

"This pain," Levi continued, "is a universal reminder of God's judgment for the sin Adam and Eve brought into the world."

"And you're saying it could be worse?" Elena swallowed. "I can't imagine that."

"More so. Sojen Micah was clear on this point—we should offer the bounty of this world as a child is born into sunshine to appease God, and through the offering, make the growth of our colony a blessing, not a curse." He leaned in a little closer. "I hear New Emile has been cursed."

Levi stood straight and took a step forward. Despite whatever crap Levi had just told her, Elena still didn't understand how so much pain could be a good thing. And it could be worse?

"One more time," the nursemaid said. "Push as hard as you can and trust in—"

"I am!" Lean screamed. "What do you think I'm doing?"

"Trust in God," Elam said.

Leah's mouth opened, but before anything came out, she released a piercing scream and pushed with all her might.

Levi raised his arms. His voice boomed in the small room. "We welcome you into the light, dear child. Born into sunshine and free now from your imprisonment, you are welcome to come forth from the womb into the new world so that you may give glory to God and prepare us all for the Great Return."

With Levi's white robe obstructing her line of sight, Elena found herself unable to witness the miraculous moment of birth. Filled with anticipation, she shifted to the right, inching closer to Elam and Ruth. The pungent combination of koralitha mingling with the distinct scent of blood and sweat saturated the surrounding air, overwhelming her senses.

As the final exertion of the mother's labor came forth, a child emerged into the world. Elena strained, rising onto her tiptoes to catch a glimpse. There, with no doubt, lay a new baby boy. A rush of joy and wonder surged through Elena, mingled with a tinge of apprehension.

Swiftly, the nursemaid severed the umbilical cord and carefully turned the infant over, presenting him to those gathered. In that moment, Leah stirred, lifting her head slightly, while Elam observed with a delicate smile gracing his lips. Nestled within the nursemaid's hands was a miracle of life.

And yet the woman's face...were those tears?

As the room fell into silence, a pallor of concern enveloped Elam. Levi, lowering his arms, revealed a look of shock, his mouth agape. The once-joyful smiles faded into a mask of worry and uncertainty.

What just happened?

As Elena looked around trying to understand, Ruth took her by the arm and ushered her outside just as the nursemaid began trying to clear the child's airway.

"I don't understand," Elena said, her voice still low. "What—"

Ruth put her finger to her lips, her face sad. "It is the way of the world. What God gives, He can also take away."

IN THE evening, with the sun setting and long shadows growing within Rephidim, Elena stood in the garden at the edge of the cliff above the waterfall. Her heart still hurt at the stillborn birth of a child. She had been trying to hide her emotions from those around her who were wary of her presence. Only Ruth had been kind enough to offer some emotional support, but she had left to attend to her own life.

Jacob burst from the Assembly. Elena turned from her mournful walk in the garden and rushed to meet him. He was angry, but when she tried to put her arms around him, he stepped back. Quickly, he looked around.

"I'm sorry," he mumbled sheepishly. "Rules."

Elena's depression quickly gave way to fury. She opened her mouth, ready to scream at anyone who would listen, but Jacob quickly put a finger to her lips.

"Not now," he said.

She bunched her hands into tight fists. "I can't believe—"

"Not now." Jacob grabbed her arm and led her away from the front of the Assembly. They hastened past other dwellings and people who could not look at them for more than a fleeting glance.

When they reached a small crevice under an overhang near the gate, Jacob stopped. He glanced around, then gave Elena a quick kiss. That was all the affection she would get if they didn't get out of Rephidim soon, not that she wanted a kiss at that moment. She wanted a shoulder to cry on.

"What happened in there?" Elena asked. She was still angry, but the kiss had tempered her slightly. "Did you tell your Elder Levi what happened?"

Jacob nodded. "It wasn't pleasant. The ass—sorry, our

grand leader wants to march on New Emile. I think it happened when he stepped away for some reason."

"There was a birth."

"Ah. That explains it. When he returned, he had made up his mind."

Elena's eyes opened wide. "He won't at least talk to Liorah? Send an ambassador to secure Gideon's release? One mistake and it's war with you people?"

With a distraught look, Jacob shook his head. "Gideon was ambassador enough. There will be no more negotiations, apparently."

"Well, what—" Elena stammered. "When is this going to happen?"

"I think Saadya swayed his thoughts. When the other elders, Malachi and Mateo, argued against such a rash decision, Levi put them on notice. One more outburst would get them thrown out of the Assembly, he said, and no stones were to be cast."

"Stones?"

Jacob sighed, as if he didn't want to have to explain what he meant. That irritated Elena more. "It's a sort of vote. There are five members of the Assembly—Malachi, Mateo, James, Gideon, and Levi. Levi is the Keeper of the Text, the One Voice of Rephidim, if you will. All five have a stone they are given when they become elders. They cast that stone in a certain direction whenever a vote is needed."

"Like a ballot. I've heard about those."

"Yes, but Levi has the deciding cast. If the Assembly is split, he casts last, which means he gets his way."

"And Levi called for no stones to be cast on this matter? On this matter of *war*?" She emphasized the last word with a scowl.

Jacob shook his head. "He claimed that without a full

Assembly, his stone is the only one that mattered. And Gideon is his son, so I kind of understand that. Parents are protective, or so I've come to learn."

"Really?" Elena scoffed. "I just met Abel's mother. You stripped her of her parental right to be protective. You stripped her of motherhood."

"I didn't." Jacob furrowed his eyebrows. "And you would be wise not to bring that up while you're inside the gate."

"I'll bring up whatever I damn well please." Elena crossed her arms. "This is outrageous. Even the Marokai are treated better than the women around here."

"'Wives, submit yourselves to your own husbands as you do to the Lord.'" Jacob suddenly looked sick for having said that.

"What the hell is that?"

"A line the Assembly reads from Father Elijah's Bible. It means—"

"I can tell you what it means. I'm not stupid."

"Then you know why mentioning anything about the treatment of women in Rephidim will get you exiled, especially coming *from* a woman."

Elena stepped back, her body shaking vigorously. "You— I can't believe—" Her voice rose higher.

"Look." Jacob reached out to touch Elena, but she took a step back. "This isn't about the women," he protested. "This is about sending the men to attack New Emile and take Gideon back by force."

"Just the men?"

"Keep your voice down."

Elena raised her voice in response. "Just the men! Why aren't the women going?"

Jacob stepped back slightly and cocked his head. He

looked utterly dumbfounded. "Women? With weapons?"

Elena's mouth dropped open slightly. She did not believe Jacob, the man she had fallen for, was agreeing with the traditions of this backward, misogynistic, homophobic tribe. Of all the...

Without another word, she turned and stormed out the gate.

CHAPTER TWENTY-THREE

Luca wished Elder Levi would settle down. The man paced the Assembly chamber like an animal, occasionally stopping to mumble something to himself and then wiping away what might have been foam at his mouth. Jacob had the right idea: it was time to leave. The man would not listen to reason. He and Diego were the only messengers from New Emile in the chamber, and the rage would fall on them. They were not Col'kasid. They were symbols of the enemy.

The other three Assembly elders, Malachi, Mateo, and James, had decided they would argue no more. They had wanted to cast their stones toward a peaceful resolution to this crisis, but Levi's words, ringing with authority, could not be ignored. In that way, Luca thought, he was very much like Liorah. She kept a council only to appear as if she considered all angles, considered all sides of a problem. That was never the case.

A shuffling from deep within the Assembly alerted Luca. He turned to see Sojen Micah step from the shadows, a man he'd briefly met only once the last time he was here. The man had founded Rephidim and was its first leader. His son, Micah the Second, had taken over when the elder became tired, but the Red Death changed everything. It left Micah's grandson, Levi, in charge.

"I will go," Micah said. He shuffled toward a bench near the eternal fire set up in the middle of the room. "I must go."

Levi stopped pacing and threw up his hands in frustration. "Absolutely not, grandfather. You wouldn't make the trip on the back of a quvianaq, and there's no telling what danger awaits us all."

"You misunderstand." Micah leaned heavily on his own ornate walking stick. "I'm not asking."

"As the Keeper of the Text and Elder of the Col'kasid, I cannot allow it. You will stay here with the women and rule in my absence."

Micah coughed once, although that may have been a chuckle. Luca couldn't tell. "Do you even know what you're getting yourself into? Wars on Earth were said to have been brutal affairs with no clear winner. If you march into New Emile as soldiers, you will be met with an equal or greater force, and my great grandson's life will be extinguished."

"Sojen Micah, please." Levi had heard this argument from the other elders, one that Luca, Diego, and Jacob had all proposed. They knew Liorah best, and she was in no way stable. "We have skills and mounts. 'The Lord your God is he who goes with you to fight for you against your enemies, to give you the victory.'" Levi waved his hand toward Luca and Diego. "And what do they have? Certainly no favor in the eyes of God. If these two are examples of what we face when we get there, we'll walk all over them."

That offended Luca but he decided it was best to keep his mouth shut. He would answer questions directed at him only. But he couldn't help but notice that the longer he and Diego were forced to say in the Assembly, the more hostile Levi had become toward them.

"These two are boys," Micah said. "It is the men you must worry about. What weapons do they have? What tactics have they been trained on? What moral code do they follow?"

"It doesn't matter." Levi spat into the fire. "I will get my son back if I have to burn New Emile to the ground."

The statement clung to the air like a heavy, oppressive fog, leaving everyone present feeling even more weighed down than they already were. The fire crackling in the center of the room seemed to lose its warmth, the dancing flames almost spectral. Luca's heart sank. He stared into the flames as an icy dread washed over him. In his periphery, shadows shifted ominously on the walls, whispering warnings of an apocalyptic end.

Maybe it wasn't the end and his mind had been conjuring exceedingly dramatic and violent scenarios, but it was something no one on Tishbe had faced before. Had they? They all heard stories, some more than others. They knew how wars had played out on Earth. Abel had said war was one of the main reasons Father Elijah had brought his followers to Tishbe.

Not that the Circle of Light was anything New Emilians believed in. No, they were told that history began at Manoach with Mother Miriam, and anything before was a fantasy, stories that could not be trusted regardless of how many bits of truth one could find. Even if Liorah occasionally discussed pre-Manoach history, did she believe any of it or was she purposefully changing the past?

The Assembly chamber transformed before Luca's eyes. The walls, a vibrant red in the light of the eternal flame, felt faded and dull. The smell of ash and smoke filled the air. It was Liorah's fault, was it not? To Luca, she'd had three options—allow Gideon to view the ancient texts in the Library, ask the Col'kasid to leave, or do as she had done and imprison them all. Despite dire warnings that the Col'kasid would not sit idly by as their future leader was bound and tortured, Liorah opted to poke the animal with a stick.

Luca shuddered, feeling as if the weight of the world was pressing down on him. He and Diego were nothing more than messengers, but every word out of Elder Levi's mouth felt like a personal attack.

"You are as dramatic as your mother," Micah said after a while. "You forget that I am Liorah's first cousin twice removed."

That was news to Luca. His eyes opened wide at that admission, as he had never once considered just how closely related New Emile and the Col'kasid were.

"There is a bond in family," Micah added.

"This Liorah is no family of mine," Levi said. "Even if that makes me her...her uncle fourth removed or something, she has threatened our way of life by kidnapping my son."

"You're her second cousin."

"I don't care!" Levi's hands closed into fists. "She brought this upon herself, and talking to her won't solve anything. We were considerate in presenting ourselves to these...these...heretics, and she responded with violent intent." Levi spun, his white robe fluttering close to the flames. "We will prepare and leave in two weeks' time. You, grandfather, will remain here as Sojen and Elder to those we leave behind. I will not be slowed."

Micah took in a deep breath and closed his eyes. Leaning slightly back, hands still on his walking stick, he appeared to be in deep contemplation. His head titled back, and from his lips came a soft, inaudible whisper. After a moment, he opened his eyes once more.

"I will go," he said.

Levi opened his mouth to protest, but Micah's hand shot up. "Patience and I brought the Col'kasid out of Manoach and into Rephidim. We built this colony with our hands, and we gave life where there was none. We were guided by the texts of the Ancients and Father Elijah's Bible, not by either separately. If there are more texts at New Emile, I must see them. If there is the slightest hope of convincing Liorah to join our two colonies as one in defense of the genuine threats on this planet, then I must be there."

Again Levi tried to interject something, and again Micah stopped him. The man was a force, even in his old age. "The strangers who came to us years ago warned that war would come to Tishbe long before the Great Return. It wasn't a false prophecy, but one based on the knowledge they possessed. They knew the Zhanshi were gathering strength in the north and that eventually they would seek to wipe out anyone who had not descended from Mathias. The strangers were not prophets but readers of history, a history written in all those texts found at Manoach."

Micah stopped and took a few more breaths. It was the most Luca had ever heard the man speak. The crackle of the fire filled the void as everyone present waited for him to continue. Finally, he did.

"I will pass into shadow soon, and my path to Eldorado leads me to New Emile. Gideon is my great grandson, and I will not abandon him. You are my son's son, and I will not abandon you. The Col'kasid can carry on without me here. If anyone should stay, it is these three elders, Malachi, Mateo, and James. Levi, you must go as well, but keep your wits about you. This is not the time for you to flex your muscle and pretend you are something you are not. You may be the current Col'kasid leader, the current Keeper of the Text, but remember that we all pass into shadow and we all return to dust."

Without another word, Micah turned and walked back into the depths of the Assembly, disappearing into the darkness.

It was settled. Luca looked around the room at those gathered. He and Diego had witnessed something that felt historic, like a moment that might be told around a fire hundreds of years from now when children gathered to hear the tale of how their lives came to be.

Something bothered Luca, however. Words he'd heard before but never put into context. Words that ate at him silently until they couldn't be ignored any longer.

Who were these strangers, and how did they know so much?

IN THE craggy embrace of rocks scattered about half a mile from the towering butte, Luca, Diego, and Jacob gathered, their silhouettes merging with shadows cast by the setting sun. The Short Moon was rising, a visible waning moon that would lend little light for the night to come. On the opposite horizon, a nearly half Long Moon would soon set. The undulating landscape around them felt like a natural barricade, an ally in their need for secrecy. Still distant from Rephidim, their voices remained soft whispers carried on the wind.

"I can't believe this," Jacob muttered. His clenched fists mirrored the turmoil that must have been within him. "Where is she? Where is Elena? I need to talk to her."

"Does it matter?" Luca asked. "I think the last time I saw her she was delivering food to Abel."

Jacob made a move to stand, but Diego put a hand on his shoulder. "Look. There are more important things to talk about, like what we're going to do. We can't very well go back. Luca would have his head on a pike, and both you and Abel would be back in the hold."

It was Luca who finally dared to voice the dangerous thought that perhaps they'd all been entertaining. "We don't have to follow the Col'kasid into this insanity," he suggested. "We can take our own path."

"Leave?" Jacob laughed, although it was devoid of mirth. "I have a duty to my father and mother, to the people here. I'm a hunter, no matter how much I protest. You may have options, but I don't have a choice."

Diego shook his head. "You always have a choice, Jacob. If you want to mend things with Elena, you'll do what's right, not what's easy or what your leaders tell you do. There's no reason you have to follow the Col'kasid creeds any longer."

"Speak for yourself. You grew up without rules. Rules are all we know."

"You don't think the Marokai have rules?"

Jacob didn't answer. As quiet descended, a khopa nudged its way out from a concealed burrow. Its fur, dusted with grains of sand, bristled in the dry air as it thrust its flattened snout into the alien world above. With a curiosity that often marked its kind, the creature swept its eyes over the terrain. Its senses, fine-tuned for subterranean life, picked up the vibrations of the three men nearby. Its nostrils flared, the peculiar scent of the strangers infiltrating its senses, raising alarm bells within its small, cautious mind. Without hesitation, it recoiled from the potential danger, the instinct to survive overtaking any inkling of curiosity. Little did it know how lucky it had been.

Luca turned to Jacob. "You've spent your whole life here. What do you know about the strangers Sojen Micah mentioned to us while we were in the Assembly after you left? Abel has mentioned them before. Who were they?"

A flicker crossed Jacob's eyes. Uncertainty, perhaps. The crease between his eyebrows deepened as he appeared to wrestle with his memory.

"The strangers," he said, his voice hushed and cautious. "I remember the stories the Assembly told. Legends, really. Sojen Micah mentioned them occasionally and always with deep respect. It was almost like he both knew and revered them."

As he spoke, his gaze seemed to focus on a point somewhere beyond the present as his mind delved into the past. "There were two of them, a man and a woman, a brother and sister, I believe. They were deeply knowledgeable about Tishbe, about the world. They gave us names for plants and animals, and they warned of us the dangers out there."

"Like the Zhanshi?"

"And others. None of what they said was written down, so you can imagine how many times their stories have changed." He paused and looked at his hands. "They spoke to Sojen Micah long before any of us were born into sunshine. It's said that Micah shared with them great secrets, great wisdom...and a past. But then they vanished, leaving no trace. They were never seen again."

"Did they pass into shadow?" Diego asked.

Jacob shrugged. "I wouldn't know, and I don't think anyone else does, either. They were just...gone. Some said they moved north, others said they moved underground. I don't suppose they ever showed up at New Emile."

"Not that I'd heard, for sure. What else did they say?" Luca's voice was anxious, but soft.

"I don't know. The Assembly never shared those details with any of us. Just that they knew more about this world and its past than anyone."

Though left with more questions than answers, Luca knew he had pried open a door to an unknown past, perhaps a path that could guide them through the chaos that awaited. He didn't know how, and as the wind swept through the surrounding rocks, one question echoed louder in his mind: If these strangers were so wise, where were they when Tishbe needed them the most?

A harsh voice echoed through the vast expanse and interrupted their conversation. "Luca! Diego!"

The sudden exclamation startled them. They turned in unison to see Saadya emerge from behind a cluster of rocks. They should have known Saadya would eventually track them down; he was a hunter, after all.

"Levi requests your presence. Immediately." Saadya snarled in the way he might have before gutting an animal. His voice was flat, yet commanding. His eyes flickered towards Jacob. "And you, wretch. Return to your post with the others. We need to get ready for what's coming."

With no hesitation, Jacob nodded, a resigned expression on his face. He cast one last look at his friends before getting up to leave. Their choices were slowly disappearing.

Maybe, Luca thought, it really is time to leave.

A DAY later, after Luca and Diego had been questioned repeatedly as to the strengths and weaknesses of the New Emilian sentinels, Saadya led one hunter team at a time into the desert in preparation to face the New Emilians. Diego had nothing to offer save what he knew of the ways in and out of the city, but Luca had been with the sentinels long enough to have some insight. Although a scout, all sentinels had been trained in the same tactics and with the same weapons. They never once considered a need to prepare for invaders, however. Their only concern up to this point had been internal threats from unhappy citizens, a revolt in the Hollows, and animals.

Following an uncomfortable grilling, Luca and Diego joined with Elena and Abel in a cave near the base of the butte, away from everyone else.

Abel threw a small twig into the smoldering embers of a fire that had recently gone out. Elena and Abel apparently had been making plans to set out toward the Barren Sea. There were rumors that the waters had receded and, if so, the ancient City of Nod would once again be accessible. There were probably supplies to be had there, and maybe a chance to establish a new home.

It had shocked Luca to hear Abel ask him if he would abandon everything for the chance at a new life, but it was even more shocking to hear that his sister would follow. Would it be possible to bring some of the Marokai along, or was that thinking too grandiose? All of them had traumatic pasts that anyone would be happy to leave behind. Why shouldn't they seek a new life? Could he approach them while they were under attack from the Col'kasid?

The fire sparked back to life under Abel's careful attention. As flickering shadows danced off the cavern walls, the muffled howls of wind outside joined the conversation. An occasional gust slipped into the cave, causing the flames to sway. The weather had turned cooler since they were last here, and while it rarely snowed in Rephidim, that didn't mean it was always warm. Some nights were downright frigid, like many nights on the moor.

Luca shared a hesitant look with Abel before turning his attention to Elena and Diego. "Maybe leaving isn't such a bad idea," he said. "We could come with you. Going our own way instead of marching back to New Emile to face a quick path into the shadows...." He trailed off. "Well, it sounds more appealing to wander aimless, if you want the truth."

Diego folded his arms across his chest and leaned back against a cold stone wall. "I'd still like to see the look on Liorah's face when the Col'kasid army marches through the gates."

Luca winced at the image, remembering Elder Levi's fiery proclamation to "burn New Emile to the ground." He looked at Elena. She was quiet, her gaze distant. "Elena?" he prompted gently. "What are your thoughts, sister?"

Elena glanced at Diego and then back to Luca. She swallowed hard. "I... I don't know. I can't help but feel like I'm abandoning Jacob."

Diego snorted. "Jacob chose his path."

"No, brother. His path was chosen for him. You know this. We may have been forced to live outside the walls of New Emile in rundown homes, but at least we always had a choice in what we did when we weren't busting rocks open or picking vegetables for the Elite." She looked at Abel. "Not here. The only choice you have is to follow — follow a leader, follow a god, or follow a book."

"Or all three," Abel said. "Jacob has been groomed one way, and it will be hard for him to break from that."

Luca looked around again at each of them. "So," he said finally. "What are we going to do?"

CHAPTER TWENTY-FOUR

JOSIAH WATCHED LIORAH PACE IN FRONT OF THE ONE window overlooking the Tree that Owned Itself. Like his, her mind was probably a cacophony of anxious thoughts, all vying for attention. Would the Col'kasid attack or use an envoy to broker a peace? Was New Emile really under threat from these invaders? Could his sentinels mount a proper defense if necessary?

Anxieties. Josiah figured she could use a vial of haelen about now. He could as well. Not only was this treatment able to cure the sick and aid in the healing of injuries, but it also had the remarkable power to calm the mind in moments like this.

Turning his attention to the council gathered around the table, Josiah's eyes fell upon Marius, the resource coordinator responsible for the colony's sustenance. Marius had just delivered the grim news that New Emile's food supplies would only last another Long Moon if no action was taken. Despite the abundance of water, the lack of a sustainable food source was a monumental issue.

Sitting beside Marius was Piper, the Keeper of the Law, who Josiah regarded with suspicion. Piper's presence was a necessary evil, his role entailing the enforcement of Liorah's edicts among the populace. Josiah couldn't help but find him unsettling, with his eerie eyes and a compliance bordering on blind obedience.

Across from Piper, the old man Alistair appeared exhausted, his face speckled with remnants of food. Although Liorah had woken him twice during the meeting, Alistair's weariness seemed to stem from something deeper, as if he carried the weight of the world on his shoulders. Josiah wondered if Alistair harbored his own doubts and concerns about Liorah's leadership.

As for Josiah, the stains of recent duties marked him with bloodied clothes and splatters of red on his face. He had just returned from handling matters that required immediate attention before joining the meeting.

"Are they still alive?" Liorah asked. She pointed at Josiah with a concerned expression. "You look like you cut them limb from limb."

"This?" Josiah pointed at his shirt. "Oh, this is not Col'kasid blood. No, we're working on the Marokai. We want to know how organized they really are."

Liorah left the window and sat. She looked at the fruit on the table and the clay jugs of wine. Naturally, Roland the Kept sat to her left and had nothing to contribute besides his body. Josiah didn't know why she just couldn't leave him in her bed.

"Did you figure out who broke in?" she asked.

"Not yet. No one will talk." Josiah motioned to his bloody clothes. "Hence the coercive techniques employed by my men."

"What about that Luca? He was with Abel most of the time they were here, and I think he has a brother or sister in the Hollows."

Liorah's obvious revulsion at the mention of the word Hollows was clear. Josiah knew the truth, but chose not to divulge it. Luca had disappeared along with his siblings, Diego and Elena. Fearing Liorah's wrath if she knew Josiah couldn't find them, he opted to tell her lies. The last thing he needed was a command to fetch the traitors.

"They've...been found, Liorah." Josiah dipped his head. "There is nothing to report."

It didn't matter. The crack in the wall in the hold had been patched. Josiah and his men had used the bodies of a few Marokai who hadn't survived his "coercive techniques" to fill the void. There would be no more attempts at escape.

"What does it really mean if the Col'kasid attack?" Alistair asked, finally coming out of his shell. "From what we've seen, they're savages who ride strange animals and wear tattered clothing. They might as well be Marokai, for all the threat they possess."

Liorah placed her arms on the table and leaned forward. "Glad you could finally join the discussion. We have haelen, and we know they can use it. They may look like savages, but I get the impression they are very strong and very organized. Have you seen the muscles on Gideon?"

Josiah saw Roland roll his eyes. He knew better, didn't he? He was kept, after all. Jealousy did not suit him.

Josiah spoke up before Alistair could continue. "From Kaius' account, the Col'kasid are very adept at hunting. He noted several weapons stores that contained well-made bows, lances, and slings. From the little time they spent in Rephidim, it appears the Col'kasid are well-equipped to mount an attack, if provoked."

"No doubt on the back of those animals," Liorah added. "But would they do so on a populace three times their size? So what if they have a few hunters?"

"Not just a few. Almost all the men. A hundred, maybe more. They stockpile weapons because of those strangers

Abel told us about. Kaius got the impression that they were ready to defend their home should a tribe like the Zhanshi come for them. They aren't a force we should turn our backs on."

"And you got all this information from Kaius?" Liorah's eyebrows furrowed. "The traitor?"

"I don't know if he is so much a traitor as a man easily persuaded."

"He is a traitor." Liorah turned away. She had banished Kaius to the Hollows as punishment for getting too close to the Col'kasid. If Liorah had her way, she would have cut off his head, but Josiah had persuaded her otherwise. He still had uses.

"What is it they really want, though?" Alistair sat up and wiped his face. "If it's simply this Gideon child, then send him out of the gates and into the moor. They can pick him up on their way. At the very least, they won't attempt to enter the city."

"I will not release Gideon or Isaiah until I am done with them," Liorah said resolutely. "They defied New Emilian custom and preach against all that Mother Miriam stood for. Besides, I think we can use them both as bargaining chips."

"Bargaining—" Alistair shook his head vehemently. "If you keep Gideon, or worse, if you *harm* him, the Col'kasid will crash through those gates on their quvi...qunia...smelly mounts and raze this city to the ground. He is their next in line, their leader's son."

"They will do no such thing." Liorah turned to Josiah but addressed everyone in the room. "We have enough men and weapons to defend against such an attack."

Josiah shifted uneasily in his chair, his voice faltering. "Y-yes, Liorah. We have men."

The room fell into a momentary silence. Liorah maintained

her gaze on Josiah, causing him to squirm even more. "We have enough men. Right? Enough weapons?"

Josiah remained silent. He knew his lack of response spoke volumes to Liorah. No, there were not enough men to defend the city. Had Liorah ever listened to his concerns the past year, she would have given him the resources he needed. Now, he was done with it, done with her.

Liorah rose from her seat and walked towards the window. From Josiah's vantage point, he saw the Long Moon shining high overhead. On these nights, the light cast an ethereal glow on the Tree that Owns Itself. Silvery haelen sparkled beneath its branches.

"What if we preempted their attack?" Liorah mused aloud. Her voice was soft and hard to hear.

Marius' voice carried across the room. "I beg your pardon, Liorah?"

Liorah turned her gaze back to the room. "The Col'kasid possess agriculture, and from what I hear, they are more advanced in this than we can ever hope to achieve. And they have those animals that could further our purposes even more."

"Yes, that is true," Alistair agreed, nodding.

Liorah continued, her voice growing more determined. "What else do they have? This... this Rephidim. What's there? What could we get from them that we do not already have?"

The question hung in the air, unanswered. Kaius claimed he had reported everything he saw before his exile to the Hollows, and attempts to gather more information about the Col'kasid from Gideon and Isaiah had been fruitless. They were unwilling to disclose any secrets. For a colony to flourish in the desert, they must possess superior knowledge that surpassed anything in New Emile. Agriculture was just the start.

Had Kaius deliberately withheld crucial information? Josiah's mind pondered the possibilities, determined to uncover the truth. He would need to talk to the man once more.

Alistair, finding his voice again, piped up with a cautious suggestion. "Perhaps we should just leave the Col'kasid alone, Liorah. If we don't provoke them, they might not pose a threat. They are miles from here, across the Wastelands. Just let Gideon and Isaiah go on the back of their mounts."

Josiah, however, remained unconvinced. "What if they perceive our hesitation as weakness? They might see it as an opportunity to strike. I have no doubt that these people would claim their god is on their side and rush in howling. They would slaughter our women and children in the name of religion."

Liorah's frustration, which must have been simmering beneath the surface, burst forth. "Enough! This is no longer about some boys disobeying me and trying to steal what is ours. This is about our survival."

She paced back and forth, her voice growing louder with each word. "I am the One Voice! No one else should dictate our actions or decide our fate. Not you, not the people, and certainly not some crazy religious hermit who lives in a desert and wants to ride through our gates on the back of an animal. As the granddaughter of our Great Mother Miriam, it is my responsibility to lead us through whatever we face and ensure our prosperity. To do that, we must stand our ground here and defend our way of life, our traditions. We cannot let these people trample our laws." She pounded a fist on the table. "*My* laws."

Her words left no room for dissent. Her authority and conviction settled upon the room, causing a brief silence to envelop them all.

All except Roland, who yawned loudly.

Liorah struck out at her kept. She grabbed a clay jar and smashed it across Roland's face, cutting into his cheeks. Blood splattered on the table and floor as the man tipped over in his chair. He struggled to right himself, but Liorah would not allow it. She kicked him in his ribs three times and once in his face.

Roland the Kept knew enough not to protest or cry. He'd been beaten before and would recover. As he lay on the floor silently, Liorah turned back to the others and steadied herself with a few deep breaths.

"We are running out of food," she announced, her voice steady. "The population is growing too fast, no matter how many people we put into the Hollows. This is unsustainable. We must seize every advantage and secure our place on this damn planet, and that includes taking whatever it is the Col'kasid have."

After a long pause, Josiah spoke again. "If Eilian were still here," he began cautiously, "he would have approached this situation differently. He had a way of seeing the bigger picture and finding common ground."

"Don't you dare say his name, Josiah," Liorah snapped, her voice laced with bitter resentment. "My father, and my brother, may have received what they deserved. Weak leaders only lead the weak."

Everyone around the table exchanged uneasy glances, sensing the weight of Liorah's words. Josiah thought he recognized a flicker of something darker lurking behind her cryptic statement. He had always known there was more to the story of Eilian's death, especially as both he and his son, Philip, had passed into shadow the same way.

Liorah reached out toward another clay jar on the table. She raised it high, her face a portrait of fury the likes of which

Josiah had only seen a few times. As the jar came crashing down on the table, Josiah jumped back, his chair tumbling away. The jar burst into pieces, scattering the contents of discarded food all over the stunned onlookers.

"Get out!" Liorah screamed. "Find me a way to stop the Col'kasid from coming through those gates. I don't care how you do it or how many people you have to enlist to get it done. Find the baker, the blacksmith. Hell, put a lance in a cook's hand. Gideon's father will not step one foot in New Emile!"

With adrenaline rushing through his system, Josiah left.

HE PUSHED past the sentinel at the gate and stormed out of New Emile. At this time of night, regardless of whether there was a Short or Long Moon in the sky, the moor was a dismal place. Darkness smothered Josiah like a blanket. How anyone could stand to live on the edge of this place in the Hollows, he didn't know.

Then again, they didn't have a choice.

In the distance, about a mile away, a few small fires showed where the Hollows were. The ramshackle buildings were barely visible. The place was so unsightly that it was a blessing in disguise that few had to look at it, and the inhabitants of the Hollows, the Marokai, were just as run-down and neglected as their dwellings.

It wasn't their fault. The ones chosen in the lottery and the others—the criminals, those who refused to renounce religion, and those who generally angered Liorah—were still just people. Yet banishment to the Hollows felt like a normal event, like the rising and setting of the two moons. There was no ceremony to it—just a kick in the ass and a good riddance. It was just one of those exiles who Josiah needed to see.

Kaius was older than Josiah by a few years, but they had

been friends long before their labor rite and long before the lottery was put into place. Of all his sentinels, Kaius was an ear upon which he felt comfortable casting his troubles.

The punishment did not fit the crime. Josiah knew that, and so did Liorah. But as the One Voice, you didn't question her decisions. His banishment to the Hollows was not just an exile. As most people in New Emile knew, the Marokai were not kind to outsiders, even if they were no longer welcome within the walls and therefore had something in common. Those with a triangle branded on their forehead were the filth to the filth, and it was common to find the body of one of these exiles in the middle of the moor. Josiah had taken enough of them out to the Wastelands to feed the animals.

He wasn't worried about Kaius, though. The man could take care of himself and was friendly enough that he would eventually work his way into the community. It was that friendliness, in fact, that had led to his exile.

At the edge of the Hollows next to a small fire, Kaius lay on his back looking up at the stars. The man before Josiah had a more peaceful demeanor than anyone he'd ever encountered despite the new mark on his forehead. It was vastly different from other sentinels who seemed to be always aware of what was going on around them, always anxious, always tense. Maybe exile would do the man some good.

"Kaius," Josiah said quietly as he approached his former sentinel and scout. "You look...comfortable."

"Should be." As Josiah stood there, Kaius steadfastly kept his eyes trained on the stars and refused to look at his former commander. "For the first time in years, I've got nothing to do and no one to tell me otherwise."

"Aren't you lonely? I mean, out here, away from the others?"

"I'm done with people for now."

Josiah chuckled and suddenly felt jealous.

Kaius sat up, propped himself on his arms. "What brings you out here?"

"Liorah."

"Did she kick you out, too? What did you do, mention something about her looks?"

Josiah smiled. "No, nothing so obvious. I came out here to ask you a few questions. I need to get your thoughts on a matter I've been puzzling over for a year."

Kaius leaned forward and sat up straight. The fire light flickered across his face. Behind him and up a small hill, a few voices filtered down through the night—Marokai who couldn't sleep, no doubt. "Let me guess. You think Eilian was murdered."

Josiah opened his eyes wide. "Either you can read minds or I came to the right place."

"You wouldn't be out here to check on my health."

Josiah sat, adjusting his crossbow and quiver. "It's never sat right with me. Eilian was healthy, yet no amount of haelen would help the man. And his son passed into shadow the same way."

"I've thought the same." Kaius threw a stick into the fire. "We have no way of finding out for sure, other than a confession on Liorah's part, but given the rumors I've heard, it's possible."

"What rumors?"

"From the Marokai who serviced the Chambers, those who became exiles recently. One of them, Ruth, had let it slip that Liorah would often send her away so the One Voice could take food and drink to her ailing father. Liorah wouldn't raise a hand if it meant work, and she certainly wouldn't serve anyone else."

"You think she poisoned them?"

Kaius shrugged. "I wouldn't put it past her. She was eighteen at the time and not very stable. You know the Great Mother had Tishbe fever, right?"

"I know that and you know it, but it hasn't been taught in schools for thirty years. One of those things that is supposed to be wiped from our history."

Kaius ran his fingers across his scalp. A little hair had come back in and if he didn't do something about it soon, the bugs would take over. "The fever affects cognitive function," he said in a tone that mimicked a teacher. "One minute you're a kind-hearted soul and the next you're gutting your children because they chewed with their mouth open."

Josiah adjusted himself. It was damnably uncomfortable to sit on the ground with a weapon slung, but he wasn't about to set it down and be unprotected in the Hollows. "Do you think she has it? Liorah, I mean."

"It runs in the family. Eilian probably did. I saw him struggle with nosebleeds and headaches in the months prior to his passing."

"I saw that, too, but I didn't really think much of it. What about Liorah's half-brother, Philip?"

"I don't think it got to him, but he had other problems." Kaius looked up the hill toward the Marokai for a second as the sounds of a squabble between lovers carried on the air. "To be honest, if Liorah assisted either of them into the shadows, it might have been a mercy."

That did not sit well with Josiah. "Eilian was my friend. We were the same age. If Liorah poisoned him and her brother so she could take over, something needs to be done. She's unfit to lead."

"That may be," Kaius said, as he leaned back and put his hands behind his head. "But what are you going to do about it?"

Josiah got the hint that Kaius was done talking. He slowly stood, repositioned his crossbow, and adjusted his tunic. What *was* he going to do about it? If Liorah had poisoned her family just to be the One Voice, what else was she capable of, and what wouldn't she do to make sure she stayed in power? Did she have the fever like her grandmother?

One thing that Josiah was certain of was that he required either proof or a confession...and he had a knack for successfully getting either from a person.

"Where is this Ruth?" he asked, looking up the hill at the Hollows. "I need to speak with her."

CHAPTER TWENTY-FIVE

GIDEON LAY SPRAWLED ON THE GRIMY FLOOR OF THE DARK, dank hold. Thankfully, the tortured he'd received had not been as bad as he originally thought. Josiah was less a physical animal than a psychological one. The torture had, however, taken a toll on Isaiah's once robust physique. The muscles in his legs had atrophied, now reduced to feeble sticks that trembled under his weight. Desperation clawed at Gideon, not for his own sake, but for the life hanging in the balance just a few feet away from him. He was sure his path to Eldorado lay here, but it didn't have to be the same for Isaiah.

They had not been shaved, and the promise of torture from the tiny bugs that fed on hair had been kept. At first, it was a minor itch in the scalp, a tingle along the legs. Within a few days, however, that tingle turned into an unrelenting fire as each hair was consumed down to its root. Gideon and Isaiah had both tried in vain to pull the hair from their heads just to stop the burning, but no matter how many clumps they yanked out, the bugs found other hair. As if Josiah's torture had not been enough, to remain unshaved in New Emile was to invite a slow and agonizing death.

Gideon's bindings were ruthless. Rough ropes of unbelievable strength bit into his flesh and tethered him to the unforgiving, cold wall. He'd pulled and thrashed, screamed and fought, but they wouldn't give an inch, much like Josiah and his heartless sentinels. For days that had morphed into weeks, they had beaten him, tortured him, stripped him of his dignity. Even so, he remained silent, his lips sealed.

Because honestly, he had nothing to offer. And as the days wore on, the torture had felt more like a punishment than necessary to elicit any information.

Gideon turned his head to the right. The sight of Isaiah was heart-wrenching. Isaiah, who had volunteered along with Jacob to join his envoy, was now a crumpled, tortured shell of a man. His body wracked by torment, he lay motionless on the filthy floor, barely able to gasp in the fetid air of the hold. His eyes were clouded over with pain, his ragged breath growing weaker with every passing second, the shadows of death creeping ever closer.

Isaiah couldn't keep down the meager scraps of food they threw at them, his body rejecting it like poison. The bowl of water they were forced to share was no better; it smelled strongly of urine, a sickly-sweet stench that made Gideon's stomach churn with revulsion. They had no choice but to drink, though, as their parched bodies craved hydration, regardless of the source.

Gideon was at a breaking point, at the precipice of madness. Every breath he took was a plea, a silent prayer to a god he was sure no longer listened. All the time spent with Father Elijah's Bible, all the time spent praying with the Assembly, all the time spent preparing for the Great Return — none of it mattered.

All he had left were questions. Had Abel, Jacob and the others made it back to Rephidim? Would his father, Levi, charge through the gates to rescue them? And where, oh where, was God now?

The lock on the door to the hold clanged, a sound that had become synonymous with pending torture. Gideon sucked in a breath through his teeth and pushed back against the wall, as if even an inch farther from the door would make a difference.

As dark as it was, it was difficult to see who was at the door as it swung open. If it had been Josiah, he would have stood there and chuckled in his maniacal way. His sentinels were quick to throw a few scraps of food on the floor or refill the water bowl. It wasn't until the person spoke that Gideon knew.

"Bring me a torch," Liorah said to someone unseen. "And leave us." Immediately, a flame illuminated the doorway and the woman standing in it. She had been down to the hold a few times in the beginning, but never without Josiah. Now, it seemed like she was alone as the sound of the sentinel retreating grew softer and softer. Her presence was as welcome as it was terrifying.

What does she want?

Liorah stepped into the room, pushing the bowl of water over with her foot. Isaiah lay on the ground, his eyes swollen shut. Gideon guessed he was either asleep or unconscious based on the slow, rhythmic sound of his breath.

"Liorah," Gideon rasped. The name felt like dust in his parched mouth. As her presence filled the grim space, the air suddenly felt heavier, the hold more claustrophobic.

Liorah tilted her head a little as she approached Gideon. She placed the torch in a holder on the wall and stood in front of him, far enough away to be safe. "Do you truly believe they're coming, Gideon?" Her voice was a chilly whisper. "After all this time?"

Gideon swallowed hard against the knot in his throat. Rather than answer, he gave a quick nod of his head.

"And yet," Liorah said, a coy lilt to her voice as she crouched, her gown pooling elegantly around her, "here you are. Left for dead, by your own faith. Your god nowhere to be found."

He flinched at her words as the suggestion hit him harder than any physical blow. But he remained silent, his eyes fixed on the dirt floor beneath him and the excrement that had never been cleaned. The truth in her words gnawed at him, but he refused to let her see his doubt.

Slowly, almost casually, Liorah reached out to trace a line up Gideon's bare arm, her touch soft against his chilled, bruised skin. Her fingers moved slowly, suggestively, up his arm and across his chest. It was a seductive dance that left a trail of fire in its wake, an unholy sensation that contradicted everything he'd been raised to believe. It was unexpected and completely inappropriate. Gideon found himself frozen under her touch. His mind raced to reconcile the teachings of the Col'kasid with the woman in front of him.

"Liorah," he whispered. But he was cut off as her fingers moved higher, tracing the line of his throat with a touch so light it made his skin tingle. The intimacy of the action was startling.

Her touch lingered, her fingers tracing the contours of his face in a gentle caress, each movement slow and deliberate. Her breath brushed against his face, and he could smell the sweet scent of her, an intoxicating mixture he remembered from long ago when things were different, when she rode the quvianaq alongside him. But there was another scent, too, something wilder, untamed.

Every fiber of Gideon's being screamed at him to recoil, to push her away. But he was pinned not only by his bindings but by her touch and the raw sensuality in her gaze. This wasn't the Col'kasid way, but it was Liorah's, and for a moment, the line between them blurred.

He did not yield. His silence became his only shield against her advances. Her caress stopped as abruptly as it began, and the silence once again fell heavy around them. Isaiah's ragged breaths and the distant crackle of the torch in its holder were the only sounds in the hold.

"Liorah," Gideon murmured, desperate to regain some control over the situation. But he was cut off once more as her fingers moved delicately over his cheekbone.

"You know, Gideon," Liorah started, her voice soft yet holding a certain authority. Her words slithered through the air, sending a shiver down his spine. "There is another way. You don't need to be a prisoner of your past, of your faith, or even of this Rephidim."

"What...what are you saying?"

She paused, her fingers tracing a path down his jawline.

"Roland bores me." Her voice lowered to a sultry murmur that stirred a confusing mix of emotions within him. "I could teach you the ways of New Emile."

Gideon's mind whirled with her words, their implications shaking the foundations of his beliefs. He could abandon the hold, the torture, the desperate hope for a rescue that seemed less likely with each passing day. But at what cost? Would he lose himself in the process? Isn't that what had happened to Liorah's Kept Roland, the strange man always at her side?

He was a man of faith, of the Col'kasid, the future Keeper of the Text. He was raised in the strict religious confines of Rephidim. Yet here he was, tied up in a grimy hold, his body scarred and his spirit broken. God was deaf to his pleas. And there was Liorah, offering a way out, a promise of a different life wrapped in a veil of seductive promises.

Liorah's touch slowly withdrew, her fingertips trailing a last, lingering path across his rough cheek before pulling away entirely. Her gaze held his a moment longer, the heat of her proximity leaving a flush on his face even as the space between them grew.

She rose gracefully, yet her gaze remained on Gideon even as she stepped back. "Think it over, Gideon," she said. Her voice echoed eerily with a promise. She would be back.

With that, she turned, her gown sweeping the filthy floor as she made her way towards the door. The flickering torchlight cast shifting shadows on her figure, transforming her into an enigma that unsettled him.

With a last glance over her shoulder and a cryptic smile, she was gone. The door closed behind her with a resounding thud.

Her departure left the hold colder, the darkness heavier. Gideon stared at the door long after her departure, her words an echo in his mind, her touch still burning his skin. Only Isaiah's labored breath kept him grounded in their harsh reality.

Despite the pain, the uncertainty, and the overwhelming fear, Gideon knew one thing—Liorah would return, and with her, the tempting promise of a different life. The thought of it kept him awake long into the night, his mind tangled in a web of faith, survival, and the seductive allure of Liorah's offer.

All he had to do was decide if he would pay the price...whatever it was.

Because temptation always comes at a price. Was he bound to take Roland's place?

THE DARKNESS was the worst, with nothing but an eerie silence. Day and night were one and the same. Gideon thought that maybe a day had passed, but it could have been two. Isaiah's condition had worsened. The shallow breaths he took were now reduced to gasping wheezes that barely disturbed the silence of the hold. It wouldn't be long until he passed into shadow and found Eldorado.

The sound of the lock disturbed the silence, and the creak of the hold door echoed through the small space. It was quickly followed by the flickering light of a torch that danced across the walls.

Liorah's silhouette filled the doorway, and her presence set Gideon's heart racing. Flickering light reflected off her eyes, giving them an almost ethereal glow. As before, she placed the torch on the wall holder and approached.

"Gideon." Her voice cut through the silence. "Have you decided what you want to do?"

His gaze moved from her to Isaiah, still motionless, his breaths coming in ragged gasps. "Can you please give Isaiah some haelen?" he asked with a dryness in his throat that made it hard to speak. "Let him heal."

Liorah stilled and her eyes narrowed slightly. "You would save a man who represents those who left you here to die?"

"He does not deserve this."

Liorah seemed to study him, her gaze probing as if trying to decipher the truth behind his words. Gideon held her stare. After what seemed like an eternity, she relented. The change wasn't visible, but Gideon sensed something in her.

"Very well," she conceded, her eyes never leaving his.

She stepped closer to him and knelt. Her fingers trailed along his chest again, their touch just as tantalizing as before. Gideon's breath caught in his throat as a sense of unsuppressed unease ignited within him.

"If that is what you wish," she whispered, her voice barely audible.

A glimmer of hope sparked within Gideon, just a small flame that flickered against the consuming darkness. It was a risk, a dangerous gamble, but for Isaiah's life and perhaps his own, he had to take it.

The silence that followed Liorah's agreement was filled with unsaid words and concealed intentions. With a measured calm that belied his inner turmoil, Gideon watched as Liorah stood and slid the fabric off her shoulders. She reached for the hem of her gown, then slowly let it fall to the ground. Her eyes never left his, challenging him, testing his resolve. He had never set eyes on a naked woman before and had only the slightest idea of what to expect. This was not it.

She knelt before him and reached for his bindings. Gideon stiffened at her touch. As her fingers danced over the ropes, he battled an urge to cry out. But she didn't untie him. Instead, her touch became suggestive, almost intimate, tracing the rough edges of the ropes, the contours of his torso.

A pang of discomfort knotted in his stomach as her hands roamed, her touch deliberately provocative. His upbringing, his beliefs, screamed at him to resist, to pull away, but he was bound, both physically and by his vow to save Isaiah. So he watched, his anguish growing under her heated gaze and wandering touch.

The dank hold became a theater of shadows and secrets. The flickering torchlight cast a macabre dance of light and darkness around them. His breath came in gasps, each intake of air laced with the stale stench of the room and the faint hint of Liorah's fragrance. With a quick jerk of his pants, she exposed him. Gideon held his breath as he hardened at her touch.

This isn't right, he thought, even as Liorah enveloped him with her body and gasped in ecstasy. *God, forgive me.*

UNCOMFORTABLE MOMENTS later, Liorah slid off Gideon and lay down next to him on the grimy floor. Her body radiated a heat that was both enticing and disturbing. With a sinking feeling, Gideon realized just how far he had been pushed. His faith, his beliefs, were under trial, and the stakes were higher than he had ever known. He had failed as the future leader of the Col'kasid, and his life would never be the same.

Yet, as the reality of his situation washed over him, Gideon held on to the flicker of hope that had sparked within him. Perhaps Isaiah would live. Perhaps, through this trial, he could find a way out of the grim hold that had become his world.

As they lay there, Liorah's fingers tracing idle patterns on his chest, her voice sliced through the heavy silence. "Tell me more about the Col'kasid, Gideon," she coaxed, her tone deceptively soft. "What are the quvianaq like? You know, during a hunt. Are they always so tied to their rider?"

The question was a reminder of the precarious nature of his situation. If his father was coming, whatever he said could be used against them. A nagging thought crossed his mind, though. They had abandoned him, hadn't they? Liorah had been right all along?

"I...I don't know much," he admitted, but the glint in her eyes told him that wasn't enough. He racked his brain for something, anything that might satisfy her curiosity.

"The...the quvianaq..." His voice faltered. He thought about the giant beasts, their formidable presence, and their power. "They...they can be distracted, which can throw the hunters off balance. The thing about the Col'kasid, though, is that they have learned best to attack from the back of their mount."

Gideon paused, his mind whirring with the implications of what he was sharing. But there was more to it, wasn't there? He thought of why she was asking, of what she might hope to get out of him. He knew this had been a ploy to extract information, but he had to admit it was a much better method than those employed by Josiah and his sentinels. She had been right—he had been abandoned and nothing he said would matter, anyway.

"They—the Col'kasid hunters, anyway—have a certain...hesitation for killing," he added, his voice barely a whisper. "It goes against our—their—beliefs. They would rather exile someone than take a life."

He could almost feel Liorah's curiosity piqued. "Exile?" she echoed.

"Yes," he nodded, the memory of countless sermons, of the scripture they lived by, vivid in his mind. "They believe the elements should decide the fate of a man. They think it's less of a sin than killing directly. If a person is truly innocent, then God will save them. If they are guilty, then the Assembly could wash its hands of the matter."

As he spoke, he realized the irony of it all. Here he was, sharing secrets, revealing vulnerabilities of his people while bound and under the mercy of his captors. But it didn't really matter, did it? Besides, it was a small price to pay for a glimmer of hope, a chance at survival for him and Isaiah.

It was, after all, that element of hope that was keeping him alive in the hold.

Gideon swallowed hard. He forced his voice to remain steady. "Liorah," he said, struggling to meet her gaze. "Isaiah needs the haelen. You promised—"

Liorah met his words with an icy silence, her touch on his chest immediately withdrawn. Her expression hardened, and her gaze became a stormy whirlpool of resentment and hurt highlighted by the flicker of the torch.

"I give you myself, and that's what you have to say?" She spat the words out, her anger boiling to the surface. The softness that had cloaked her was gone, replaced by a chilling fury.

Without another word, she rose and put her gown on. It swept the grimy floor as she stormed out of the hold, the heavy thud of the door echoing ominously in the silence she left behind.

It had been so quick. All of it.

And then there was nothing.

Alone in the cold, dank room, Liorah had left Gideon with his thoughts. Regret and guilt gnawed at him. The air was still heavy with the lingering scent of sex, the aroma of Liorah's body. It was a haunting reminder of the choices he had made, like a ghost that had enveloped his soul.

The emotional dam within him broke. Tears trickled down his cheeks, silent testimonies of his torment, the physical pain from his wounds a dull echo in comparison. With each sob that wracked his frame, he could taste despair. The heavy scent of Liorah clung to his skin, once an intoxicating and confusing mix of passion, now a nauseating reminder of the lengths he had gone to in order to protect Isaiah.

In the grim solitude of the hold, he allowed himself to weep. His tears mingled with the dirt and sweat on his face.

The future was bleak, and the weight of his choices was now a crushing burden on his conscience. As his cries echoed in the hold, Gideon felt the full impact of his predicament. He had been forced to play a dangerous game, one he was ill-equipped to navigate.

But he had no choice, did he?

MUCH LATER, the heavy clanging of the hold door reverberated through the room, jarring Gideon out of his thoughts. His eyes darted towards the entrance as he half-feared, half-hoped Liorah had returned. Instead, a burly sentinel stepped into the dimly lit room. In his hand was a small vial, its contents shimmering in the faint light from a torch just outside the door.

"Haelen," Gideon whispered to himself. A flicker of relief washed over him.

The sentinel grunted as he approached Isaiah. His hulking figure cast a long shadow over the unconscious man. As Gideon watched, his eyes were glued to the vial in the sentinel's hand. The man uncorked it, then gripping Isaiah's jaw, he tilted his head back and forced the liquid down his throat. Isaiah spluttered and coughed, but managed to swallow.

Gideon watched as Isaiah's ragged breath steadied. It was a minor victory, but it was enough. Isaiah was still alive, for now.

What more would Gideon have to do to keep him that way?

As the sentinel left, slamming the door behind him, Gideon sank back against the wall. The taste of relief was sweet, yet also tainted by the bitter aftertaste of what he had done.

His body felt leaden, his heart heavy with remorse yet relieved that Isaiah would live another day. The scent of Liorah was still on his skin like a rash that wouldn't heal. As he closed his eyes, he could still feel her touch, her fingers tracing over his chest, her words echoing in his ears, her body consuming him.

If he had gone this far, what else would he do against the Col'kasid, against God?

And, too, when would she be back?

CHAPTER TWENTY-SIX

IN THE FOUR WEEKS SINCE THE UNEXPECTED APPEARANCE OF Russant and his men from New Emile, the Zhanshi had been far from idle. Aside from finally testing their new projectile—which worked flawlessly with the corral of pua'a ono obliterated in a flash—Chen had dispatched scouts to follow the path taken by the gulao. His hope was to uncover signs of their origin, a path that would lead the Zhanshi to victory. One team had recently returned with intriguing news—signs of human passage to the northwest, near the river's shallowest point and upstream from the canyon that had so vexed the Zhanshi scouts before.

At the moment, Chen found himself deep in deliberation with his lieutenants in his dwelling. His men, Lucien, Martin, and Lin Xi were arrayed around him, their collective focus on the rough map spread before them. Luke was present as well, but he opted to stay in the shadows, still seemingly upset at Chen's desire for bloodshed.

"We must seize the moment, Zhuren," Lucien insisted. "They do not know we are coming, and an army of our men led by you could quickly bring about the end you seek."

Martin echoed his sentiment. "We cannot afford hesitation. The path ahead was given to us by this...gulao." He spit the word out. "It is their mistake, and now that we have our weapons, we will be unstoppable."

Ever the voice of reason, Lin Xi countered. "Haste should not cloud our decision. Should it, Zhuren? We must consider all possibilities."

"Such as?" Martin asked. He was tired of this conversation, but Chen would not allow a decision to be made without hearing everyone's opinion.

"What if they are stronger than we expect?" Lin Xi continued. "If we have been successful in advancing technology in Yaolan, what is to say that this New Emile has not also perfected weapons? They may be more of a threat than those left at the temple. As we all heard from the stories of our great Zhuren Mathias the Third, those he encountered were sickly and weak." Lin Xi paused before continuing. "I do not think that would be the case here. Intelligence should lead before weapons."

"Intelligence is a big word for you." Martin's sarcasm filled the room. "Are you sure you know what that means?"

Chen listened intently. He valued the input of his lieutenants—needed it, really—but ultimately the decision would be his. His gaze drifted to the map, his fingers tracing the lines that represented their land, their valley, their home. Beyond what was known, all was blank.

He turned from the map and looked into a corner of the room where Russant watched, bound and useless. His other men had succumbed to torture far too fast and were set ablaze outside the valley where the stench of their burning bodies would be carried away. Russant had been resolute, however, unwilling to answer questions as to where this New Emile was, what type of weapons they possessed, and how powerful their men were. Still he hung on.

It was annoying.

The meeting was abruptly broken by one of the scouts

who had ventured to the northwest in search of Russant's path. "Zhuren," the boy, no older than fifteen, looked as if he'd just run a thousand miles to deliver news. "We have found signs of human passage. Camp remains, footprints, and...strange stacks of rocks."

Chen considered his words. "Where the three rivers run?"

"Yes, Zhuren."

With a nod that Chen knew meant more to the scout than any thank you, he measured his next move. "Anming, is it?" he asked.

"Yes, Zhuren."

"Take a few of your more capable comrades and follow these...stacks of rocks, these cairns."

"Cairns?" Anming echoed, his expression puzzled.

Chen nodded. "They are markers, Anming, created by travelers to guide the way or to signify something important. They are markers left in error by our guest here." Chen pointed to the corner of the room where Russant looked crestfallen.

Anming straightened up. "Understood, Zhuren," he responded dutifully.

"Look for signs of civilization, especially any that would point to this New Emile," Chen added. "If you find anything, anything at all, I want you to return immediately and report. Do not engage. Do not approach to where you might be seen. Our advantage is in knowledge and preparation." He turned to Lin Xi. "As has been pointed out, intelligence must lead an army."

Anming nodded. "We will not fail you, Zhuren."

"No." Chen gave a curt nod. "You will not. Stay safe and vigilant, Anming. As our history tells us, these gulao cannot be trusted."

Chen dismissed Anming and watched him depart from the room. As soon as the door closed, a deep sigh echoed in the room. He turned to see Luke leaning against a wall. He looked troubled.

"Zhuren." Luke said. "Are you certain about this course? Is it not better to let the past remain buried?"

Chen sighed, rubbing his temples. "We have had this discussion many times. The gulao must pay for what they have brought to our world."

Luke nodded, his weathered face stern. "I know. But remember what your father said. Vengeance is a fire that consumes all, and no decision should be made solely on its heat."

"No?" Chen's tone turned bitter. "My father was a wise man. This is without a doubt. But tell me, what choices do the gulao leave us, Luke? Should we not stand for ourselves, for those who suffered at the hands of their ancestors? Or should we let history repeat itself, again and again?"

"Of course not, Zhuren, but the path of conflict is filled with uncertainties and loss. Loss is a beast we know too well. We are Zhanshi, warriors indeed, but we are also protectors, guardians of our people. I fear our quest to avenge Mathias will lead to terror in the valley."

Chen stared at Luke for a long moment, wrestling with the wisdom in the elder's words. "I wish there was another way," he said finally, his voice quiet. "But we cannot protect by merely hiding and hoping to be left alone. If this fool found us, others will follow. What then?"

Luke nodded slowly before bowing his head. "May the spirits of the Zhuren guide us right."

Chen silently nodded his head before turning from Luke and looking at their prisoner.

"Russant." Chen's voice echoed.

Russant stirred, looking up at him. Cracked lips and dried blood parted, but no words came out.

"It seems as if you have made a fatal error, my friend."

Russant's face went pale. When he finally spoke, his voice was bitter and harsh. "What is so important about New Emile that you are willing to invade? We have nothing."

Chen's gaze hardened. "I take it your leader, your One Voice as you call her, has never told you of the history of our people."

"Liorah didn't know about you until recently. What stories would she tell us?"

"My great grandfather, Mathias," Chen began, his voice steady, "was a man of peace. When the original Circle of Light colonists came to this planet you refer to as Tishbe—your ancestors, I should add—Mathias extended the hand of friendship."

He paused, waiting for a reaction. But the man simply watched.

"He offered them food," Chen continued, "ways to get resources, a chance to come together as one to build and populate a new world of peace. He tried to build bridges between our people, to coexist in harmony. But what did he get in return? Exile. Humiliation." His voice grew harsher with each word. "Mathias was thrown out, mocked, treated as an outcast. Despite everything he did for your kind, for Elijah's people, they turned their backs on him, on us. They drove us away and into this valley. And now, you come here, hoping for what? Sympathy? Forgiveness?"

"We were only on Discovery, curious," Russant answered weakly. "We only wanted to know if the rumor of a third tribe was true."

Chen's eyes widened. He was silent for several long moments as he processed this revelation, his brows furrowing in thought. Finally he spoke again, his voice hushed. "Did you say...a third tribe?"

CHEN'S HANDS remained steady as he applied another round of punishment to the frail figure before him. The small, enclosed room was filled with the acrid scent of sweat and fear. Russant had been hung on a beam upside down in a corner of Chen's chambers. His body swayed with each agonizing breath. Around his belly, a cage had been attached and inside, a small rodent had been feasting on the man's flesh.

"Once more," Chen said, his voice cold and hard. "Who are the Col'kasid, this third tribe you have mentioned?" His eyes bored into Russant's.

Russant's head lolled, the blood pooling in his face, his breath ragged. When he attempted to meet Chen's gaze, there was defiance still in his bloodshot eyes. He opened his mouth to speak, but nothing came out.

Chen clenched his jaw. The stubborn resistance irked him. His hand found the hilt of his dagger, but he did not wield it against Russant. Not yet, anyway. "You try my patience, Russant," Chen said through gritted teeth. "It does you no good to take your secrets to your grave."

Despite the dire situation, Russant chuckled, a dark, bitter sound. "You...don't...know..."

His words trailed off, and his body convulsed. Chen watched as Russant's eyes rolled back. His breath came in quick gasps before finally falling eerily silent. The body swayed gently, casting long, grotesque shadows on the chamber walls while the rodent squealed in delight.

"No!" Chen roared, his voice echoing throughout the room. He lunged at the now lifeless body, hands balled into fists. "You will not die on me! Not yet!"

But it was too late. Russant was gone, and so too was any chance at learning more about the Col'kasid.

Chen's rage flared, his vision blurred with a red haze. He kicked over a table, scattering tools of torment. The loud crash filled the room, but did nothing to dull his anger. He balled his fists, his knuckles turning white from the force.

"You coward!" He screamed at the corpse. His anger gave way to raw, seething frustration. He ripped the rodent cage off the man, tossing the feasting animal to the side. With a grunt, he pulled his dagger from its hilt and lashed out, slicing Russant's stomach open. Entrails fell from the gaping wound and plopped onto the floor. With renewed fury, he jabbed the dagger into Russant's chest and punched his torso repeatedly, not caring about the blood that covered his arms, his neck, his face. His father had always warned him about the futility of anger, but right now, it did not matter.

As Zhuren Chen, leader of the Zhanshi, lost his composure, the rodent took the opportunity to flee leaving small trails of bloody footprints.

Finally, Chen's breath slowed, his pulse no longer a thundering cacophony in his ears. He pulled the dagger out and stared at it, its blood-soaked metal gleaming in the dim light. He turned from Russant at last, leaving the lifeless body to sway gently.

Chen was left with nothing but unanswered questions and an unresolved threat. For that, he hated the gulao even more.

He turned and stood before the shrine of the past Zhuren in silence. The sacred artifacts of the Zhanshi sat before him, radiating a sense of ancient wisdom. Illuminated by flickering candlelight, they seemed to scrutinize him, their symbolic presence more oppressive than comforting. His breathing exercises helped quell the storm of emotions within him, but they could not eliminate the nagging uncertainty gnawing at his gut.

Who were these people?

Chen contemplated his journey to this point. He had inherited the legacy of his tribe, tales of bravery and courage, wisdom passed down through generations. They were stories that molded him into the leader he now was, a Zhuren, a warrior. Yet, they did not prepare him for this—the uncertainty of an imminent confrontation with a previously unknown band of gulao who had escaped his grandfather's wrath. With two tribes of gulao, what was he to do?

He clenched his fists, nails digging into his palms. Russant's death, although expected, was a loss, not a victory. It was a door slammed shut, leaving him in darkness. He had not relished the man's suffering. Each scream, each grimace, had reflected his own failure as a leader. Every time he had hoped that the next question, the next prod, would reveal a way to avenge his people, fulfill the promises he had made when he had taken the mantle of Zhuren. But now, that hope was gone.

The scent of burning incense filled his nostrils, grounding him in the moment. He studied the sacred tools and symbols, each carrying tales of former Zhurens cast in the soft glow of candlelight. They had faced their own trials, their own moments of indecision, yet they had also led the Zhanshi to where they were now—a thriving community, self-sufficient and strong, despite their isolation.

Reflecting on the legacy of Mathias the First, Chen could almost hear his great-great-grandfather's voice as if channeled through the tales and wisdom passed down through the generations. He'd never met the man, something he had long regretted. "Strength does not come from the absence of fear," he wrote once, "but from the will to face it."

Yes, he thought. *Have the will to face it.* He extinguished the candles, their smoke spiraling upward, carrying with it silent promises to his people. His path was not clear, but that was okay. He would face this unknown future, not with fear, but with courage, just as his ancestors had before him.

The room fell into darkness, broken only by the faint glow of moonlight filtering through the solitary window. Chen moved towards it and contemplated the path that lay ahead for him and his people. Yaolan was quiet this night, but that would have to change.

The mention of a third tribe had unnerved him. He had lived his life believing there were only two tribes—the Zhanshi and those who had escaped his grandfather's wrath, those who had descended from the Circle of Light. The existence of another was a shock. It threatened to upend the order of the world as he knew it. He remembered his grandmother's stories about the victory, the way she would describe his grandfather, Mathias the Third, returning home with the spoils of their conquest and the anger of its incompleteness.

So, who were these Col'kasid? How had they survived his grandfather's wrath? Had they also turned to technological advancement, like the Zhanshi, or had they followed a path of faith and devotion, like the old Circle of Light which had turned its back on Mathias the First?

Chen felt both dread and excitement. On the one hand, the revelation brought with it potential problems and dangers. Yet it also represented an opportunity. If this tribe was peaceful and enemies of this New Emile, would they be willing allies?

The enemy of my enemy?

But if they weren't peaceful, if they were hostile...

Chen shook his head and forced the worrying thoughts

away. It was useless to speculate without information. He needed facts. He needed to know more about the Col'kasid—their culture, their capabilities, their intentions. Only then could he make an informed decision about how to approach. Intelligence should lead before weapons, as Lin Xi had said.

He needed to send another scouting team, stronger and more capable.

Chen called in a young scout, Jin, whose eyes shined with pride. The boy was fifteen, but ready to prove himself, much like his brother Anming.

"Jin." Chen kept his voice commanding but steady, firm yet tinged with a sense of urgency.

The young scout bowed his head respectfully. "Yes, Zhuren."

"I have a task for you. Are you ready?"

"Yes, Zhuren. I am ready."

"There have been rumors of a...possible third tribe hidden from our view. Have you heard anything?"

Jin's eyes widened. "No, Zhuren. Only of the gulao my brother seeks."

Chen nodded. "I want you to find them for me. Take a few of those you trust and arm yourself."

Jin's face revealed his apparent nervousness. "But Zhuren, where should I begin? How will I find them?"

Chen took a moment to steady his thoughts before answering. He recognized the significance of the task he was assigning, as well as the inherent difficulty in chasing a rumor. "Do you know how to get to the shore of the Barren Sea?"

"Yes, Zhuren. My brother and I have ventured there many times."

"Good, good. Follow the shore to the southwest. There you will find the old gulao settlement, a place they called the

City of Nod. Continue south past it until your path takes you east."

Jin nodded, absorbing the wisdom offered by his leader. "And I will find this new tribe there?"

"I doubt it, but it will be a starting point." Chen considered all the possible things that might lie in the young boy's path. "Travel south, away from the shore. If you find something—signs of civilization or settlements—observe. Do not approach. Do not reveal yourself. Is this understood?"

"Yes, Zhuren. I understand. I will not disappoint you."

Chen's expression softened. "I believe in you, Jin, just as I believe in your brother. May the spirits of the Zhuren guide your steps and grant you safe passage."

Jin straightened his posture and bowed.

As Jin left, Chen turned toward the corpse of Russant still hanging in the corner of his chambers. The rodent had returned and was now nibbling on the man's entrails.

He would not be the last gulao to suffer this fate.

No.

All of them would.

CHAPTER TWENTY-SEVEN

GIDEON'S FACE WAS TWISTED INTO A GUILT-RIDDEN EXPRESSION, not that anyone could see that in the dim light coming through the cracks in the door to their prison. He studied Isaiah, whose constitution had remarkably improved in just a week from his previously near-death state. Despite not being at full strength, Isaiah had a revived spirit that was hard to overlook. Haelen was indeed a miracle.

"Gideon," Isaiah said, interrupting the silence. The creases on his forehead gave away his awareness of the discomfort Gideon was going through. "You look like you're on the road to Eldorado and you've lost your way."

Gideon was in turmoil. How could he bring himself to articulate the enormity of his mistake? "I screwed up," he said weakly.

Isaiah looked at Gideon. "Go on."

"I...I was scared for you," he stammered. "I...I did what I thought I had to do."

Confusion flickered in Isaiah's eyes. "What do you mean?"

"I was with Liorah." Gideon's voice trembled slightly at the mention of her name. An involuntary shiver ran through him. "She...she helped save you. But in return, I may have told her too much about us, given her ideas. About the quvianaq. About our people."

The ensuing silence was oppressive. What Gideon had confessed to Liorah was nothing more than what Josiah had attempted to pry from them both through painful force.

Isaiah's expression was unreadable.

"I'm scared, Isaiah," Gideon admitted. "I fear what might happen if the Col'kasid decide to attack New Emile. We won't survive. Not after what I've done." His hands clenched tight in his lap.

Isaiah didn't respond immediately. He looked weakened, his eyes glossed over with a pained understanding as he stared at Gideon, who sat in the half-light wrestling with his conscience. The silence stretched, aching and heavy, and Gideon was left to contend with his thoughts alone.

He was more than just a leader, more than just an ambassador to New Emile, more than just Levi's son. He was to be the Keeper of the Text, the spiritual guide of the Col'kasid. And yet, he had been tempted by the touch of Liorah, had bartered his people's secrets for his personal desires. He had strayed from his sacred path and allowed his heart to rule his mind. How could he face his father, his people, after such a transgression? It was these actions that warranted expulsion from Rephidim.

"Gideon." Isaiah finally broke the silence, his voice weak. "We all make mistakes."

Gideon looked at him, desperate for some form of absolution. "Not like this, Isaiah. This was betrayal."

Isaiah shook his head. "You were scared. You made a choice in a moment of desperation. Who can fault you for that?"

"But was it the right choice? Or was it selfish? Was I thinking of the Col'kasid or was I thinking of myself, of Liorah?"

Isaiah was quiet for a moment. "Only you can answer that, Gideon," he said gently, despite the evident struggle to speak. "We all seek our own path through trial. You are no different."

As soon as the words left Isaiah's lips, his body gave in to exhaustion and he slumped back onto the filthy floor, unconscious. The frail light from under the door danced across his face, highlighting the lines of fatigue and illness that marked his skin. Gideon, left alone once again, could only stare at Isaiah's tranquil form, the man's words echoing in his mind.

He needed to seek his path. Seek guidance in the Text, not that he had access to it now. But how could he reconcile that with the lingering memory of Liorah's touch, the magnetic pull he still felt towards her even amidst the burden of his guilt? He couldn't deny that his actions had been born out of personal desire as much as desperation.

The room closed in on Gideon as he grappled with his conflicted feelings.

Was it too late?

The prospect of his father, Levi, arriving brought with it a twinge of fear. He dreaded the disappointment he was sure to see in his father's eyes when the truth was revealed. He was not a forgiving man, despite all the sermons to the contrary. He was, in a word, a hypocrite. He could only pray that his father and the New Emilians could negotiate a peaceful solution. The thought of his people engaging in a futile attack was unnerving. His actions had set these events into motion, and now it was beyond his control. There was no undoing the damage.

As Isaiah's chest rose and fell, Gideon grappled with the weight of his actions. Making things much worse, though guilt plagued him, he longed for Liorah's touch again, reliving each caress. Caught between duty and desire, Gideon faced a long journey of redemption and self-discovery. Beneath his titles, he hoped to find his true path again when the dust settled.

Isaiah's weak stirrings interrupted the silence and his eyes fluttered open.

"Has...has Liorah been back?" Isaiah rasped out.

Gideon shook his head. "No." He wondered if his answer sounded like disappointment to his friend. Damn it, though. He missed her. It was a longing that contradicted his duty, a dangerous ache that gnawed at him. He really *wished* she would come back.

Isaiah studied him quietly. "Gideon," he said, the words a clear struggle. "Longing and duty...they often pull us in different directions. But remember this—duty is what we owe to others, to our people. Longing...that's a debt we owe to ourselves."

Biblical lines suddenly echoed in Gideon's mind, their words mocking his inner turmoil. He murmured them, more to himself than to Isaiah, "For what shall it profit a man, if he shall gain the whole world, and lose his own soul?"

The words danced around his thoughts, a cruel irony as he weighed the cost of his longing against his duty.

"I wouldn't say you lost your soul," Isaiah said with a slight mirth in his voice. "You just made love to a woman. I have to say...I...I'm jealous."

In that moment Gideon felt himself break. A laugh escaped from deep within and resounded off the stone walls. "It wasn't long enough to be called love."

GIDEON HAD requested to see Liorah again, had made his plea as politely and as desperately as he could. But as the hours crawled by, his hope waned. There had been no response, no acknowledgment. It was as if Liorah had disappeared from his world as suddenly as she had entered.

Not seeing her was becoming more painful than seeing her again.

"Gideon." Isaiah's voice punctured his thoughts, sounding startlingly clear despite his frailty.

Gideon turned, a knot forming in his chest. He didn't need to voice his thoughts; the distress in his eyes said it all.

Isaiah regarded him quietly. "Sometimes," he said, his voice barely more than a whisper, "we have to face the consequences of our actions to truly understand their magnitude. We all play the fool, Gideon. It's what we learn from it that defines us."

But as he spoke, the light in his eyes dimmed, his words gradually tapering off into nothing more than a hushed whisper. Gideon watched in a growing panic as Isaiah's breaths became shallow, each exhale longer than the last.

"Isaiah," Gideon said, his voice rising in alarm. Isaiah's eyelids fluttered, his consciousness teetering on the edge.

He was passing into shadow.

"No, no, Isaiah," Gideon babbled, his hands shaking as he reached out to his friend. The man needed more haelen. But what would it take to get some? Another betrayal?

As if in answer, the bolt dislodged, and the door creaked open. Gideon's head whipped around, and his heart pounded in his chest not only for the life passing before him, but for the fear of who might be coming.

Framed in the doorway was Liorah, her eyes solemn.

A glimmer of hope ignited within Gideon. As she stepped into the room, the tension of the past hours eased, replaced by a silent prayer that it wasn't too late.

"Is this what your friend needs?" Liorah asked, her tone almost playful. She withdrew a vial of haelen and let it dance between her delicate fingers. "What payment should I take this time?"

Her words sent a jolt through Gideon. The levity in her voice was in stark contrast to the situation.

"Help him," Gideon said, swallowing his pride.

A devilish smile graced Liorah's lips as she moved closer. "Only if you help me." She placed her hand on his chest. "After you, Roland is...boring. There's nothing like being here...with you."

Gideon's breath quickened as her hand traveled down his chest, across his stomach, and reached between his legs. He gasped...not because it was shameful to be aroused anymore, but because he wanted it more than anything else in the world.

Because he wanted her.

"Anything," Gideon whispered. "Just give him the vial."

PART IV: THE CONVERGENCE

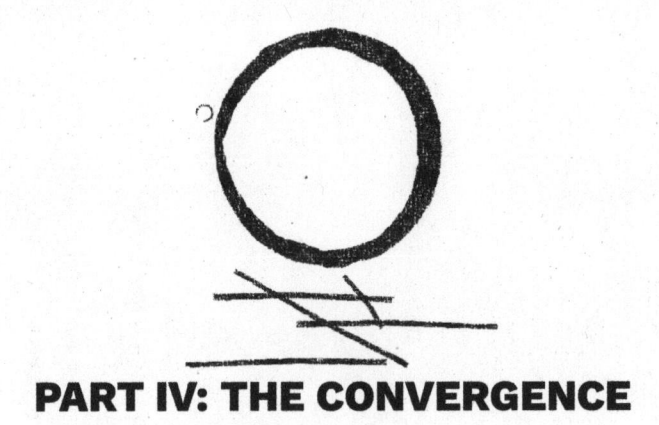

Cycle 16, Day 15, Year 96

"It was like the eve of a battle; the hearts beat, the eyes laughed, and they felt that the life they were perhaps going to lose, was after all, a good thing."

— Alexandre Dumas, *The Three Musketeers* (1844)

CHAPTER TWENTY-EIGHT

ABEL SAT TALL ATOP HIS QUVIANAQ, EYES SCANNING THE line of hunters as it wove its way through the merciless expanse of the Wastelands. New Emile was ahead. Seventy-five Col'kasid hunters, one New Emilian fugitive, two Marokai and an exile marched on, a battalion of untested warriors bound by their shared allegiance, if not to Gideon, then to his father Elder Levi and the people of Rephidim.

That wasn't exactly true. Abel didn't feel he had any allegiance, only a fear of the unknown and no other choice. That fear was only slightly tempered by the presence of those he had come to trust, to love.

To his right, his partner Luca exchanged hushed words with his sister Elena, their heads bent close together. Behind them, Diego, Elena's twin, sat in pensive silence, his focus squarely on the barren landscape ahead. Each of them bore their own fears and concerns about the looming battle. As Marokai, Elena and Diego had nothing to lose. It was Jacob, who rode his quvianaq behind Abel, who was the most troubled. Jacob and Gideon had been friends, and he had confessed just how haunted he was by the thoughts of what might be happening inside the hold where their future leader was either still alive with Isaiah...or had long since passed into shadow.

"We're marching into a trap," Diego suddenly said, breaking the tense silence. His tone was darker than it had ever been, his eyes hollow as he stared out at the desolate landscape. "There's no way Liorah won't be prepared. She has to know that her actions were utterly stupid."

Abel sighed. "As much as I had to admit it, I think I understand Elder Levi's position. He wouldn't just abandon Gideon. He is, after all, the next Keeper of the Text and his son."

"But at what cost, Abel?" Luca asked. His eyes met Abel's in a silent plea for understanding. "I was a sentinel and I like to think I know how Josiah thinks. We're risking the lives of seventy-five of your men—nearly half of your colony—for the sake of one person."

Jacob abruptly turned in his saddle. "He's more than just one person, Luca. He's our friend, our next leader. You may not be one of us, but that doesn't mean you can't empathize. If we don't fight to get him back, what then?"

Before anyone could respond, Elena spoke up. "Elder Levi isn't just fighting for Gideon," she said. "He knows Liorah has haelen, and you told him what it can do to the Red Plague. I fear that this has become more than just a rescue mission. It's a raid."

There was a pause as her words sank in. Jacob knew. They all knew. They were caught in a web of conflicting goals...and not everyone had the same idea. Not for the first time they all thought they should have left, looked for a home somewhere else. Maybe the edge of the Barren Sea or even back to Manoach.

Abel glanced at Luca before turning his attention back to the group. "We knew the risks when we agreed to this," he said with as much conviction as he could muster. "There's no turning back now. Let's just hope Liorah is in a talking mood."

AS THE sun set, it painted the horizon with an array of vibrant hues. Elder Levi in the lead with Saadya held up his staff. It was time to halt their march for the night. The vast expanse of the Wastelands seemed less desolate in the twilight, and the stark shadows softened the harshness Abel recalled from his previous travels to and from Rephidim. Even the quvianaq seemed to welcome the reprieve. Their massive bodies sank to the snow-covered ground as the riders dismounted. Coos and clucks filled the air as they spoke to each other in their own way.

Abel looked out over the unforgiving terrain, trying to guess just how far they come, how far they had to go. Not that he could tell in a landscape of white.

Luca answered his unspoken questions. "We've made it about halfway," he said, a note of relief in his voice. They had been marching for a little over two weeks, covering a distance that had previously taken them at least three weeks on foot. Despite the brutal conditions as the temperature had dropped and snows fell every other day, they were making good time.

With a snarl, Saadya approached Luca. "What meat should we be looking for, outsider? We do not have much of our bison left."

Abel wanted to suggest the ku'vatar, that nasty creature which had killed Ivan so long ago on his first journey to New Emile. He knew it was a dangerous gamble, one that might put Saadya at risk. That was, of course, the point. The man had been a thorn in their side, and a part of him relished the thought of the ass getting what he deserved.

Before he could voice his thoughts, Elena cut him off. "There are plenty of creatures in this part of the Wastelands. Tufted reekbirds—who don't fly, by the way—and fanged zhetus are the most common. Some moles, as well, which is where you'll find the zhetus. They may not taste great, but they'll keep us full."

Saadya spat on the ground next to Elena. "You're lucky you're an outsider," he said. "Women shouldn't speak out of turn."

Elena bunched her fists, but Diego held her back from doing anything that might make the situation worse.

"Elena," Diego said gently as Saadya walked away. He put his arm around his sister's shoulder, offering a silent reassurance. "Now's not the time."

With a restrained growl, Elena spun away from Diego and walked off, her feet crunching in the snow.

UNDER THE glow of both a half Short Moon and a crescent Long Moon, Abel and Luca worked in quiet unison setting up their shared tent. Each movement was careful and deliberate, something they had done many times before in the past few cycles of the Short Moon. But Abel also knew they couldn't be seen together, and each night of this trip had been a disaster waiting to happen.

A few feet away, Elena and Diego prepared their own sleeping quarters. Elena, though feeling better about her relationship with Jacob, was forced to abide by the stringent Col'kasid rule that an unmarried woman could not share quarters with a man who was not a relation. Diego had agreed to stay with her, and Jacob had no choice but to stay with the rest of the hunters.

As the Col'kasid settled in for the night, Abel gathered among his companions. He surreptitiously slipped his hand into Luca's, then quickly withdrew it as Sojen Micah approached. The man walked uneasily on the uneven ground using his walking stick with great care. Abel quickly stood and helped the founder of Rephidim make the final few steps toward their tiny fire.

"Thank you," he said as both Abel and Elena helped Micah to the ground. "It's easier walking in the desert than it is out here. There are holes everywhere."

The five of them sat in silence watching the fire crackle and burn. The air had a chill to it, and the ground felt cold. More snow was on its way, and Abel silently prayed it wouldn't slow them down. He was anxious to get this over with, to find some normalcy once again.

Micah turned to Luca on his left. "What can we expect when we get to New Emile, son?"

Luca rubbed his forehead and grimaced. "My guess is that Josiah, the sentinel commander, has been preparing his men. This isn't something we ever prepared for, so their numbers may not be strong."

"No one expected this." Micah shifted himself on the ground to get more comfortable. "Before Manoach, before the flood, I recall Eldress Glenda giving a lesson about many of the culture clashes that happened on Earth centuries before Transit. It never ended well."

"How so?" Elena asked.

"Usually the side with the most weapons would overwhelm those who had made some place their home. If it looked like it had more resources, people would fight for it. Diplomacy was rarely used."

Abel asked a question that had been burning in the back of his mind for quite some time. "Sojen Micah," he said slowly. "Did the strangers ever mention New Emile? Did they ever tell you who was out there?"

"That's been bothering me, too," Diego added. "Jacob said that he was told stories, but they had changed so much no one really knew the truth. He said you rarely mentioned them."

Micah took in a few deep breaths before answering. "Petra and Nemeth were not strangers, and I don't know why that term was ever adopted. No, they didn't mention New Emile, only the Zhanshi and what they observed from afar. After the genocide at Manoach, they made it their duty to warn Miriam, but first they had to know where the threat came from."

"They never made contact?"

Micah shook his head. "Too dangerous. They followed the Zhanshi back to their home village, a place called Xin Shijie de Yaolan, where they discovered just how much hate festered in the hearts of the people there. Staying in the shadows, they learned how advanced the Zhanshi had become, much further than we ever thought. They were on the verge of figuring out how use electric power, make incendiary weapons, and develop batteries made from algae. They were—are, I should say—truly ahead of our time."

"Why didn't they find New Emile?" Abel threw a few sticks onto the fire. Sparks rose and joined the stars in the sky. "The city isn't exactly hidden."

"They tried. By the time they found the Col'kasid in Rephidim, they had been many places, always searching for wherever Miriam ended up. But Tishbe hadn't been kind to them and most of their travels were underground."

"Underground? You mean like in tunnels?" Abel looked down at the ground where he sat, as if he could see though the dirt.

Micah nodded. "According to them, there is a network of tunnels under our feet. They aren't well marked, and had we known about them before the flood, we could have saved so many more people." His voice trailed off as moisture filled his eyes. Abel waited for a moment for the man to gain his composure again. "By the time they came to me, years had passed."

"What did they tell you?"

Micah coughed and wiped his mouth with the back of his hand. "They said the Zhanshi were determined to be the only people left, that Tishbe was their home which, by the way, they had named Huolong Yaosai. We had to be on the lookout always, but thankfully the Barren Sea at that time was still full of water. The ancients—the sa'ja'veil and sa'ja'peet—were unable to help in any way."

"Why not?" Luca's eyes opened wide. "Are they still around?"

"I never got an answer to that question, but my impression was that their numbers had dwindled so far it wouldn't have made a difference. Still, they left instructions for technology left behind."

At that, Elena perked up. "Instructions? For what?"

"Machines that would help us, ways to cultivate food, methods for expansion. None of it mattered to us."

"None of it...mattered? Wouldn't you want to follow their instructions?"

Micah shrugged, then smiled at Elena. "I wanted to, but after Petra and Nemeth left, we simply fell back into our own patterns. A few made use of what they were told, but they didn't get very far. It was almost as if something was missing. Truth be told, we had everything we needed in Rephidim, child. Petra and Nemeth left as quickly as they had come, hoping once again to find Miriam. I was convinced my cousin hadn't made it, that the reason they hadn't been found yet was because they had all passed into shadow." He stopped and looked out over the vast dark landscape. "That's not true, though. Is it?"

NOT EVERYONE in the camp had fallen asleep, and some of the hunters acted as guards against any nocturnal hunters. Abel's eyes were heavy, the travel wearing on him.

"You." Saadya's voice cut through the night air. "Sleep

at the edge of camp. Exiles have no place here."

Before Abel could protest, Luca was on his feet. "He stays here, Saadya!" The fierce defiance in Luca's voice only seemed to amuse the man. He chuckled in a way that severely unsettled Abel. He'd heard that laugh before.

"You both can go to hell, for all I care." Saadya spat not at the ground but on Abel's feet.

The audacity of his words and action sparked a flame within Elena. She rushed forward, trying to push Saadya away from her family, but he was an immovable force against her slender frame.

Elena fell back, anger burning in her eyes. "We're done here." She dragged a silent Diego and the seething duo of Luca and Abel behind her. "You don't need our help anymore."

But before they could take another step, a commanding voice filled the night, halting them in their tracks. "Enough!" Levi raged. With purposeful strides, Levi placed himself in front of Saadya, his eyes narrowing. "Saadya! They carry knowledge we need. We cannot cast them out regardless of their past or future offenses."

Saadya fell silent under Levi's glare.

Levi turned to face the departing group of outsiders, addressing Abel directly. "You will remain among us, but you shall sleep alone. Your...partner shall remain with me. I have some questions to ask."

Luca made to speak, but Abel shook his head briefly.

"Remember this," Levi said now addressing everyone who had gathered. "'Behold, how good and how pleasant it is for brethren to dwell together in unity.' We cannot march divided into New Emile; we must remain united. For 'every kingdom divided against itself is brought to desolation; and every city or house divided against itself shall not stand.' Let us not forget this as we tread the path that lies ahead."

Elena's face said she didn't believe a word Levi said. Abel couldn't disagree. If they wanted unity, the first thing the Col'kasid needed to do was accept the Marokai for who they were and put Abel's supposed transgressions aside.

A QUIET rustling of fabric stirred Abel from a fitful sleep. An ominous shadow loomed over him, bringing with it an overwhelming sense of dread. As he blinked himself awake, the grim, scarred face of Saadya emerged from the darkness.

"Awake, are we?" Saadya's voice was low in the silence of the night.

"Why...what do you want?" Abel pushed himself up to a sitting position, the chilly ground beneath his hands rough and uneven.

Saadya leaned in closer bearing a malicious smile. The glint of moonlight off metal told Abel that a knife was in the man's hand. "Once this little escapade is over, exile will not save you."

Abel felt a chill crawl down his spine. He knew this man was not one for empty threats.

Saadya's eyes glinted, a dangerous promise of pain dancing within their depths. "You remember Asher, don't you? Or did you forget him the minute you dropped your pants for that New Emilian atrocity?"

A cold knot of fear formed in Abel's stomach at the mention of his former lover. Levi and the council had voted them into exile, but Saadya was the man physically responsible for kicking them out of Rephidim, ensuring there was no way they could be together again. He was not the judge. He had been the executioner.

"I remember what I did to him," Saadya continued, his tone almost casual. He used the tip of his knife to pick at something under a fingernail. "You should have heard the screams in the orchard. You should have seen the life draining from his eyes."

In a flash, Saadya placed the tip of his knife at Abel's throat and held it with enough pressure that any movement the boy made would draw blood. "That's what's also waiting for an abomination like you, Abel," Saadya whispered. There was a cruel delight in his voice. "Something I should have done long ago."

With that, he retreated into the night, leaving Abel alone with his terror. The threat was the only thing that remained, echoing endlessly in the cold night air.

CHAPTER TWENTY-NINE

Chen led the march of the Zhanshi out of Yaolan, each footfall on the foreign soil a step closer to justice. Far from their home, lost in a sea of wilderness and unfamiliar topography, they marched, guided by the austere gray stone piles of Russant's cairns. The man had been good for something after all.

A line of algae-powered vehicles, acting as beasts of burden, strained against the weight of their cargo—four enormous explosive-filled projectiles mounted on sleds. The batteries in the vehicles would require near-constant sunlight to remain charged, but if they were to fail, Chen knew his men would be willing to pull in their absence.

The path to New Emile was long, the trek estimated at five arduous weeks, according to Russant, and they were halfway into their journey. A hundred men and boys were each armed with crossbows whose bolts bore deadly tips that sparked into flame upon impact. Their lances, sharpened to a deadly point, bore a deadly gift—a coating of potent poison made from the blood of river leaches found in and around the valley. While the poison wouldn't kill, it would paralyze anyone on the wrong end of the lance.

Chen allowed himself a moment to marvel at the resolve in the eyes of his men, their willpower carving out his path towards retribution. He was not blind to their vulnerability, however. There was no way to know just how powerful the gulao had become in the fifty-five years since his grandfather had almost wiped them from the face of the planet.

As he walked, his thoughts circled back to the tales told about his great-great-grandfather, Mathias the First. They were stories of humiliation and torment at the hands of the original Circle of Light settlers whose descendants had founded New Emile. Each step Chen took was a promise to the spirit of past Zhuren that those sins would not go unanswered.

He envisioned the city in his mind, the heart of sin and humiliation, soon to be transformed into a smoldering pyre of justice. As the sun dipped below the horizon, painting the unknown land in front of them with strokes of crimson and gold, Chen fell into stride beside Martin.

"Zhuren," Martin said. "We should consider what defenses we might face at New Emile."

The hint of a smile played on Chen's lips. "Do you think a city of gulao, ignorant of the harshness of our world, can stop the Zhanshi?"

"Their ignorance is not something we should rely on," Martin countered. "Even the meekest creature can show its fangs when cornered."

Chen had to respect Martin's concern, but he held a different perspective.

"New Emile may show its fangs," Chen conceded, "but fangs are useless against an avalanche. We are that avalanche, Martin. Unstoppable, inevitable."

Chen stared out towards the horizon once again, imagining the impending confrontation. "Let them prepare," Chen said after a moment. "It will not change the outcome. And I do not believe they even know we are coming. So much the better for us in the end."

As Chen and Martin continued their discussion about the impending clash with New Emile, Luke joined their side with a wearied expression, one that he had worn since the day they left the village. Perhaps longer.

"Zhuren," Luke interjected, his voice tinged with caution. "I understand the desire for justice, but have we truly exhausted all other options? Must we confront them head-on?"

Chen turned his attention to Luke. How was this old man able to make this journey? And yet Chen felt honored that he did. "Waiting for New Emile to come to us is an act of passivity. We are the Zhanshi—warriors. It is our duty to bring justice to our ancestors."

Luke's eyes shifted. "But the risks, Zhuren," he said. "We have made progress in Yaolan. We have built a community which grows every day. Is it worth jeopardizing all of that for vengeance?"

"In our valley, Luke. This is our *world*, and the gulao have staked a claim that is not theirs."

Martin spoke up. "Luke, the Zhanshi have carried the weight of injustice for generations. There comes a time when we must confront the source of our suffering, even if it means stepping into the unknown."

Luke nodded. "I understand the need for justice. I was with the great Zhuren Mathias the Third on the day we cleansed the rainforest. Those men were weak, beaten down by a world their minds could not understand. But let us not underestimate the passage of time. The gulao have likely grown as much as the Zhanshi, and we must be prepared for what lies ahead."

Chen refused to be influenced, even by the words of the only man who had previously encountered the threat. "We have trained our men well, Luke. We possess both power and the will to overcome any obstacle in our path. New Emile will tremble in the face of the Zhanshi, and Mathias will be avenged."

The trio fell into silence as the wind whispered around them. Luke may have been wise to express his concern, but in the end it would not matter.

TWO DAYS later, their journey took an unexpected turn as they stumbled upon a swamp. The air grew thick with moisture, and the ground beneath their feet became mired in murky water.

As the Zhanshi pressed forward, the buzzing of insects filled the air, growing louder with each step they took. The once calm landscape had transformed into a scene of imminent danger. Dark clouds of flies swarmed above and soon descended on the soldiers. Tiny, needle-like mouths pierced the flesh of the Zhanshi, injecting a venomous poison which spread through their veins like wildfire.

Chen's men recoiled in agony, screaming as the venom took hold. Two men fell, then three. While several came to their aid, they too succumbed to the poison, their limbs growing weak and unresponsive. Panic rippled through the ranks as men writhed on the ground, voices choked with fear and pain. As Chen watched, helpless, he knew every moment counted. A failure to act here, weeks from their destination, would be devastating.

"Veer to the south!" Chen called out as he swatted away a swarm that threatened to engulf him.

The Zhanshi altered their course. Men pulled paralyzed men through the difficult terrain. Chen remained at the forefront, and as the Zhanshi emerged from the treacherous marshland, the sun shone high above. There was an unacceptable disorder to the ranks.

"Listen to me!" Chen bellowed. He turned to face his men. His gaze swept over the weary and beaten Zhanshi. "This was a test. A reminder of the trials our ancestors endured and overcame. They rose from their tribulations stronger, and so shall we."

He paused, letting his words hang in the air. The surviving Zhanshi nursing those who had been paralyzed by the insects, turned their eyes towards their leader. Chen looked at them, each man and boy beset by the day's ordeal.

"These flies, these insects...they are nothing more than a reflection of the gulao. They bite, they sting, they cause us pain. We will not retreat. We are the Zhanshi. We have known hardship, and we have grown stronger with each passing day."

He moved to the center of his men, his voice louder with each step. "Let this be a reminder to us all that the path to justice is treacherous. But it is a path we must tread. Victory seldom comes without pain, and it is the strong who come out on top."

He paused once more. Coughs and cries floated in the still humid air. "These trials stand between us and justice. But remember this — they are but obstacles in our path, stones in the river. And like all obstacles, they will be overcome. We will march on. Let the gulao tremble at the sound of our approach."

The echo of Chen's speech faded into the air as he surveyed his men. Some of them looked as if they understood, others still appeared terrified. They had never encountered anything like this before, not in Yaolan, not in the surrounding hills and valleys. As his gaze roved, it fell upon a cluster of men at the edge of the ragged formation, their shoulders slumped with a weight heavier than exhaustion.

Martin and Lin Xi knelt in the churned-up muck,

cradling a figure between them. The sinking sun threw elongated shadows across their hunched bodies.

As Chen approached, the figure became clear.

Luke lay immobilized in their arms, his skin paled to an ashen gray. But it was the eyes that caught Chen's attention— once steady and strong, they were now clouded with pain.

As he looked down at Luke, Chen felt something turn in his gut. His heart beat a fraction slower, its rhythm faltering in concert with the man who had stood by his side, had been there as he grew from a boy to a man. His palms tingled with a sudden coolness, a stark contrast to the fiery words that had filled his speech moments before. As his boots sunk into the mire, a bitter taste crawled up the back of his throat.

His jaw tightened, and he took a moment to swallow the bile that rose within him. His pursuit of justice had brought his advisor to this painful state. There was a sudden rush of guilt, each inhale laced with the weight of his decisions, each exhale shrouded with unspoken regret.

As the silent seconds crept by, his eyes narrowed and anger took over. He clenched his fists, turning his knuckles white. It was not the swamp or the insects that had ignited this fury within him. No. It was them—the gulao.

SEVEN BODIES had to be burned that night. Among them was Luke. Chen watched as the pyre was lit and flames danced higher into the night sky. He would have burnt joss paper if he were home, but out here, the smell of wood and burning flesh would have to do.

In the morning, they moved on. New Emile had become both a symbol of their past grievances and a beacon of retribution. It represented the culmination of generations of suffering and injustice, and Chen carried the weight of that history on his shoulders.

As the silence of their grief hung heavy, Chen noticed Martin's attention diverted to a place behind them. He turned to see the algae-powered vehicles that were their war engines. His eyes widened as he took in what was missing.

"Zhuren," Martin pointed towards the vehicles. "One of our projectiles. It is gone."

Chen noted the void where a fourth enormous explosive-laced projectile should have been. The missing weapon was a gut punch.

"Lost to the swamp," Martin added.

Lin Xi strode over, confusion on his face. "What do you mean, lost? We can go in and retrieve it, right?"

Chen took a deep breath in and sighed. Obstacles. He shook his head, a bitter taste crawling up his throat. "Are you willing to go back into that swamp, Lin Xi?"

Lin Xi fell silent. No, he was not willing to go.

"We will have to adapt our strategy," Chen added. "We cannot risk another loss. We need to ensure our remaining weapons reach New Emile."

Chen looked to the sky where clouds had been gathering throughout the morning. The weathered landscape was unforgiving, unpredictable, and unyielding. If they failed to keep the batteries of the vehicles charged, he would need to assign men the task of pulling the heavy projectiles on foot.

"Obstacles," he said to himself. "Stones in the river. Come, we must move away from this place."

CHAPTER THIRTY

IN THE HAZY PRE-DAWN HOURS, JOSIAH STOOD AT THE RIM OF the quarry, his silhouette a solitary figure against the pale, dim light. Below, tethered by thick, reinforced chains, was a quvianaq, one of the creatures Gideon had brought with him on his ill-fated ambassadorial quest to...

Why did they come to New Emile in the first place?

The beast was an imposing sight, standing eight feet tall on two muscular legs, its gray skin tough and thick. Underneath its massive body, six retractable limbs hung limply, a grotesque parody of any other creature's arms. Its bulbous head was crowned with a long, squarish snout, and several rows of sharp teeth lurked within. This was a predator, and according to Gideon, the only known natural adversary to the mysterious rychat he'd heard about long ago when tales of Mother Miriam's journey were told to children.

Opposite the quvianaq stood the sound generator, the harmonic transducer, a beast of its own. Made of alien technology and constructed from materials not found around New Emile, the hulking machine had never been moved. Instead, Marokai brought the stones to it so that they could be lifted out of the quarry. It hummed with a subtle energy, a continual thrum that resonated deep into the bedrock beneath. Its presence was felt more than it was heard. The vibrations seeped into the bones of those near it, an omnipresent undercurrent in the daily life of the quarry.

Engineered according to principles of wave manipulation foreign to New Emile's scientists, its functions were a series of conjectures and educated guesses rather than fully understood facts. Since its discovery forty-two years ago, no one had so much as developed a working theory of why it performed the way it did. At its heart was a patterned metasurface, a bizarrely decorated layer that was the active part of the transducer. This was the conductor to the symphony of sound waves it manipulated, an artificially engineered surface designed to interact with, guide, and control the powerful ultrasonic waves produced.

Despite its mysterious origins, the inhabitants of New Emile had discovered early on one critical property—the transducer could manipulate objects larger than the wavelength of its produced sound, and it was this principle which had been harnessed to move the colossal rocks in the quarry, contactless and powered by the machine's internal source. Once the rocks were out of the quarry, teams of Marokai laborers would place logs under them and roll them to a construction site.

However, the lack of a comprehensive understanding meant it was an asset as volatile as it was useful. Josiah knew that, in theory, the harmonic transducer should be able to direct the ultrasonic waves in any direction, controlling the acoustic force exerted on an object. For all its power, it was damnably difficult to move. He was not the only one who believed it was far too risky to move both out of the quarry and into the path of the oncoming army of Col'kasid hunters.

With a signal from Josiah, the device's pitch rose, the frequencies escalating. Josiah put his hands to his ears. Marokai onlookers, told to stop working for the moment, did the same. The quvianaq screamed, its cry of pain sending shivers up Josiah's spine. When the scream stopped, so did the animal—frozen in a rictus of fear and pain. It was an abrupt shift, the creature's inherent predatory vigor seizing up as if a switch had been flipped. Its eyes glazed over, and its body stiffened. Moments later, it collapsed, convulsing violently as it succumbed to an apparent seizure.

A wave of discomfort washed over Josiah as a few of the Marokai onlookers let out a collective gasp of disgust. This was a test, but it was a cruel one, even for a creature like this.

Josiah signaled for the harmonic transducer to be cut off. With a final shudder, the quvianaq stilled, and the seizure subsided as abruptly as it had started. The test was over, but the implications hung in the air. The animal wasn't dead, but it could easily be killed in such a state of disarray.

A hunter off his mount was, according to Gideon, unbalanced.

An unbalanced hunter would be easy to kill.

The Col'kasid could be stopped before they ever approached the gate.

With a deep breath in, Josiah turned away from the scene. This had sickened him in a way he could not understand, but he would need to carry out further testing later. Torturing animals was apparently far different from torturing Marokai and it disgusted him.

For now, though, Liorah had asked to see him, and she was not a woman you told to wait.

JOSIAH MOVED through the heart of New Emile, the streets of the city echoing beneath his boots. He was enroute to the Chambers, a summons he had received too many times to count. But this time, a quiet sense of dread hung heavily in his gut. Each step closer to the Chambers tightened an invisible noose around his neck and reminded him of the lengths to which Liorah had gone to rise to power.

Eilian had been his friend.

Around him, the city teemed with life; familiar faces weaved in and out of the crowd, some bearing names he knew, others anonymous souls contributing to the city's daily rhythm. There was the baker, the blacksmith, the seamstress, and the butcher. And over there, the man who had crafted his boots. Under different circumstances, Josiah would find comfort in these signs of everyday life. But now, every interaction, every moment, felt stained by a grim revelation that threatened to shatter his world.

Liorah was a murderer.

Ruth, the Marokai, had brought forth a claim at once fantastical and yet also too critical to dismiss. Her words, spoken in hushed tones and anxious glances, painted a picture Josiah could not get out of his head. Ruth had accused Liorah of poisoning her father, Eilian, and her half-brother, Philip, a claim that had turned the power dynamics of New Emile on its head.

Eilian had been more than a ruler to Josiah. He had been a trusted friend, and while Josiah didn't always see eye to eye with Eilian, he didn't doubt his decisions like he did with Liorah. To think that Master Eilian could have been a victim of his own daughter's ambition was a concept Josiah struggled to grasp. It felt like a cruel joke, but with Ruth's confession, the seeds of doubt had been sown.

As he navigated through the sea of faces and stone buildings, the echo of Ruth's words kept pace with him like a chilling background noise to his inner turmoil. The image of Eilian, a ghost of a friend, loomed in the back of his mind, shaping doubts into a chilling reality.

Josiah now grappled with his role as the sentinel

commander. It was a title that came with the responsibility and trust of the city, a mantle he'd borne with conviction for many years. He was to protect the One Voice at all costs. However, Ruth's revelation had seeped into Josiah's core. It gnawed at the corners of his mind and eroded the foundations of his loyalty, turning it into a thin sheet of uncertainty and suspicion. Now, each interaction with Liorah was tainted with this newfound knowledge, a mirror that reflected a warped image of the woman.

Meanwhile, the burdens of his role did not abate. The weight of impending external threats added another layer of complexity to his predicament. New Emile's defenses were untested, their vulnerabilities increasingly clear the more he prepared his men to defend the walls. The risk of the Col'kasid mounting a rescue attempt for Gideon was growing with each passing day. It was no longer a matter of *if* it would happen, but *when*.

With Gideon held captive in their city for three cycles of the Short Moon, the once vibrant walls of New Emile had come to feel like a hold of its own. Each passing day brought them closer to the inevitable confrontation, and while his trust in Liorah was gone, his duty to New Emile was not. Amidst the turmoil of doubts and suspicions, he trudged on, the city's safety and future hinging on his ability to navigate through the waters of betrayal and conflict.

As Josiah approached the wooden door of the Chambers, the cityscape of New Emile fell behind him, its unique blend of human and alien architecture now just a silhouette against the Tishbian sky. He paused, allowing the weight of responsibility to settle on his shoulders once more. But even as he embraced this commitment, the echo of Ruth's words whispered persistently in the creases of his mind. The revelation, like a pebble cast into a still pond, had sent ripples of uncertainty through him and raised questions he had never thought of before, ones that loomed larger with each echo of Ruth's words.

How far would he go to seek justice for his friend Eilian?

What lines would he cross to unmask the poisoner of his former leader?

And in seeking justice, how could he ensure the safety of New Emile and its citizens, a task with which Eilian had entrusted him?

With a last glance at the streets of New Emile, Josiah reached out and pushed open the wooden door to the Chambers.

LIORAH PACED in front of the window overlooking the Tree that Owns Itself and the haelen pond. "Tell me your men can defend the city from these...these Col'kasid."

"It will be difficult, Liorah." Josiah weighed his next words carefully. "We could certainly use more hands and more weapons."

Liorah's eyes flickered. "More hands? From where?"

Josiah swallowed, aware of the bitter pill he was about to offer. "The...Marokai, Liorah. They can fight, and they have a reason—"

"The Marokai?" Liorah's face showed the scorn Josiah knew she felt. "I'd rather the city fall than allow the...the *filth* to step foot inside our walls. No, the Marokai are fine where they are. To bring them in to help your pathetic excuse for sentinels is to give them ideas that they can stay here."

"Then perhaps," Josiah said, "we should prepare for the city to fall."

Josiah saw Liorah's emotions fluctuate as she struggled to control them. The mention of the need to defend New Emile had her visibly shaken, but it was his allusion to the

Marokai that caused her to recoil in apparent disgust. Despite her outward appearance, he could see through her facade, however. Something was off.

As he stared at her, Josiah's mind threaded together a tapestry of conspiracy. He'd seen her frequent visits to the hold, the supposed need to "converse" with the prisoners. Her trips weren't going unnoticed, and they suggested a shift in her loyalties, or at the very least, a fraying of her indifference.

A smile played at the corners of his mouth as an idea took shape. Liorah, for all her strength, had a vulnerability, a blind spot—a growing fondness for Gideon. That was something he could use to his advantage.

As much as he wanted to seize this moment to upend Liorah's composure for good, he needed to bide his time and wait. Liorah, in her weakness, had offered him a priceless opportunity...once this mess with the advancing Col'kasid was done. Her reign suddenly felt unstable, and Josiah knew he had a chance to overthrow her. If he waited, he could rid New Emile of this poisoner who had taken what was not rightfully hers.

The seed of Liorah's demise, Gideon, was still locked up in the hold. Josiah had subjected Gideon and Isaiah to regular bouts of "persuasion," yet Liorah's visits had become too frequent. That connection was a vulnerability Josiah intended to exploit.

Liorah turned. "What of this harmonic transducer, the one used in the quarry? Gideon mentioned the effect it had on the quvianaq when they arrived. I assume you've tested it on one of those beasts."

Josiah nodded, although he still felt slightly uncomfortable at the sight of the quvianaq seizing.

"We need every advantage, Josiah." There was an urgency

in her voice that prickled his skin. "The religious fanatics from Rephidim will be attacking on the backs of those beasts. Can't we turn this in our favor somehow? Knock them down on the moor?"

Josiah furrowed his brows. The potential was there, but moving the transducer was risky. If it broke because of mishandling, they would have no way to remove the stones from the quarry. Construction would cease. "It's...plausible," he finally admitted slowly. His hand reflexively rubbed his shaved head. "But the transducer is stationary by design, and it's heavy. Shifting it might break the damn thing."

Liorah did not respond. Minutes ticked by, and yet still Liorah remained quiet, her eyes locked on a distant void. Josiah shifted uncomfortably, the silence amplifying the beat of his heart in his ears. The room suddenly felt smaller.

Liorah moved her hand slowly, tentatively, until it rested on her belly. Her eyes shifted, once again looking out through the window towards the Tree that Owns Itself. Her body stiffened and her grip tightened around the fabric of her dress.

For just a fleeting moment, Josiah saw something more than the One Voice, more than a ruler who had gained her power through unforgivable sins. There was a glimmer of vulnerability, an intimate, private fear that humanized her. She was a woman grappling with the uncertainties of the future.

He swallowed. The silence was once again oppressive. This time, it felt different. It wasn't merely the absence of noise, however, but the anticipation of a thousand unsaid words and emotions.

"Bring me Gideon," Liorah finally said, her voice barely above a whisper. "I need to talk to him."

CHAPTER THIRTY-ONE

SOMETHING BAD WAS ABOUT TO HAPPEN, AND KAIUS KNEW IT. He sat with Ruth and her child, Lika, deep in the Hollows. It had been a week since Josiah used his extensive interrogation techniques to extract information she would have been willing to share readily if he'd simply asked.

Liorah did, in fact, poison both her father and half-brother. Philip was the first to go. All of New Emile was stunned when he passed into shadow at just thirty-eight. He had been healthy all his life, albeit aided by haelen, just like any other member of the Elite. When their father Eilian passed—Mother Miriam's only child—of exactly the same ailment, rumors circulated. Was it possible that both Eilian, the One Voice, and his heir Philip had met with foul play? If so, who would have orchestrated such a feat?

The title of One Voice had been immediately conferred on Liorah at just eighteen years old despite her lack of political experience, and it wasn't long before the populace of New Emile questioned her leadership. As payment for those questions, the loudest of the voices had been marked and exiled to the Hollows or put in the hold. Some of them were never seen again.

As the handmaiden to Liorah prior to her ascension to power, Ruth had been witness to many of the events within the Chambers. All of it was from the point of view of Liorah, but Ruth had seen how horribly she had been treated by her father and half-brother. She was the child of a concubine of Eilian's, and her mother had disappeared shortly after she'd been born into sunshine. While granted rights to live among the Elite, they did not expect her to become anything more than a sister or a daughter.

According to Ruth, Liorah's treatment by her brother was hideous. She was tormented constantly and abused in ways that no girl or woman should have to suffer. Ruth had seen it all, so it was not surprising when she had been asked by Liorah to bring her the venom of a river leach to "teach her brother a lesson." Ever the dutiful handmaiden, Ruth did as asked, and within a cycle of the Long Moon—a quarter of a year—Philip had become something less than human. He could barely eat, could not speak, and his muscles had atrophied so much from a constant paralysis that he was eternally bedridden. He passed into shadow within a year.

Master Eilian was devastated and vowed to have another son. This sent Liorah into a rage with Ruth as the unwitting target. Without being asked, Ruth then produced another vial of venom and left it with Liorah. The hint was obvious. Eilian took nearly two years to pass into shadow, all the time paralyzed and unable to lead effectively. Liorah had taken on the role of the One Voice temporarily...knowing well that it would only be a matter of time.

For all of Ruth's obedience to Liorah, she was marked and permanently banned from ever entering New Emile. Liorah could not bring herself to execute Ruth, but she couldn't have her remain in the Chambers with a secret such as this. No, she had to go.

All of this had been told to Josiah. It took little in the way of coercion. Despite the pain inflicted on her, she shared all she'd witnessed and provided the proof Josiah needed. Liorah had murdered her father and half-brother in order to ascend to the role of One Voice.

Ruth still suffered, however, and Kaius had taken it upon himself to care for her and her child. He was just as guilty as Liorah, after all. He distinctly remembered the day he had escorted her to be marked with a triangle on her forehead and then to the gates for the final order of banishment, forcing a loyal handmaiden to a permanent life in the Hollows.

As he held Lika in his arms and sat next to a blanket where Ruth was stretched out recovering, Kaius thought back to those years—no, decades—when he had been a sentinel. He had escorted many of the Elite's targets to the gates. Those chosen by the lottery, those singled out for ambiguous offenses—it didn't matter. Once you became filth in the eyes of the One Voice, you were no longer welcome within the walls. Now he was among them, at first an outcast of the outcasts. Just recently, however, he had learned of something else.

The Marokai were organized, and Kaius had been thrown right in the middle of their final plans to overthrow the Elite and take control of the haelen.

The original orchestrators of the plan, Elena and her twin brother Diego, had not been seen for almost three cycles of the Short Moon. It was rumored that they had been involved in the escape of Abel and that other Col'kasid ambassador, Jacob, who had come with Gideon and Isaiah. The rumor mill had generated enough usable information for Kaius to discern that Luca had abandoned his post and gone with Elena and Diego, Gideon and Isaiah were still in the hold, and the Col'kasid were on the march to rescue their future leader.

This had put the Elite into a state of disarray. Josiah had been attempting to bolster the defenses, but as Kaius knew, that wouldn't be easy. There were not enough weapons and very little in the way of strategy should someone attack. No one had ever considered that a possibility. For years, New Emilians had been taught that history began at Manoach and the only humans left on Tishbe lived in and around the moor. What would they need to defend against?

A few Marokai quarry workers had just reported that Josiah was attempting to leverage the harmonic transducer to stun or paralyze the quvianaq. The alien machine was not as mobile as Josiah would have liked, and some of the Marokai suggested that might play to their advantage. As the muscle to redirect the harmonic transducer toward any oncoming horde of Col'kasid hunters, it might be possible to reverse that and send sound waves into the walls of New Emile. It may not destroy the walls, but it would certainly weaken their defenses.

As a former sentinel with a high standing, Kaius had been pulled under duress into the nightly planning sessions of the Marokai leadership. With the Elite confused and their attention diverted elsewhere, now was the perfect time to oust Liorah and take control of the only resource worth having—the haelen. It was long believed that there was enough in the pond where the Tree that Owns Itself grew that no one should have to be ill again. It was selfish that only the Elite were allowed ready access and only the sentinels were given a vial to keep with them. The Hollows had been running through a host of diseases that could have been easily cured by the haelen, and no one seemed to care.

Enough was enough.

A man approached. Like many of the others in the Hollows, he was young, his clothes a tattered array of filth. "Kaius," he said. "The council would like a word."

"I have a child to tend to, Jeremiah." He raised the bundle in his arms. "Unless you'd like to take over babysitting duties."

"Bring her. We're in the final stages and need some advice."

"You're wasting your time."

"Come." With no further argument, Jeremiah left. Kaius gingerly rose to his feet and stepped out from under the cheap blanket which Ruth had called home. He was amazed anyone could live like this. Even a six-week long Discovery mission had felt more comfortable.

The council met around a small fire near the edge of the Hollows and slightly down a hill, hidden from view from the sentinels along the top of New Emile's walls. There were nine present with Kaius rounding the number to ten. Eleven, if one counted the child still in his arms. All of them were relatively young except for Cain, a brutish man of fifty who had found himself on the wrong side of Liorah's graces two years ago for sneaking a bowl of haelen to save his ailing wife. The rest ranged in age from maybe thirteen to twenty-five.

Previously led by Elena and Diego, the council was now under the leadership of Jeremiah and Angela. They stood near to the fire while all the others sat around it. In front of them lay a crude drawing in the dirt of the streets of New Emile with rocks for buildings. The largest rock, frequently pissed on by the Marokai, represented the Chambers or, more specifically, Liorah.

There was no love for the woman here.

"Kaius," Angela greeted him coldly as he approached. The flames of the fire danced in her eyes. "Glad you could join us."

"Let it rest, Angela," Jeremiah said. "We may need him."

Angela crossed her arms and turned her back to Kaius. It had been the same ever since he had arrived after his exile.

"Let's get right to it." Jeremiah used a small twig and traced an imaginary line from the Hollows to the Chambers on the rough sketch in the dirt. "We need to know the best time and way to get into New Emile. As one of them, you should know best."

Kaius studied the crude map, memories of patrol routes and sentinel changes flooding back. "Dusk," he said absentmindedly. "There's a shift change then, and that moment of confusion could buy you some time. At least you'll be through the gates."

"So we go at dawn," Angela chimed in.

"You're not helping, Angie."

"I don't care. I don't want him here and I've made my point several times."

"What happens once we're in?" Cain asked, cutting Angela off. His weathered face did not hide his skepticism. "I'm pretty sure the path to the Chambers will be quickly secured."

"With enough of us," Jeremiah said, "we can overwhelm any resistance."

"So you think." Cain pointed to Kaius. "I'm sure our outsider here would disagree."

Kaius found that remark a little offensive. He and Cain had grown up together and played in the streets of New Emile when they were young. Then their two paths diverged, and Kaius was left with a job that would eventually lead to escorting him out through the gates. He had always regretted that.

"We'll push through," Jeremiah said, an air of finality around his words.

A youthful voice piped up from the shadows. "But what then?" Kaius didn't know his name. In fact, he didn't know most of their names. "Do we kill her?"

A silence fell over the group. The flames crackled and filled the void. Kaius had to say something.

"Liorah's death will solve nothing," he said as Lika's tiny

hand clutched his rough fingers in her sleep. "It'll only breed more chaos."

"So, we let her live?" The young boy looked heartbroken.

"We can," Angela suggested. "For now, anyway. We confine her, question her, use her. Kill her later."

Cain threw his hands in the air. "Use her? She's more venomous than a river leach."

Arguments exploded, voices rising and falling in a symphony of discord. Words danced between hope and fear, courage and doubt, change and the painful sting of the familiar. Kaius sat back and took it all in.

"With Liorah out of the Chambers," Kaius said after a while, "we'll be all safer."

"We're supposed to trust you, Kaius?" Cain's voice sliced through the chatter, drawing all eyes to him. He glared at the former sentinel, the firelight deepening the furrows on his hairless brow. "You stood by while my wife suffered. She passed into shadow because you escorted me out."

Kaius met his gaze without flinching. "Yes, I did. And it's a burden I bear every day."

"Burden?" The young boy scoffed, a note of bitterness in his voice. "You banished us, forced us to live in this godforsaken place."

"I had orders, as we all did," Kaius said calmly. "I was not the only one, either. If I could walk you back into the city and give you all homes, I would." His gaze shifted to the dirt map, lingering on the crude depiction of the city he once swore to protect.

"Orders..." Jeremiah muttered under his breath. He shook his head.

Kaius shifted Lika in his arms, the child still asleep through the tension. His anger had been growing, despite his attempts to remain still.

"We're wary of you," Angela said with no emotion. "You were one of them, Kaius. And now you're here with us, telling us not to kill Liorah. It's a bit...difficult to stomach."

"I don't hold a grudge against Liorah," Kaius said, his voice flat.

"Of course you don't," the young boy said. He stood and spat at Kaius' feet.

Kaius took a moment to calm himself. "Hate only breeds more hate. That's something I think you all should have learned by now."

Cain grunted, crossing his arms. "Sounds like something an Elite would say."

"No, Cain. It's something someone tired of violence would say."

The argument shifted again away from Kaius and onto how many Marokai they could get ready by the following dusk. Kaius listened, Lika stirring a little, but still not awake.

After a while, Kaius' voice cut through the chatter. "Wait."

"Wait?" Angela asked. "For what?"

"Wait to enter the city."

She sneered and crossed her arms tightly over her chest. "And just why should we do that?"

"Just until the Col'kasid arrive," Kaius answered calmly, trying to maintain eye contact with each member of the council.

"That's not even guaranteed to happen."

"You don't think their Elder Levi, the leader of the Col'kasid, will want to rescue his son? They're on their way."

"You've lost your mind." Cain rose from his seat, his fists clenched. "You want us to trust your word?"

"Once the Col'kasid hunters get here, the sentinels will be occupied. Josiah will need all his men to defend against an attack."

"Can you be certain of this?" Jeremiah narrowed his eyes. "Who told you this?"

Kaius paused, his mind racing. He couldn't reveal his source, not without igniting their fury at him once again. Yet he couldn't afford to lie either.

"I...I heard it from Josiah."

A wave of angry mutters rippled through the group. Cain's eyes bulged with rage, Jeremiah's face twisted in surprise, and Angela's expression hardened further.

"You've been consorting with Josiah?" Cain roared, storming toward Kaius. "The very beast who tortures our people?"

Lika stirred at the commotion, a cry emanating from her. Kaius adjusted the child in his arms. "I wasn't—"

"Josiah told you this?" the younger boy asked. "Are you expecting us to stake our lives on his word?"

"It's not—"

"You're still working for her," Angela cut in, her voice icy. "You weren't exiled."

"No! Enough!" Kaius roared, his voice echoing in the Hollows. Silence fell like a shroud. Their accusing eyes fixed on him. Lika wailed at the noise. "I was exiled, and this isn't about allegiance to one person. It's about survival. It's about strategy and exploiting the circumstances in our favor. I want her gone as much as you, but we need to wait until the time is just right."

Doubt filled the air. But the night was far from over, and it seemed only shadows and uncertainty were present.

The Col'kasid were coming. Kaius knew that. He also knew there would be only one opportunity to topple Liorah and take control of New Emile.

The Marokai had to do this right.

"Take your weakest," Kaius said, "and put them somewhere."

"What are you suggesting?" Angela crossed her arms. "We hide?"

"No. I'm suggesting we try a different tactic to get in. The Col'kasid will no doubt march on the gates, so getting in that way will be a problem. As I said, all of Josiah's men will be engaged, attempting to hold them back."

He looked past Angela at the young boy who had spit at Kaius. "I heard there was another way into the city. Is this true?"

The younger boy shifted uneasily. He glanced at Jeremiah and then at Angela, apparently unsure of how much he should say to Kaius.

"Why are you asking him?" Jeremiah asked.

"Look." Kaius adjusted Lika in his arms and attempted to rock her back to sleep. "You may not like me, and I understand that. But there are things I know that you don't. I know the Marokai have been sneaking into the city to steal grain and other things, but what you don't know is that most sentinels have purposefully turned their back on that and let you."

"I don't know what you're talking about," Angela said. She obviously did and was making a poor attempt at denying what Kaius already knew.

Kaius ignored her. "What we were never sure of was how many tunnels or other small entrances you had to get into the city. So I'm asking: where are they?"

"So you can shut them down?" Jeremiah's face turned red.

"No. So we can use them to get around what's going to happen at the gates. The sentinels will be preoccupied, and if you want the best chance of getting to Liorah—and holding her—you'll send a few people in through those tunnels and keep the rest at a safe distance and away from the Hollows."

The young boy looked nervously at Jeremiah. It was frustrating to have to deal with so much mistrust, but could Kaius really blame them after so many years of banishment by the Elite?

"There are two tunnels," Jeremiah said finally. "One in the north, one in the east." He pointed to the crude drawing of the streets of New Emile. "The north tunnel will be the best option and has the clearest path to the Chambers. Two or three people can go in at a time."

CHAPTER THIRTY-TWO

THE COL'KASID HUNTERS GATHERED ON A HILL, THEIR EYES fixed on the city of New Emile, a strange place built in a strange land. The vast moor stretched before them, and to the right, the large hole that Abel knew was the quarry, oddly deserted even at this early morning hour.

In fact, everything looked deserted. An eerie stillness imbued the air.

Elder Levi was convinced the only course of action was to storm the city and take Gideon back by force. Talk was useless. He figured if the New Emilians had no mounts similar to their quvianaq, there was no way the sentinels could stand against them. The Col'kasid were a tribe of hunters and gatherers, and the gatherers stayed behind. Seventy-five men charging in with weapons drawn would certainly put the fear of God into anyone, especially someone like Liorah.

A woman, no less. Abel hated the way Levi looked down on women and treated them as inferior.

After Gideon was rescued, Levi had agreed with Sojen Micah that he would attempt to speak with Liorah. But he would not do so if she could still use his son as a bargaining tool. No one treated the future Keeper of the Text in such a way. Talks would only happen on Levi's terms.

Abel felt a knot tighten in his stomach as he surveyed the scene. The absence of any people at all—from the sentinels normally at the gates to the workers preparing to move rocks from below—sent a wave of unease through him. It was as if the heart of the moor had been silenced, its rhythm disrupted by an unknown force. To the left and shrouded in a low fog, the Hollows appeared just as empty.

Where had everyone gone?

The hunters exchanged worried glances. They had come all this way, braving the journey through foreign lands, only to be greeted by a city that appeared devoid of life. The Col'kasid's anticipation of a battle shifted as uncertainty and a growing sense of foreboding took hold.

Abel peered closer, his eyes squinting in the morning light. The gates of New Emile, usually open and welcoming, now stood firmly shut, yet no sentinels were present. The walls that Abel once thought he could call home now felt like barriers which shielded secrets and hidden dangers.

A surge of doubt washed over him. He turned to Luca, mounted on a quvianaq beside him. "What the hell is going on?" he asked. "The sentinels. The Marokai. Where is everyone?"

Luca's face showed he did not have an answer. The situation was as strange to him as it was to Abel. Even Diego and Elena looked nervous.

"Did we march into a trap?" Elena asked. She kept her voice low, as if to say anything at all would make it true.

Elder Levi approached atop his quvianaq, Saadya beside him. "Is this it?" He pointed to the city across the moor. "Doesn't seem like a very busy place."

"Something isn't right," Abel said.

Levi said nothing. His silence created a stark contrast to Abel, who felt like a whisper in the wind. Saadya grinned slightly.

"Luca," Levi said, ignoring Abel entirely. "What would you normally see out there?"

Luca knitted his eyebrows. "At the very least, two sentinels at the gates."

"Hmm." Levi stared at the city on the moor. Abel, not as angry at being ignored as he might have been a year ago, looked around. The Col'kasid hunters sat high on their quvianaq, their grip on their crossbows and lances tight. They had trained for this, prepared themselves for whatever lay ahead. And while unnerving to Abel, the stillness of New Emile did little to quell their apparent resolve.

Levi turned to look at Saadya. With a barely perceptible nod, he gave the signal. As one, the Col'kasid descended the hill, their mounts' footsteps the only sound.

Abel looked at the eerie yet quiet city, the walls he yearned to make his home, and the quarry that should have been filled with life. Jacob marched with the other hunters, according to his position, while Luca, Diego, and Elena remained with Abel.

As the quvianaq descended into the moor, their massive forms stepping carefully through the rugged terrain, the tension among the Col'kasid heightened. Abel gripped the reins of his mount tightly, his eyes fixed on the path ahead. The rhythmic thuds of their footsteps resonated in his chest.

As they stepped onto the solid path that led through the mushy moor, a sudden cacophony shattered the stillness. The surrounding air crackled with an unseen force, and Abel felt a wave of disorientation wash over him. He knew exactly what had just happened. The harmonic transducer, hidden somewhere within New Emile, had been activated.

A disorienting low rumble erupted from the direction of the quarry, engulfing the moorlands in a relentless assault of noise. The effect was immediate and devastating. The quvianaq faltered in their steps, their bodies paralyzed by frequencies that assaulted their sensitive ears.

Abel's heart sank as he witnessed the scene unfold. The Col'kasid hunters, their expressions twisted in confusion, fought to maintain control of their quvianaq. The animals writhed in pain, their primal instincts overridden by the relentless assault on their senses.

As each quvianaq succumbed to the excruciating agony caused by the harmonic transducer, chaos erupted. The creatures convulsed and spasmed uncontrollably. The impact was crushing. Riders were thrown from their mounts, their bodies tumbling through the air, crashing to the ground with bone-jarring force.

Abel desperately clung to his quvianaq's reins, his hands slick with sweat as he fought to maintain his grip. The world around him blurred in a whirlwind of motion and disorientation. The moorlands became a chaotic scene of quvianaq bucking and riders desperately trying to stay on, human shouts adding to the pandemonium.

Panic and confusion gripped the air as injured hunters struggled to crawl away from the thrashing quvianaq, desperate to find safety amidst the chaos. As each animal succumbed to the sound and fell to the ground paralyzed, some hunters disentangled themselves and scrambled away. Others were not as fortunate, caught in the tangled mess and pinned under the massive weight of the mounts.

Through the chaos, Abel's gaze darted, searching for Luca, for Diego, for Elena, for any glimmer of hope. He spotted Luca to his left, injured but alive. He looked to be pulling his sister out from under her paralyzed quvianaq. Quickly, he joined with Jacob and both ran to help.

As suddenly as it had started, the paralyzing attack from New Emile ceased.

SAADYA'S EYES bore into Luca, his voice dripping with seething anger and betrayal.

"You!" The man's voice was filled with contempt. "You were a sentinel, and now a traitor in our midst. I should kill you right now. You set us up."

Luca recoiled, his own gaze wavering under Saadya's intensity.

"I left the sentinels," he said, his voice cracking. "I am no more New Emilian than I am one of you."

Saadya's lip curled into a mocking smile. "Oh, how convenient. You think you can simply shed your skin and expect us to believe you're a changed man, beholden to no one? Your betrayal disgusts me."

Luca's jaw clenched, his fists tightening at his sides. "I risked everything to bring Gideon's message to you. I wouldn't be here if I didn't care as much as you."

Saadya took a step closer, their faces mere inches apart, his voice low. "You risked *nothing*. You knew this was possible. You knew the quvianaq would be harmed, and you set us up to fail."

A fire ignited in Luca's eyes as Saadya's anger flared even hotter. Abel stepped forward, a protective glare in his eyes.

"Enough, Saadya!" Abel kept his voice firm, but laced with a touch of warning. "There is no way Luca could have known the New Emilians would use the quarry's harmonic transducer on the quvianaq. He couldn't have predicted it."

Saadya's gaze shifted from Luca to Abel, his nostrils flaring. "Stay out of this, abomination! You are as much at fault as your...lover." He spit at Abel's feet. "You both deserve the edge of my blade."

"Luca may be a New Emilian," Abel continued without

blinking, "but he has done nothing to harm the Col'kasid. He's fighting alongside us now, risking his life just like the rest of us."

"There is no us! You have no right to speak, no right to stand here, no right to even live!" With a swift motion, Saadya pulled his knife from his belt.

"Stop!" Sojen Micah's voice cut through the tension. With his ornately carved walking stick, he pushed his way past Col'kasid hunters desperately trying to revive their quvianaq or dust themselves off. "Saadya! Get your men and their mounts back, behind the hill."

Saadya didn't move, but Abel saw a tremor in his eye. He wouldn't strike out now, not in front of this legendary man.

"Did you not hear me?" Micah stopped next to Saadya and put a hand on the man's knife-wielding arm. He lowered his voice but kept it firm. "Get everyone back and regroup. You and Levi have some plans to make, and they do not start with the slash of your blade."

Saadya's scowl deepened, but he reluctantly obeyed. As his knife went back in his belt, his gaze lingered on Abel a moment longer. Finally, he turned away and barked orders to his men.

Micah turned to Abel and Luca. His body shivered. "I am sorry for Saadya," he said after a moment. "Blame is often cast in the wrong direction."

"This isn't safe for you, Sojen." Abel looked around at the melee. "You'll surely be injured."

Micah nodded. "I don't intend to ride through those gates with you, child. I'm starting to feel it was a mistake to be here at all."

As THE quvianaq were guided back, Levi looked over the assembled hunters. His eyes finally rested on Luca, Abel, and Diego.

"I need to speak with you," Levi said, pointing at Luca only.

Abel exchanged glances with Luca. Elena stood and took a position by Jacob, her expression adamant. "You need to speak to all of us," she said.

Levi turned to her, surprise evident in his eyes and the undercurrents of patriarchal bias clear. "Elena, this isn't the place for a wo—"

"I've been here from the beginning!" Elena shouted, cutting him off with a raised hand. "You need all the help you can get if you expect to get into the city, rescue your son, and come back out alive." Her eyes blazed fiercely. "I've earned my right to be here, with Luca and with Abel."

Abel thought he saw a flicker of respect in Levi's eyes. Still, the Col'kasid Keeper of the Text spoke quickly through gritted teeth. "A woman should learn in quiet and full submission."

"What the hell is that?" Elena bunched her fists and tried to pull out of Jacob's sudden grip on her.

"It is the word of Timothy from the text of our Lord. 'I do not permit a woman to teach or to assume authority over a man; she must be quiet.'"

Before Elena could throw a punch, Levi stepped back. Elena strained again to get free from Jacob's hold on her, but the man would not relent.

"Let her hear what you have to say," Jacob said finally. "She knows ways into and out of the city walls."

Elder Levi stood firm, his hand on his walking stick. The wind picked up a few strands of peppered hair and let it blow in front of his face. The six of them stood in silence, five pairs of eyes locked on the man whose son was at the heart of all of this. Abel saw in Levi a face strained with worry and pain. Levi's free hand clenched into a fist, knuckles turning white from the effort.

With no further argument, Levi finally appeared to relent. He glanced at the Col'kasid hunters still wrangling their quvianaq mounts back behind the hill.

"I came here for one reason," Levi said, his tone more pensive. "New Emile has Gideon, and we are not leaving without him." Turning to Luca, his brows relaxed. "Luca, you know New Emile better than any of us. Could you sketch a rough map of the city? If we can't charge through the gates on our quvianaq, perhaps there are other ways to get to Gideon."

Luca nodded, swallowing a lump in his throat. The city's layout was etched into his mind. Using a bolt from a quiver on his back, he drew the outline into the dirt. He sketched the high walls, the now closed gates, the silent quarry. He marked the sentinel posts, the routes across the moor, the farms, and finally the Hollows.

"What is that?" Levi asked, pointing to a group of circles in the dirt.

"Home," Elena said coldly. "Or what used to be home. We call it the Hollows."

"That's where you're from? Not from inside the city walls?"

Elena sighed. "No. Diego and I are never allowed inside the city after we were picked in the lottery."

Levi's eyes grew wide. "I don't understand. Why not, if you are New Emilian?"

Elena did her best to paint a picture of the Marokai, and what it meant to be an outcast. While she spoke, Levi listened, seeming both amazed and disgusted.

When she was finished, the Col'kasid leader sat down and looked out over the moor. "Jacob said that you know other ways into the city. Is this true?"

Elena nodded. "There are a few tunnels on the other side

that the Marokai use to sneak in and get grain or other things we use to survive. We don't raid the place or the sentinels would come after us. Instead, one or two of us sneak in every few weeks, take a few small things, and come back out."

Levi looked to be considering all Elena had to say. He had been softening to her, and Abel had to wonder if the man was weakening his stance on women. Too bad he couldn't do that for everyone. "Where do these tunnels lead?"

"There's only one that will lead to the hold where Gideon is being kept, but there's no guarantee he's still there."

"The crack in the quarry that you mentioned earlier? How you rescued Jacob?"

"And Abel, yes."

Before she could say more, Luca cut in. "I'm sure the sentinels have closed that off," he said. "There's no way Josiah would allow it."

Levi studied the map closer. "Where are they? The tunnels your thieves use?"

"They aren't thieves," Abel said. "They are people trying to survive."

Ignoring him once again, Levi turned to Elena. "You said there were a few. Where are they?"

Furious at his mistreatment, Abel turned away. He looked out at the moor once again. One of these days, the Col'kasid would learn. They couldn't base their rules on a strict interpretation of the texts left by Father Elijah. He wanted to say more, needed to tell the man how backwards his thinking was, how hurtful. For a man who preached love and forgiveness, all Abel saw was hate and banishment.

Abel suddenly froze, his gaze fixed on a distant point to the east of New Emile. Something was there—a shadowy mass moving slowly, casting up dust.

"What is that?" Abel whispered, his voice just above a

breath. Luca stepped away from the map and followed the direction of Abel's outstretched finger. "To the east. Do you see it?"

In seconds, all of them were looking in that direction, their eyes fixed on the rising dust cloud.

None of them had an answer.

"It almost looks like..." Abel wasn't sure enough to finish his sentence. It looked a little like the clouds that the Tishbe bison would kick up around Rephidim.

But there were no animals that large out here.

Standing next to him, Levi shielded his eyes from the sun. "Is that a...another...army?"

CHAPTER THIRTY-THREE

U NDER THE GLARING BRILLIANCE OF THE SUN, CHEN AND the Zhanshi stood on a hill overlooking the city of New Emile. They had made the march in just under five weeks, skirting mountains and lakes to the north. Their misfortune of stumbling through the swamp near the Three Rivers clung to their clothes in the form of mud and stink.

Chen's gaze narrowed. "This is the day we seek retribution for the Zhanshi."

As he turned his attention to his men—all made haggard by the experience but more ready than ever to fight—he felt a sense of pride, like a father might for a son. These were his people, the Zhanshi, and they were on the cusp of victory after decades of abandonment. A cacophony of various sounds filtered through the air—men sharpening their swords and lances, filling their quivers with magnesium-tipped bolts, and mentally preparing themselves for what was to come. It was invigorating.

Martin's voice snapped Chen back to reality. "Zhuren." He stepped closer, apprehension on his face.

Chen motioned toward a boulder nearby, and Lin Xi and Lucien quickly joined them. It was time to solidify plans. As they huddled together, a myriad of choices lay before them, each with their advantages and risks—a ballistic attack on the eastern wall, hurling projectiles into the heart of New Emile, or a daring foot advance towards the city gates. The later choice pleased Chen the most, but he needed to hear out his advisors.

"The eastern wall," Lucien proposed. "If we puncture it, we'll have an entry point. We may not know the layout of the city or how many of their men are armed, but our numbers and surprise might work to our advantage."

Lin Xi interjected. "We could launch one or two projectiles over the wall. That will sow chaos and allow our men smooth entry."

Chen rubbed his chin pensively. "Neither of those are guaranteed, and approaching the gates on foot is no less risky. I believe we may need some sound intelligence before we decide. If you lack knowledge of your enemy, you will suffer defeat, even in victory."

He scanned his warriors until he finally spotted Jiang, a nimble Zhanshi Chen had admired for his stealth and perception. The younger man had frequently sought information in the tightest of places and was well trained. "Jiang," Chen said, waving the man over. "I need you to scout the city. Circumnavigate it, look for any weaknesses in their defenses, and report back. If you see an opening in the wall, perhaps one not guarded, note the location."

Jiang stood tall, his sharp eyes gleaming with resolve. "Yes, Zhuren." He nodded and gripped his lance. Without wasting another moment, Jiang darted off, melting seamlessly into the surrounding landscape like a ghost.

Chen watched him disappear. This was the moment he had been waiting for, the culmination of years of patience and preparation. Despite all his attempts at cultivating an inner calm, however, Chen felt an electric surge of anticipation. Every muscle tensed, ready to spring into action. He had to steady his breathing, knowing he could not afford to be careless now.

As the sun began its descent, casting long, dancing shadows over the terrain, Chen stood alone on a slight ridge overlooking the city of New Emile, the home of the gulao. A soft wind rustled his hair as he squinted against the last rays of the day, his thoughts filled with strategies and the haunting memory of Luke's voice. If only he could have properly honored him in death.

Silence reigned around him, punctuated by the distant hum of the Zhanshi preparing for the night. As the sky darkened, he felt an urge to join his comrades, to take some respite before the impending clash. Yet, his heart held him in place, waiting for the silhouette of his scout to reemerge from the shadows. Clouds in the north hung ominously. They had been greeted on this journey already with bouts of snow, though never enough to slow their travels.

Would it be good to advance under the cover of a storm?

If conditions were right, tomorrow they would make their move. Tonight, however, was a moment of uncertainty. The city seemed stoic, unyielding against the purple and green twilight, its shadow stretching out toward them. Chen could not help but marvel at the paradox of it all—the looming victory versus the tranquil evening, his sense of honor against the pangs of loss, the anxious anticipation of the next move and the peaceful quiet before the storm.

His eye caught objects to the southwest which seemed out of place. Chen strained his vision against the dwindling daylight, trying to discern its exact nature. There seemed to be a cluster of tents, not large enough to be an army but significant enough to raise his suspicion. A group of men, perhaps? Camped just over a hill, obscured from the city's view?

Russant's mention of a third tribe, the Col'kasid, came to his mind.

Could this be them?

Rather than dispatch another scout, he waited for Jiang's return. Whoever it was, Col'kasid or someone else, Jiang would spot them. Chen could not afford to alert this potential third party, not when their intentions remained shrouded in mystery. The fact there was a third tribe had been bothering him for weeks. It changed the course of a victory, from the need to eliminate just one population to the threat of facing a different one.

How advanced were they?

He moved away from the ridge, back towards the heart of his camp, his mind buzzing with questions. He yearned for the simplicity of earlier times when straightforward vengeance was enough to spur him on. As he walked, Chen glanced one last time at the shadowy outline of the encampment in the distance. He felt a knot in his stomach, a premonition of yet another challenge they would have to face. The goal had been clear from the start: leave no gulao alive.

Lightning flashed in the distance. In a few hours, snow would fall.

Tonight, the storm gathered. Tomorrow, it would break loose.

THE SUN had slipped below the horizon and disappeared behind the approaching clouds when Jiang returned.

"There are two gates, Zhuren," Jiang said, his words swallowed up by the steady hum of the camp being set up. "Both are closed and, from what I could tell, heavily reinforced with wood and metal. To the west of the city, there appears to be an abandoned village. The buildings are falling apart, but it could provide us some cover."

Chen digested this information, his mind already mapping out strategies and alternatives. The presence of two gates implied a double-edged problem, but the dilapidated village offered an interesting opportunity...and another worry. Were the residents expecting an attack, and if so, had they all fled to safety inside the walls?

"No guards?" he asked, keen to understand the city's apparent lack of defenses. He would never think of leaving Yaolan open to an attack. Even now, boys who were too young to make the five-week trip to New Emile were armed and in place in the valley.

"None that I could see," Jiang confirmed.

New Emile might seem unguarded, but war is deception. He recalled a book his father had left in his keeping, one stolen from the original settlers during the time of Mathias the First. "When we are able to attack," he said, quoting the text as he remembered it, "we must seem unable; when using our forces, we must appear inactive; when we are near, we must make the enemy believe we are far away; when far away, we must make him believe we are near."

"I am sorry, Zhuren," Jiang said after a moment. "I do not understand."

Chen did not answer. Rather, he pointed toward the southwest. "The camp on the hill. Did you get a good look at those men?"

Jiang paused, a frown creasing his forehead. "No, Zhuren. I did not get a clear look, as they were at a considerable distance. But what I can confirm is that it appeared they had large beasts with them...and all of the men had hair."

Hair? This peculiar detail caught Chen off guard. The revelation deepened the mystery of the camp. Russant and his men had been shorn of all hair, and the Zhanshi were the same except for those who were old enough—as his advisor Luke had been. His mind swirled with questions, each more puzzling than the last.

"Thank you, Jiang," he said finally, offering a nod of approval to his scout. "Your information is invaluable. Rest now. We have a long day ahead of us."

As Jiang retreated, Chen gazed once more at the dim outlines of New Emile in the distance. His desire to avenge Mathias the First and eliminate the gulao was only further fueled by the new information. No matter who stood in their way, not a soul in the vicinity of New Emile would live to see another sunset. Of that, he was determined.

Chen gestured for his lieutenants to join him once again. In the light of a hastily constructed fire, stark shadows painted their faces, the dancing flames emphasizing lines of anxiety.

"Where is Lucien?" Chen asked.

"He is adjusting the projectiles as we speak." Martin nodded toward New Emile. "Trying to get the right angles for an attack."

"Very well." Chen relayed Jiang's findings. "Two gates, a deserted village, and...a camp of hairy men with large animals. That is our situation."

Martin's eyes narrowed. "We could still consider launching a projectile over the wall, as Lin Xi suggested. This might give us an advantage."

"What is this abandoned village?" Lin Xi asked. "Are there no residents?"

"None that Jiang saw," Chen said.

"Could we use the village as a distraction, then? We cause a commotion there and draw out their guards."

"That does not address the hairy men on the hill." Chen looked toward the southwest, where a few small fires could be seen. "We need to consider them, too. If they are the Col'kasid mentioned by our guest prior to his passing, then we may need a second front."

A silence stretched between them, filled with the crackling of the fire and the murmurs of men and boys about to go to war. Chen's mind raced, forming and rejecting plans with each passing moment.

Eventually, he broke the silence. "We stick to our first plan," he said decisively. "We launch the projectile on the eastern wall and breach it. That will be our point of entry." He turned to Martin. "Was Lucien close to being done aligning the projectiles?"

"Yes, Zhuren. They await only your word."

He paused. "I will lead a team through the breach. We will take them by surprise. I would like a smaller team to remain behind and watch for any unexpected development from those on the hill, from the Col'kasid."

Lin Xi and Martin exchanged glances before nodding. "It is a risk to leave some men back," Lin Xi said, "but I agree it will be our best option."

The fire cast long shadows over the Zhanshi warriors. For a moment, Chen allowed himself to imagine the city of New Emile, its walls crumbling under the force of their projectile, the gulao screaming for mercy as their lives were cut short in payment for all the atrocities their ancestors committed.

"Rest now," Chen said at last. "We will attack at dawn."

As Chen stared at the fire, he steeled himself for what was to come. A new dawn would bring a new battle, a new chance to avenge Mathias the First.

And New Emile would not know what hit it.

PART V: THE RECKONING

Cycle 1, Day 1, Year 97

Do not weep, maiden, for war is kind.
Because your lover threw wild hands toward the sky
And the affrighted steed ran on alone,
Do not weep.
War is kind.

—Stephen Crane, "War is Kind" 1899

CHAPTER THIRTY-FOUR

LIORAH'S REVELATION FIVE DAYS AGO STILL HUNG OVER Gideon like a heavy fog. The weight of her words bore down on him, challenging the very fabric of his reality.

A child? *Their* child? He had been questioning Liorah's confession for days, unsure of the truth. At least he was permitted out of the hold and allowed to heal.

Isaiah had not been so lucky.

"Are you sure about this?" Gideon's voice wavered, his eyes searching Liorah's face for any sign of deception. It would make sense—lie about something like this to gain some sort of leverage. She had shown some mercy, however, allowing him enough haelen to feel once more like himself. Except for the bugs still gnawing at his hair, he'd remarkably improved.

Liorah's eyes showed both vulnerability and anger. "Roland the Kept cannot father children, Gideon. It's a well-known fact that he is nothing but a toy, something I can use when I feel like it." She shifted her gaze away for a moment. "And besides, I have only been with you since you arrived." Her voice quivered with a raw honesty that left Gideon momentarily speechless. "You've...infested my thoughts more than I would have liked."

Gideon's mind was a maelstrom of doubt and confusion,

much like the snow falling outside the window. The cold air blew a few flakes inside, but at least there was a warm fire to keep out the worst of it.

As he searched Liorah's face, he saw no hint of deceit. Her apparent vulnerability told him more than any words could say. This was not a trick. This was their reality, woven with threads of uncertainty and possibility. Not only had he sinned against the Lord, he had become a traitor to his people, and now seeded the enemy. Gideon grappled with the implications of both treason and fatherhood. The weight of some responsibility he was not prepared to accept settled on his shoulders and mixed with his tumultuous feelings for Liorah. He hated her for what she did to him, yet there was a magnetic pull that drew them together—and it was now mirrored in the life growing within her. His mother had once said that the line between love and hate is thin.

She wasn't wrong.

There was fear, guilt, anxiety, shame...and in that, a small glint of happiness. He had always seen himself as a guardian, a protector of his people. He was the next Keeper of the Text, after all. But now? Was it possible that his role could extend beyond Rephidim and bind both the New Emilians and Col'kasid together? He was to be a father, responsible for nurturing and shaping a life that would carry their legacy forward.

Gideon reached out to take Liorah's hands in his, but she recoiled and stepped back. Her brow knitted. "You do not have the right to touch me without my permission. I don't care if you are the father of my child."

Suddenly that happiness he had felt, that sense that the future was in their hands, was gone. All that remained was guilt, fear, and anger. Standing in Liorah's Chambers, Gideon felt an oppressive silence that made him think the hold would be a better place. Even the cold air felt colder.

"I...I don't understand," he said. "If I am to be the father of this child—"

"You are the *seed* of this child, yes." Liorah folded her arms. "But do not think for a minute that puts you in my bed or allows you a seat at my table. You are no better than the men at the gates, your Col'kasid."

Gideon blinked. "The men— My *father* is here?"

Liorah nodded. "And when we're done with them, you will remain. I assume you know how to raise a child."

Stay in New Emile? How could he entertain such a thought when his father, Levi, and the Col'kasid hunters were just outside? They had come to rescue him and Isaiah. But if there was to be a battle, how safe would Liorah be? How safe would his child be?

"What do you intend to do with the Col'kasid?" Gideon asked. He watched Liorah closely, searching for any sign of uncertainty or hesitation.

Liorah's gaze was unreadable, but behind those eyes Gideon thought he saw a spark of the maniacal. Her grandmother had contracted Tishbe fever. Had she as well? "New Emile is mine. The haelen is mine. You are mine, and I will protect all of it at all costs. Your father poses a threat, and I will not negotiate or show any sign of weakness."

Gideon's heart sank. There it was. There was no way this woman was going to let him go. He was now torn between his loyalty to his people and the newfound responsibility of fatherhood, regardless of how much Liorah acted as if she despised him. Admitting to such a sin to his father would get him exiled. Yet should the hunters march into the city, Liorah's safety and the life they had created would be at risk.

The room fell into silence once more. The image of Levi, his father, leading the Col'kasid hunters across the moor, through the gates, and to the doors of the New Emilian Chambers loomed large in his mind. For the longest time, he had imagined just such a scenario and relished in the prospect of release. He fervently prayed it would happen. Yet now, because of a prolonged lapse of reason, the responsibility he felt toward his people and the joy of being set free clashed with a new fierce protectiveness he suddenly felt.

Gideon ran through options in his mind. When he finally spoke, his voice was strained. "What if I talk to my father? Explain everything."

"Explain what? That you and your men attempted to steal from us? That you rode in here on your smelly animals and tried to assert your values on us?"

"I cannot turn my back on the Col'kasid. They are my blood, my heritage. But—" Gideon weighed his next words carefully. "If I agree to stay here and raise our child, would you let them be, allow them to return to Rephidim unharmed?"

The crease between Liorah's eyes deepened. "What makes you think you have a choice between staying here and leaving?"

"I don't think that." Gideon held his hands out. "But I don't think attacking my father or my people will solve anything. This is the first time in our recorded history that two distinct tribes have met. Not since Manoach have we all been together. Do you want to be remembered as the harbinger of war?"

"Harbi— War?" Liorah stuck her finger into Gideon's chest. "You brought this on your people. And may I remind you—I am the One Voice. History is what I make of it."

Gideon's gaze met Liorah's. He understood Liorah's struggles, the practicality of not being able to handle an increase in population within New Emile. Yet, a truce hinged upon the establishment of some sort of trade for sustenance. Did it not?

"Liorah," Gideon said. He attempted to keep his voice steady but also laced with empathy. "I understand the challenges New Emile faces, and I know you must prioritize the well-being of your people. If establishing trade for food can secure their survival, then let me talk to my father, explain the situation with your grain, your out-of-control population, your need for resources."

A flicker of frustration crossed Liorah's features. She opened her mouth to argue, then closed it again as if she was seriously considering the possibility of saving New Emile. "If I let you talk to your father now," she said finally, "you will not return. Our child will have no father." Gideon thought he heard a crack in her voice.

"What if I promise to stay, to accept my responsibility and raise this child?"

"Why? Your father groomed you to take his place. Your allegiance will always be with your family, with the Col'kasid. You will forever look to the south and pine for a home."

"My home can be with you." As Gideon said that, he felt a twinge of sickness at the thought of living with Liorah in her chambers. She had locked him in a hold, had him and his friends tortured, and threatened his people. Despite all that, was there a chance they could mend this relationship, even if only to raise a child properly? It was doubtful, but also impossible to see another way.

He stood straight and put his hand on Liorah's. This time, she did not pull away. "I will not abandon our child or the responsibility I bear as its father. Allowing me to talk to my father, to negotiate, is not solely for the benefit of the Col'kasid but for the preservation of your people, the citizens of New Emile."

"Do you think your father will allow you to remain here, to be a part of our child's life?" Her hand felt warm. "As far as I can see, the Col'kasid despise our way of life, our rejection of your beliefs. Which, by the way, is something I will not allow to infect New Emile. Your father will not tolerate your defiance."

"I will face my father." Gideon took in a deep breath, knowing exactly what that really meant. "Children deserve to be raised in a world free from the type of hatred that pervades my people, and I believe this is an opportunity that may allow this to happen."

Liorah withdrew her hand from Gideon's and stepped back. "He won't allow it, and as a leader, I wouldn't either."

"I won't let fear or my father's disapproval dictate our path. We make our own decisions generation after generation. If we remain on the road carved out for us by our ancestors, we will never change."

Liorah's eyes suddenly gave way to anger. "Your idealism blinds you, Gideon! You can't see the consequences, the danger you put yourself in attempting to negotiate with your father. Your defiance of him will only bring destruction and chaos, more so than if I merely keep you in the hold myself."

Gideon did not match Liorah's anger, but kept his voice soft. It wasn't easy. "Liorah, I understand your concerns, but I will fight for what I believe in, for what I believe should be the way of the world. My father does not speak for my morality. We can secure a truce and create a better future for New Emile. You just need to let me talk to him."

Gideon's chest hurt, torn between his new responsibility and a gnawing—almost annoying—sense of duty to the Col'kasid.

Liorah's anger dissipated quickly as her gaze softened.

"You are stubborn, Gideon." She sighed. "But perhaps that stubbornness will be a strength. Let me think on this some more. I..." She turned away from Gideon and toward the window. "I don't want to lose—"

An explosion ripped through the Chambers, shaking the very foundation of the room. Gideon rushed to grab Liorah instinctively and threw her to the floor as small rocks fell from the ceiling. She immediately attempted to pull away, but Gideon held tight.

Something was terribly wrong.

As he held Liorah, Gideon tried to make sense of the chaos unfolding around them. The Col'kasid hunters, led by his father Levi, didn't possess weaponry capable of causing such a devastating explosion. While they had attempted to make explosives that would clear away large blocks of stone or fell trees, to Gideon's knowledge, no one had succeeded.

That left only one chilling possibility.

His voice barely above a whisper, Gideon voiced his thoughts. "Liorah, it's the Zhanshi. They're attacking."

Liorah stopped struggling and clung to him, her grip tight even as they both stood. Her voice quivered. "But how? What hell is this?"

Gideon's mind attempted to piece together all he knew. "We were warned by the strangers years ago. The Zhanshi are relentless. They won't stop until they've destroyed everything."

"What the hell for? What did we ever do to them?"

"I don't think it matters. Whatever reason they have is reason enough."

The surrounding air thickened with smoke and snow filtering in from the outside. It choked their lungs and clouded their vision. Panic swirled and fear coursed through his veins. "We need to find safety. Is there someplace we can go?"

"I will not run from this!" Liorah pushed Gideon away. "I am the One Voice and this is my home. No one will take that from me."

"Fine, fine." Gideon looked around. "But if the Zhanshi breach the Chambers, you—and our child—will be killed on sight. I'm not saying we run like cowards. I'm saying we find some damn protection."

The sound of rushing footsteps filled the air, cutting off Liorah's response. Josiah burst into the Chambers. His face showed surprise at seeing Gideon in the room with Liorah, but he wasted no time in delivering the news that had brought him running.

"Liorah," Josiah panted, his voice strained. "The eastern wall has crumbled. Strange men armed with weapons are pouring into the city. My men are doing their best to hold them back, but we must get you to safety. They are cutting down anyone they see."

Liorah's body tensed. "No, Josiah! I won't hide while my city burns."

Josiah's expression twisted in concern. "Liorah, I understand your bravery, but we can't very well risk your life."

Gideon was amazed that despite the trauma she must have felt and the fear that had to be there, Liorah would not relinquish her grip on power. "Don't tell me what I can and can't do!" she cried.

Her gaze shifted from Josiah to the city beyond the window. Screams filtered through the air, each one suddenly cut short.

"I am the One Voice, Josiah," she said resolutely. "Leaders stand with their people, even in the face of danger. Would my father, Master Eilian, have run? No, no, no. I will not abandon my home. Your job is to protect me until the threat is gone or you breathe your last."

Josiah's face registered something that Gideon couldn't quite place. It was neither surprise at Liorah's decision nor fear of the Zhanshi attack. Instead, it looked like...anger, rage directed at the One Voice.

"Whatever you say." Josiah bowed mockingly. "Whatever you say."

CHAPTER THIRTY-FIVE

THE DEAFENING ROAR OF THE DETONATION REVERBERATED through the streets of New Emile as the dust settled. A tremendous cloud rose in a towering column, threaded with trails of black smoke. Through it all, men emerged, dressed in black battle garments, their heads shaved, brandishing weapons of war. As they stormed through the breach in the eastern wall, the sky unleashed a torrent of snowfall and wind.

Josiah readied himself as his sentinels stood their ground. This was not what he had expected. With all the attention devoted to the Col'kasid to the southwest, there had been no preparation. Although he'd only heard rumors and stories told by Gideon and Abel, Josiah knew this had to be the Zhanshi, a third tribe of descendants of the Circle of Light who had nothing but bloodlust in their eyes. Each of them was a force unto himself, armed with swords, crossbows loaded with bolts that appeared aflame, and lances pointed threateningly forward. As they flooded into the city, their goal was obvious—slay any New Emilian in their path.

Josiah staggered back. A wave of terror coursed through the citizens at the realization of their plight; mothers clung to their children as they scrambled for cover, while fathers grabbed whatever weapons were at hand to defend their homes. Sticks, bars of metal, stones—anything was better than facing death empty-handed. Everywhere Josiah looked, he heard screams and saw anguish, blood, and smoke. The clash of steel on steel filled the air and muffled the cries of those caught in the chaos.

The brutal combat of men against men, metal against metal, was merciless, swallowing screams whole, and consigning them to oblivion. The once bustling city, filled with the sounds of life and laughter, was now replaced by the sounds of hell. The city's lifeblood dripped red onto the stone streets. Splattered with crimson, the freshly snow-covered ground became a canvas of death, each drop of blood a future extinguished, a dream shattered.

Josiah's hands were tight around his weapons, a shield in one hand and a sword in another. His jaw tightly clenched as he surveyed the scene before him. People ran, screaming and knocking each other over to flee. Josiah stepped forward, cutting through the noise with a steely voice. "Hold them back!" he shouted. "We're the only defense!"

Josiah's sword arm ached from the strain, and sweat cascaded down his face despite the chill. He watched as his men pushed forward against overwhelming odds, thrusting spears and swords at the Zhanshi raiders. An enemy crossbow bolt grazed by his leg, and he stepped back in surprise as a fellow sentinel cut down a Zhanshi warrior who looked to be only fifteen.

A cluster of Zhanshi warriors broke away from the main force and descended upon a home sheltering a group of terrified New Emilians. Josiah spotted the imminent threat and, with a small contingent of those nearest him, sprinted towards the endangered household.

Crossbow bolts hissed through the smoke-choked air, their tips alight with an ominous glow. Josiah did not understand how the flames could remain lit, but it didn't matter. Each shot brought death and drew a stark trail of doom across the sky. When they struck an object, be it building or person, flames expanded outward. Josiah and his men reacted swiftly, raising their shields to intercept the fiery projectiles. The bolts impacted with a shower of sparks but did not extinguish.

"Shield wall!" Josiah bellowed over the cacophony. They had practiced this, and his men responded in perfect unison. They interlocked their shields, forming an impenetrable barrier between the terrified inhabitants and the Zhanshi.

To the left, several sentinels counterattacked, their arrows singing through the air, finding purchase in the flesh of their aggressors. Each thud of an arrow that hit its mark was a minor victory.

A guttural roar of triumph from the Zhanshi tore through the din of battle as they breached the sentinels' line. Josiah was thrown back, and in seconds, the home was overrun. The shrill cries of those inside were cut chillingly short. As Josiah regained his feet, the echoes of their terror sent a shiver down his spine.

With a renewed anger, Josiah pivoted toward another offshoot of Zhanshi warriors. Five of them had skirted past a mass of his own men, and behind them, a horde of their comrades followed. They were headed for the Chambers, the center of power, the heart of the city. Knowing of Liorah's deception made the idea of saving her unpleasant, yet there were other Elite in that building—Piper, Alistair, Marius—not to mention a host of servants. He knew what he had to do. It was his duty—the Chambers, if not Liorah, had to be protected.

"Regroup!" Josiah's command sliced through the clamor of battle, drawing the attention of his scattered men. "Shield wall at the Chambers! Now!"

With renewed vigor, they regrouped, shields interlocking with a resounding clash. Each man stood tall, their weary bodies pushed to the limit, death looming ominously over them. For many of them, this would be their road to Eldorado, and they accepted it. In the heart of the chaotic battlefield, twenty-five sentinels of New Emile stood firm, a human fortress poised before the approaching wave of Zhanshi warriors.

The Zhanshi launched their assault. The fire-tipped bolts from their crossbows whistled through the air. As the first wave of bolts crashed against their shield wall, the sentinels held firm, yet the Zhanshi were upon soon on them, their weapons raised.

Swords met in a flurry of sparks. Men fell from both sides, lives cut short in the street. Behind them, the Chambers loomed large. Josiah glanced back toward the one window that overlooked the haelen pond, but could not see Liorah. Perhaps she had taken his advice and found shelter.

The sentinels fought ferociously despite their exhaustion. Josiah hoped the unyielding courageousness guiding their actions wasn't solely driven by their desire to protect themselves, but also their comrades and the city. He didn't know how many of these Zhanshi warriors had come through the eastern wall, but the New Emilians would need to fight until the very end.

In the throes of the battle, Josiah suddenly felt a firm grip on his shoulder. Jerking around, his sword at the ready, he met the wide eyes of a fellow sentinel, sweat-streaked and splattered with blood. The man's breath came in ragged gasps, condensing in the cold air like puffs of smoke.

"Josiah," the sentinel huffed. "The Col'kasid...have gathered at the southwest gate. I think they plan to break it down. We need more men, or the gate won't hold."

The news disrupted Josiah's momentum. His mind raced as he quickly assessed the situation. His men were barely holding back the Zhanshi, the New Emilian formation slowly thinning under the constant onslaught. The thought of dividing his already outnumbered force was a gamble he was loath to take, but he also knew that leaving the southwest gate unguarded was not an option.

With a curt nod, he decided. "Get four men. Hold the gate as long as you can. Arrows and oil from the parapet. The rest stay here." His gaze swept over the man before him. "Fight like hell."

The sentinel rushed off to rally his men, while Josiah took a moment to survey the chaotic scene before him. The street was littered with corpses, Zhanshi and sentinels alike. The survivors among his own men were battered and bloodied. They were not prepared for something like this. Some threats were internal—the Marokai, uprisings, rebellions. This was different. It wouldn't be long before they would fall, overwhelmed by sheer numbers.

The need to divide their meager forces was a clear sign of how desperate things had become.

With a deep breath, he jumped back into the fight, calling for his remaining men to stand strong. Arrows flew and swords clashed against shields. Josiah had no other option but to concentrate on what was ahead of him, despite the possibility of the Col'kasid breaking through the southwest gate and making things that much worse. With every step his men took backwards, Josiah felt his resolve wavering. He had to push them forward and out or all would be lost.

THERE WERE seventy left, seventy Col'kasid hunters who had not been injured by the tragedy that befell the quvianaq. Abel stood watching the southwestern gate of New Emile. He had entered that gate several times, never once thinking of it as a barrier. Now, though, the city, once a symbol of freedom and safety for him, was an obstacle that had to be overcome.

As one, the Col'kasid hunters unleashed a battle cry that shattered the tranquility, something that obviously meant stealth was not in their plan. Abel had heard that cry before, but never in such numbers. These men, these hunters, were not an army, though, despite being armed with lances, crossbows, axes, and a handful of swords forged in Rephidim. How would they work together as a team, especially without being on their mounts? While none of the quvianaq had died, they all appeared stunned, their coos and clucks mere whimpers. They were useless.

They had traveled for four arduous weeks from their homeland of Rephidim to arrive here with the sole purpose of forcing Liorah to release Gideon and Isaiah...or avenge their deaths. Past battles were not in their history; the Col'kasid was a peaceful tribe, and this marked their first onslaught against anything human. As they had never set foot in the Wastelands nor gazed upon a moor such as the one New Emile was built on, it had to be frightening for all.

Abel was different. He had walked through these lands before, guided by Kaius and joined by Luca. Now Luca was with him. Were his former friends, Kaius, Raphael and Nico, on the other side of that wall?

While not possessing the same familiarity with New Emile as Luca, Elena, and Diego did, Abel still felt as if he were returning home. With that came a strange blend of apprehension and nostalgia. It was a peculiar sensation, stepping into a territory that was at once alien yet familiar.

Despite being exiled from the Col'kasid, Abel had to admit his sentiments still lay with them. He held no grudge against the New Emilians, but his allegiance was to his kind.

Liorah had imprisoned Gideon and Isaiah for nothing more than disobeying a ridiculous rule. Now, as one, they were about to venture into the unknown, with Saadya leading the charge. It was time to rescue Elder Levi's son, Gideon, the future Keeper of the Text and Abel's friend.

He was ready.

Sort of.

Abel reached out and look Luca's hand. As the tension thickened while they waited for the command to move forward, their focus returned to the city gates. Their path was set, but did it lead to Eldorado? Whatever came next, at least they would face it together.

Luca broke away and approached Elena and Diego standing slightly apart from the main group. They looked resolved to join in this fight, but there was also a sense of unease.

"Why was the Hollows abandoned?" Luca's question sent a ripple of surprise through Abel. Either he never noticed the Marokai's absence or he put it to the back of his mind in the heat of the moment. "Did they know something?"

"They know enough to hide," Elena said with some reservation.

"Where?"

"North of the farms on the other side of the city."

Luca sighed as if he wished he were among the Marokai now. His shoulders slumped, and he cast a last look at the southwestern gate of New Emile. A stab of sympathy hit Abel—Luca was also an exile from his homeland, another hated cast off looking for a place to rest his head. Why couldn't they have just gone their own way, found a place to call home together?

With no more hesitation, Saadya gave the command to destroy the gate, and the Col'kasid launched their assault.

They ran through the moor, doing their best to stay on more solid ground. With snow falling and dirt rising around them, they gave another unsettling cry and crashed against the sturdy gate. One after one, they pounded with rocks, with their hands, with whatever they could find in order to weaken the barrier. The thunderous drumming of their collective efforts reverberated and marked the beginning of a relentless onslaught. Each impact jarred the gate and sent tremors that rattled its strongholds. Wood splintered and flew, shards whipping through the air like arrows turned awry.

Abel watched as the gate was slowly reduced to a trembling bulwark, suffering under the repeated strikes of the Col'kasid hunters. Around him, the air was thick with snow, now blowing horizontally and in swirls, often at the same time. The wind was brutal and stung Abel's exposed skin. Each second stretched out in anticipation of the gate's eventual collapse. They knew it was just a matter of time before the last barrier between them and their objective would fall. Every strike brought them closer to their goal.

But what then? What waited for them on the other side? What had Josiah and his sentinels set up?

As splinters continued to fly, the gate showed the first signs of imminent collapse. A low creak echoed as the formerly impenetrable defense looked ready to succumb to the pressure. Despite the swelling fear threatening to consume him, Abel looked up towards the ramparts. Barely visible through the snow and in the dark, he saw five sentinels defending the gate, but they looked determined. Were Raphael and Nico up there?

Suddenly, the whistling sound of loosed arrows cut through the air, swiftly followed by sharp thuds as they found their targets. Three of the arrows embedded deep into the bodies of unfortunate Col'kasid hunters. Blood spurted from wounds as the men fell.

In a second, it all became too real.

Abel looked back up. There was a subtle shift among the sentinels, yet the assault on the gate continued unabated. The sturdiness of the defense was being tested, but Abel knew, as the sentinels above likely did, that this was only the beginning. The real battle, the desperate fight to rescue Gideon and Isaiah — if they still even lived — was yet to come.

From his vantage point, Abel saw the sentinels above shift again. The walls built around New Emile were made for defense, and even in the face of overwhelming odds, those who had a high ground had an advantage. Even as more arrows descended from the sky, containers of hot oil fell, their contents spilling over and cascading down the walls. They shattered on impact, the oil instantly igniting upon contact with torches held by the Col'kasid.

Abel recoiled as the scent of burning flesh filled his nostrils. It was a smell not unlike the funeral pyres in Rephidim, one that clung to clothes and created a lasting memory. An unrecognizable hunter screamed and stumbled backward, his hands covering his face. The smell stung Abel's eyes and created a scratching at his throat. He glanced towards Saadya and the rest of the Col'kasid hunters up front, half expecting to see them retreat.

Yet, they stood strong. The sound of crackling fire and pained grunts filled the air. Hunters, illuminated by the flames, continued to pound on the beleaguered gate. Abel, though standing in the heart of the Col'kasid formation, couldn't help but empathize with the tortured creaking of the wooden structure.

He could only imagine the rising dread among the sentinels who watched as their last line of defense, their physical barrier against the invaders, was slowly but steadily chipped away. Each splintering chunk of wood represented a fading hope.

As if sensing the gate's imminent surrender, the Col'kasid rallied, their efforts rejuvenated with monstrous vigor. Their guttural roars reverberated through the cold air. Abel, amidst the ear-splitting noise of war cries, felt another chill seep into his bones.

The Col'kasid were animals.

Amidst the chaos, though, there was a sudden shift in the Col'kasid's battle cries. Their unified roar was now accompanied by another set of war cries, higher pitched and more sinister. Abel turned his attention to where the sound originated and saw what he feared the most...

...a horde of Zhanshi warriors charging through the blizzard and headed straight at the Col'kasid.

CHAPTER THIRTY-SIX

INSIDE THE CHAMBERS, GIDEON STOOD STILL, PANIC ENVELOPING him as Liorah paced back and forth. Despite the danger, she refused to run away or seek safety elsewhere. Instead, she waited for word. The sounds of battle mixed with howling winds filtered in through the window uninterrupted.

Josiah marched into the room, his boots echoing loudly on the stone floor. Normally composed, he looked unhinged.

"What news?" Liorah asked. "Did you hold them off?"

Josiah took one look at Gideon, furious. "Why is he here?"

"Because I want him here." Liorah stepped away from the window and approached Josiah. "Answer my question. Did you hold them off?"

"We held back the Zhanshi, for now." Josiah's eyes never left Gideon. "They're regrouping, though. I think we have a little breathing room."

"Allowing them to regroup is not a victory."

"We're down about five men."

"That is not my concern. Use what you have to keep them away from here, from me." She looked at Gideon. "And make sure Gideon's father doesn't get through the southwest gate."

Josiah furrowed his brow. "We don't have the men to hold New Emile from two fronts. We're doing the best we can."

"Your best isn't good enough. I don't care if you have to pull every woman and child from their homes and give them a weapon. You find a way to keep me safe."

Josiah stiffened. "You would be safe down below, where I told you to go."

"And I told you I wouldn't abandon my home."

In a moment of anger, Josiah's face hardened, his fists clenching. "Your home, Liorah? Or your power?"

Liorah's icy gaze bore into Josiah, but she didn't respond. She merely stood, her head held high, chin jutted out in defiance. Her silence was a challenge, and Josiah took it as an invitation.

"You...you disgust me, Liorah." Josiah took a step toward Liorah. "You poisoned your own father and half-brother to gain this power, to become the One Voice. You took their lives, and for what? You will never be like Mother Miriam."

Gideon's eyes widened as he observed the heated confrontation, but before he could process anything he'd just heard—*Liorah murdered her family?*—Josiah advanced. Instinct kicked in, and Gideon stepped in front of Liorah, his body shielding her from this man who had spent so long torturing him for information he didn't have.

Josiah, his face flushed with anger, didn't slow his approach. He got close—too close—and shoved Gideon aside with a force that sent him stumbling backward. It wasn't hard to do, given how weak Gideon had become since being thrown in the hold. But even if Liorah disgusted him—now more than ever—she carried his child. He would have to do something to defend her.

Gideon quickly regained his balance and whirled back to face Josiah, who was now dangerously close to Liorah. The leader of the sentinels put his hand on the hilt of his sword.

"Don't." Gideon's voice was quiet, but there was an undercurrent of threat, of warning. He stared at Josiah, his body tense, ready to act if necessary.

Liorah's icy demeanor was unbroken. All at once he was able to reconcile this image of her with the ruthless actions Josiah had just accused her of. The mother of his child had a darkness that Gideon was only beginning to understand.

Suddenly, faster than Gideon could have ever expected, Liorah's hand flashed. A glint of cold steel caught the Chamber's dim light, a small but deadly blade concealed within the folds of her gown now in her hand.

"Power is not given, Josiah. It is taken." Liorah's voice was colder than any Gideon had heard before.

Before Josiah could react, Liorah lunged forward. The dagger sliced through the air between them. Josiah, so caught up in his rage and shock at her audacity, didn't have time to draw his sword or step back.

The sound of the dagger at it slashed through Josiah's throat was barely a whisper. His eyes bulged, surprise replacing the anger that had been there just moments before. His hands rose to his throat and grabbed at the wound, blood squirting between his fingers. As Josiah staggered, Gideon saw the light in the man's eyes fade.

With surprising force, Liorah pushed Josiah backwards and out of the window. Gideon did not see the man land, but heard a loud crunch on the street below. Words of shock erupted from those on the ground who had just witnessed the execution of their commander.

Gideon stared at Liorah in shock. Fear gripped him, but so too did an unsettling sense of relief. She stood still, the dagger clenched in her hand. Her gaze was as icy as ever, but there was also a flicker of something else, something Gideon couldn't quite place.

Regret? Or was that the same relief he suddenly felt?

Liorah dropped the bloodied dagger on the stone floor. Crimson droplets splattered her gown, the fabric slowly staining a chilling red. She wiped her hand, now slick with blood, across her dress with a sense of casual nonchalance, as if she had merely spilled a glass of wine. She turned to face Gideon, her eyes changing to something tender, almost gentle. It seemed completely at odds with the chilling scene that had just unfolded.

She really had killed her father and brother. Of that, there was no longer any doubt in Gideon's mind.

"Gideon," she said softly. It was as though a completely different person had taken Liorah's place, the ruthless leader replaced by a tender lover. "It was self-defense."

Gideon swallowed as he looked from her face to the blood on her dress and back to her eyes. "Self-defense?" he echoed. He couldn't help the disbelief in his voice.

"Josiah was going to kill me, Gideon. Kill our child. You saw it." She stepped towards him and caressed his face with her bloody hand.

"But—" Gideon's mind raced.

"I won't turn on you, Gideon." Her words cut him off, her tone insistent. Her fingers traced the contours of his face, a tender touch that was eerily at odds with what had just happened. "You don't need to fear me. You're safe with me."

The way she said it—with such conviction and certainty—it was almost as if she truly believed it, as if the blood on her hands, the life she had just taken, were mere details in a grander scheme.

That was what frightened Gideon the most.

A shiver ran down his spine as he stared into her eyes, sensing more than feeling Josiah's blood now smeared on his cheeks. He shook away his fear and tried to focus on anything else—the flicker of candlelight in the corner of the room, the chill of the air, the chaotic battle raging outside.

"We're not safe here, Liorah," Gideon said, bringing his attention to the problem at hand and trying to push the horror he'd just witnessed to the back of his mind. "I heard Josiah mention tunnels below our feet. We could escape, get out of here before the Zhanshi come."

Liorah chuckled amidst the chaos. "My dear Gideon, we're not the ones who need to escape. They are." She turned to look out the window, to the battlefield outside. The danger didn't bother her at all.

"Josiah's passing." Gideon's voice was desperate, imploring. "It's created a fracture in New Emile's defense. The Zhanshi will exploit that, and soon. They won't stop until they reach us. We need to go. Now."

"And abandon my city?" Liorah's tone was incredulous as she turned back to Gideon. "New Emile is my home. It's where my child will be born into sunshine and where he—or she—will rule as the One Voice."

There was no swaying Liorah, not when it came to her city, her power. Her vision was all-consuming, blinding her to the reality that New Emile was about to be overthrown not only by the Zhanshi, but by the Col'kasid as well.

"Your rule means nothing if we've passed into shadow."

"Then that won't happen." There was a simplicity in her words, a conviction that was as terrifying as it was mesmerizing.

"You can't predict that," Gideon argued. "But we can make choices that increase our chances of survival. The tunnels Josiah mentioned. They could be our way out."

Liorah's gaze softened. "Gideon, my love, we are not the ones hiding. We are not the ones running." She moved closer, and her fingers traced a gentle path along his jawline. He wanted to swat her hand away but couldn't. "Our destiny isn't in some dark tunnel like cowards, hiding away with Piper, with Marius and Alistair. It's here. Trust me."

He wanted to believe in her, to share in her unshakeable faith, but the reality was a much harsher, crueler thing.

As the sounds of battle grew in intensity outside, the walls felt more and more like the hold. They were trapped, and their enemies were closing in.

Suddenly, the door burst open. Two figures, both ragged and grimy, stormed in. Shadows concealed their faces, but their intent was clear.

They were here to kill Liorah.

Gideon knew these two were Marokai from the desperation in their eyes, the tattered clothes on their thin frames, the grime smeared across their faces. These were the people Liorah relegated to the fringes of society, pushed to live in squalor.

Liorah's expression quickly changed from one of tenderness back to maniacal, deadly. "You're a long way from the Hollows, filth."

The larger of the two, a man, drew his weapon.

Gideon's stomach twisted, but as before, he positioned himself between this new threat and Liorah.

The woman, smaller but equally fierce, sneered at Gideon. "Whoever you are, step away from Liorah."

Before Gideon could react, a third figure stepped into the light. Kaius. He was as Gideon remembered him from their journey together from Rephidim, but his face was now gaunt, etched with struggles he could not imagine — plus a triangle brand which now marked his forehead.

"Angela, Jeremiah," he said to the Marokai calmly. The introduction gave names to the faces. "You don't have to do this."

"Ever the traitor," Jeremiah said, taking a step toward Liorah. "Should have left you outside the walls."

"There are more problems than just Liorah." Kaius put his hand on Jeremiah's shoulder. "Killing her won't help anyone."

Gideon stole a glance at Liorah. Her mood had changed once again, and was now calm, almost serene. "Remember Gideon," she whispered in his ear, "power is not given, it is taken."

Gideon kept his focus on Jeremiah and Angela. Liorah's words echoed in his mind, but he wasn't entirely sure what they meant.

Power is not given, it is taken.

Without another thought, Gideon stepped forward, placing himself squarely between the Marokai and Liorah. The look in Jeremiah's eyes was fierce and Angela's was just as ruthless.

"No one else needs to die today," Gideon said, his voice steady despite a tremble in his legs. He felt the blood of Josiah drying on his skin.

Jeremiah laughed, a hollow sound that did nothing to ease the tension in the room. "Your misplaced loyalty, boy," he sneered. "Defending a whore like this is going to be the death of you."

With a roar, Jeremiah lunged forward, his weapon swinging at Gideon. Anticipating the move, Gideon sidestepped, barely avoiding the blade. His own hand was empty, but he had spent enough time with the hunters in Rephidim to know how to defend himself. He swung his fist, connecting with Jeremiah's jaw. The man staggered backward but quickly recovered, his gaze wilder than before.

Angela sprang at Gideon from the side. He spun away, but her claws scraped across his arm, tearing through fabric and skin alike. Pain flared up his arm.

Out of the corner of his eye, Gideon saw Liorah. She stood like an icy statue, her gaze fixed on the unfolding scene with a surprising calm. The blood on her gown stood out, red against white, a brutal reminder of Josiah's fate.

Regaining his footing, Gideon rushed at Angela. He grabbed her wrists and used his momentum to throw her off balance. She tumbled to the ground, cursing. Before Gideon could make another move, Jeremiah was back on him, his face contorted in rage.

Gideon dodged the man's attack, returning with his own blows. They were ragged and desperate, born out of survival rather than technique. He was no trained fighter, but the will to protect the mother of his child—as flawed as she was—fueled his every move.

Jeremiah slashed his weapon through the air in wild arcs as Gideon continued to evade him. Every near miss reminded Gideon of the thin line he was walking between life and death, between sunshine and shadow.

A howl echoed outside, followed by screams of shock and alarm. The Zhanshi were close.

Gideon glanced toward the screams and gave Jeremiah an opening. The man's blade sliced through his side, ripping a hot path across his skin. Gideon bit back a cry, staggered, but didn't fall.

But the sounds outside had distracted the Marokai as well. Summoning his last reserves of strength, Gideon saw his opportunity. He surged forward, tackling Jeremiah. The two of them went down in a tangle of limbs, the man's blade skittering across the floor.

Gideon pinned Jeremiah, his hands around the man's neck. His vision blurred from the pain in his side, but his grip didn't falter. Jeremiah's eyes bulged, his breaths coming out in ragged gasps.

"Stop!" Angela's voice sliced through the chamber, holding a note of desperation. Gideon looked up, his gaze meeting hers. She had a blade pressed against Liorah's throat, her eyes flicking between Gideon and her captive.

Gideon's grip on Jeremiah loosened. His gaze, however, didn't leave Angela. At the moment, he was helpless, and the sinking feeling of that realization felt like a punch to his gut.

"Angela," Kaius' voice was firm, resonating in the tense silence. "That's not the way we'll win this."

She sneered. "And you have a better plan?"

"We need everyone to fight against the Zhanshi. Killing each other only weakens us, does their job for them. And killing her leaves a vacuum."

Angela's eyes darted to Jeremiah, now pinned beneath Gideon, then back to Kaius. A flicker of uncertainty crossed her face, which Kaius seized upon. "Liorah is the One Voice. You don't want to know what will come after her. We can get her to listen to reason, but you can't do that if her blood is on your hands."

Reluctantly, Angela's grip on the knife loosened, the blade inching away from Liorah's throat. The tension in the room eased a fraction, but Gideon didn't dare breathe easily. For now, Liorah was unharmed, and that was a small victory in itself.

As Angela lowered her weapon, Kaius took a step forward. "The Zhanshi have split into two fronts," he said. "They're assaulting the Col'kasid at the southwest gate."

Hearing this news was like a physical blow for Gideon, knocking the wind out of him. His father and his tribe were under attack, and here he was, trapped in a standoff within New Emile's walls. He held Jeremiah beneath him, the two locked in a stalemate. It suddenly seemed insignificant compared to the chaos unfolding outside.

"We need to help them," Gideon said. The words tasted suddenly bitter in his mouth. He didn't know if he meant the Col'kasid or New Emile or everyone else caught up in this war.

Kaius nodded. "I agree. The Col'kasid won't last long against the Zhanshi. We need the Marokai to come to their aid."

Gideon allowed Jeremiah to sit up. The man's eyes were wary, flicking between Gideon and Kaius, while Angela stood rigid, her weapon still clutched in her hand.

"This is a mistake," Jeremiah said, his voice hoarse. "Aligning ourselves with the Col'kasid — with you —"

"But necessary," Kaius cut in.

"The Marokai don't have weapons. Not anything that will help."

"What other choice do we have?" Kaius demanded. "If we don't help, the Col'kasid will be run over and we'll all pass into shadow."

Angela scoffed. "And why should we believe you? You've given us no reason."

Kaius drew in a deep breath. "Do you remember what happened at Manoach?"

"I don't care."

"You will. What happened there is what will happen here. The Zhanshi don't negotiate. They don't show mercy. They simply kill. And if we don't unite, if we don't fight back, we're next."

"And how do you propose getting word to the Col'kasid?" Liorah asked. She stepped away from Angela, but Gideon saw the small dagger in her left hand — the same one she'd used on Josiah and must have somehow picked up again.

Kaius must have seen it, too. He moved silently between the two women.

"Free Isaiah," Gideon said, thinking as fast as he could. He knew Liorah would never let him go. He was too valuable. "He's well enough to run, and the Col'kasid will look for any reason to cut down whoever isn't like them." Gideon pointed to his head. "That means people with no hair."

"I will not release a prisoner who violated my laws," said Liorah.

"You may not have a choice." Gideon studied Liorah's expression. He wondered if she thought of their child, or if her refusal to back down was simply defiance in the face of imminent death.

"Liorah," Gideon continued. "I know you have your laws, your ways. But right now, we need all the help we can get."

"He's a criminal, just like you," Liorah snapped. Her eyes flashed with barely restrained anger. "The only reason I haven't thrown you back in the hold is because I haven't had the chance." She glanced at Angela. "I've been distracted by the filth."

Gideon swallowed hard, pushing away the sting of her dismissive tone. "He's not a threat, Liorah. You have an option—one option. Use it."

"He disrespected our customs and chose his fate. What kind of One Voice would I be if I gave a pass to those who defy me?"

"This isn't about Isaiah, is it?" Gideon said quietly. "This is about you, Liorah. About your pride, your unwillingness to bend even when New Emile—and our child's life—are at stake."

There was a slight pause in the room followed by a collective gasp. The fact that Liorah was pregnant was not known, and Gideon had just let loose a secret the One Voice may have wanted to keep.

Liorah's face hardened, her eyes cold. "I am doing what's best, Gideon. The sentinels are perfectly capable of taking care of this...this infestation. I don't need the help of the filth or the Col'kasid. I can handle things myself."

Frustration bubbled in Gideon. "Can you, Liorah?" He struggled to keep his voice even. "Or is it that you can't stand the idea of accepting help from those you consider beneath you?"

Liorah recoiled. "How dare you—"

"No, Liorah," Gideon cut her off, stepping closer. "How dare you? You're so blinded by your hatred, by your prejudice, that you can't see the bigger picture." He gestured toward the window and the hell that raged outside. "New Emile is under attack, Liorah. Your city is dying. The Marokai, the Col'kasid... You may not like them, you may not trust them, but right now, you *need* them."

Liorah's gaze dropped to the floor, her hands clenched. The room was silent, the only sound the chaos unfolding outside and the relentless wind. Finally, Liorah looked up, her gaze meeting Gideon's.

"Fine," she said, her voice steady. "I'll release Isaiah and accept the aid of the Marokai and the Col'kasid. But only until the Zhanshi are dealt with. After that, nothing changes."

"That's all I'm asking."

"Kaius!" Liorah's voice rose. "You know the way to the hold. Get Isaiah and bring him back here, but don't think for a minute that means I've forgiven you."

ISAIAH WAS a pitiful sight. His clothes hung off his skeletal frame, his skin a sickly shade of pale. While Gideon had suffered some of the same, Isaiah was far worse off. Sores covered his body, no doubt where the little hair mites, the mitters, had taken root.

Gideon glanced at Jeremiah briefly, wondering if he intended to start the conversation or talk at all. When Jeremiah said nothing, Gideon cleared his throat. "The Col'kasid are outside the southwestern gate."

Isaiah's bloodshot eyes widened. "The Col'kasid are here?" he asked, unable to hide the joy in his voice, the hope of eventual freedom.

Gideon nodded. "Yes, but they're under attack by the Zhanshi. And New Emile is on the brink, too. The Zhanshi have breached the eastern wall with some sort of weapon and are now pushing toward the Chambers."

"What about the Marokai?" Isaiah looked between Gideon and Jeremiah. "Where are they?"

"Currently away from the Hollows," Jeremiah said.

Gideon continued. "We need to work together. All of our survival depends on us standing as one—Col'kasid, Marokai, and New Emilians. No one force can stand on their own."

As Gideon explained the task at hand, Isaiah listened attentively, his gaze steady. "Elder Levi," Isaiah echoed. "And Elena and Diego, the Marokai who are among the Col'kasid. I need to convince them to rally their people and aid us."

Isaiah's eyes lit up. "Wait. How am I supposed to get to the Col'kasid, to Elder Levi? I'll be killed on sight."

This was a problem, and Isaiah was right. The sentinels who were at the southwestern gate would attack him immediately. There had to be another way.

Gideon turned to Jeremiah. "How did you get in here?"

Jeremiah looked at Angela, then at Liorah. "There are tunnels under the city. Ways to get in and get out unseen."

Liorah's reaction was immediate; her eyes narrowed in response. "I knew it. The filth can't be satisfied with what I give them, so they come to steal."

"What you *give* us?" Angela countered. "You hoard resources. You left us out there on our own and expect that we will make do with whatever we can find."

"As it should be. The lottery is fair, and there is no place for Marokai in New Emile."

"Liorah," Gideon interrupted. Frustration gnawed at him between the animosity on display and the desperate need to get a message to his father. "Can we shut down the harmonic transducer? You've used it to disable the quvianaq, but we need the Col'kasid at their full strength if we stand a chance against the Zhanshi. We need them back on their mounts."

Liorah waved her hand, a look of resignation on her face. "Fine. But don't forget—once the Zhanshi threat is over, we return to our former stances. The Marokai and the Col'kasid will no longer be allies, but threats."

As Liorah's words echoed away, Angela made a move. She was a blur of motion, a streak of passionate fury lunging forward. In her grip, the dagger glinted in the light.

Perhaps instinctually, Kaius moved to intercept and threw himself into the path of the oncoming danger. The blade found a mark, sinking into Kaius' side, carving a crimson path through his cloth and flesh. A pained grunt slipped through his gritted teeth. His face twisted in a grimace, but he remained still, a force to be reckoned with, eyes never leaving Angela.

Gideon jumped. He lunged at Angela and clamped his hand around her wrist as tightly as he could. The struggle was quick, and the dagger clattered to the floor. As if seeing his own opening, Jeremiah charged towards Liorah.

Despite his frail, near skeletal frame, Isaiah mustered enough strength to throw himself into Jeremiah's path. Isaiah stood firm, his body alive with renewed strength, while Jeremiah fell to the side.

Liorah looked between an injured Kaius and the still angry figures of Jeremiah and Angela. Her eyes betrayed her fear, but her face remained calm and collected, as if nothing had happened.

Kaius, blood seeping through his fingers where he clutched his wound, struggled to his feet and positioned himself uneasily in the center. He was in pain but remained upright, a physical barrier to further escalation.

Gideon broke the tense silence. "Isaiah," he said, his voice urgent. His eyes never left Jeremiah and Angela. "Go. Get some haelen then exit the city through the tunnel. Find Elder Levi then bring Elena and Diego to our cause. We're relying on you. Be quick about it."

"How will I find Elena and Diego?"

"Just look for the bald heads in a sea of hair."

CHAPTER THIRTY-SEVEN

As Isaiah stepped out of the tunnel on what Jeremiah said was the northern wall of the city, he took in a deep breath filled with smoke and the scent of death. For so many cycles, he'd been a prisoner in a dank hold under New Emile. Now, in what seemed like the most unlikely scenario, he was free.

He turned toward the southwestern gate, the same way he'd come into New Emile so long ago. By his estimate, he needed only to follow the wall of the city to reach his target. His legs, unused to movement after so long, burned with exertion. Nevertheless, he'd been given a message to deliver to Elder Levi. Following that, he was to find Elena and Diego, two Marokai he'd only briefly met during the rescue of Abel and Jacob. He hoped he could pick them out of the crowd.

Just look for the bald heads.

As Isaiah approached the southwestern gate, the sounds of battle intensified and fear gnawed at his insides. The clash of metal against metal, the cries of pain and defiance, and the acrid smell of burning flesh filled the air. The Col'kasid had been putting up a fierce fight, but he saw the Zhanshi were overpowering, if not in numbers, then in ferocity. Bodies lay in the moor, covered in blood, some Col'kasid and some Zhanshi. He recognized the faces of some of the fallen—

hunters he'd been with, friends he'd known in Rephidim. He wanted to mourn, to fall on his knees and curse God for all that had happened in the past year. It was a scene of utter devastation, but if there was to be any hope at all, the Col'kasid would need all the help they could get.

Isaiah gathered both his strength and the battle axe of a fallen comrade, steadied his nerves, and charged headlong into the fray of the unfolding events. Swords clashed and men screamed, but there ahead was the first part of his mission. Elder Levi, Gideon's father, was engaged in a fight with a Zhanshi warrior who had to be only fifteen or sixteen years old. With a quick thrust, Levi drove his sword into the boy and pushed his body into the muddy ground.

"Elder Levi!" Isaiah shouted. The man turned to face Isaiah and his eyes opened wide.

"Isaiah?" Levi rushed toward the man. "Gideon? Where is he? Is he alive?"

Isaiah nodded. All the exertion since leaving the hold had left him breathless. "Yes...but we need to talk. He's...he's with Liorah, but there are problems."

Levi appeared to struggle with his words. "Liorah? I...I had lost all hope of ever seeing him again," he said with a quivering voice. "This is a gift beyond measure, but I won't believe it until I see him with my own eyes."

"Yes, but...the problems."

"What is it?" A flurry of activity to Levi's left grabbed their attention. Quickly, Levi pulled on Isaiah's arm and led him back away from the fight. When they were relatively safe from the danger, he wiped blood off his face with a rag. "What is it?"

Isaiah spoke rapidly. "The Zhanshi have broken through the eastern wall and are engaged with the New Emilian sentinels. Gideon has requested your help in pushing them back."

"But we're barely holding on here."

"That's why I need to find..." Isaiah struggled to remember the names of the two Marokai. "...to find..."

"Elena and Diego? The Marokai?"

Isaiah's eyes lit up. "Yes, that's it. If they can rally support from their people, you might have a better chance here."

"Not without the quvianaq." Levi looked around. "Fighting on the ground is proving harder than I imagined."

"Liorah has ordered that the harmon... the sound machine be shut off so you get back on your mounts. With the help of the Marokai, you should be able to push the Zhanshi back here and then again inside the city."

"Why would I want to help them?" Levi gestured toward New Emile. "This Liorah kidnapped you and my son and earlier had her men pour hot oil on us."

"There's no other option. The Zhanshi are determined to kill everyone, regardless of tribe. It doesn't matter to them."

"I don't understand."

"Manoach."

Levi's eyes grew wide at the mention of Manoach. "That was a long time ago. These are the same men? The same people?"

"If not the same, then their descendants. They have only one purpose in mind and the only way to protect the Col'kasid is to help New Emile push the Zhanshi back to wherever they came from."

Levi looked around then pointed toward the other side of the fight. "Go, Isaiah. You'll find Elena and Diego near the quarry. If they really can rally the Marokai, we might have a chance."

ISAIAH PUSHED through the battleground, narrowly avoiding the deadly swings of blades wielded by both Zhanshi and

Col'kasid. Every step was a dance between life and death as he maneuvered through the chaos toward Elena and Diego. The overwhelming sounds of clashing metal, the shrill cries of pain, and the pungent smell of blood and burning assaulted him from all directions. A fleeting thought entered his mind—being in the hold felt safer than freedom.

At first he was dismayed by the amount of bald heads he saw, all Zhanshi. He didn't know how he was going to find two Marokai out of many. Relief washed over him as he spotted a bald woman dressed differently from the others—Elena, he presumed. Next to her was a bald man setting a bolt in a crossbow, perhaps Diego. And behind them both was Luca, wiping blood off the tip of a lance. Where was Abel? Isaiah called out their names, but the noise of the battle drowned his voice. He had to get closer.

Ducking and weaving, Isaiah dodged a group of fighters locked in combat. Finally, he reached Diego and grabbed his arm to get his attention.

Seeing Isaiah, Diego's eyes widened with surprise as he turned to face him. Despite the chaos surrounding them, Diego's concern for the emaciated man standing before him was obvious. How could he have recognized Isaiah after only seeing him briefly in the dark hold?

Hair. And a stink that was probably worse than anything on the moor.

"You're...free?" Diego asked. "What about Gideon?"

"He's with Liorah right now. We need your help."

Elena stepped up. "I hope you're not suggesting we help Liorah."

"Not just Liorah," Isaiah said. "All of New Emile, the Marokai, and the Col'kasid."

"And just how are we going to do that?" Elena waved her hand over the battlefield. "You see what's going on."

Isaiah took a deep breath and recited the message he gave to Elder Levi. "The Zhanshi have broken through the eastern wall and are engaged with the New Emilian sentinels. If they aren't stopped, everyone dies. Jeremiah—"

Elena held her hand up. "Wait. What about Jeremiah? You saw him?"

"Him and Angela. At least, I think that was her name. They were the ones who told me to come find you."

"Whatever for? We can't very well march into the Chambers right now and rescue them."

"No, but Jeremiah said you could sway the Marokai. Get them to help the Col'kasid push the Zhanshi back. From there, all of you could then move into the city to help the sentinels."

Diego shook his head. "Not possible. What are they going to fight with? Sticks and hoes? The Marokai are not fighters."

"I'm just relaying the message."

Elena looked at Diego, and it seemed as if messages were being passed between them. Finally, she turned back to Isaiah. "I'll go. I know where they are."

"Can you turn off that thing?" Isaiah asked. "Whatever is paralyzing the quvianaq?"

Diego looked toward the quarry opening. "Abel went down there to do just that. Jacob had to fight off a few New Emilian watchers who were stuck here when the fight started."

As they stood amid the chaos, the sounds of clashing weapons and screams of combatants echoed in the background.

"Come with me," Elena said, pulling on Isaiah's arm. "We might be able to get a few of them to help."

Isaiah followed Elena's lead as she glided effortlessly

through the chaos. They weaved between fighters engaged in intense combat, narrowly avoiding swords and axes. Isaiah's eyes darted around, searching for any sign of danger nearby. The last thing he needed was to face a Zhanshi warrior with an axe he could barely wield. He did feel much better after getting a vial of haelen before leaving the Chambers, but it wasn't instantaneous.

In the melee, a crossbow bolt flew, finding its mark in Isaiah's leg. With a sharp cry of pain, he collapsed onto the ground in agony. Without a word, Elena pulled him across the moor and out of harm's way. With the last reserves of his strength, he urged Elena to continue. "Get them," he said through gritted teeth. "Bring whoever you can."

Elena wrapped a cloth torn from her garment around the wound and the protruding bolt, then ran off. Isaiah's vision blurred as he fought to stay conscious. The pain in his leg was agonizing, but he pushed the bolt through his flesh. Thankfully, bone did not get in the way, but there was no questioning the amount of effort it took him to push it out. With a final scream, he turned and crawled toward relative safety—a slight rise of the hill where he could better dress his wound.

He hadn't been freed from the hold to pass into shadow on a battlefield. No, this was not going to be his road to Eldorado.

CLIMBING OUT of the quarry with Jacob, Abel looked around and felt the weight of the night settle on the moor as the snow storm abated. Fires from New Emile cast an eerie red glow over everything, lending an ominous air to the scene. The Col'kasid were in the middle of a fight to the death against the Zhanshi, but at the very least, they'd successfully disabled the harmonic transducer. It was a minor victory, but Abel would take anything.

As the last long drawn out note of the harmonic transducer ceased, a moment of anticipation hung in the air, and it felt as if the noise of battle had become muted. The sound had been directional, away from the city and toward the hill where the Col'kasid had first arrived. Had they known, they might have attacked from a different direction. As it was, the Col'kasid, unsure of what had just happened, looked around.

Ahead of him, about fifty feet away, Elder Levi must have noticed it as well. He turned to Saadya and called out urgently, "Saadya! Fall back and get the animals from over the hill! We can remount the quvianaq and turn the tide of this battle!"

Saadya nodded in acknowledgment and swiftly made his way to execute the order. A few of the Col'kasid hunters formed a protective line between the battle and the hill, allowing Saadya and several other men to make their way to where the quvianaq had fallen.

Abel watched with anxiety itching at his heels. It seemed to take forever, time they didn't have—but there they were, several hunters cresting the hill on the backs of their quvianaq. The animals looked unsteady at first, but with each step, they gained confidence. The ground shook as the animals passed through the moor, the claws on their six arms extended to levy the most damage. Hunters wielding axes from on high slashed through stunned Zhanshi warriors while the quvianaq clucked and cooed in their own language. For all the claims the Col'kasid had against killing another person, it seemed as if in the throes of battle, morality was pushed aside.

Surprised by the resurgence of the Col'kasid, the remaining Zhanshi faltered for a moment, their formation breaking under the overwhelming assault. To Abel, it was clear they had never seen hairy men on the back of monstrous beasts. Their attention was diverted for just long enough.

And there, across the battlefield, a mass of Marokai surged forward with makeshift weapons of roots and stones. Some grabbed axes and lances that lay scattered around the fallen warriors.

Immediately, Abel and Jacob ran toward the hill to retrieve their own quvianaq. With Diego and Luca close behind, they mounted their animals and charged back into the fight, their movements suddenly fluid. With cries of anger, they were on top of several retreating Zhanshi warriors. Abel lowered his lance and aimed at the enemy. His quvianaq charged headlong, seeming to know the target. With a scream borne of frustration, Abel's lance was driven into and through the man, slipping out of his grip and skewering him on the moor. He'd lost a weapon but there were more everywhere he looked.

Luca's war cry echoed beside him as he dispatched two Zhanshi foes with a neat precision. Abel was not so accurate, but that didn't deter him. Jacob swung an axe, cutting through a line of Zhanshi warriors.

As they fought side by side, Abel sensed a unity between the Col'kasid and the Marokai, their once-separate identities melding into a single force equally despised by Liorah. Yet that seemed to be no longer an issue; they were warriors fighting for a common purpose—the survival of not only New Emile, but anyone who was not Zhanshi. Together, they pushed the enemy back, gaining ground with each passing moment. The Zhanshi, now disoriented and overwhelmed, struggled to mount a cohesive defense against the unyielding onslaught of the united forces.

As they advanced, Abel felt the tide of the battle shifting in their favor. The eerie red light of the fires in New Emile bathed the moor in a haunting glow, and the night was filled with the clash of weapons, the sounds of the quvianaq, and the cries of battle. It was a symphony of chaos, but amidst the noise and fury, Abel felt a sense of purpose and solidarity with the Marokai and with those who had cast him out.

As the battle continued, the Col'kasid and the Marokai gained more ground, driving the Zhanshi further away from New Emile. Every step they took brought a hope that this would end soon enough.

Amidst the chaos, Abel glimpsed Isaiah being carried to safety. He hadn't known the man had escaped the hold, but there he was. Where was Gideon in all of this? Had he made it out, and if so, was he fighting alongside his father?

As the night wore on, the battle raged, and the Zhanshi's numbers dwindled. The quvianaq, now fully unleashed from the control of the quarry's harmonic transducer, dominated the battlefield. The Zhanshi retreated into the darkness, the battle-scarred moor the only thing remaining.

Abel, breathless and weary, looked around at the Col'kasid and Marokai beside him. Their eyes, beaming with the light of victory and unity, were the only bright spots on bodies covered in dirt and blood. Fallen hunters, some of whom Abel knew, lay among the bodies of those Zhanshi who had fallen.

"That's it?" Abel didn't believe it.

"Only the beginning," Diego said as his quvianaq came alongside Abel. "We're supposed to help inside the city now."

"What?" Abel looked toward the southwest gate. Two sentinels were opening it. "Aren't we here to rescue Gideon?"

"Yes, but it was Gideon who apparently told Isaiah to deliver the message. Between the Marokai, the Col'kasid and the New Emilians, we might have a chance of sending the Zhanshi into the shadows."

CHAPTER THIRTY-EIGHT

WITH SAADYA AT THE FOREFRONT RIDING ATOP HIS quvianaq, the combined forces of the Col'kasid and Marokai were ready for a fight. They charged toward the collapsed eastern wall, opting to flank the Zhanshi from the south, while inside the city, the New Emilian sentinels were still engaged in a fight of their own, attempting to drive the enemy back with every ounce of strength they had left. The surrounding buildings and what remained of the wall reverberated with the clash of metal against metal, but the relentless attacks were taking their toll on everything. It seemed as if the Zhanshi had run out of their flaming bolts, not that the rest of them weren't as deadly.

On the outside, the Col'kasid and the Marokai fought in unison. Bolts flew from crossbows, lances speared the air, axes swung from on high. The Marokai—empowered by a new focus that had the potential to improve their lives immensely—fought with whatever they could find, from the weapons of the fallen to farming tools swiped from the fields to the jawbones of animals slaughtered as food for the Elite.

Although they had only been together for a short period, the Col'kasid and Marokai alliance had already become a force. Abel hoped it was enough to show the Zhanshi that their grip on New Emile was slipping away. Yet the Zhanshi refused to yield, and with a surge of brute force, launched a relentless counterattack.

—

Saadya scanned the battlefield, assessing the situation and strategizing the best approach. The sentinels inside the eastern wall were fighting with everything they had, but the sheer number of Zhanshi threatened to overwhelm them.

"We can't hold them back much longer." A Col'kasid hunter atop his own mount guided his quvianaq next to Saadya.

Saadya's jaw tightened. Time was running out, not to mention a decrease in the number of men he had available to him. They needed another way to bolster their defense, reinforce the sentinels inside the walls, and turn the battle in their favor.

"Fall back!" Saadya called out. "We need to create a diversion, draw their attention away from the walls."

Without hesitation, the Col'kasid hunters retreated, moving swiftly and silently to the flanks of the battlefield. The Marokai, still engaged in their own battle on foot, followed. Crossbows remained nocked with arrows, ready to strike.

As the hunters regrouped at the edge of the moor, Saadya signaled for a barrage of arrows to be unleashed upon the Zhanshi's rear ranks. The sudden downpour of death from above diverted the invaders' attention, forcing them to pivot and confront the new threat.

INSIDE THE eastern wall, the sentinels seized the opportunity to push the Zhanshi back even more. Severely depleted in numbers, the distraction had given the New Emilians the space they needed. Zhanshi warriors slowly inched toward the wall where they'd broken through, the streets now covered in blood. So engaged were the sentinels in the fight to save themselves, their families, and their city, no one seemed to notice their leader, Josiah, was no longer with them.

Between the Col'kasid and Marokai in the rear and New Emilian sentinels in the front, the united force had gained the upper hand. The resurgence had thrown the Zhanshi warriors into chaos as men and boys broke their ranks, defying everything they had been taught.

AS THE first rays of sunrise painted the battlefield in hues of gold and crimson, Abel and Elena fought side by side. Nearby, Jacob was engaged in a battle of his own, fighting off a man covered with blood and nearly twice his size. The clash of steel and the cries of war filled the air. Abel glanced over.

The Zhanshi warrior, eyes filled with malice, delivered a swift, merciless blow to Jacob with an axe. Abel's friend and Elena's partner fell to the ground, his life slipping away like the fading stars in the morning sky.

"Elena, no!" Abel shouted as he saw her rush to Jacob's side. He blocked an incoming attack from Jacob's assailant, then thrust a lance into the man's side.

Elena knelt beside Jacob. Her hands trembled as she tried to staunch the flow of blood from his wounds. Her eyes widened with surprise, then shock, as the reality of the situation set in. In the morning light amidst all the chaos, Abel saw a single tear trace a path down her dirt-streaked cheek.

Abel struggled to keep his footing. Jacob had been his friend and one of the few Col'kasid who accepted him for who he was. With a renewed fury, he struck out at anyone nearby, his stomach burning with anger at the man who had caused this pain. He wanted to pick up the man's axe and pulverize his body into the moor.

Abel saw Elena's shock slowly turn to anger. The sight of

her love now lifeless surely fueled a fire within her, just as one would burn inside Abel if that had been Luca. With rage, Elena rose and channeled her pain into every strike, every swing of her sword. With a primal cry, she lunged at the nearest Zhanshi warrior, her blade finding its mark with deadly accuracy. The man's stomach opened up as the life in his eyes disappeared. While Abel nearby ensured no one else came close to Jacob's body, she attacked again and again. Each swing of the sword was a year she would not have with Jacob.

Amid the chaos, time slowed for Abel. He saw the fear in the eyes of their enemies, and he knew they had the advantage. The Zhanshi warriors were faltering as anger overtook their thirst for blood.

Abel caught Elena's eye. Her grief was clear, but he saw something else — a hatred that sent a chill down his spine. She was a leader, a force of one avenging Jacob but also defending her homeland. She nodded at Abel, then turned to dispatch yet another invader.

And then another and another.

THE TISHBIAN sun climbed higher in the sky and bathed the battlefield in an unforgiving light. Abel was tired. How much longer could the Zhanshi hold out until they retreated? How much more of this did they have to endure? It was as if no matter what happened, the Zhanshi would not relent.

He turned and saw Luca fighting nearby. Their eyes met, and for a moment, a flicker of hope surged through Abel. When this was over, they could be together in a world that did not care who they were. There was a moment of clarity, of a future that grew brighter with each passing minute. It was something Abel had not felt in a long time, something he lost the day the Col'kasid exiled him from Rephidim.

But that hope was short-lived as an arrow soared through the air, finding its mark on Luca's chest.

"No!" Abel cried out in horror. Luca stumbled and fell as Abel's heart shattered. In a second, the world had changed once more, God himself seeing that whatever future Abel thought he could have was no longer possible. The battlefield became a blur as anger, grief, and desperation surged through him like a tidal wave.

Elena rushed to join Abel. Her eyes widened in shock at seeing Luca lying motionless on the ground.

"No...not Luca," she whispered. Her voice trembled with sorrow. "Not my brother."

SAADYA CAUGHT sight of Abel. A dark hatred flickered in his eyes as he locked onto the young man, the exile, the abomination. Abel represented everything Saadya believed was wrong with their people — a stain on their traditions and purity, a birth defect who should have passed into shadow long ago.

As the battle raged on, Saadya found himself drawn to Abel. He wanted to crush this supposed abomination and rid their tribe of the disgrace. Every fiber of his being urged him to strike the young man down and wipe away the memory of his existence. It was the perfect moment, easily excused by the surrounding chaos.

Who would know?

For the moment, Saadya was preoccupied, forced to focus on the onslaught of the Zhanshi warriors. The fight for New Emile's survival demanded his attention and his prowess as a hunter. His desire for revenge would have to wait.

Saadya's quvianaq reared back and extended one of its arms, slashing across the face of an approaching threat. With a swift downward strike, Saadya planted his axe in the enemy's head and kicked his body over in the bloody moor. Rage drove his actions, not so much for the collective goal but for the one that had burned inside for so long. The dead warrior was Abel. They were all Abel...and Abel was going to die.

Elder Levi guided his quvianaq beside Saadya. "Stay focused," he said sternly. "Our only priority right now is what's in front of us."

Saadya gritted his teeth, torn between his duty to the tribe and his overwhelming hatred for Abel. He wanted so much to defy Levi's orders, to hunt down the exile and bring him to justice. He pivoted on his mount and looked back toward where Abel and that Marokai woman were engaged in a battle of their own.

It sickened Saadya. There was Abel, unaware of just how much hatred there was for the boy, for his actions. He fought well, perhaps as someone might who had once been an outcast fighting for the right to be seen as an equal, to prove his worth. But that in no way changed how Saadya saw him.

Yet, as he allowed his anger to consume him, Saadya's vigilance waned. He became blinded to the battle's ebb and flow, unaware of the incoming danger.

A sudden bolt struck Saadya in the head, an arrow sent from within the enemy's ranks. Shadows overtook him, and the world went dark. A calmness washed over him, and the all-consuming rage that had been inside for so long was finally silenced.

He slipped off his mount and crumpled to the bloody ground, his once-burning hatred now extinguished.

CHEN STOOD in the center of the battlefield, his eyes fixed on the unified front born from some alliance between various tribes. Anger and frustration coursed through his veins. This was not the outcome he had envisioned for the fall of the gulao.

"Send a projectile into the middle of them!" Chen's voice thundered. "Break their ranks!"

"Zhuren," Martin said, his face covered in blood. "We cannot do that. Our own men are intermingled with theirs. We will cause heavy casualties among our own forces."

Chen clenched his fists. "I do not care. Victory demands sacrifice, and our soldiers are expendable if it leads us to triumph over these gulao."

Lin Xi stepped forward, his expression one of concern. "Zhuren, we understand your desire for victory, but we must consider the consequences. Our men are already stretched thin, and we risk losing even more if we act recklessly."

Chen's resolve would not yield. No, he had waited his entire life for the chance to avenge Mathias the First and to finish what his grandfather Mathias the Third set out to do. "There is no room for hesitation. The gulao's unity threatens to overthrow us. Tell Lucien to launch a projectile. Break. Their. Ranks."

To Lucien, it felt as if he were preparing his own grave.

After double-checking that his calculations were correct, he gave the order to send their weapon into the fray, hoping to disrupt the enemy and sow chaos among their forces. But fate had other plans. With an otherworldly rumble, the projectile misfired and exploded without ever leaving the sled.

Lucien and Martin, along with many others surrounding the launch point were caught in the blast, their lives lost in an instant.

CHEN'S HEART pounded with shock and horror at the unintended consequence of his orders. The anger and frustration that had driven him were now replaced by a deep sense of remorse and guilt. He had not only sacrificed his own men, but had also lost two of his trusted advisors who had tried to reason with him.

Once the smoke and dust had settled, the only things left were burned corpses and a crater. Bodies lay strewn across the ground, some motionless, while others moaned in agony. The landscape was a macabre tapestry of pain and suffering.

Chen fell to his knees, his spirit broken.

As the shock wore off, remorse took its place. Chen berated himself for allowing such a catastrophic mistake to occur. The weapon that gave the Zhanshi an advantage had become their own downfall.

Amid the chaos, the gulao seized the opportunity. They charged forward, emboldened by the turn of events. The Zhanshi struggled to regroup as attack after attack of men on the backs of magnificent animals sent shockwaves through Chen's forces.

Chen clenched his fists, torn between grief and a burning desire to turn the tide once more. This was no longer about vengeance, though. It was about survival. Yaolan had been virtually emptied of defenders. What would become of them now?

"What have I done?" Chen muttered, his voice barely audible.

Chen's mind raced, trying to salvage what remained of his crumbling strategy. Without his trusted advisors, he felt a weight of responsibility that threatened to overwhelm him. The loss of Lucien and Martin had left him vulnerable, along with the spirits of Zhuren past, those who now chastised him from beyond.

"Retreat!" Chen's voice rang out, commanding the Zhanshi to fall back. "We will return!"

The remaining Zhanshi soldiers, disheartened by their losses and the apparent turning of the tides, reluctantly obeyed their leader's order. They withdrew from the battleground, stepping back from the relentless assault of the gulao.

ABEL WATCHED as the Zhanshi disappeared into the darkness, emotions swirling within him. Victory was theirs, but it had come at a great price.

Luca and Jacob were both gone.

The moor, once a fierce battleground, now fell into an eerie stillness. The fires from New Emile still burned, but the chaos of war had given way to somber reflection.

Elena and Diego approached Abel, their faces grim and tired. Their shoulders sagged under the weight of the day's events and their own losses. The survivors of the battle tended to the wounded and mourned their fallen comrades.

The eastern wall, once the frontline of a fierce conflict, now stood as a solemn testament to the sacrifices made in the name of New Emile's survival. For now, the threat of the Zhanshi had receded, but everyone knew that this was only the beginning.

The Zhanshi would be back, and the world would never be the same.

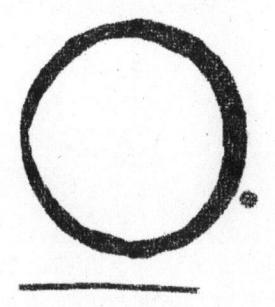

PART VI: THE REVELATIONS

Cycle 1, Day 3, Year 97

"I am no bird; and no net ensnares me; I am a free human being with an independent will, which I now exert to leave you."

— Charlotte Brontë, *Jane Eyre* (1847)

CHAPTER THIRTY-NINE

IT WAS SUPPOSED TO BE A CELEBRATORY MEAL, BUT AN UNEASY undercurrent cut through the dinner. Liorah, seated at the head of the table with only Alistair at her side, listened intently as Gideon and Isaiah recounted the wonders they had discovered in the city. They spoke some of the healing water, haelen, and its potential to save lives, but mostly about the ancient texts found in New Emile's library, written in the same mysterious language as those at Manoach.

Micah, finally allowed entry into the city after the dangers had passed, sat next to his grandson Levi. The pair exchanged intrigued glances. For him, the prospect of deciphering the ancient texts was captivating, something he hadn't done in a long time. His eyes sparkled with excitement, as if he knew that whatever was contained in those texts could bring their colony one step closer to unlocking the truths of the planet their ancestors had settled.

Something amazing was in there.

On the other side of the table, the Marokai listened with skepticism. Jeremiah, Angela, Elena, and Diego sat in silence, amazed Gideon and Isaiah would even agree to this dinner. Liorah had locked them in the hold and now it seemed as if the past was already forgotten. For the Marokai, only ending the damned lottery and opening the gates of New Emile mattered.

That, and access to the ample supply of haelen. The Elite did not deserve to hoard such a miracle. That they were even invited to the table was a wonder and one mostly likely arranged by Gideon. Liorah would have never agreed to it on her own. Elena, still grieving the loss of Jacob and Luca, found her mind wandering to the healing properties of haelen. Could it have saved them if they'd had access to it on the battlefield? While her thoughts consumed her, she tried to lessen the pain by focusing on the moment, on the discussion happening around the table.

Liorah waved her arms, cutting off Gideon's recital of what New Emile offered. Her displeasure was obvious to all. "And what would I gain from sharing these resources with you?" She looked unenthusiastically at Gideon, Levi, and Micah. "If Alistair here could not translate a single page of those books in all his years, what makes you think you have any chance at all?"

Alistair shifted uneasily in his seat. A servant, dressed in brown rags, approached and removed the empty plate from in front of the man.

Sojen Micah spoke, his eyes darting around the room. "Fifty-five years ago, back when my cousin Miriam and I both lived in the temple at Manoach, we worked together to decipher what we could from the books that were left behind there. And we made progress. We learned many things about who built the temple, these buildings here in New Emile, and even learned a little about how the Well was created."

"The Well?" Liorah leaned forward. "There were no mentions in the Great Mother's writings that speak of anything like that."

Micah cleared his throat. "History tells us that our ancestors traveled to Tishbe through a device created by a race called the sa'ja'veil. When they arrived, the device was disabled, but texts found at Manoach indicated there was a way to fix it, to return everyone back to Earth."

Liorah snorted. "Why would we ever want to go to a planet that we have heard is filled with the same hate we just witnessed outside?"

"Another cousin, Joel," Micah said slowly and then visibly swallowed. "He had taken people with him into the Barrier Mountains to find the material needed to repair the Well."

"What happened to him?" asked Liorah.

"The strangers who visited us long ago told a horrific tale of their murder just before..." Micah trailed off, a deep sadness clear in his eyes.

"The Zhanshi?" Gideon asked. "The same people who caused the genocide at Manoach?"

A silence settled over the table as the question lingered in the air. Micah shifted a little in his seat and appeared uneasy with the conversation. Finally, after a moment, he nodded and spoke, but quickly changed the subject. "The texts you have, Liorah. They are readable, but it would take a concerted effort and Father Elijah's Bible."

"The Bible will not leave Rephidim," Levi said with conviction. "You know this as well as I, and I see no need for you to attempt something that will aid us in no way. Liorah is right—this is a foolish conversation, and I think it is time the Col'kasid return. Our women are lost without us."

"But what do you think the ancient texts contain?" Alistair asked. "If it is even possible to interpret them."

Micah perked up. "There were many wonders found in the temple at Manoach. Tales that told of journeys, descriptions and uses of plant life, which animals to avoid. The map that led Miriam here—that was found tucked away in one of the texts by her husband, Tobias. Imagine what else—"

"That name will not be spoken here," Liorah said quickly, cutting Micah off. "That was the first thing the Great Mother decreed, and we have honored it ever since."

Micah looked confused but didn't press the issue. "I suspect that there are many other things to be found in your library. Your harmonic transducer, for example. Do you know how it operates? What makes it run without electric power?"

Alistair shook his head. "That has been a mystery from the day it was first discovered. The few engineers who had traveled with the Great Mother learned what it did but could never figure out how it worked."

"What if those texts tell you something? Wouldn't that be worth the time it took to translate?"

"I don't really care," Liorah said. "Do whatever you feel you need to do, but nothing leaves New Emile. Alistair will help you, if you must dig into them."

Levi shook his head. "You're not staying here, Grandfather. You are coming back to Rephidim with me."

"And who are you to tell me what I should do?" Micah rapped his knuckles on the table. "You may be the Keeper of the Texts, but you are not the keeper of me." Micah's voice rose. "You will learn your place, Levi."

"But Sojen Micah," Levi said, his voice lower. "It is not safe for you here."

"And why is that?" Micah pointed to Liorah. "She offered. I have no utility in Rephidim. Patience has passed into shadow and there's nothing more for me to do. You go."

"But..."

"That's final. You go, and when I've discovered the secrets of the universe, I'll send a note."

"Soje—"

Liorah cleared her throat. "What else would you and Alistair need, Sojen Micah?"

Micah turned from Levi, his gaze softening. "A scribe or two. Do you have any?"

Alistair nodded. "I have a few under my employ, but they are young."

"Then they will learn." He glanced back at Levi. "And I will take Abel, too."

Elena watched Levi's jaw tighten and his knuckles turn white as he seethed with clenched fists. "The abomination—"

"He is not an abomination, Father!" Gideon called out. "He was the best scribe the schools of Rephidim produced, and just because you can't stomach the fact that—"

Levi turned and pounded a fist on the table. "You will not speak to me like that, son. The boy was exiled in all fairness after the stones were cast. He does not deserve mercy and certainly shouldn't be working around or near Sojen Micah."

"You are an ass," Micah said.

Levi spun back around, his mouth open wide. Before he could say anything in response, Micah continued.

"You've always been an ass. You read the texts the way you want to read them, with no thought for what they really mean. You look for ways to pervert the Word of God to fit your narrow view of the world and then you force that down upon the Col'kasid as if only you know the meaning. Well, you don't. You never have, but I didn't stop you. I let you lead, and I let you make your own damn mistakes."

Levi rose from the table quickly, knocking his chair over. "I will not be spoken to like this. Not from you." He looked at Gideon. "And certainly not from my son. We are done here."

Just as he turned to go, Liorah called out. "Wait, Elder Levi."

"What?"

Liorah's voice remained steady. "Before you go, I really need to know what you can offer me?"

"Offer you?" Levi's eyes narrowed. "For what? Kidnapping my son and locking our ambassadors away for your pleasure? Harboring an abomination and rejecting our religious rights?"

"First of all, we have not discussed your religious rights, nor do I care." Liorah's voice was firm. "Secondly, your ambassadors, as you call them, violated the edicts of New Emile. For that, they still must be punished. And I am not speaking of the past, I am speaking of the future. Gideon here has told me that your Rephidim possesses a great deal of knowledge about agriculture. Is that true?"

"We have orchards and gardens, yes." Levi sat back in his chair. Elena noted for the first time that he hadn't eaten a bite of food. "But that's knowledge. Certainly nothing we could offer in trade with the distance between our two cities."

"I understand that, but seeds perhaps, and the knowledge of how to grow them. We are running low on grain in the city stores and our farms do not produce enough to supplement the needs of New Emile."

Elena was just about to add "or the Hollows," but Levi cut in.

"We could provide seeds, yes," he said. "But what are you offering in return?"

A coy smile played on Liorah's lips. "What do you need?"

"The Water of Life, for starters."

"Haelen?" Liorah glanced at Alistair before continuing. "I suppose we could...part with a few vials. If that's something that would really be of value to you."

"A few vials?" Jeremiah rose from his chair. "There is enough haelen in that pond to heal every person who lives in New Emile, Rephidim, and the Hollows now and for decades to come."

Liorah kept her composure, but Elena saw her hands close in a tight fist. "Please sit, Marokai. We will discuss your needs in a moment."

Elena put her hand on Jeremiah and gently urged him to sit back down. His temper could be volatile, and if what she'd heard was correct, he'd already tried to kill Liorah once.

"The haelen," Levi said, "would help us with the Red Death. I'm sure my son has told you all about that."

Liorah nodded. "He has." She looked at Gideon for a moment, and Elena didn't miss the spark in her eyes. Had she...fallen for him? "What about a few of your quvianaq? Your mounts? We could raise them here and use them as work animals for our fields."

"As long as you don't torture them with your sound device."

"Of course not. Now that we know, we can ensure their safety. Perhaps we can offer you a few laborers to help you build up more homes in Rephidim? Animals for—"

Elena interrupted, her anger suddenly piqued. "Laborers, Liorah? You mean Marokai."

Liorah shrugged. "Why not? Perhaps the change in scenery will do the fil— the Marokai some good."

"Sounds to me like you see this as an opportunity to clear the Hollows."

Liorah smiled menacingly. "Of course not. I could use a few laborers here, too."

"And if we all left?" Elena seethed. "Who would you marginalize then? Who would work in your quarry or till your fields? Who would serve your damn dinner?"

"Your anger is misplaced. It was fate who decided where you live. What do you want?"

Jeremiah slammed his fist on the table. "We're not asking for charity, and personally, I wouldn't want to live within a mile of your smell."

Elena put her hand on Jeremiah's arm...just in case. She took a deep breath, trying to keep her composure. "We want the chance to live freely, to contribute and be valued members of this society. All we seek is cooperation, not confrontation. End the lottery and turn the sentinels away. They have other things to worry about now, like when the next attack will come."

Liorah seemed unyielding, but Elena saw a flicker of doubt in her eyes at the mention of another attack. "And how am I supposed to trust any of you after what happened earlier? You broke into these Chambers, *my* home." She pointed at Angela. "That woman put a knife to my throat. Your labor is in the quarry and the fields, and your place is in the Hollows."

Gideon cleared his throat and leaned forward. "Liorah. What harm would come in preparing for the next attack? You saw how a combined force of Marokai, Col'kasid, and your sentinels pushed the Zhanshi back. If—no, *when*—they return, they will be stronger and more prepared. Perhaps with even greater weapons we cannot imagine."

Liorah turned on Gideon. "And what would you have me do? Welcome these...these people into my home? They will raid the haelen pond and steal what little grain we have left. Who would protect me then?"

"Why is it always about you?" Angela threw her hands in the air. "There are hundreds of people living within the walls and hundreds more outside. Your reign, if you want to call it that, covers all the moor, not just who you pick."

Liorah rose, her fists clenched tight. "I will not have any of you talk to me in this way. I am Liorah, the One Voice, the holder of the vials of haelen, and granddaughter of the Great Mother Miriam. Your presence here is at my mercy, and now you may leave." She pushed her chair back and straightened her gown. "We are done. Thank you all for your support and defense of the city. When the next attack comes, I am sure you will be as motivated in your defense of New Emile as you were the other day."

With that, she turned and walked out. Levi rolled his eyes, but to Elena, Gideon looked conflicted, as if he should run after Liorah or stay with his father.

"I wouldn't be so sure we'll help the next time," Elena said.

GIDEON STOOD at the end of Liorah's bed where he had stood before when she called to him. She had been crying, something he didn't think he'd ever see. The room was a place he'd only recently been allowed, and it felt more sinister the longer he stayed in it. Her bed was high, a mattress stuffed with fibers and grasses comfortable yet pungent smelling. A table held vials containing a liquid of which Gideon could never guess, and on the walls there were blankets draped on hooks. One of them, he knew, had belonged to Liorah's grandmother, Miriam. Yet despite his awkward feeling, it still felt comfortable, more a home than anywhere else he'd recently been. Certainly, it was better than the hold, and the few times he had lain with her in this room had been more...passionate, if that was the word he could use.

At least for Liorah. Not that he really had a choice.

Gideon was curious. There was a new vulnerability to Liorah. She was young, and the pressures of leadership had to weigh heavily on her. New Emile had suffered great losses—over a hundred citizens killed within the walls alone.

Outside on the moor, the bodies were still being counted and carried toward a single pyre that would eventually light up the Tishbian sky. While Liorah claimed not to have cared how many Col'kasid hunters or Marokai had lost their lives in the city's defense, Gideon felt there was remorse, nevertheless. On her watch and at her command, many people had passed into shadow.

She was evil, though. That was clear. She was also inexperienced, and there were certain traits about her that one might consider selfish. These combined were not a good fit for a leader. She had poisoned her father, Eilian, and her half-brother in order to gain power. She had killed Josiah in what she claimed was self-defense. Yet every so often, despite his revulsion, Gideon saw in her a sadness that belied her cruel exterior. With power comes hard choices, and perhaps she truly regretted her actions.

Gideon looked around. In the corner of the room a crib would eventually sit, holding their child. There would no doubt be nursemaids, but he didn't know how much of a mother she would be. It pained him to think he had to let his father know about the pregnancy soon, as he was sure to demand he return to Rephidim and reclaim his seat in the Assembly.

He no longer wanted that. To be the Keeper of the Text meant being the voice of a tribe who abided by rules that seemed counter to the acceptance that was on display in New Emile. Abel was a good example of that, and his thoughts drifted to the pain the boy must be feeling now at the loss of Luca. Once more, a love had been taken from him. Once more, God had punished him for being who he was—just a man who loved another man, a man who deserved the same rights as everyone else.

It was similar to how the Marokai were treated, was it not? They were outcasts for being nothing more than unlucky in a lottery that should never have been implemented in the first place. So many New Emile wasn't as accepting as he thought.

Liorah stirred. She wiped tears from her cheeks and sat up on the bed. Her mask of anger was gone, replaced by a tenderness that confused Gideon. "Why didn't you tell your father?" she asked. It was not a question directed in anger, but out of honest curiosity.

"When I'm ready."

"You don't think he'll be happy? Didn't you say the Col'kasid revered large families?"

"Yes, but not this way." Gideon wanted to move closer to the bed, but needed the distance. "In my father's eyes, I have sinned in such a way that would guarantee exile from Rephidim."

Liorah twisted her lips. "For what? Creating another human being? Your god gave you this power. I don't understand the pull of this religion."

"As any member of the Assembly would say, God works in mysterious ways."

Liorah sat straighter and shook her head. They'd had this conversation before, and would likely do so many more times in the future. But the Col'kasid's faith was unshakeable. Liorah must have sensed that.

"You want to go back," she said.

"No," Gideon finally relented and sat on the edge of the bed, resigned to this life. He couldn't imagine living here with Liorah, but he couldn't abandon his responsibility, either. "My life is here with our child."

"Then why don't you tell your father now? If he'll be so upset, perhaps he'll leave right away. Does that bother you? Do you think you'll miss him?"

Gideon couldn't answer that question. Would he miss his father? Sure, but not the rules, not the constant reminders of living a life that was free from temptation and sin. "It doesn't matter what I feel. If I am to be a father, I will not be one that remains distant and eventually so wrapped up in the dealings of the Assembly that I cannot take part in his rearing."

Liorah smiled. "*His* rearing? What makes you think this child will be a boy? I could very well have another Liorah running around. What would you think of that?"

Gideon didn't answer. If the child was another Liorah, she wouldn't be raised to poison her father. No, someone had to teach her morals, and they wouldn't come from the mother.

"What are you going to do about the Hollows, about the Marokai?" he asked, attempting to change the subject. "Elena, Jeremiah. They were looking for answers at dinner."

Liorah's smile faded, but not immediately. She slowly inched across the bed toward Gideon and wrapped her arms around him. "What would you do, my love?"

Gideon involuntarily shivered. The question was unexpected, and to call him "love" was so unlike her. Did she even know what that word meant? "I...I don't know. You use the Marokai as labor to help with the quarry and the farms. Why not give them freedom in the city?"

"They will come after me."

"Not if they see you as benevolent. I know you can't let them live within the walls since there is no space, but perhaps they can build real homes in the Hollows, extend the border of New Emile to more firm land. With the seeds my father promises, you'll need larger farms, more workers. Not to mention, if you raise quvianaq, you'll need ranchers."

"And this will keep them from slicing my throat while I sleep?"

"Nothing will prevent that, but if you give them what they want and treat them as equals, they will have less of a reason."

Liorah reached up and took Gideon's face in her hands. Her eyes bore into him in a way that made his stomach bubble with both anticipation and abject fear. Could she not see how much he despised her? "You're a sensible man, Gideon," Liorah said softly. "You have a gift of compassion that escapes me. Perhaps we can come to...to some sort of arrangement."

"An arrangement?"

Liorah's lips turned down and her eyes filled with tears. "I am Liorah, the One Voice, the holder of the vials of haelen, and granddaughter of the Great Mother Miriam." She paused as her voice caught. "I made my bed, and it is mine to sleep in. I am alone, but that does not mean I should remain so. At my core, I need someone to go through life with, someone with whom I can walk toward the shadows on our way to Eldorado."

Gideon perked up. "You know of Eldorado?"

"My grandmother told the poem to my father and my father to me." Her eyes drifted away from Gideon for a moment.

"'And as his strength,
Failed him at length,
He met a pilgrim shadow.'"

Gideon swallowed. Was she really asking him to stay with her? The thought was terrifying and yet...invigorating at the same time.

Liorah continued.

"'Shadow, said he,
Where can it be —
This land of Eldorado?'"

He didn't know what to say, yet his mouth opened involuntary to finish the verse.

"'I will ride, boldly ride

Over the mountains of the Moon,
Down the Valley of the Shadow...'"

"'...to stay with me forever?" A tear traveled down Liorah's cheek.

Gideon did not answer. He felt trapped in a hold worse than any he'd been in before.

"To stay with me forever...right?"

THE FUNERAL pyre burned into the night. All counted, thirty-two Col'kasid, seventeen New Emilian sentinels, and twenty-nine Marokai gave their lives in the defense of not only the city but of their way of life. They were placed atop the one hundred twenty New Emilian citizens who had passed into shadow at the hands of the Zhanshi. Among the one hundred ninety-eight bodies piled atop each other, Luca and Jacob burned together.

Gideon rubbed his newly shaved scalp and stood to the side of the fire with Isaiah. Elena and Diego were next to them, but Abel was alone. It pained Gideon to see that in more ways than he could say. Abel deserved someone in life, but so far, all life had given him was emptiness.

It was not New Emilian custom to burn bodies but take the remains into the Wastelands to feed the animals. Gideon had insisted on the pyre, however, not only to clear the moor but to solidify the binds that held the New Emilians—to include the Marokai—and the Col'kasid together. Liorah agreed, provided the bodies of the Zhanshi were not included. Those, she said, could be ground into fertilizer for their new farms for all she cared. They did not deserve any respect.

By the morning, all that remained was a smoldering pile of ashes, smoke rising high into the cold air contrasting with the snow that covered the rest of the landscape. Clouds portending another coming storm were far off on the horizon, and the Col'kasid would need to leave soon if they were to beat the weather.

Eight quvianaq would stay behind. At first, Elena and Diego, who had experience with the animals, would care for them and—hopefully—breed more. It wasn't guaranteed, but they said they'd make an attempt with a few tips from some of the Col'kasid hunters. Elder Levi finally agreed to send seeds and agricultural information from Rephidim when the seasons changed. In exchange, at least twenty Marokai volunteered to find a new life with the Col'kasid. Naturally, Levi felt it necessary to baptize them in the ways of their faith, but for a chance at absolute freedom, the Marokai were happy to oblige. Anything to get away from life on the moor.

As the funeral ended, Gideon turned to find his father who had already packed a saddle bag as the Col'kasid hunters gathered for their final meal before leaving. It was time to tell him the truth.

"Father," Gideon said with a hesitant voice.

Levi turned, a frown on his face. "Where is your gear, son, and what did you do to your hair? I've heard the bugs only infect the unclean, and you are not one of them. This is no time for games. We're leaving within the hour."

"I...I'm not going with you," Gideon stammered, barely able to look his father in the eyes.

There was a moment of silence, long enough for Gideon to question whether what he'd just said had really registered. But before Gideon could repeat himself, Levi laughed.

"Your humor is something your mother and I have long admired." Levi patted Gideon on the shoulder. "But really, we must be going. We do not want to be stuck in this God-forsaken place when the snows come again."

It was time to spit it out. "Liorah is pregnant."

"And? Should I care? A harlot like that always gets what she deserves."

"The child is mine."

Levi stared at his son for a moment, and there seemed to be another hint of incredulous laughter. Instead, he swallowed it down. "Are you telling me the truth?" Levi asked, his voice wavering between anger and disbelief.

Gideon nodded solemnly. "As a father, I cannot leave now. It is only right that I remain here."

"You..." Levi looked around as if the words he wanted to say were somewhere else. "You have committed the most *egregious* sin, Gideon!" he shouted. His voice carried and several people nearby looked on. "You bring shame upon our family and shame upon God!"

Gideon's hands shook. He'd been trapped, but there had to be a glint of hope left. "Father, I beg you. Forgive me. I...I never meant for any of this to happen, but you're going to have a grandchild soon. Shouldn't that amount to something?"

"Forgive you?" Levi spat, recoiling from his son. "I cannot forgive a sin like this, Gideon. You knew the consequences of your actions, and yet you defied our ways, spit in the face of the Almighty Father."

"Please—"

"Your path into the shadows is chosen, Gideon," he replied, his voice low and pained. "As the Keeper of the Text, I cannot—will not—condone your actions. You have forsaken your duties, your family, and your people."

Levi's dark eyes were alight with fire. Gideon swallowed hard, trying to find the right words, but fear and shame held him back.

"By your actions," Levi continued, "you have forever tainted the Col'kasid. You will never become Keeper of the Text."

Gideon flinched, his father's words striking him like a physical blow. He had decided he didn't want to become Keeper of the Text long before any of this, but the words were hard to hear.

"Your child will be a bastard without rights or privileges among our people. You have brought this upon yourself, Gideon."

He knew what he had done would make his father angry, but he never expected the consequences to be this severe. In the back of his mind, there was always the hope that his father would accept things as they were.

"Father, I—"

Levi raised a hand, silencing him.

"Do not speak to me. Do not say you are sorry." Levi's eyes showed pain, disappointment, but also the duty to uphold the laws of the Col'kasid. "From this day forth, you are no longer my son. I disown you and exile you permanently from Rephidim. My stone is cast."

The finality of his father's decision hit Gideon hard. He felt utterly alone in that moment. There would be no more protest, no further explanation.

"Then this is goodbye," Gideon said, his voice firm. "Elder Levi, I wish you and your Col'kasid safe travels."

With that, he turned away and headed for the gates of New Emile and his new life.

CHAPTER FORTY

ABEL HAD NO IDEA WHERE TO START. THE TEXTS IN THE LIBRARY were not arranged in any way that made sense to him, but Allistair assured him that their placement had never been changed in all the years the New Emilians had attempted to translate them. Placement, according to Sojen Micah, mattered, as did whatever was written on the first page of each book.

"There will be a keyword in each of the books," Micah had said, "something you can probably find in Father Elijah's Bible."

"But Elder Levi won't release the Bible." Abel had taken a seat at a table with one book in front of him. Micah, across the table, suddenly looked decades younger, as if he'd finally found a purpose in his old age. "How will we know what to look for if we don't have a starting point?"

"Here." Micah pulled a paper out from his satchel and dipped a quill in an inkpot. "There are several symbols I remember, ones that were etched in my memory. The first—" he drew three lines with a squiggle and dot, "—represent the authors of the text, the sa'ja'peet."

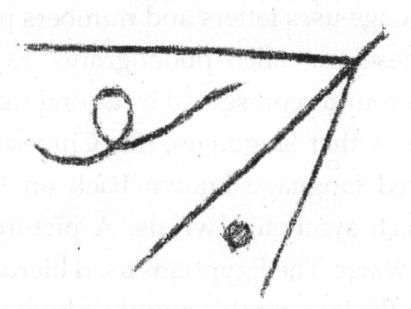

"The second represents the sa'ja'veil." He drew another shape very similar in appearance, but with a slight deviation in the squiggle.

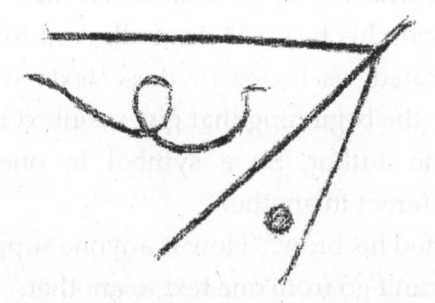

Abel studied what Micah had drawn. Alistair stood over Micah's shoulder and looked on in wonder. "I've seen these many times," he said. "In just about every text. How can you tell the difference?"

"The little curl on the right of the squiggle." Micah pointed. "My cousin Joel and I believed that the lines and dot were more like a marker that said 'in the category of species I give you...'. At first, we didn't see the difference either, but each logogram is drawn in exactly the same way so that eventually there could be no doubt. It was actually the Elder Marcus Michaels, your Mother Miriam's grandfather, who interpreted these symbols."

"What do you mean by logogram?" Abel asked.

"Our language uses letters and numbers put together to form ideas. These are called phonograms. Every once in a while, we see a sound represented by a combination of letters like 'th' or 'chr'. Other languages, like Chinese, which is the oldest translated language known back on Earth, contain logograms which symbolize words. A picture of a tree. A symbol for the water. The Egyptians used hieroglyphs, which combined both the logographic and the phonographic. If you look at the language of the sa'ja'peet, there are characters that represent ideas, and those ideas are not easily translatable."

"So it's not a straightforward translation?" Alistair sat down next to Micah and opened the text he had been holding.

Micah shook his head. "Not at all. And to make things more complicated, each one of these texts will contain a keyword near the beginning that gives context to the rest, all specific to the author. So a symbol in one may mean something different in another."

Abel knitted his brow. "How is anyone supposed to read it, then? You can't go from one text to another."

"No, you can't, but there are similarities." Micah tapped the paper with the two symbols. "These are the same no matter where you look."

The Library fell quiet for a moment. Alistair had brought in Micah and Abel, but also one of his own scribes, Simon, to learn from Sojen Micah. He rationalized that the combination of four brains might be better than just two or three, and if they could get a start—maybe even put together a dictionary of sorts—their translation efforts might yield some results soon. Liorah did not seem to care, but she had repealed her edict about who could enter the Library. For now, she had more problems to deal with, including the reconstruction of the eastern wall and the razing of those buildings which had been burned and become uninhabitable.

Sojen Micah drew another symbol on the paper. "There is another species that my wife Patience found."

"An animal?" Alistair asked.

"No. Animals are rendered with many other symbols, but it appears as if intelligent species are given the three lines and dot."

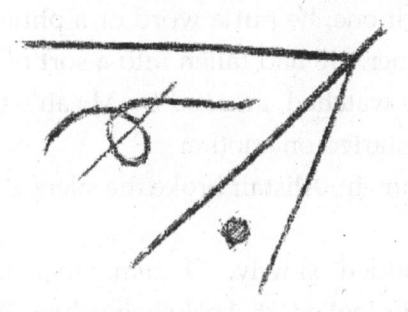

Abel shook his head. "I don't understand. In all the histories, we've never heard of a third species before. Who are they?"

Micah shrugged. "This was found in only one text in the library in the temple at Manoach. But I have a feeling you'll see it here, too."

Alistair pushed back from the table and reached out to another one of the many texts on shelves nearby. When he returned, he opened the text to a specific page and set it down on the table. "This is what you mean." He pointed to a symbol that looked like the one Micah had just drawn. "It shows up in several texts around this one."

Micah closed the text he had been looking through and pulled the new one closer to him. His eyes danced across the page as if he could read exactly what was written. Abel knew that it had been fifty-five years since anyone in Rephidim had seen one of the texts. Those they brought from Manoach had been lost in the deadly dunes to the north during the event in which Micah's sister Candice had passed into shadow. It was a tale told by the Assembly around the fires frequently. However, now it appeared that Micah recognized much more than just that one symbol. Had he secreted away one of the texts for himself?

Micah's eyes grew wide as he jotted down a few more symbols, starting at the front and then turning the pages gently. For each one, he put a word or a phrase under them on his own paper. He had fallen into a sort of trance, and as the other three watched, amazed by Micah's focus, he filled the paper and started on another.

After a moment, Alistair broke the silence. "You can read that?"

Micah nodded slowly. "I remember most of these logograms." He looked at Abel sheepishly. "I haven't been entirely honest with you."

Abel blinked. "How so?"

"The strangers, as you call them—Petra and Nemeth—returned one of the texts we thought we had lost in the dunes. I've been studying it for years."

"Why didn't you say anything?"

Micah paused before answering. "I guess it really didn't matter in the end. Anyway, when you have nothing to do for decades, you stay in your memory for a long time. They became like old friends, and when I lost the texts, I turned to Father Elijah's Bible where he had written many other translations in the margins of the pages. After a while, even a language such as this becomes...familiar."

"What does it say?" Simon, Alistair's scribe, asked. He was as young as Abel and maybe even as eager to learn.

"Not now, Simon," Alistair said gruffly. "Let our guest work."

"No, it's okay." Micah sat back. "I think I understand a little of what this one is telling us."

Simon and the other scribe both looked at each other, excitement written all over their faces and plainly visible in the light of the oil lamps in the Library. Alistair himself had that same childlike wonder in his eyes. They had probably spent so long in this very room looking over the texts with no luck, that any word or symbol translated was like the largest victory.

"I don't know everything, of course," Micah said. "If I had Father Elijah's Bible or the key I copied over I might figure out more." Micah looked at the paper on which he had made his notes. "The keyword here is unique to this author, but it's the same keyword that was in many of the texts in the temple at Manoach." He pointed to one of the first symbols he had written, under which he had written "history author A."

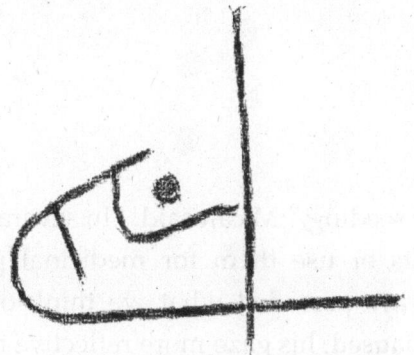

"The author of this text was at Manoach. This is a history covering some sort of conflict between the sa'ja'veil and sa'ja'peet with that third species mixed in."

"How do you know there was a conflict?" Simon asked.

"Let the man speak," Alistair scolded.

"Many of the texts at Manoach were histories. They told stories of battles and some travels throughout Tishbe taken on by the sa'ja'peet. There are also mentions of...other places."

Abel sat up straight. "Other places? You mean like New Emile or Rephidim? Other cities out there?"

Micah slowly nodded. "Not only that, but other...I don't know the best word to use, but other planets is the best I can come up with."

The room fell into a silence that was broken only by the noise filtering in from outside. Hammers pounded and people shouted instructions at each other. Dust motes seemed suspended in the air, caught in the light of the oil lamp. Simon and Abel both looked at each other while Alistair reviewed the notes Micah had written on the paper.

Other planets?

"What is this?" Alistair pointed to another symbol or logogram, as Sojen Micah called them. "The five dots."

"Seeds or seeding," Micah said. "In several texts on how to grow plants or use them for medicinal purposes, that logogram always preceded what we think of as the word sow." Micah paused, his gaze more reflective than usual. "In this case, seeding is associated with that third species."

Abel considered that for a moment, parsing through the jumble of information he'd taken in so far. "So it's possible," he said slowly, "that the third species—whoever they were—was seeded or planted."

Micah shrugged. "At this point, your guess is as good as mine. But if what I'm reading is correct, then the sa'ja'veil were responsible, which led to a conflict with the sa'ja'peet."

"And this one?" Alistair pointed to another, which had nothing written under it. It looked like a circle with a dot in the middle and squiggle underneath."

"That, my new friend, means Well."

"Like the one that brought our ancestors to Tishbe?"

Micah nodded. "And like the one that's currently underneath your fine city."

MICAH HAD learned of the Well under New Emile from a conversation he'd had with Luca during their journey from Rephidim. Unable to get the image of the green light he had seen in the crack which led from the quarry to the hold during the rescue of Abel and Jacob, Luca approached Sojen Micah one night at Abel's prodding as they rested under the stars.

Abel had opted not to join him, which depressed Micah a little. He liked the boy in as much as he saw himself in him as a younger scribe. It was a shame Levi had to be so rigid in his interpretation of Father Elijah's Bible.

"What do you think?" Luca had asked Micah while sitting around a small fire set up away from the main camp.

Micah looked up at the night sky and pointed. "My grandfather used to tell me stories of life on Earth, of what things were like there."

Luca followed Micah's gaze toward the vast sea of stars. "Where is Earth?"

"Elder Marcus could never point out the star around which the planet rotated, but he always said it was visible to us. Every once in a while, he would tell me how much he had regretted following Father Elijah into the Well. He would look up, point, sigh heavily, then mumble on about something else."

"What was the Well?"

"A device of sorts. I'm not really sure how it worked or what it did, but my cousin Joel was fascinated with it. There were more than a few ancient texts in the temple at Manoach which referenced the Well, and with each new finding, Joel learned more."

"Such as?"

"From what we could tell, the sa'ja'veil had built the Well to transit from one place to another. It was the sa'ja'peet who built a ship around it. It had to be contained, or they just worshiped it. No one knows for sure."

"How could something like that transport people from Earth here?"

Micah smiled. "I have no idea. Joel tried to explain it to me once, but I never could wrap my mind around it. I was a scribe—still am, by the way—and all engineering is magic to me."

"Did you ever see it?"

"No, but my father did." Micah poked at the fire with a stick and watched as the sparks floated up. "Most children back in the day, long before the Barren Sea flooded, would often play in places that were off limits—the holes in the Barren Sea, Harper's Forest, and the Circle of Light ship."

Micah paused, his eyes reflecting the fire. Remembering his childhood was easier than remembering anything after the exodus. "From what my father told me, he was younger and out exploring with his cousin Tyrone. They had gotten bored with the holes and decided to climb into the COL ship."

"Is that when they saw it? The Well?"

Micah nodded slowly before continuing. "My father had this shiny rock with him in his bag. As they were walking across a bridge of sorts, the rock started to glow. It got so bright that it shone through the cloth, and the closer they got to the middle, the brighter it became. My father was scared out of his wits."

He paused again, reflecting more on the memory of his father than on what he said. "I guess he thought the thing was going to catch fire and burn them all alive. So, he pulled the bag off his shoulders and tossed it over the railing. Down it went, into the Well. When he and his cousin looked over to watch it fall, they saw the rock—which we learned later was called scandium—grow brighter and brighter. It lit up the sides with this weird green glow, not unlike the glow you have described to me."

"So..." Luca appeared to weigh his words. "So, the glow I saw. It was another Well?"

Micah shrugged. "Maybe or maybe not. At Manoach, there was a greenish glow to the walls, too, a sort of bioluminescent goo that came from the trees around the temple. You could have seen that."

THAT CONVERSATION had been a long time ago, but it had stayed with Micah during the rest of the trip toward New Emile and all the time he sat in safety while the battle with the Zhanshi raged on. Seeing confirmation of the Well in the ancient texts in the Library in New Emile had made him rethink many things.

Was it possible there was a second Well under the city, and if so, did it work?

And where would it lead?

Micah left Alistair, Abel, and Simon alone with the texts while he took a walk. It was something he rather enjoyed, especially on the days when he needed to think. While the weather around Rephidim was more pleasant, Micah didn't care. His grandson, Levi, had already left to head back to Rephidim taking the Col'kasid with him. Micah would never return, and that was okay. Patience was gone, and there was no place for an old scribe any longer.

The air was chilly after a quick bout of snow that had covered the landscape in a pleasant white powder. Tracks of people and animals crisscrossed the moor, some leading away from New Emile, others to the quarry, and more to the Hollows. There was so much life here, and for a moment Micah felt proud at what his cousin Miriam had accomplished. She had brought a large group of people out of Manoach, through a dangerous rainforest filled with rychat, across a canyon, through the Wastelands to this place here. She did what she set out to do...and he couldn't be happier for her.

There was a lot he didn't know about that trip or what happened after, but he could still feel a sense of pride. He knew their grandfather, Marcus, would have been proud as well. What had started so innocently as a little flood on the Barren Sea had led to a mass exodus, a dash for safety in high ground, and a complete overhaul of the society that the original Circle of Light settlers had made.

Far past the gates to New Emile and up on a hill on the edge of the moor, Micah paused, leaning on his walking stick for support. He looked around at everything and took it all in. This was the legacy of Miriam and, by extension, the legacy of Father Elijah...just as Rephidim and the Col'kasid had been the legacy of Micah.

As the wind gently caressed his face, Micah couldn't help but marvel at how quickly time had flown by. The world around him had changed so much since his youth. The bustling life of New Emile was a reminder to him that his time to contribute to such endeavors had passed. The moor was a canvas for his thoughts, a place of solace where he could escape to reflect. He could not return to Rephidim and as much as he wanted to know more about the possible existence of a second Well, he suddenly realized he could not remain here, either.

He felt it—Eldorado beckoning to him like a distant call.

Yet still, he resisted. He didn't feel like his life's work was done. Not now, not after being gifted this chance to uncover all the secrets that Tishbe had kept hidden.

What else lay beyond the horizon?

Out of nowhere, a man and a woman appeared next to Micah, startling the old man. He turned to regard them and instantly smiled.

The strangers had returned.

"Petra." Micah swallowed. "Nemeth."

Petra was much older now, yet there was a glow about her that belied her age. Nemeth, too, appeared...radiant.

"I don't...I don't understand." Micah felt his legs weaken. "Why are you here?"

"Come," Nemeth said, holding his hand out. "Come and see."

Compelled by an inexplicable force, Micah took Nemeth's hand.

Together, the three stepped away from New Emile, venturing into the vast expanse of the Wastelands beyond. The air became colder, and as they walked, the world around them seemed to shift and blur, reality itself bending to accommodate their presence. It was a mesmerizing mixture of memories and dreams, of past and present, all intermingling in a surreal dance.

Although he knew it was not possible, Micah thought he saw Patience in the mist.

A man appeared next to Petra and Nemeth, someone he thought he'd never see again. A lump formed in Micah's throat as he looked upon Asher, the man exiled along with Abel so long ago.

Asher's voice when he spoke was filled with genuine delight. "Hello, Sojen. How is Abel?"

Micah's carved walking stick, which he had used since

the days of the flood and upon which had been carved so many memories, fell to the side. Just as he bent to retrieve it, Petra put a hand on his shoulder.

"You won't need that any longer," she said with a smile. "Not where we're going."

APPENDICES

DRAMATIS PERSONAE

Rephidim (Col'kasid)
Ages are listed for Tishbe (T) and also relative to Earth (E)

Abel (T: 17/E: 21): An exiled member of the Col'kasid tribe; once a scribe who wrote down the stories told by the Assembly; banished for his sexual orientation along with his lover Asher

Gideon (T: 16/E: 20): Levi's son and future leader (Keeper of the Text) of the Col'kasid tribe; Sojen Micah's great grandson; the youngest member of the Prelatic Assembly

Levi (T: 34/E: 43): Leader (Elder) of the Col'kasid tribe and keeper of religious texts; Gideon's father

Isaiah (T: 21/E: 26): A Col'kasid hunter who accompanies Gideon to New Emile

Jacob (T: 19/E: 24): A Col'kasid hunter who accompanies Gideon to New Emile; develops a relationship with the Marokai Elena

Saadya (T: 32/E: 41): the Keeper's help, leader of the hunters; Saadya has a scar which runs diagonally down his face, given to him as an honor

Asher (T: 18/E: 22): Abel's lover, also exiled for the same reason; Asher was sent north and presumed to have passed into shadow, while Amos was sent west toward the mountains

New Emile

Liorah (T: 20/E: 25): The most high, the One Voice, holder of the vials of haelen, and granddaughter of the Great Mother Miriam

Josiah (T: 46/E: 58): Commander of the New Emile sentinels under Liorah; childhood friend of Kaius and of the former leader Eilian

Kaius (T: 49/E: 62): A sentinel/scout from New Emile who finds and rescues Abel; childhood friend of Josiah

Luca (T: 21/E: 26): A New Emilian sentinel who falls in love with Abel; the older brother of the Marokai Elena and Diego

Alistair (T: 56/E: 70): An elder in New Emile who oversees the Library of ancient texts and other special projects; the oldest member of Liorah's council

Russant (T: 36/E: 45): A New Emilian constructionist, responsible for the growth of the city; sent by Liorah to explore and gather information on the Zhanshi

Marius Holmes (T: 41/E: 51): A New Emilian responsible for managing food resources

Piper Lucientes (T: 37/E: 46): Keeper of the Laws; a member of Liorah's council responsible for enforcing Liorah's edicts

Roland the Kept (T: 18/E: 22): Liorah's companion and bedmate; not permitted to talk; assumed to be bisexual

Raphael (T: 22/E: 27): A sentinel from New Emile

Nico (T: 21/E: 26): A sentinel from New Emile

Ivan (T: 24/E: 30): A sentinel from New Emile

Eilian (deceased): Miriam's son and father of Liorah; second ruler of New Emile

Philip (deceased): Eilian's first born, expected to take over from Eilian until his passing; half-brother to Liorah

The Hollows (Marokai)

Elena (T: 18/E: 22): Twin of Diego and younger sister to Luca; Elena leads an underground resistance in the Hollows along with her twin brother; falls for the Col'kasid hunter Jacob

Diego (T: 18/E: 22): Twin of Elena and younger brother to Luca; Diego and Elena are inseparable and both were exiled to the Hollows as a result of the population lottery; they work in the quarry freeing stones so they can be moved by the harmonic transducer

Angela (T: 20/E: 25): A strong voice for the resistance within the Marokai; exiled to the Hollows as a result of the population lottery

Jeremiah (T: 20/E: 25): Part of the Marokai resistance; exiled to the Hollows as a result of the population lottery

Cain (T: 50/E: 63): Part of the Marokai resistance and a childhood friend of Kaius; Cain was exiled to the Hollows after attempting to steal haelen for his ailing wife

Ruth (T: 22/E: 27): Once a handmaiden of Liorah, Ruth was exiled to the Hollows most likely because she was aware of what Liorah had done; recently gave birth to a child Lika who was saved by haelen Elena had conned out of a sentinel in the quarry

Zhanshi

Apart from the Zhurèn – the master or leader – no member of the Zhanshi is permitted a surname

Chen Tseng (T: 34/E: 43): Zhurèn of the Zhanshi; the grandson of Mathias Tseng III and great grandson of Mathias Tseng; determined to avenge his great grandfather's treatment by the gulao—anyone who is not Zhanshi

Luke (T: 80/E: 101): Former right hand of Mathias Tseng III; current advisor to Chen Tseng and the oldest Zhanshi by far
Lucien (T: 33/E: 41): Lieutenant and most trusted advisor of Chen Tseng
Martin (T: 27/E: 34): One of Chen Tseng's lieutenants
Lin Xi (T: 25/E: 31): One of Chen Tseng's lieutenants
Tye (T: 21/E: 26): One of Chen Tseng's lieutenants

Elders
Long since deceased, but are mentioned as founders or prophets in varying degrees

Father Elijah Jonas: The leader of the Circle of Light cult, Elijah Jonas, originally named Norman Oakes; devised the plan that became Transit after being rescued and nursed back to health by a mysterious man following a suicide attempt. Elijah passed into shadow following the colonists' arrival on Tishbe, but never saw the new world.

Elder Jackson Liao: Elijah's right-hand man as the COL was preparing for Transit. Jackson took over as leader—the first Manager of the City of Nod—following Father Elijah's passing. Under Elder Jackson's leadership, the colonists built the city, established farms and created a functioning society. He was also the force behind the creation of the Labor Rite.

Elder Marcus Emile Michaels: Originally a navigator/mathematician onboard the COL ship prior to Transit responsible for translating the alien manuals Father Elijah had found. Aided by tivas root, Elder Marcus is the oldest elder within the City of Nod and the man responsible for the traditions and societal mores of the colonists. Namesake of New Emile.

Elder Zachary Miller: One of the members of the dive team tasked with recovering the bodies of the COL cult when

Father Elijah executed his grand plan. Along with Elder Thomas and Eldress Kayla, Zachary was one of the Remainders, a small group of friends and relatives of the members of the Circle of Light cult. Zachary was tasked by Elder Jackson to form and lead the scouts, a group of armed colonists originally set up to ensure the safety of all those living within the walls of the City of Nod.

Eldress Claire Miller: Zachary Miller's sister and wife of Elder Marcus. Claire, a medic, was responsible for stealing the mineral ore needed to power the Well of the COL ship that enabled Transit, inadvertently tipping Mathias off on the location of the COL ship. Upon arrival on Tishbe, Claire married Elder Marcus and help him devise ways to get the colonists to work together.

Eldress Kayla Boyer: Deaf and mute, Eldress Kayla was a geointelligence analyst on Earth who discovered inconsistencies in the reports coming out about the Circle of Light cult. As a result, Eldress Kayla formed the Remainders and enlisted the help of several of the relatives and friends of those supposedly deceased.

Elder Thomas "Tigger" Jones: One of the Remainders. Tigger, a Marine on Earth, suffered from PTSD after a tour in Syria. Tigger formed the Cazador, a group of hunters who were, like the scouts, charged with keeping the colonists safe. Tigger married Eldress Kayla following Transit. He passed into shadow by his own hand after the birth of one of his children.

Mathias Tseng: The leader of a Chinese terrorist cell on Earth, Mathias stowed away onboard the COL ship just prior to Transit, murdering one of the crew members. Mathias escaped after Transit and hid out in the forests to the north, eventually forming the Zhanshi and a village named Xin Shijie de Yaolan.

Third Generation Characters Mentioned or Appearing in
The Widening Gyre

Further information can be found in the preceding books
Miriam Page (Michaels) (deceased): Granddaughter of Elder Marcus Michaels and Eldress Claire Miller. First cousin of Joel Page and widowed wife of Tobias Page. Miriam founded and named New Emile and developed the governmental system. Mother to Eilian (deceased) and grandmother of Liorah and Philip (deceased).
Tobias Page (deceased): Former husband of Miriam and once a scout. Tobias' name was banned from New Emile on the order of Miriam after Tobias betrayed her during their long trek from Manoach.
Joel Page (deceased): Grandson of Elder Marcus Michaels and first cousin of Miriam. Joel, an engineer, attempted to set up a mining camp in the Barrier Mountains to find the material needed to power the Well inside the COL ship. He was killed by Mathias III.
Petra Cooper (T:77/E:97): A natural resources engineer who went with Joel to scout out a new place to live in the mountains and build a mining camp. Sister to Nemeth Cooper and mother of an unknown child. Petra was saved by Nemeth following the Zhanshi attack on Joel's group in *All We Leave Behind*.
Nemeth Cooper (T:68/E:86) Petra's brother. Born mentally disabled, both Nemeth and Petra lost their parents during the Exodus or Second Transit. Nemeth's intelligence was dramatically increased through a mysterious connection with the Orinate.
Christina Grigsby (deceased): A medical assistant before the Exodus and later the person in charge of a medical duties at

Manoach. Christina was the love interest of Micah Victor, but passed into shadow as a result of an attack in the temple near the end of *Sunshine and Shadow*.

Micah Victor (T:69/E:87): First cousin of Miriam, Joel, and Aaron. The Chief Scribe for the remaining colonists at Manoach and founder of Rephidim. Given the honorific of Sojen after abdicating his rule. Husband to Patience and father of Micah II (deceased). Grandfather of Levi and great grandfather of Gideon.

Candice Victor (deceased): Micah's younger sister who passed into shadow during the Micah's flight from Manoach to Rephidim.

Patience Victor (Grubbs) (deceased): Micah's wife who passed a few years prior to the events of *The Widening Gyre*; Patience was instrumental in helping Micah found Rephidim.

Aaron Jones (deceased): Grandson of Elder Thomas Jones and Eldress Kayla Boyer. Aaron was the first cousin of Isaac who he murdered. Additionally first cousin to Miriam, Joel, and Micah. Aaron joined with the Zhanshi after abandoning his people at Manoach. Killed in the genocide in *All We Leave Behind*.

Mathias Tseng III (deceased): Past leader or Zhurèn of the Zhanshi and the grandson of Mathias Tseng who snuck aboard the COL ship prior to the First Transit.

DEFINITIONS/GLOSSARY

Throughout the Transit *series, not specific to* The Widening Gyre

A

Aichmiri (ack-MEER-ee): see *vermillion aichmiri*

B

Baca: A root that grows around Rephidim, with a green spike on top filled with water. Under the ground there's a purple bulb. A sweet root once roasted, it grows near the Reed Sea but only on elevated surfaces.

Barren Sea: The name given the dry lakebed on which the COL ship came to rest after the First Transit. The Barren Sea is full of holes, which are actually burrows for the Barren shrimp who hibernate during the Dry Period of the Shift.

Barren shrimp: These "shrimp" are extremely large and carnivorous. They hibernate under the Barren Sea during the Dry Period. During the Wet Period, they awaken and emerge from the holes hungry.

Brewer's Forest: The name given the forest west of the City of Nod, named after Adrienne Brewer, who was found murdered when the COL ship arrived on Tishbe.

Brother or Sister: Adults of the second generation are often referred to as "Brother" or "Sister." The terms started after Transit when Jackson Liao decided he needed a way to bring everyone together as a family. This is also where the term "Father Elijah" came from. When the societies split, the tradition died.

C

Cazador (KAZ-a-door): A group of hunters and gatherers assigned by Council during the Labor Rite. The Cazador are responsible for bringing food—primarily meat—to the colonists. Founded by Thomas "Tigger" Jones at the request of Jackson Liao and at the same time as the scouts, the Cazador was initially set up to be a defensive measure against danger. It was later converted to a hunter/gatherer type of labor.

Chroma Toad: A small creature that lives in the undergrowth of the forest around Manoach. It is a symbiote who uses its lights to attract prey then paralyzes that prey so other animals can eat the flesh away. When the bones are left, the chroma toad is able to eat the calcium from the bones.

Circle of Light: The name given the fake religious cult dreamed up by Elijah prior to the First Transit. Called the COL for short, it refers more to the ship Elijah was shown by We-yal-up, the mysterious stranger who rescued Elijah after he attempted suicide.

City of Nod: The first settlement of the colonists of Tishbe after the First Transit. Located about two miles from the shore of the Barren Sea, the City of Nod was named after the place Cain settled after he killed his brother (east of Eden).

COL: Circle of Light. May refer to the religious "cult" started by Elijah Jonas or the ship surrounding the Well.

Col'kasid: A religious tribe meaning "followers of the Circle of Light" formed by Micah after the exodus from the temple and their wanderings to find a new home.

Crocowolf: An animal found in the forest west of the City of Nod with the body of alligator and the fur of a fez. The ridiculous name was given to the animal by elders who were "too tired" to more appropriately name newfound animals.

Cycle: The time it takes for the Short Moon to revolve around Tishbe, which is approximately 25 days. A cycle is analogous to a month on Earth, and there are 16 cycles per Tishbian year.

D

Discovery: A term used by the New Emilians referring to an extended trip in any direction to look for resources which might help with their cities growth.

Dry Period: The period of time in which any rain which falls is absorbed by the Barren Sea. The Dry Period, opposite the Wet Period, may last for decades.

E

Elder/Eldress: During the events of *Sunshine and Shadow* and *All We Leave Behind*, first generation settlers are referred to as "elders" with the males prefixed as "Elder" and the females prefixed as "Eldress." After the establishment of New Emile and Rephidim, Elder was rarely used.

Elder Pine: Much like a pine tree, the elder pine has "needles on its needles" and can injure a person who gets too close. It is found in Brewer's Forest west of the City of Nod closer to the foothills as the elevation rises.

Emilians: Or New Emilians, these are the residents of New Emile. Emilians are a secular tribe who rely heavily on science and observation than any sort of faith. Emilian law states that any belief in something unseen or something which cannot be proven is outlawed.

F

Feast of Elijah and the Circle of Light: An annual ceremony where three elders selected by the aldermen to relay their stories. It typically occurs during the last cycle of the year and includes an exchange of gifts. The Feast lasts for three days, with each day focused on one elder. If the elder has already passed into shadow, a direct relative tells the story as they heard it. All stories are written down by the Chief Scribe.

Fez: A deer-like creature found on Tishbe. Useful for food, leather and clothing, but horrendously ugly with a vertical mouth and wide-set eyes.

Fez face: A common insult the third generation uses. In reference to the ugliness of a fez. Not used very often after the events in *All We Leave Behind*.

First Transit: The First Transit is the name given to the events at the end of *Out of Due Season* when the settlers activated the Well inside the COL ship and arrived on Tishbe.

G

Great Return: The Great Return is an event in which the more religious of the colonists have come to believe is their eventual destiny. Elder Jackson Liao ambiguously declared during the earliest years of life on Tishbe that: "A time may come when humans will return to Earth, to spread the great news of the paradise we have found and bring with us those who believe. This Great Return may be initiated by us or because of us, but it will happen."

H

Haelen/Water of Life: Originally found in a pool in the temple at Manoach where it was called the Water of Life, a similar source was found in New Emile. Haelen contains a bacteria that has healing properties and is prized by the New Emilians.

Harper's Forest: The name of the forest found north of the City of Nod, named after Georgia Harper, an agricultural technician who died during the First Transit.

Helen's Esker: Eldress Helen Pallen, a geologist during the First Transit, identified an esker to the west of the City of Nod. The esker—a winding long ridge of gravel and other sediment—had likely been deposited by meltwater from a retreating glacier or ice sheet that could still be seen in the highest points of the Barrier Mountains. Helen's Esker marks the western edge of safety for the colonists and is approximately 300 miles long.

Huǒlóng: A terrorist cell on Earth active in the early part of the 21st century. The name translates from the Chinese to "fire dragon" and was led by Mathias Tseng. In honor, Mathias named the new world Huǒlóng Yàosài or "home of the fire dragon."

I

Into Sunshine/Into Shadow: Terms used for "birth" and "death," one of the many social mores Jackson Liao established at the suggestion of Marcus Michaels during the first few years after the First Transit.

J

Jivara (ji-VAR-ah): A type of yellow and red grass which is prevalent in the Wastelands and surrounding New Emile. Jivara has many construction uses when it is weaved together, although it is often still not strong enough to be used as a roofing material in the Hollows.

K

Khopa (KO-pah): A small burrowing animal found in the deserts around Rephidim. Khopa stay in families and their dung is used as a healing remedy for the Col'kasid, much in the same way haelen (or the Water of Life) is used in New Emile.

Koralinth (KOR-a-lynth): A fragrant grass which grows in shaded areas around Rephidim. The Col'kasid believe the smoke from burning the grass has healing powers.

Ku'vatar (KOO-va-tar): A muscular animal found in the Wastelands with red and yellow spotted fur; runs fast and changes direction quickly. Across its muscular neck are stripes which spiral down onto its spine. Has a slender body that can slither into tight spaces.

L

Labor: work

Labor Rite: A ceremony performed when a child turns sixteen in which a labor is assigned by the Council. This rite was abolished after the events in *All We Leave Behind*.

Long Moon: The second moon with an orbit of approximately 101 days. The Long Moon is larger than the Short Moon. Tishbians use the moon as a seasonal indicator as four occur within a Tishbian year.

M

Maldoric (mal-DOOR-ik): A small bird, about three inches long with four wings. They are extremely numerous on Tishbe, and sometimes gather in swarms. The down of the infantile maldoric can be used for many things, to include stuffing for pillows or to help insulate a coat.

Manoach (man-OH-ack): The name given the temple found by the refugees. Manoach is a Hebrew word meaning "a resting place, state or condition of rest." It was built by the sa'ja'veil, once inhabited by the sa'ja'peet, and abandoned for reasons unknown.

Marokai (MARE-oh-ky): The name given to those who live in the Hollows outside the wall of New Emile. There are three ways an individual becomes Marokai: losing the population lottery, as a sentence for a crime committed against the One Voice, or because they were born there. Losers of the population lottery are branded on their foreheads with a line. Criminals and those disliked by the One Voice have an additional triangle brand applied over the line.

Michus (MY-kus): The name Aaron gave to a small creature with gray fur and a foot-long tail he found on his trek through the rainforest toward the north away from Manoach. They have small bodies but provide little meat.

Mirakulu (Mee-ra-KOO-loo): Trees which grow in an orchard near Rephidim. Mirakulu trees produce small red berries, which Col'kasid women turn into wine.

Mitter: A tiny mite that feeds on human hair up to, but not including, the follicle. The reason the New Emilians and Marokai shave all hair off their body.

N

New Emile: The city found and populated by Miriam Michaels after she led a group of people out of the temple. It was named after Miriam's grandfather, Marcus, whose middle name is Emile.

O

Orinate (OR-in-ait)): see *sa'ja'peet*

P

Pahira (pa-HEER-ah): A large swamp animal that curls into a ball for both protection and rapid movement. Pahira have large mouths with multiple tendrils used for foraging. They are omnivorous, preferring meat, but can sustain themselves on plant life found in the swamps to the northeast of Three Rivers.

Poralima (por-a-LI-ma): Trees which grow in an orchard near Rephidim. Poralima trees produce a long fruit that, while slightly bitter and has the consistency of dirt, is filled with nutrients.

Pit badger/Huan: Much like an Earth badger, the pit badger is a ferocious creature without fear. It is about two to three feet long and has a desire to attack anything larger than itself. Its most distinctive feature is its four eyes, two on the side of a pink nose and two near tiny ears.

Pua'a ono (pu-a-a-O-no): An animal that looks similar to a boar on Earth, but with floppy ears. The meat tastes like bacon. Pua'a ono translates from Hawaiian to "tasty pig."

Q

Quvianaq (KOO-vin-ak)/Strider: Once called a strider when first found, the quvianaq is a massive creature that stands on two thick legs and is eight to ten feet tall. It's skin is gray and has six retractable limbs held limply under the animal's chest. A bulbous head caps the animal, and a long, squarish snout holds a mouth of several rows of sharp teeth. It is the only natural predator to the rychat.

R

Reekbird: A grounded bird with colorful tufts of feathers on its head. Found in the Wastelands.

Rephidim (REF-a-deem): The settlement founded in the desert by Micah after their wandering. Meaning stay, rest or support. Rephidim was mentioned in Exodus 17:1-7.

River leach: A leach about ten centimeters long. It lives in the rivers and waters of the rain forest. The bite contains a paralytic that incapacitates a human for a day. The poison from the leach is later used to amplify the harm of a weapon.

Rychat (RYE-kat)/Green Growler: An animal that on Earth would be similar to a panther or jaguar with six legs and a scorpion-like tail. It is originally given the nickname "green growler" by Micah during the search for a new home. The animal was renamed rychat by Eldress Glenda during the trip to the temple, from a Russian word meaning "growl.". Rychat, which are intelligent and hunt in packs, live in the rain forest west of the Barrier Mountains. They are relentless in their attack on the refugees on their way to the temple, killing several people. However, their growl is a warning sign the refugees quickly learn. In addition, the meat contains an oil which has both a psychogenic and healing effect on humans.

S

Sa'ja' (sah-yah)—: Roughly translated to "race", sa'ja' prefixes a species. It was invented by linguists who arrived on Tishbe with Father Elijah.

Sa'ja'peet (sah-yah-PEET)/Orinate (OR-in-ait)): The race of alien who wrote the manuals in the COL ship and the texts found in the temple. Their language is difficult but not impossible to translate, consisting of logograms, phonograms and other glyphs. While Elijah had been able to read a few of the manuals when he was first shown the COL ship, the translation of the rest had lagged behind. Eventually, only Marcus could translate some of it, and he did not want to for reasons revealed during *Sunshine and Shadow*. Sa'ja'peet/Orinate, it its later revealed, are very short. They built the COL ship around the Well, which is why the ceilings were so low.

Sa'ja'veil (sah-yah-VALE)/Ikolī (EE-ko-lie): The race of alien who built the Well, mentioned by the sa'ja'peet/Orinate in the texts found in the temple and the manuals in the COL ship. Sa'ja'veil/Ikolī, it is later revealed, are very tall. They built the temple, which the sa'ja'peet/Orinate later occupied. However, they did not build the ship around the Well.

Scouts: originally, a labor which was set up to ensure the safety of the City of Nod, founded by Zachary Miller; later, a labor adjunct to a sentinel for the city of New Emile; scouts are sent out on Discovery—a means to find resources that might be needed for growth.

Shift: After the "rainy season" (Wet Period) when the Barren Sea fills and floods most of the land, the "dry season" (Dry Period) starts. Both periods last several decades in a cyclical pattern known as The Shift. When the colonists first arrived, it was the beginning of the Dry Period. Fifty-one Earth years later, the world floods and the Wet Period begins. During the Dry Period, the assumption is that that water is diverted away from the Barren Sea to some unknown part of the planet. When the holes (and the Barren Sea) fill, this is the apex of the period. The water recedes slowly, eventually leaving the Barren Sea dry again. This is not a world-wide phenomenon, but a localized one. However, to the colonists, it seems global since they have had no way to explore the planet they are on.

Short Moon: The first moon with an orbit of approximately 25 days. The Short Moon is smaller than the Long Moon. Tishbians use the Short Moon as a cycle indicator, with 16 cycles making up a Tishbian year.

Skookum: Legendary dwarves and evil spirits mentioned by We-yal-up as the builders of the COL ship and the reason why there are northern lights. This is based on a story told by the Makah Indians of the Strait of Juan de Fuca. The skookum are the sa'ja'peet, a fact implied in the second novel but not stated outright.

T

Tigris: The river the refugees from the City of Nod followed to the temple at Manoach. While the refugees never named it, Aaron does after his escape from the temple. The Tigris flows from the mountains to the canyon.

Tishbe (TISH-bee)/Ena'tuviya Kolic (en-a-TOOV-ee-ya KO-lick)/ Huǒlóng Yàosài (HOO-o-long YOW-sye): The name given to the new world by Jackson Liao who wanted to honor Elijah Jonas. Tishbe is the birthplace of the biblical Elijah. The Orinate called the world Ena'tuviya Kolic, while the Zhansi called it Huǒlóng Yàosài (Home of the Fire Dragon). It is unknown what the sa'ja'veil/Ikolī ever called it, as their language was never known.

Tishbe Bison: An animal with floppy ears and wide-set eyes that looks somewhat like an Earth bison with wool that can be shorn and skin like a rhinoceros. Raised by the colonists for food and leather to make clothes and shoes.

Tishbe Oak: Wood from what appears to look like an oak tree from Earth. The exact family and genus of the tree was never given as the primary botanist on board the COL ship during the First Transit was killed shortly after arriving on the planet.

Tishbian: A human born and raised on Tishbe.

Tishbian Mole: a small, sandy-furred mammal perfectly adapted to life underground in the Wasteland; Tishbian moles carve extensive burrow systems with strong claws and feed on roots and invertebrates; although it bathes itself in familial urine, its meat is tasteless

Tishbian Year: Tishbe's rotation around its star is 403.873 days with a rotation of 27 hours 26 minutes. This equates to one Earth year being 78.9% shorter than one Tishbian year, thus a person who is 10 on Earth is 7.89 in Tishbian years. A person who is 26 in Tishbian years, would be 32.95 in Earth years.

Tivas (TEE-vas) root: A plant found on Tishbe, the root of which contains healing properties. The settlers learned quickly to make tea out of tivas root as a medicinal remedy. The name is derived from the Spanish *curativas* meaning "healing."

U-V

Vermillion aichmiri (ack-MEER-ee): Sometimes shortened to aichmiri, this is a variety of fruit grown naturally in the ground around the City of Nod and in places north of New Emile. The rind is spiky, but inside the fruit is sweet and sticky. About the size of a small apple, aichmiri are light, easily tossed about on the wind.

W

Well: A mysterious device built by the sa'ja'veil that brought the humans to Tishbe. Not much is known about how it operates, only that it requires certain coils made from scandium. The COL ship housing the Well under the lake in northwestern Washington was rebuilt and populated by Elijah Jonas.

Wet Period: The period of time in which any rain which falls is not absorbed by the Barren Sea and is augmented by water rising out of the holes (where Barren ship hibernate during the Dry Period). The Wet Period, opposite the Dry Period, may last for decades. While the initial flooding reaches the Barrier Mountains, it recedes to an equilibrium within a cycle or two, leaving the forests fresh and still standing.

X

Xialiti (zah-LEE-tee): A cold-blooded animal that lives in the mountains and rocks around Rephidim; xialiti weigh 100-150 pounds, have scales, live alone, and spit to paralyze prey. The often slither or crawl, preferring to use their short legs for jumping when necessary.

Xin Shijie de Yaolan: The village set up by Mathias after the First Transit far north of Harper's Forest. The name translates from the Chinese to "cradle of the new world."

Y

Yaolan: see *Xin Shijie de Yaolan*

Z

Zarcoa: A large carrion bird with an eight-foot wingpan found in the deserts around Rephidim; the bird does not have feathers in the traditional sense; its skin is typically green with orange spots and is feared for its aggressiveness.

Zhanshì (zan-SHEE): A nomadic warrior tribe formed from the descendants of Mathias Tseng. The name translates from the Chinese to "warrior" or "soldier."

Zhetus (ZEE-tus): A fanged serpent-like creature with fur instead of scales. Zhetus are commonly found around Tishbian mole burrows in the Wastelands.

Zhurèn (joo-REN): The honorific given to the current leader of the Zhanshi. The name translates from the Chinese to "director, head."

Ziz: A massive, griffin-like bird with a wingspan of over three meters which live in the high treetops of the forest to the west of the City of Nod. Named by early settlers based on a creature in Jewish mythology.

DIFFERENCES BETWEEN WORLDS

	Earth	Tishbe
Rotation	23:56	27:26
Orbit	365.256 days	403.873 days
Total Hours in a Year	8741.7936	11,079.586
Age at 10	10	7.89
A person who is 26 on Tishbe is ___ on Earth	32.95	26
One hour is...	60 minutes	60 minutes
There are __ hours in a day	24	30
The calendar is based on:	12 months	16 "cycles"
Moon/orbit	1/28 days	2/25 days & 101 days

YEAR 96 MOON PHASE CALENDAR

Short Moon (25 days) then Long Moon (4 cycles)

ACKNOWLEDGMENTS

To say this has been a neck-whipping journey would be an understatement.

The *Transit* series has been outlined out to nine novels, meaning this one, *The Widening Gyre*, is not quite at the halfway point. And at first, everything flowed smoothly. I wrote book one. Book three followed two, and then I started in on four. Sometime around the end of writing the fourth book, I got it in my head that I needed to finish my schooling. That is, I needed my doctorate. And so I began what is not an easy process. As a student and practitioner of industrial-organization psychology, I suddenly needed to compartmentalize my time a little more between writing, schooling, and work. The benefit, of course, it being able to psychoanalyze my characters.

Thankfully, years of failing to do many things has resulted in me putting support systems in place. Being an author is a lonely business, and yet it can be surrounded by a strong network. That's an oxymoron, but it's true. There are alpha readers, beta readers, ARC readers, cover designers, copy editors, proofreaders...the list goes on. For all of them, I am appreciative. They took time out of their day to refine and polish what initially came out of the folds of my brain...folds that are now full of many other things that need to be done.

My first acknowledgment is to my wife, Jesse, who has remained with me as I wrote all of these novels, offering her suggestions and providing much of the framework for the psychological undertones found in the story.

Many other gracious readers took a look at this novel during its development and were once again truly instrumental in making sure plot holes and inconsistencies were patched. Craig Strickland has followed this story from the beginning and has made sure the new characters were as well-rounded as the older ones, and the older ones that survived since the third book stayed true to who they were. Ira Johnson provided me with a solid early review that was key to making sure the harmonic transducer — which is a real thing, by the way — made sense. And Lou Kemp pointed out where there were missing pieces, a few ugly holes, and things I would rather not admit were wrong in the version I sent. Finally, for those who supported this novel during the launch — thank you!

Pepper and Tucker, my two dogs, are still keeping my seat warm, and Minnie the cat has been more loving. I think age has something to do with it.

Benjamin X. Wretlind
Colorado Springs, 2024

BIOGRAPHY

BENJAMIN X. WRETLIND IS A SPECULATIVE FICTION AUTHOR WHO writes science fiction, dark fantasy, magical realism, and some horror. Infusing his writing with a heavy dose of philosophy and epistemology, he is the author of several novels, novellas, and creative writing books and is a full member of the Science Fiction and Fantasy Writers Association (SFWA).

While not writing, Benjamin builds and teaches leadership and professional development courses for staff at Yale University. Owing his life's viewpoint to Bob Ross, he has also painted a few things, thrown a few paintings away, and probably has a painting on an easel right now. Oh, and he loves woodworking, too. It's all about creating.

Benjamin lives with his wife Jesse in Colorado.

BIOGRAPHY

BENJAMIN X. WALD LAND IS A SPECULATIVE FICTION AUTHOR WHO writes science fiction, dark fantasy, magical realism, and some horror. Infusing his writing with a heavy dose of philosophy and epistemology, he is the author of several novels, novellas, and creative writing books and is a full member of the Science Fiction and Fantasy Writers Association (SFWA).

While not writing, Benjamin builds and teaches leadership and professional development courses for staff at Yale University. Owing his life's viewpoint to Bob Ross, he has also painted a few things, thrown a few paintings away, and probably has a painting on an easel right now. Oh, and he loves woodworking, too. It's all about creating.

Benjamin lives with his wife Jesse in Colorado.